BLOOD THIRST

100 Years
of
Vampire Fiction

EDITED AND WITH AN INTRODUCTION BY
LEONARD WOLF

NEW YORK OXFORD
OXFORD UNIVERSITY PRESS
1997

Special thanks to Greg Cox for his contribution
to the headnotes and section heads. —L.W.

Oxford University Press

Oxford New York
Athens Auckland Bangkok Bogota Bombay
Buenos Aires Calcutta Cape Town Dar es Salaam
Delhi Florence Hong Kong Istanbul Karachi
Kuala Lumpure Madras Madrid Melbourne
Mexico City Nairobi Paris Singapore
Taipei Tokyo Toronto Warsaw

and associated companies in
Berlin Ibadan

Compilation copyright © 1997 by Byron Preiss Visual Publications, Inc.
Introduction copyright © 1997 by Leonard Wolf
Illustrations copyright © 1997 by Max Douglas

Published by Oxford University Press, Inc.
198 Madison Avenue, New York, NY 10016

Oxford is a registered trademark of Oxford University Press

Library of Congress Cataloging-in-Publication Data
Blood thirst: 100 years of vampire fiction / edited and with an introduction
by Leonard Wolf
p. cm.
ISBN 0-19-511593-7 (alk. paper)
1. Vampires—Fiction. 2. Horror tales, English. 3. Horror tales, American.
I. Wolf, leonard.
PR1309.V36B58 1997
823'.0873808375—dc21 97-15366
CIP

1 3 5 7 9 8 6 4 2

Printed in the United States of America
on acid-free paper

CONTENTS

INTRODUCTION

by LEONARD WOLF

Bram Stoker's novel *Dracula* appeared in 1897, one hundred years ago. Since its publication, the book has never been out of print and its title character, Count Dracula, has become an icon of terror familiar to many millions of people. All the world knows the count's name and for what he is famous. He has lost his status as a character in a work of fiction and has become instead a figure embedded in our subconscious.

Perhaps because Stoker's Dracula evolved into such a mythic figure, subsequent writers of vampire fiction have failed to invent a character of comparable grandeur. Regardless of the explanation, there have been very few vampire novels of distinction published since 1897; of more than one hundred fifty, only a handful is of literary merit.

That handful includes George Sylvester Viereck's *House of the Vampire* (1907), Dion Fortune's *The Demon Lover* (1927), Richard Matheson's *I Am Legend* (1954), Theodore Sturgeon's *Some of Your Blood* (1961), Raymond Rudorff's *The Dracula Archives* (1971), Fred Saberhagen's *The Dracula Tapes* (1975), Stephen King's *Salem's Lot* (1975), Anne Rice's *Interview with the Vampire* (1976), Chelsea Quinn Yarbro's *Hôtel Transylvania* (1977), Tanith Lee's *Sabella or the Bloodstone* (1980), Suzy McKee Charnas's *The Vampire Tapestry* (1980), and Whitley Strieber's *The Hunger* (1981).

Of that small list*, the works that most engage our attention are those by Stephen King, Anne Rice, Suzy McKee Charnas, Tanith Lee, and Chelsea Quinn Yarbro, all of whom are included in this anthology.

King, author of a single vampire novel (*Salem's Lot*), has won a loyal and enormous following with his compelling plots and unpretentious style. Rice has created a five-volume series of vampire novels, the Vampire Chronicles, in which she develops a kind of epic vampire theogony. Her lush prose and polymorphous eroticism have enchanted millions of readers. Both writers are monuments on the horror fiction scene.

Charnas and Lee are both accomplished prose stylists. In Charnas's work, the idea of the vampire transcends its usual limitations as an armature for a horror fiction, becoming (as it does, for example, in J. Sheridan Le Fanu's *Carmilla*) a means of investigating the most dangerous, if also the most exalting, of human experiences: being in love. In Lee's hands, vampire fiction can feel darkly sumptuous even as it is curiously otherworldly, sweetly dreamlike.

*Derived from the chronological list in *V is for Vampire* (Plume, 1996).

Yarbro created Count Saint-Germain, the noblest of the sympathetic vampires who began to appear in fiction in the 1970s. Saint-Germain, the hero of *Hôtel Transylvania,* is a model of decency, grace, and intelligence. He is also a superb lover who, in his long life, has learned erotic secrets that render his lovers (they are not exactly his victims) weak with gratitude for his attentions. He is a rather wonderful mix of the Scarlet Pimpernel—heroic, witty, wise, distinguished, and dedicated to doing good—and the demon lover for whom women, in fiction at least, are presumed to be wailing endlessly.

If the writers of vampire novels have not, by and large, produced works of real literary merit, short story writers in this century have produced a rich array of vampire fiction, as the stories collected here demonstrate.

Before turning our attention to these stories, I want to deal with a literary critical—and perhaps psychological—problem that has vexed me for more than three decades: What is there about the image of the vampire that makes it such a singularly attractive genre to twentieth-century readers and moviegoers? If we look at popular culture fiction, what do we see? In murder mysteries, we are interested in variations on the "who done it?" theme. In sword-and-sorcery fiction, the interplay of derring-do and the supernatural holds our interest. In the so-called women's Gothic fiction (the bodice-rippers), the pulsing eroticism beneath the story line draws in the reader. And in mainstream horror, the reader's interest is focused on the variety of gruesome ways in which human lives are threatened, tormented, or ended.

But vampire fiction, which has elements of all the above genres, exerts an amazing pull on readers for a reason that we may find disturbing.

To begin with, any vampire fiction has blood as its primary metaphor. As the mad Renfield in Stoker's *Dracula* says, quoting the Bible, "The blood is the life," a fact impressed upon any of us who have ever bled or seen someone else bleed copiously. Beyond that, as Havelock Ellis explained long ago, "There is scarcely any natural object with so profoundly an emotional effect as blood."[*]

Over the eons, blood has acquired a variety of social meanings. The Bible memorializes the first shedding of human blood in the story of Cain and Abel. A bond of blood, as between members of different clans, stands for close relationship, for brother- or sisterhood. We say of particularly cruel people that they are bloodthirsty. There are cultures in which menstrual blood is regarded as taboo and others in which it is supposed to bring good luck. Folk tradition has it that pacts with the devil must be signed in blood. In the Catholic Christian tradition, there is the profound mystery of the salvational power of wine transubstantiated into the blood of Christ.

---

[*]*Studies in the Psychology of Sex,* Second edition, Vol. 3 (F. A. Davis Inc., 1927).

Blood can also represent our identity. Speaking proudly of a child or a grandchild, we say, "My blood flows in his or her veins."

Some years ago, I thought I had a key to the power of the vampire image. In an essentially sociological reading of Stoker's *Dracula,* I was willing to believe that the vampire count stood for the modern industrialized world's fascination with "energy without grace, power without responsibility."* I saw in Dracula a symbol of the unbridled, and often exploitative expansion in the twentieth century of industrialism and the factory system. The phrase "energy without grace" referred to the contemporary tendency to admire vitality for its own sake, regardless of its intended use.

When America was still involved in the war in Vietnam I had no trouble seeing in Dracula an apt symbol of that disastrous and bloody conflict. It seemed to me, too, that Dracula stood for the American fixation on youth and for our well-known unwillingness to confront the reality of our own death.

I have not entirely abandoned such views, but now the appeal of vampire imagery to me seems less global and more personal. Contemporary readers and filmgoers are drawn to vampire imagery because it speaks to them about deeply inner (and especially sexual) temptations and doubts.

The point is—and in recent years, it has been made again and again by many commentators on the genre—that the blood exchange represents every variety of sexual union: men with women, men with men, fathers with daughters, mothers with sons, women with women. Moreover, the vampire's embrace is perceived as an intimate entry. In Stoker's novel, the innocent Lucy, "vampirized" by Dracula, acquires the looks and manners of a sexually experienced whore. Even the blood donations Lucy gets from the male heroes are perceived by the donors as making them, in a sense, Lucy's husbands. And, when Dracula takes Mina Harker's blood and forces her to drink his, he uses the language of the marriage ceremony: "She is blood of my blood, flesh of my flesh." Because she has Dracula's blood in her veins, Mina has a psychic bond with him, enabling her to guide his enemies to him.

In addition to the erotic implications of the blood exchange, vampire fiction has psychological and spiritual meanings as well. In nineteenth-century stories (especially in Stoker's novel), the vampire's victim is spiritually tainted because the vampire is defined as a creature of the devil.

Stoker's Dracula, when we first meet him, is a loathsome, white-haired old man with bad breath and hair on the palms of his hands. He recaptures his youth and sustains his immortality by drinking the blood of his victims. In twentieth-century fiction, particularly that written in the second half of the century, the religious content of the imagery has progressively

---

*Wolf, Leonard. *A Dream of Dracula* (Potter, 1992).

diminished, and the vampire, more and more frequently, is seen as a thief of psychological energy rather than as a threat to the immortal soul.

Not only have late-twentieth-century vampires been secularized, but they have also been more and more explicitly eroticized. The vampires imagined for us by writers like Rice and Yarbro and filmmakers like Francis Ford Coppola are handsome, youthful, romantic, and sensuous.

I have begun to think, too, that the vampire embrace fascinates late-twentieth-century readers because of the gracefulness with which it is usually depicted. One thinks of the dreamlike stillness of the vampire's lovemaking. A vampire bends over his or her victim; there is a not particularly painful little bite, and the victim's face takes on a look of bliss. How different—and to some readers, how soothingly different—that is from the usual, and essentially awkward, tumults of sex.

Finally, there is the special meaning that the vampire idea has acquired in our minds since the coming of AIDS. Because it is a blood-transmitted disease, AIDS has re-emphasized the ways in which blood, sex, and death are linked, giving an additional meaning to our reading of vampire fiction. The vampire was seen simply as a monster who could endanger a victim's life and taint his or her immortal soul. Now, in the age of AIDS, the blood exchange between vampire and victim, still deadly, has the new and very modern implication of a death preceded by a lingering and incurable disease.

Stories about vampires existed long before Stoker. There is a vampire episode in Lucius Apuleius's *The Golden Ass,* a second-century Latin classic, and there is no dearth of vampire folklore in Europe. It was not, however, until the nineteenth century that *The Vampyre,* the first vampire novel in English, appeared. *The Vampyre,* by John Polidori, an ambivalent friend, traveling companion, and physician of George Gordon, Lord Byron, was written in answer to a challenge Byron made to his guests in the Villa Diodati on a rainy summer evening in Geneva in 1816. Those guests included Polidori, Percy Bysshe Shelley, and Mary Shelley, all of whom Byron challenged to write a ghost story. Byron himself never wrote more than a fragment. Percy Shelley did not make the attempt. Mary Shelley's response to the challenge was the novel *Frankenstein.*

Polidori's *The Vampyre* appeared in 1821 and had an impact, particularly on the European stage, far beyond its apparent merit. Polidori's vampire is Lord Ruthven (a thinly disguised Byron), a pallid English nobleman who befriends a young gentleman named Aubrey. Ruthven "vampirizes" Aubrey's sister even as Aubrey—bound by an oath not to reveal for a year what he knows about Ruthven—is unable to save his sister from her fate. Since neither Aubrey nor his sister are characters with much individuality or vitality, and since the plot of the novel turns on Aubrey's keeping a ridiculous promise, one can only be surprised at the story's durability in theaters on the Continent in the first half of the nineteenth century.

The next major fictional vampire character to appear in print was *Varney the Vampyre* (1847), for a long time attributed to Thomas Preskett Prest but actually written by James Malcolm Rymer. Although excessively long and frequently ridiculous, the novel is dear to my heart. I am enchanted by the author's endlessly ingenious wordiness, and by the novel's almost infinite number of subplots.

Rymer's prose is high pitched and breathless. We have helpless heroines and a "tall, gaunt figure in hideous relief . . . a long, gaunt hand which seems utterly destitute of flesh . . . the figure turns half around . . . it is perfectly white—perfectly bloodless . . . her beautiful rounded limbs quivered . . . he seizes her neck in his fang-like teeth—a gush of blood, and a hideous sucking noise follows. . . ."* Readers of Rymer's prose must be endlessly patient and tolerant of drawn-out suspense. The blood-thirsty Varney is as memorable as he is unbelievable. But here, unlike the more well-known *Dracula,* there is some sympathy for the vampire.

From the unintentionally comic and seemingly endless pages of *Varney the Vampyre,* we move next to J. Sheridan Le Fanu's 1872 novella *Carmilla,* a superbly literate, beautifully crafted story by a man who, like Stoker, was an Irishman. The vampire in *Carmilla* is a woman, as are her victims. This fact has led many readers, critics among them, to conclude that this is a novella whose primary focus is lesbianism. I do not share that view. I am convinced that the power and the literary value of Le Fanu's story lies in its study of the fragility of human love. Of course, there is a deep undercurrent of Eros in this story, as there is in all love stories. But Le Fanu's focus is on the tragic fact that betrayal, too, is an essential element in love—not on the fact that the vampire's victim is a woman. As Carmilla describes it, "as I draw near to you, you, in your turn, will draw near to the others, and learn the rapture of that cruelty, which yet is love. . . ."

The next novel to appear was Stoker's, in 1897. When I describe Count Dracula as "embedded in our subconscious," I may, without intending it, seem to imply that the novel alone broadcast the image of the count to the world. That is not what happened.

Stoker's novel, conceived originally as a "shilling shocker," did not reveal to its first readers the layers of meaning that late-twentieth-century critics have since found in it, and which have made subsequent readers acknowledge the novel's greatness. Read only for its plot, as it originally was, *Dracula* is still a first-rate adventure tale in which a group of devoted and high-minded heroes pursue and finally destroy an evil Transylvanian creature of the night who menaces British womanhood. Stoker added to that plotline another not particularly complicated element. The antagonist, Count Dracula, is depicted as a satanic creature, the Primal Dragon, and

*Varma, Devendra P., ed. *Varney the Vampyre* (Ayer, 1972).

his pursuers as a sort of composite St. George doing battle with the dragon.

Stoker did not attempt anything like character analysis. His characters are two dimensional, his humor is a step above music-hall comedy, his heroes are heroic, his women are beautiful and good (until Dracula taints their purity). Dracula himself is a minion of Satan and is wholly villainous.

On the other hand, Stoker—who spent most of his adult life in the service of Sir Henry Irving, England's most famous actor, and who heard fine stage prose being spoken almost daily—had an ear for high-sounding speech, which he imitated with considerable success in *Dracula*. He was served by his slight knowledge of the historical Vlad Tepes, a fifteenth-century Transylvanian tyrant whose cruelties are notorious. He had also read a wonderful travel book by an Englishwoman named Emily Gerard, *The Land Beyond the Forest* (1888), in which he found most of the vampire lore he used in *Dracula*.

Stoker also possessed an extraordinarily lucid vision of the psychological implications of his central metaphor. I do not say he understood them. To see clearly is not the same as to understand what one sees. Stoker's story, as he gave it to us, has left us wrestling ever since with its varied meanings.

Though *Dracula* in its time sold reasonably well, it did not become a best-seller until after Stoker's death. However, it was films based on Stoker's book, that eventually made Dracula a household word.

It should not surprise us that films based on Stoker's novel have never been faithful to his text. Stoker's story, though it makes for dramatic reading, has far too many characters and far too many incidents to sustain a filmgoer's interest for very long. In any case, film fiction is not the same art form as print fiction. Film has to show what a print reader can imagine. We need not then grade our film versions of the Dracula story on whether they are or are not faithful to the book.

The German film *Nosferatu* (1922), made by Prana Films, is a pirated, thinly disguised version of Stoker's story. F. W. Murnau, the film's director, believed that by making superficial changes to the names of Stoker's characters, he could appropriate the story. An outraged Florence Stoker sued and eventually prevailed in the German courts, which ruled that all copies of the film were to be destroyed. Fortunately for us, some copies survived.

In Murnau's silent film, the vampire is seen as a caricature of a monster. Max Schreck, the actor who plays Count Orlock, the vampire, is given the pointed ears of an animal, long fingernails, a face with hideously distorted features, and glazing eyes. If he resembles any literary character at all, it is Varney the Vampyre, but in fact he is simply meant to look like a monster.

Nosferatu, despite the deficiencies of comparatively primitive filmmaking technology, is one of the world's greatest horror films. The sequences in which Orlock appears feel like authentic transcriptions from nightmares. The climactic scene in which Orlock comes to "vampirize" Nina (Mina Harker in Stoker's *Dracula*) is terrifying in the extreme and, as in Stoker's *Dracula,* has religious implications, as Nina assumes the role of a sacrificial figure who will die for the sake of humanity.

Although *Nosferatu* is indeed frightful, it would be nearly ten years before the film appeared that would give the world the Dracula it would never forget.

In 1931, Universal Pictures released Tod Browning's *Dracula* with Bela Lugosi in the title role. The film, based on the Hamilton Dean/John Balderston stage play adaptation of the novel rather than on the novel itself, is marred by comic interludes meant to appeal to theater audiences. I have taken critical potshots at this poorly edited film in my time, but despite its jerky pacing and wooden performances by David Manners (John Harker), Helen Chandler (Mina Harker), and Frances Dade (Lucy Weston [sic]), it is still, because of the unsurpassed achievements of Lugosi as Dracula and Dwight Frye as Renfield, the most memorable Dracula yet made. Lugosi's face and accent will spring to mind whenever the name Dracula is mentioned. With this film began the mythologizing of the name Dracula. Who can ever forget Lugosi's magisterial "I do not drink . . . wine," or his "Listen to them, children of the night. What music they make"?

The Lugosi film created for us the Dracula we now experience as an archetype: the vampire in tie and tails who is a supremely civilized yet unmistakably feral being who can be drawing-room charming but may also take on the guise of a bat or a wolf. Always he (or she) is an irrepressible force whose dynamic energy is profoundly attractive.

That attraction has been presented to us on screen in a variety of guises. Christopher Lee's Dracula in the English Hammer Films productions of the late 1950s and 1960s is cold, aloof, immobile, and implicitly violent. Gloria Holden's title role in *Dracula's Daughter* (1936) is brooding, anguished, and profoundly dangerous. Frank Langella's theatrical Dracula (1979) is playful, witty, charming, and utterly cuddly. John Carradine, in *Billy the Kid versus Dracula* (1965), is as funny as the characters who appear in opéra bouffe, while William Marshall, in the exploitation film *Blacula* (1972), is dignified and dynamic with the look in his eyes of a man who has suffered an incurable inner wound. Gary Oldman, in Francis Ford Coppola's *Bram Stoker's Dracula* (1992), had the difficult task of playing several roles in that film: the fierce fifteenth-century warrior Vlad Tepes, the aged nineteenth-century Count Dracula, the blood-revivified youthful count, and, at intervals, the demonic version of that self.

I have described at length the part that the film industry has played in the development of our ideas about vampires because, since 1922, the eroticism of the vampire embrace has been rendered in film more and more explicitly; and, almost as a corollary, the vampires themselves have been reimagined for us as sympathetic creatures: as Byronic heroes, as admirable outlaws, as heroic antagonists of God himself.

That tectonic moral shift in the perception of vampires on movie screens has had its impact on the vampire fiction that has appeared in print. The distance between Stoker's conception of his evil Count Dracula and Yarbro's elegant, fastidious, and admirable Count Saint-Germain is exemplary. For Stoker, Dracula, an unmitigatedly evil creature in the service of the devil, preyed not only upon Christian lives but also on Christian souls. Saint-Germain, who actually wears a cross, is infinitely wise and decent. If Dracula eroticizes women to procure their damnation, Saint-Germain does the same to give them supreme pleasure.

In a century in which God and Satan have become increasingly irrelevant in the popular arts, there has been an accompanying secularization of the vampire idea. There has been a shift in interest on the part of readers and filmgoers. While in the earlier books and films the vampire's victim suffered from his or her embrace, in more recent works the focus is on the erotic sensuality of the embrace. Death may be the result but, as in Coppola's film interpretation of Stoker, it is a small price to pay for the ecstasy and the immortal life and youth that is the vampire's gift. Not surprisingly, for hasty readers and filmgoers, the grace of God is less appealing than a sublimely sensual passion.

The stories in this collection were selected with two goals in mind: first, to give readers as much pleasure as a single anthology can be expected to provide; second, to display the evolutionary shift in the treatment of the vampire.

Though literary theory is not my strong point, that has not kept me from noticing that the tales can fall into six descriptive categories. But a reader should be warned: categories are rhetorical devices, useful in making suggestive distinctions. The reader should not be surprised that one or another of the tales in this book could fall into a category other than the one to which it is assigned. For instance, "Shambleau," by C. L. Moore, could easily fit in any of four categories: The Classic Adventure Tale, the Psychological Vampire, the Science Fiction Vampire, or the Non-Human Vampire. But Moore was chiefly a science fiction writer, so I feel most comfortable calling her tale science fiction.

The categories, then, are:

• **The Classic Adventure Tale,** for which the narrative line of Stoker's novel is the model. In such tales, the tension of the plot derives from the antagonism that exists between the entirely evil vampire and the good people on whom he or she intends to feed. The designated victims, singly or with help, fight back and are usually triumphant. Examples include "The Blood Is the Life," by F. Marion Crawford, and the excerpt from Stephen King's *Salem's Lot*.

• **The Psychological Vampire.** This category, it should be noted, does not appear as a distinct genre until the mid-twentieth century, the age of

Freud. In the tales under this rubric, the word "vampire" is more nearly a metaphor than it is a literal description of the antagonist. The vampires in these stories do not drink blood. Instead, they are thieves of energy. In Mary E. Wilkins-Freeman's "Luella Miller," Luella literally, without turning a hand, drives those who help her into early graves.

• **The Science Fiction Vampire.** In this category, the stories take place within a recognizable science fiction ambiance: time travel, intergalactic voyages, genetic mutations, chemical constructs. Often such stories, lacking psychological or allegorical resonance, are, from a fictional point of view, comparatively weak. Both C. L. Moore's "Shambleau" and Suzy McKee Charnas's "Unicorn Tapestry" are powerful exceptions to that rule. "Shambleau" renders, almost unbearably, the "slimy, dreadful, and wet" physical attraction of monstrous couplings, while "Unicorn Tapestry" focuses on the intellectual attraction of the vampire.

• **The Non-Human Vampire.** Stories in which non-human vampires appear normally do not inspire much reader sympathy; low-grade humor is what such stories usually achieve. It is hard to care for the fortunes of cat-vampires, dog-vampires, plant-vampires, rabbit-vampires, or, as in one amazing comic book, a cow-vampire. For *Blood Thirst,* however, I have gathered tales of non-human vampires that outwit this general principle, such as Hanns Heinz Ewers's "The Spider" and Tanith Lee's "Bite-Me-Not or, Fleur de Feu." In "The Spider," the mimetic gestures that the vampire and her victim exchange between their facing windows become a hypnotic ballet performance whose graceful form adds horror to the tale. With "Bite-Me-Not . . ." it is Lee's suave and romantic prose that gives the story depth.

• **The Comic Vampire.** One would suppose that it would be hard to find humor in a genre of fiction in which blood drinking is a central theme. Still, there are vampire jokes and there have been a considerable number of quite funny vampire films. Not the least among them are *The Fearless Vampire Killers* (1967) and *Love at First Bite* (1979), which spoof both vampirism and the shibboleths of the Love Generation. Then too, Abbott and Costello have exploited vampirism for such laughs as they could get. In this anthology there are some funny short stories, such as filmmaker Woody Allen's "Count Dracula" and Frederic Brown's "Blood."

• Finally, we have **The Heroic Vampire.** The tales in this category, like those listed as Psychological Vampire stories, are latecomers to the vampire fiction scene. Here we have the diametric opposite of Stoker, with the vampire no longer representing absolute evil. Instead, the reader is meant to sympathize with the creature. We have Edward Bryant's "Good Kids," Anne Rice's "The Master of Rampling Gate," and the tale of a vampire photographer with a deadly artistic ambition in Laura Anne Gilman's "Exposure." The charm of the latter story lies in the delicious paradox that its vampire protagonist, a creature of darkness, is desirous of capturing a sunrise on film.

Here, then, is *Blood Thirst: 100 Years of Vampire Fiction,* a collection of vampire tales written in the century following Bram Stoker's *Dracula.* Sometimes the tales are grotesque, sometimes sublime. Sometimes whimsical, and sometimes profound. The startling variety of the stories gathered here is proof of the paradox that, though Stoker's fictional vampire could cast no shadow, his literary shadow hovers over all the tales in this book. Who'd have thought the old man had so much blood in him?

THE CLASSIC ADVENTURE TALE

Prior to literature of the twentieth century, vampires were depicted as unrepentant monsters, heartless creatures of hell who threatened the innocent and tested the courage of brave men and women. As the stories in this section show, there is still a lot of life left in such old-fashioned fiends. *Dracula* remains the model for such adventure tales, pitting Dr. Van Helsing and his hardy band of vampire-hunters against the seemingly unstoppable menace of the undying count. This type of conflict has been slavishly imitated ever since in inferior sequels and copies.

Still, several subsequent writers have crafted novels exploring ingenious variations on this theme of heartless vampire and earnest foe. *Progeny of the Adder* by Leslie H. Whitten (1965) updates the traditional adventure tale, and gives it a new sense of contemporary verisimilitude, by changing the hero to a big-city cop and disguising an old-fashioned vampire story as a police procedural. Jeff Rice accomplished much of the same feat in *The Night Stalker* (1973), which inspired two TV movies and a short-lived TV series about a spook-chasing reporter named Carl Kolchak. Stephen King's best-selling *Salem's Lot* (1975, excerpted in this volume) effectively transfers Stoker's plot to a small New England town. *Necroscope* by Brian Lumley (1986) is a gleefully gory mixture of science fiction, espionage, and full-blooded vampire fighting that has spawned at least nine sequels and is still going strong. Other successful tales of Good versus Undead Evil include *The Light at the End* by John Skipp and Craig Spector (1986) and *Bloodletter* by Warren Newton Beath (1994).

In these novels, and in the stories that follow, there is little of the moral ambiguity seen in much of today's vampire fiction. The vampires are dastardly and dangerous, and the humans are resourceful and in peril.

Of these tales, Stephen King's vampire and his good-guy opponents follow the Stoker formula most closely. In M. R. James's "Count Magnus," the count is more a force than he is a person, but he is an evil force.

It is the sheer, fear-inspiring threat of supernatural evil that propels these stories. The Classic Adventure Tale works now, as it did in Bram Stoker's time, because it taps into our primal fear of blood-sucking creatures from beyond the grave.

LAFCADIO HEARN
(1850–1904)

Patricio Lafcadio Tessima Carlos Hearn, the great interpreter of Japanese culture to the Western world, was born in Greece and spent his childhood in France, England, and Ireland. He was, for many years, a journalist. Among his other literary achievements are his translations of Théophile Gautier into English. Gautier, it will be remembered, is the author of La Morte Amoureuse *("Amorous Love"), one of the finest vampire tales ever written.*

Hearn began his career in America as a reporter for the Cincinnati Enquirer *and soon started, along with his friend Henry Farney,* Ye Giglampz, *a journal of social satire. The publication lasted for only a few months, but Hearn went on to more successful writing ventures, including* Chita: A Memory of Last Island *(1889), with which he made his mark among American writers. His works are gathered in many posthumous volumes, including* Editorials *(1926),* Essays on American Literature *(1929),* Barbarous Barbers and Other Stories *(1939), and the sixteen-volume* Writings of Lafcadio Hearn *(1922).*

From 1890 to 1894 Hearn lived in Japan, where he seems to have found his spiritual home. Kwaidan *(1904), Hearn's collection of Japanese folktales and ghost stories, was the basis for Masaki Kobayashi's wonderful film of the same name (1964).*

The tales in Kwaidan *reflect the view that everything in the world, living or not, is sentient and capable of exercising will, whether for good or evil. It is a view we will see reflected in Algernon Blackwood's "The Transfer." Hearn's tales are notable for their lucidity, for a simplicity of narrative style that we tend to think of as "Japanese."*

Here, in "The Story of Chūgorō," the narrator assumes that supernatural creatures inhabit the natural world, and that they hunger to experience human life. Without reaching for psychological detail or intricate plot development, the story, in the form of an allegory about a succubus, describes what the ingredients are for unhappiness in love: a desiring man, a beautiful and charming woman, and a difference between their two natures so great that disaster is inevitable. Like other examples of the Classic Adventure Tale, it is also an elemental tale of ordinary humanity confronting a dangerous supernatural force.

THE STORY OF CHŪGORŌ

A long time ago there lived, in the Koishikawa quarter of Yedo, a *batamoto* named Suzuki, whose yashiki was situated on the bank of the Yedogawa, not far from the bridge called Naka-no-hashi. And among the retainers of this Suzuki there was an *ashigaru* named Chūgorō. Chūgorō was a handsome lad, very amiable and clever, and much liked by his comrades.

For several years Chūgorō remained in the service of Suzuki, conducting himself so well that no fault was found with him. But at last the other *ashigaru* discovered that Chūgorō was in the habit of leaving the yashiki every night, by way of the garden, and staying out until a little before dawn. At first they said nothing to him about this strange behavior; for his absences did not interfere with any regular duty, and were supposed to be caused by some love-affair. But after a time he began to look pale and weak; and his comrades, suspecting some serious folly, decided to interfere. Therefore, one evening, just as he was about to steal away from the house, an elderly retainer called him aside, and said:—

"Chūgorō, my lad, we know that you go out every night and stay away until early morning, and we have observed that you are looking unwell. We fear that you are keeping bad company and injuring your health. And unless you can give a good reason for your conduct, we shall think that it is our duty to report this matter to the Chief Officer. In any case, since we are your comrades and friends, it is but right that we should know why you go out at night, contrary to the custom of this house."

Chūgorō appeared to be very much embarrassed and alarmed by these words. But after a short silence he passed into the garden, followed by his comrade. When the two found themselves well out of hearing of the rest, Chūgorō stopped, and said:—

"I will now tell you everything; but I must entreat you to keep my secret. If you repeat what I tell you, some great misfortune may befall me.

"It was in the early part of last spring—about five months ago—that I first began to go out at night, on account of a love-affair. One evening, when I was returning to the yashiki after a visit to my parents, I saw a woman standing by the riverside, not far from the main gateway. She was dressed like a person of high rank; and I thought it strange that a woman so finely dressed should be standing there alone at such an hour. But I did not think that I had any right to question her; and I was about to pass her by, without speaking, when she stepped forward and pulled me by the sleeve. Then I saw that she was very young and handsome. 'Will you not walk with me as far as the bridge?' she said; 'I have something to tell you.' Her voice was very soft and pleasant; and she smiled as she spoke; and her smile was hard to resist. So I walked with her toward the bridge; and on the way she told me that she had often seen me going in and out of the yashhiki, and had taken a fancy to me. 'I wish to have you for my husband,' she said;—'if you can like me, we shall be able to make each other very happy.' I did not know how to answer her; but I thought her very charming. As we neared the bridge, she pulled my sleeve again, and led me down the bank to the very edge of the river. 'Come in with me,' she whispered, and pulled me toward the water. It is deep there, as you know; and I became all at once afraid of her, and tried to turn back. She smiled, and caught me by the wrist, and said, 'Oh, you must never be afraid with me!' And, somehow, at the touch of her hand, I became more helpless than a child. I felt like a person in a dream who tries to run, and cannot move hand or foot. Into the deep water she stepped, and drew me with her; and I neither saw nor heard nor felt anything more until I found myself walking beside her through what seemed to be a great palace, full of light. I was neither wet nor cold: everything around me was dry and warm and beautiful. I could not understand where I was, nor how I had come there. The woman led me by the hand: we passed through room after room,—through ever so many rooms, all empty, but very fine,—until we entered into a guest-room of a thousand mats. Before a great alcove, at the farther end, lights were burning, and cushions laid as for a feast; but I saw no guests. She led me to the place of honor, by the alcove, and seated herself in front of me, and said: 'This is my home: do you think that you could be happy with me here?' As she asked the question she smiled; and I thought that her smile was more beautiful than anything else in the world; and out of my heart I answered, 'Yes. . . .' In the same moment I remembered the story of Urashima; and I imagined that she might be the daughter of a god; but I feared to ask her any questions. . . . Presently maid-servants came in, bearing rice-wine and many dishes, which they set before us. Then she who sat before me said: 'To-night shall be our bridal night, because you like me; and this is our wedding-feast.' We pledged ourselves to each other for the time of seven existences; and after the banquet we were conducted to a bridal chamber, which had been prepared for us.

"It was yet early in the morning when she awoke me, and said: 'My dear one, you are now indeed my husband. But for reasons which I cannot tell you, and which you must not ask, it is necessary that our marriage remain secret. To keep you here until daybreak would cost both of us our lives. Therefore do not, I beg of you, feel displeased because I must now send you back to the house of your lord. You can come to me to-night again, and every night hereafter, at the same hour that we first met. Wait always for me by the bridge; and you will not have to wait long. But remember, above all things, that our marriage must be a secret, and that, if you talk about it, we shall probably be separated forever.'

"I promised to obey her in all things,—remembering the fate of Ura-

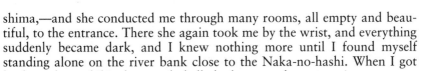

shima,—and she conducted me through many rooms, all empty and beautiful, to the entrance. There she again took me by the wrist, and everything suddenly became dark, and I knew nothing more until I found myself standing alone on the river bank close to the Naka-no-hashi. When I got back to the yashiki, the temple bells had not yet begun to ring.

"In the evening I went again to the bridge at the hour she had named, and I found her waiting for me. She took me with her, as before into the deep water, and into the wonderful place where we had passed our bridal night. And every night, since then, I have met and parted from her in the same way. To-night she will certainly be waiting for me, and I would rather die than disappoint her: therefore I must go. . . . But let me again entreat you, my friend, never to speak to any one about what I have told you."

The elder *ashigaru* was surprised and alarmed by this story. He felt that Chūgorō had told him the truth; and the truth suggested unpleasant possibilities. Probably the whole experience was an illusion, and an illusion produced by some evil power for a malevolent end. Nevertheless, if really bewitched, the lad was rather to be pitied than blamed; and any forcible interference would be likely to result in mischief. So the *ashigaru* answered kindly:—

"I shall never speak of what you have told me—never, at least, while you remain alive and well. Go and meet the woman; but—beware of her! I fear that you are being deceived by some wicked spirit."

Chūgorō only smiled at the old man's warning, and hastened away. Several hours later he reentered the yashiki, with a strangely dejected look. "Did you meet her?" whispered his comrade. "No," replied Chūgorō; "she was not there. For the first time, she was not there. I think that she will never meet me again. I did wrong to tell you;—I was very foolish to break my promise. . . ." The other vainly tried to console him. Chūgorō lay down, and spoke no word more. He was trembling from head to foot, as if he had caught a chill.

When the temple bells announced the hour of dawn, Chūgorō tried to get up, and fell back senseless. He was evidently sick,—deathly sick. A Chinese physician was summoned.

"Why, the man has no blood!" exclaimed the doctor, after a careful examination;—"there is nothing but water in his veins! It will be very difficult to save him. . . . What maleficence is this?"

Everything was done that could be done to save Chūgorō's life—but in vain. He died as the sun went down. Then his comrade related the whole story.

"Ah! I might have suspected as much!" exclaimed the doctor. . . . "No power could have saved him. He was not the first whom she destroyed."

"Who is she?—or what is she?" the *ashigaru* asked,—"a Fox-Woman?"

"No; she has been haunting this river from ancient time. She loves the blood of the young. . . ."

"A Serpent-Woman?—A Dragon-Woman?"

"No, no! If you were to see her under that bridge by daylight, she would appear to you a very loathsome creature."

"But what kind of a creature?"

"Simply a Frog,—a great and ugly Frog!"

M. R. JAMES
(1862–1936)

Montague Rhodes James, a lifelong bachelor, was a master ghost-story writer as well as a polyglot scholar, primarily of the medieval world. He was for many years a fellow at Cambridge University in England until, in 1914, he was elected provost of Eton.

Though he would not absolutely acknowledge a belief in ghosts, he nevertheless mastered the ghost-story genre. His best-known ghost stories are "The Ash Tree," "Canon Alberic's Scrapbook," "Oh Whistle and I'll Come to You, My Lad," and, of course, "Count Magnus," reprinted here. His collections include Ghost Stories of an Antiquary (1904), Collected Ghost Stories (1931), A Thin Ghost (1919), and A Warning to the Curious (1926).

In addition to his achievements as a ghost-story writer, James is important in the history of the horror literature genre because he was an early appreciator of the talents of Sheridan Le Fanu, a collection of whose stories (Madame Crowl's Ghost) he edited. Le Fanu was the author of "Carmilla," an influential early vampire story.

Purists who think a vampire's diet is, by definition, liquid, may object that "Count Magnus," who does not drink blood, is flying under false colors in an anthology of vampire fiction. The objection is valid. My two-part defense must be, first, that "Count Magnus" is such a splendid example of James's masterful pseudorealistic ghost fiction that I could not resist including it. Second, though the count does not drink blood, he does, like every other vampire, suck away the life of his victims.

James's horror tales owe much of their effectiveness to the tension he is able to create between his realistically described settings and the supernatural events that take place there. In "Count Magnus" James slowly, slowly lets his story meander from England to Stockholm, and from there to Vestergothland. Gently, almost imperceptibly, our attention shifts from what would seem to be the protagonist, Mr. Wraxall, to the Raback family history, and from that, finally, to Count Magnus himself.

"Count Magnus" borrows from Stoker the technique of keeping his horrid creature offstage through most of his tale. The supernatural climax of the story, told in the even tones of a scholarly narration and coming after so many pages of unsurprising detail, is particularly horrible. As in other tales of this nature, there is little attempt at metaphor or ambivalence or psychological complexity; the reader is simply meant to be frightened by the unhappy fate of an ordinary man who unwittingly falls prey to a malevolent vampire.

COUNT MAGNUS

By what means the papers out of which I have made a connected story came into my hands is the last point which the reader will learn from these pages. But it is necessary to prefix to my extracts from them a statement of the form in which I possess them.

They consist, then, partly of a series of collections for a book of travels, such a volume as was a common product of the forties and fifties. Horace Marryat's *Journal of a Residence in Jutland and the Danish Isles* is a fair specimen of the class to which I allude. These books usually treated of some unknown district on the Continent. They were illustrated with woodcuts or steel plates. They gave details of hotel accommodation and of means of communication, such as we now expect to find in any well-regulated guide-book, and they dealt largely in reported conversations with intelligent foreigners, racy innkeepers, and garrulous peasants. In a word, they were chatty.

Begun with the idea of furnishing material for such a book, my papers as they progressed assumed the character of a record of one single personal experience, and this record was continued up to the very eve, almost, of its termination.

The writer was a Mr. Wraxall. For my knowledge of him I have to depend entirely on the evidence his writings afford, and from these I deduce that he was a man past middle age, possessed of some private means, and very much alone in the world. He had, it seems, no settled abode in England, but was a denizen of hotels and boarding-houses. It is probable that he entertained the idea of settling down at some future time which never came; and I think it also likely that the Pantechnicon fire in the early seventies must have destroyed a great deal that would have thrown light on his antecedents, for he refers once or twice to property of his that was warehoused at that establishment.

It is further apparent that Mr. Wraxall had published a book, and that it treated of a holiday he had once taken in Brittany. More than this I cannot say about his work, because a diligent search in bibliographical works has convinced me that it must have appeared either anonymously or under a pseudonym.

As to his character, it is not difficult to form some superficial opinion. He must have been an intelligent and cultivated man. It seems that he was near being a Fellow of his college at Oxford—Brasenose, as I judge from the Calendar. His besetting fault was pretty clearly that of over-inquisitiveness, possibly a good fault in a traveler, certainly a fault for which this traveler paid dearly enough in the end.

On what proved to be his last expedition, he was plotting another book. Scandinavia, a region not widely known to Englishmen forty years ago, had struck him as an interesting field. He must have alighted on some old books of Swedish history or memoirs, and the idea had struck him that there was room for a book descriptive of travel in Sweden, interspersed with episodes from the history of some of the great Swedish families. He procured letters of introduction, therefore, to some persons of quality in Sweden, and set out thither in the early summer of 1863.

Of his travels in the North there is no need to speak, nor of his residence of some weeks in Stockholm. I need only mention that some *savant* resident there put him on the track of an important collection of family papers belonging to the proprietors of an ancient manor-house in Vestergothland, and obtained for him permission to examine them.

The manor-house, or *herrgard*, in question is to be called Råbäck (pronounced something like Roebeck), though that is not its name. It is one of the best buildings of its kind in all the country, and the picture of it in Dahlenberg's *Suecia antiqua et moderna,* engraved in 1694, shows it very much as the tourist may see it today. It was built soon after 1600, and is, roughly speaking, very much like an English house of that period in respect of material—red-brick with stone facings—and style. The man who built it was a scion of the great house of De la Gardie, and his descendants possess it still. De la Gardie is the name by which I will designate them when mention of them becomes necessary.

They received Mr. Wraxall with great kindness and courtesy, and pressed him to stay in the house as long as his researches lasted. But, preferring to be independent, and mistrusting his powers of conversing in Swedish, he settled himself at the village inn, which turned out quite sufficiently comfortable, at any rate during the summer months. This arrangement would entail a short walk daily to and from the manor-house of something under a mile. The house itself stood in a park, and was protected—we should say grown up—with large old timber. Near it you found the walled garden, and then entered a close wood fringing one of the small lakes with which the whole country is pitted. Then came the wall of the demesne, and you climbed a steep knoll—a knob of rock lightly covered with soil—and on the top of this stood the church, fenced in with tall dark trees. It was a curious building to English eyes. The nave and aisles were low, and filled with pews and galleries. In the western gallery stood the handsome old organ, gaily painted, and with silver pipes. The ceiling was flat, and had been adorned by a seventeenth-century artist with a strange and hideous "Last Judgment," full of lurid flames, falling cities, burning ships, crying souls, and brown and smiling demons. Handsome brass coronae hung from the roof; the pulpit was like a doll's-house covered with little painted wooden cherubs and saints; a stand with three hour-glasses was hinged to the preacher's desk. Such sights as these may be seen in many a church in Sweden now, but what distinguished this one was an addition to the original building. At the eastern end of the north aisle the builder of the manor-house had erected a mausoleum for himself and his family. It was a largish eight-sided building, lighted by a series of oval windows, and it had a domed roof, topped by a kind of pumpkin-shaped object rising into a spire, a form in which Swedish architects greatly delighted. The roof was of copper externally, and was painted black, while the walls, in common with those of the church, were staringly white. To this mausoleum there was no access from the church. It had a portal and steps of its own on the northern side.

Past the churchyard the path to the village goes, and not more than three or four minutes bring you to the inn door.

On the first day of his stay at Råbäck Mr. Wraxall found the church door open, and made these notes of the interior which I have epitomized. Into the mausoleum, however, he could not make his way. He could by looking through the keyhole just descry that there were fine marble effigies and sarcophagi of copper, and a wealth of armorial ornament, which made him very anxious to spend some time in investigation.

The papers he had come to examine at the manor-house proved to be of just the kind he wanted for his book. There were family correspondence, journals, and account-books of the earliest owners of the estate, very carefully kept and clearly written, full of amusing and picturesque detail. The first De la Gardie appeared in them as a strong and capable man. Shortly after the building of the mansion there had been a period of distress in the district, and the peasants had risen and attacked several chateaux and done some damage. The owner of Råbäck took a leading part in suppressing the trouble, and there was reference to executions of ring-leaders and severe punishments inflicted with no sparing hand.

The portrait of this Magnus de la Gardie was one of the best in the house, and Mr. Wraxall studied it with no little interest after his day's work. He gives no detailed description of it, but I gather that the face impressed him rather by its power than by its beauty or goodness; in fact, he writes that Count Magnus was an almost phenomenally ugly man.

On this day Mr. Wraxall took his supper with the family, and walked back in the late but still bright evening.

"I must remember," he writes, "to ask the sexton if he can let me into the mausoleum at the church. He evidently has access to it himself, for I saw him tonight standing on the steps, and, as I thought, locking or unlocking the door."

I find that early on the following day Mr. Wraxall had some conversation with his landlord. His setting it down at such length as he does surprised me at first; but I soon realized that the papers I was reading were, at least in their beginning, the materials for the book he was meditating, and that it was to have been one of those quasi-journalistic productions which admit of the introduction of an admixture of conversational matter.

His object, he says, was to find out whether any traditions of Count Magnus de la Gardie lingered on in the scenes of that gentleman's activity, and whether the popular estimate of him were favorable or not. He found that the Count was decidedly not a favorite. If his tenants came late to their work on the days which they owed to him as Lord of the Manor, they were set on the wooden horse, or flogged and branded in the manor-house yard. One or two cases there were of man who had occupied lands which encroached on the lord's domain, and whose houses had been mysteriously burnt on a winter's night, with the whole family inside. But what seemed to dwell on the innkeeper's mind most—for he returned to the subject more than once—was that the Count had been on the Black Pilgrimage, and had brought something or someone back with him.

You will naturally inquire, as Mr. Wraxall did, what the Black Pilgrimage may have been. But your curiosity on the point must remain unsatisfied for the time being, just as his did. The landlord was evidently unwilling to give a full answer, or indeed any answer, on the point, and, being called out for a moment, trotted out with obvious alacrity, only putting his head in at the door a few minutes afterwards to say that he was called away to Skara, and should not be back till evening.

So Mr. Wraxall had to go unsatisfied to his day's work at the manor-house. The papers on which he was just then engaged soon put his thoughts into another channel, for he had to occupy himself with glancing over the correspondence between Sophia Albertina in Stockholm and her married cousin Ulrica Leonora at Råbäck in the years 1705–10. The letters were of exceptional interest from the light they threw upon the culture of that period in Sweden, as anyone can testify who has read the full edition of them in the publications of the Swedish Historical Manuscripts Commission.

In the afternoon he had done with these, and after returning the boxes in which they were kept to their places on the shelf, he proceeded, very naturally, to take down some of the volumes nearest to them, in order to determine which of them had best be his principal subject of investigation next day. The shelf he had hit upon was occupied mostly by a collection of account-books in the writing of the first Count Magnus. But one among them was not an account-book, but a book of alchemical and other tracts in another sixteenth-century hand. Not being very familiar with alchemical literature, Mr. Wraxall spends much space which he might have spared in setting out the names and beginnings of the various treatises: The book of the Phoenix, book of the Thirty Words, book of the Toad, book of Miriam, Turba philosophorum, and so forth; and then he announces with a good deal of circumstance his delight at finding, on a leaf originally left blank near the middle of the book, some writing of Count Magnus himself headed "Liber nigrae peregrinationis." It is true that only a few lines were written, but there was quite enough to show that the landlord had that morning been referring to a belief at least as old as the time of Count

Magnus, and probably shared by him. This is the English of what was written:

"If any man desires to obtain a long life, if he would obtain a faithful messenger and see the blood of his enemies, it is necessary that he should first go into the city of Chorazin, and there salute the prince . . ." Here there was an erasure of one word, not very thoroughly done, so that Mr. Wraxall felt pretty sure that he was right in reading it as *aëris* ("of the air"). But there was no more of the text copied, only a line in Latin: *Quaere reliqua hujus materiei inter secretiora.* (See the rest of this matter among the more private things.)

It could not be denied that this threw a rather lurid light upon the tastes and beliefs of the Count; but to Mr. Wraxall, separated from him by nearly three centuries, the thought that he might have added to his general forcefulness alchemy, and to alchemy something like magic, only made him a more picturesque figure, and when, after a rather prolonged contemplation of his picture in the hall, Mr. Wraxall set out on his homeward way, his mind was full of the thought of Count Magnus. He had no eyes for his surroundings, no perception of the evening scents of the woods or the evening light on the lake; and when all of a sudden he pulled up short, he was astonished to find himself already at the gate of the churchyard, and within a few minutes of his dinner. His eyes fell on the mausoleum.

"Ah," he said, "Count Magnus, there you are. I should dearly like to see you."

"Like many solitary men," he writes, "I have a habit of talking to myself aloud; and, unlike some of the Greek and Latin particles, I do not expect an answer. Certainly, and perhaps fortunately in this case, there was neither voice nor any that regarded: only the woman who, I suppose, was cleaning up the church, dropped some metallic object on the floor, whose clang startled me. Count Magnus, I think, sleeps sound enough."

That same evening the landlord of the inn, who had heard Mr. Wraxall say that he wished to see the clerk or deacon (as he would be called in Sweden) of the parish, introduced him to that official in the inn parlor. A visit to the De la Gardie tomb-house was soon arranged for the next day, and a little general conversation ensued.

Mr. Wraxall, remembering that one function of Scandinavian deacons is to teach candidates for Confirmation, thought he would refresh his own memory on a Biblical point.

"Can you tell me," he said, "anything about Chorazin?"

The deacon seemed startled, but readily reminded him how that village had once been denounced.

"To be sure," said Mr. Wraxall; "it is, I suppose, quite a ruin now?"

"So I expect," replied the deacon. "I have heard some of our old priests say that Antichrist is to be born there; and there are tales—"

"Ah! what tales are those?" Mr. Wraxall put in.

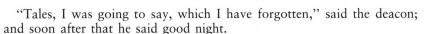

"Tales, I was going to say, which I have forgotten," said the deacon; and soon after that he said good night.

The landlord was now alone, and at Mr. Wraxall's mercy; and that inquirer was not inclined to spare him.

"Herr Nielsen," he said, "I have found out something about the Black Pilgrimage. You may as well tell me what you know. What did the Count bring back with him?"

Swedes are habitually slow, perhaps, in answering, or perhaps the landlord was an exception. I am not sure; but Mr. Wraxall notes that the landlord spent at least one minute in looking at him before he said anything at all. Then he came close up to his guest, and with a good deal of effort he spoke:

"Mr. Wraxall, I can tell you this one little tale, and no more—not any more. You must not ask anything when I have done. In my grandfather's time—that is, ninety-two years ago—there were two men who said: 'The Count is dead; we do not care for him. We will go tonight and have a free hunt in his wood'—the long wood on the hill that you have seen behind Råbäck. Well, those that heard them say this, they said: 'No, do not go; we are sure you will meet with persons walking who should not be walking. They should be resting, not walking.' These men laughed. There were no forest-men to keep the wood, because no one wished to live there. The family were not here at the house. These men could do what they wished.

"Very well, they go to the wood that night. My grandfather was sitting here in this room. It was the summer, and a light night. With the window open, he could see out to the wood, and hear.

"So he sat there, and two or three men with him, and they listened. At first they hear nothing at all; then they hear someone—you know how far away it is—they hear someone scream, just as if the most inside part of his soul was twisted out of him. All of them in the room caught hold of each other, and they sat so for three-quarters of an hour. Then they hear someone else, only about three hundred ells off. They hear him laugh out loud: it was not one of those two men that laughed, and, indeed, they have all of them said that it was not any man at all. After that they hear a great door shut.

"Then, when it was just light with the sun, they all went to the priest. They said to him:

" 'Father, put on your gown and your ruff, and come to bury these men, Anders Bjornsen and Hans Thorbjorn.'

"You understand that they were sure these men were dead. So they went to the wood—my grandfather never forgot this. He said they were all like so many dead men themselves. The priest, too, he was in a white fear. He said when they came to him:

" 'I heard one cry in the night, and I heard one laugh afterwards. If I cannot forget that, I shall not be able to sleep again.'

"So they went to the wood, and they found these men on the edge of the wood. Hans Thorbjorn was standing with his back against a tree, and all the time he was pushing with his hands—pushing something away from him which was not there. So he was not dead. And they led him away, and took him to the house at Nykjoping, and he died before the winter; but he went on pushing with his hands. Also Anders Bjornsen was there; but he was dead. And I tell you this about Anders Bjornsen, that he was once a beautiful man, but now his face was not there, because the flesh of it was sucked away off the bones. You understand that? My grandfather did not forget that. And they laid him on the bier which they brought, and they put a cloth over his head, and the priest walked before; and they began to sing the psalm for the dead as well as they could. So, as they were singing the end of the first verse, one fell down, who was carrying the head of the bier, and the others looked back, and they saw that the cloth had fallen off, and the eyes of Anders Bjornsen were looking up, because there was nothing to close over them. And this they could not bear. Therefore the priest laid the cloth upon him, and sent for a spade, and they buried him in that place."

The next day Mr. Wraxall records that the deacon called for him soon after his breakfast, and took him to the church and mausoleum. He noticed that the key of the latter was hung on a nail just by the pulpit, and it occurred to him that, as the church door seemed to be left unlocked as a rule, it would not be difficult for him to pay a second and more private visit to the monuments if there proved to be more of interest among them than could be digested at first. The building, when he entered it, he found not unimposing. The monuments, mostly large erections of the seventeenth and eighteenth centuries, were dignified if luxuriant, and the epitaphs and heraldry were copious. The central space of the domed room was occupied by three copper sarcophagi, covered with finely-engraved ornament. Two of them had, as is commonly the case in Denmark and Sweden, a large metal crucifix on the lid. The third, that of Count Magnus, as it appeared, had, instead of that, a full-length effigy engraved upon it, and round the edge were several bands of similar ornament representing various scenes. One was a battle, with cannon belching out smoke, and walled towns, and troops of pikemen. Another showed an execution. In a third, among trees, was a man running at full speed, with flying hair and outstretched hands. After him followed a strange form; it would be hard to say whether the artist had intended it for a man, and was unable to give the requisite similitude, or whether it was intentionally made as monstrous as it looked. In view of the skill with which the rest of the drawing was done, Mr. Wraxall felt inclined to adopt the latter idea. The figure was unduly short, and was for the most part muffled in a hooded garment which swept the ground. The only part of the form which projected from that shelter was not shaped like any hand or arm. Mr. Wraxall compares it to the tentacle of a devil-fish, and continues: "On seeing this, I said to myself, 'This,

then, which is evidently an allegorical representation of some kind—a fiend pursuing a hunted soul—may be the origin of the story of Count Magnus and his mysterious companion. Let us see how the huntsman is pictured: doubtless it will be a demon blowing his horn.' " But, as it turned out, there was no such sensational figure, only the semblance of a cloaked man on a hillock, who stood leaning on a stick, and watching the hunt with an interest which the engraver had tried to express in his attitude.

Mr. Wraxall noted the finely-worked and massive steel padlocks—three in number—which secured the sarcophagus. One of them, he saw, was detached, and lay on the pavement. And then, unwilling to delay the deacon longer or to waste his own working-time, he made his way onward to the manor-house.

"It is curious," he notes, "how, on retracing a familiar path, one's thoughts engross one to the absolute exclusion of surrounding objects. Tonight, for the second time, I had entirely failed to notice where I was going (I had planned a private visit to the tomb-house to copy the epitaphs), when I suddenly, as it were, awoke to consciousness, and found myself (as before) turning in at the churchyard gate, and, I believe, singing or chanting some such words as, 'Are you awake, Count Magnus? Are you asleep, Count Magnus?' and then something more which I have failed to recollect. It seemed to me that I must have been behaving in this nonsensical way for some time."

He found the key of the mausoleum where he had expected to find it, and copied the greater part of what he wanted; in fact, he stayed until the light began to fail him.

"I must have been wrong," he writes, "in saying that one of the padlocks of my Count's sarcophagus was unfastened; I see tonight that two are loose. I picked both up, and laid them carefully on the window-ledge, after trying unsuccessfully to close them. The remaining one is still firm, and, though I take it to be a spring lock, I cannot guess how it is opened. Had I succeeded in undoing it, I am almost afraid I should have taken the liberty of opening the sarcophagus. It is strange, the interest I feel in the personality of this, I fear, somewhat ferocious and grim old noble."

The day following was, as it turned out, the last of Mr. Wraxall's stay at Råbäck. He received letters connected with certain investments which made it desirable that he should return to England; his work among the papers was practically done, and traveling was slow. He decided, therefore, to make his farewells, put some finishing touches to his notes, and be off.

These finishing touches and farewells, as it turned out, took more time than he had expected. The hospitable family insisted on his staying to dine with them—they dined at three—and it was verging on half past six before he was outside the iron gates of Råbäck. He dwelt on every step of his walk by the lake, determined to saturate himself, now that he trod it for the last time, in the sentiment of the place and hour. And when he reached the summit of the churchyard knoll, he lingered for many minutes, gazing at the limitless prospect of woods near and distant, all dark beneath a sky of liquid green. When at last he turned to go, the thought struck him that surely he must bid farewell to Count Magnus as well as the rest of the De la Gardies. The church was but twenty yards away, and he knew where the key of the mausoleum hung. It was not long before he was standing over the great copper coffin, and, as usual, talking to himself aloud: "You may have been a bit of a rascal in your time, Magnus," he was saying, "but for all that I should like to see you, or, rather—"

"Just at that instant," he says, "I felt a blow on my foot. Hastily enough I drew it back, and something fell on the pavement with a clash. It was the third, the last of the three padlocks which had fastened the sarcophagus. I stooped to pick it up, and—Heaven is my witness that I am writing only the bare truth—before I had raised myself there was a sound of metal hinges creaking, and I distinctly saw the lid shifting upwards. I may have behaved like a coward, but I could not for my life stay for one moment. I was outside that dreadful building in less time than I can write—almost as quickly as I could have said—the words; and what frightens me yet more, I could not turn the key in the lock. As I sit here in my room noting these facts, I ask myself (it was not twenty minutes ago) whether that noise of creaking metal continued, and I cannot tell whether it did or not. I only know that there was something more than I have written that alarmed me, but whether it was sound or sight I am not able to remember. What is this that I have done?"

Poor Mr. Wraxall! He set out on his journey to England on the next day, as he had planned, and he reached England in safety; and yet, as I gather from his changed hand and inconsequent jottings, a broken man. One of the several small note-books that have come to me with his papers gives, not a key to, but a kind of inkling of, his experiences. Much of his journey was made by canal-boat, and I find not less than six painful attempts to enumerate and describe his fellow-passengers. The entries are of this kind:

24. Pastor of village in Skane. Usual black coat and soft black hat.
25. Commercial traveler from Stockholm going to Trollhättan. Black cloak, brown hat.
26. Man in long black cloak, broad-leafed hat, very old-fashioned.

This entry is lined out, and a note added: "Perhaps identical with No. 13. Have not yet seen his face." On referring to No. 13, I find that he is a Roman priest in a cassock.

The net result of the reckoning is always the same. Twenty-eight people appear in the enumeration, one being always a man in a long black cloak and broad hat, and the other a "short figure in dark cloak and hood."

On the other hand, it is always noted that only twenty-six passengers appear at meals, and that the man in the cloak is perhaps absent, and the short figure is certainly absent.

On reaching England, it appears that Mr. Wraxall landed at Harwich, and that he resolved at once to put himself out of the reach of some person or persons whom he never specifies, but whom he had evidently come to regard as his pursuers. Accordingly he took a vehicle—it was a closed fly—not trusting the railway and drove across country to the village of Belchamp St. Paul. It was about nine o'clock on a moonlight August night when he neared the place. He was sitting forward, and looking out of the window at the fields and tickets—there was little else to be seen—racing past him. Suddenly he came to a cross-road. At the corner two figures were standing motionless; both were in dark cloaks; the taller one wore a hat, the shorter a hood. He had no time to see their faces, nor did they make any motion that he could discern. Yet the horse shied violently and broke into a gallop, and Mr. Wraxall sank back into his seat in something like desperation. He had seen them before.

Arrived at Belchamp St. Paul, he was fortunate enough to find a decent furnished lodging, and for the next twenty-four hours he lived, comparatively speaking, in peace. His last notes were written on this day. They are too disjointed and ejaculatory to be given here in full, but the substance of them is clear enough. He is expecting a visit from his pursuers—how or when he knows not—and his constant cry is "What has he done?" and "Is there no hope?" Doctors, he knows, would call him mad, policemen would laugh at him. The parson is away. What can he do but lock his door and cry to God?

People still remember last year at Belchamp St. Paul how a strange gentleman came one evening in August years back; and how the next morning but one he was found dead, and there was an inquest; and the jury that viewed the body fainted, seven of 'em did, and none of 'em wouldn't speak to what they see, and the verdict was visitation of God; and how the people as kep' the 'ouse moved out that same week, and went away from that part. But they do not, I think, know that any glimmer of light has ever been thrown, or could be thrown, on the mystery. It so happened that last year the little house came into my hands as part of a legacy. It had stood empty since 1863, and there seemed no prospect of letting it; so I had it pulled down, and the papers of which I have given you an abstract were found in a forgotten cupboard under the window in the best bedroom.

F. MARION CRAWFORD
(1854–1909)

Francis Marion Crawford was born in Italy, and was raised both there and in America. The son of a sculptor father and a novelist mother, he was educated in Italy and at Cambridge University. In 1879 he went to Allahabad, India, to edit the Indian Herald. *Crawford then traveled to the United States to seek work in the literary field with the aid of his uncle Samuel Ward, a famous gourmet and lobbyist. He later chose to live in Italy, but remained a U.S. citizen.*

Crawford's stay in India provided the inspiration for Mr. Isaacs: A Tale of Modern India *(1882), the story of a diamond merchant whose sale of a unique stone brings protest from Britain. This was his first novel, and it marked the beginning of a prosperous career. Crawford's popularity with his readers has often been overlooked by critics, mostly due to the fact that his career coincided with those of Mark Twain and Henry James. Readers of the time, however, seemed to prefer his vivid characterizations and settings to the "masters' " work. All forty-five of his novels were bestsellers, as were the three collected editions of his work.*

Crawford also ventured into other literary genres, and was a critic, lecturer, playwright, and historian. One of the most important nonfiction works he authored was The Novel: What It Is *(1893), in which he stated his belief that the purpose of most novels should be to amuse the reader from an intellectual standpoint, not to be instructional. This was a point of contention between himself and other novelists of his day, including William Dean Howells, and was commonly misinterpreted to mean that novels should be entertainment and nothing more.*

His best works are set in the Italy he loved, including Saracinesca *(1887),* Sant' Ilario *(1889), and* Don Orsino *(1892), part of a series about the effect of social change on an Italian family during the late 1800s. He also wrote many unforgettable short stories, among them "The Upper Berth" (1894), "The Screaming Skull" (1911), and the story reprinted here, "For the Blood Is the Life" (1911).*

The latter stretches the boundaries of the Classic Adventure Tale by providing a measure of sympathy for its vampire. Its undead revenant, Christina, starts out as an innocent gypsy girl cruelly murdered through no fault of her own. Although she did not ask for her fate, the now-vampiric Christina poses just as much a threat as any other traditional vampire.

FOR THE BLOOD IS
THE LIFE

We had dined at sunset on the broad roof of the old tower, because it was cooler there during the great heat of summer. Besides, the little kitchen was built at one corner of the great square platform, which made it more convenient than if the dishes had to be carried down the steep stone steps, broken in places and everywhere worn with age. The tower was one of those built all down the west coast of Calabria by the Emperor Charles V early in the sixteenth century, to keep off the Barbary pirates, when the unbelievers were allied with Francis I against the Emperor and the Church. They have gone to ruin, a few still stand intact, and mine is one of the largest. How it came into my possession ten years ago, and why I spend a part of each year in it, are matters which do not concern this tale. The tower stands in one of the loneliest spots in southern Italy, at the extremity of a curving rocky promontory, which forms a small but safe natural harbor at the southern extremity of the Gulf of Policastro, and just north of Cape Scalea, the birthplace of Judas Iscariot, according to the old local legend. The tower stands alone on this hooked spur of the rock, and there is not a house to be seen within three miles of it. When I go there I take a couple of sailors, one of whom is a fair cook, and when I am away it is in charge of a gnomelike little being who was once a miner and who attached himself to me long ago.

My friend, who sometimes visits me in my summer solitude, is an artist by profession, a Scandinavian by birth, and a cosmopolitan by force of circumstances. We had dined at sunset; the sunset glow had reddened and faded again, and the evening purple steeped the vast chain of the mountains that embrace the deep gulf to eastward and rear themselves higher and higher toward the south. It was hot, and we sat at the landward corner of the platform, waiting for the night breeze to come down from the lower hills. The color sank out of the air, there was a little interval of deep-gray twilight, and a lamp sent a yellow streak from the open door of the kitchen, where the men were getting their supper.

Then the moon rose suddenly above the crest of the promontory, flooding the platform and lighting up every little spur of rock and knoll of grass below us, down to the edge of the motionless water. My friend lighted his pipe and sat looking at a spot on the hillside. I knew that he was looking at it, and for a long time past I had wondered whether he would ever see anything there that would fix his attention. I knew that spot well. It was clear that he was interested at last, though it was a long time before he spoke. Like most painters, he trusts to his own eyesight, as a lion trusts his strength and a stag his speed, and he is always disturbed when he cannot reconcile what he sees with what he believes that he ought to see.

"It's strange," he said. "Do you see that little mound just on this side of the boulder?"

"Yes," I said, and I guessed what was coming.

"It looks like a grave," observed Holger.

"Very true. It does look like a grave."

"Yes," continued my friend, his eyes still fixed on the spot. "But the strange thing is that I see the body lying on the top of it. Of course," continued Holger, turning his head on one side as artists do, "it must be an effect of light. In the first place, it is not a grave at all. Secondly, if it were, the body would be inside and not outside. Therefore, it's an effect of the moonlight. Don't you see it?"

"Perfectly; I always see it on moonlight nights."

"It doesn't seem to interest you much," said Holger.

"On the contrary, it does interest me, though I am used to it. You're not so far wrong, either. The mound is really a grave."

"Nonsense!" cried Holger, incredulously. "I suppose you'll tell me what I see lying on it is really a corpse!"

"No," I answered, "it's not. I know, because I have taken the trouble to go down and see."

"Then what is it?" asked Holger.

"It's nothing."

"You mean that it's an effect of light, I suppose?"

"Perhaps it is. But the inexplicable part of the matter is that it makes no difference whether the moon is rising or setting, or waxing or waning. If there's any moonlight at all, from east or west or overhead, so long as it shines on the grave you can see the outline of the body on top."

Holger stirred up his pipe with the point of his knife, and then used his finger for a stopper. When the tobacco burned well he rose from his chair.

"If you don't mind," he said, "I'll go down and take a look at it."

He left me, crossed the roof, and disappeared down the dark steps. I did not move, but sat looking down until he came out of the tower below. I heard him humming an old Danish song as he crossed the open space in the bright moonlight, going straight to the mysterious mound. When he was ten paces from it, Holger stopped short, made two steps forward, and then three or four backward, and then stopped again. I knew what that meant. He had reached the spot where the Thing ceased to be visible—where, as he would have said, the effect of light changed.

Then he went on till he reached the mound and stood upon it. I could see the Thing still, but it was no longer lying down; it was on its knees now, winding its white arms round Holger's body and looking up into his face. A cool breeze stirred my hair at that moment, as the night wind began to come down from the hills, but it felt like a breath from another world.

The Thing seemed to be trying to climb to its feet, helping itself up by Holger's body while he stood upright, quite unconscious of it and apparently looking toward the tower, which is very picturesque when the moonlight falls upon it on that side.

"Come along!" I shouted. "Don't stay there all night!"

It seemed to me that he moved reluctantly as he stepped from the mound, or else with difficulty. That was it. The Thing's arms were still round his waist, but its feet could not leave the grave. As he came slowly forward it was drawn and lengthened like a wreath of mist, thin and white, till I saw distinctly that Holger shook himself, as a man does who feels a chill. At the same instant a little wail of pain came to me on the breeze—it might have been the cry of the small owl that lives among the rocks—and the misty presence floated swiftly back from Holger's advancing figure and lay once more at its length upon the mound.

Again I felt the cool breeze in my hair, and this time an icy thrill of dread ran down my spine. I remembered very well that I had once gone down there alone in the moonlight; that presently, being near, I had seen nothing; that, like Holger, I had gone and had stood upon the mound; and I remembered how, when I came back sure that there was nothing there, I had felt the sudden conviction that there was something after all if I would only look behind me. I remembered the strong temptation to look back, a temptation I had resisted as unworthy of a man of sense, until, to get rid of it, I had shaken myself just as Holger did.

And now I knew that those white, misty arms had been round me too; I knew it in a flash, and I shuddered as I remembered that I had heard the night owl then too. But it had not been the night owl. It was the cry of the Thing.

I refilled my pipe and poured out a cup of strong southern wine; in less than a minute Holger was seated beside me again.

"Of course there's nothing there," he said, "but it's creepy, all the same. Do you know, when I was coming back I was so sure that there was something behind me that I wanted to turn round and look? It was an effort not to."

He laughed a little, knocked the ashes out of his pipe, and poured himself out some wine. For a while neither of us spoke, and the moon rose higher, and we both looked at the Thing that lay on the mound.

"You might make a story about that," said Holger after a long time.

"There is one," I answered. "If you're not sleepy, I'll tell it to you."

"Go ahead," said Holger, who likes stories.

Old Alario was dying up there in the village behind the hill. You remember him, I have no doubt. They say that he made his money by selling sham jewelry in South America, and escaped with his gains when he was found out. Like all those fellows, if they bring anything back with them, he at once set to work to enlarge his house; and, as there are no masons here, he sent all the way to Paola for two workmen. They were a rough-looking pair of scoundrels—a Neapolitan who had lost one eye and a Sicilian with an old scar half an inch deep across his left cheek. I often saw them, for on Sundays they used to come down here and fish off the rocks. When Alario caught the fever that killed him the masons were still at work. As he had agreed that part of their pay should be their board and lodging, he made them sleep in the house. His wife was dead, and he had an only son called Angelo, who was a much better sort than himself. Angelo was to marry the daughter of the richest man in the village, and, strange to say, though the marriage was arranged by their parents, the young people were said to be in love with each other.

For that matter, the whole village was in love with Angelo, and among the rest a wild, good-looking creature called Cristina, who was more like a gypsy than any girl I ever saw about here. She had very red lips and very black eyes, she was built like a greyhound, and had the tongue of the devil. But Angelo did not care a straw for her. He was rather a simple-minded fellow, quite different from his old scoundrel of a father, and under what I should call normal circumstances I really believe that he would never have looked at any girl except the nice plump little creature, with a fat dowry, whom his father meant him to marry. But things turned up which were neither normal nor natural.

On the other hand, a very handsome young shepherd from the hills above Maratea was in love with Cristina, who seems to have been quite indifferent to him. Cristina had no regular means of subsistence, but she was a good girl and willing to do any work or go on errands to any distance for the sake of a loaf of bread or a mess of beans, and permission to sleep under cover. She was especially glad when she could get something to do about the house of Angelo's father. There is no doctor in the village, and when the neighbors saw that old Alario was dying they sent Cristina to Scalea to fetch one. That was late in the afternoon, and if they had waited so long, it was because the dying miser refused to allow any such extravagance while he was able to speak. But while Cristina was gone, matters grew rapidly worse, the priest was brought to the bedside, and when he had done what he could he gave it as his opinion to the bystanders that the old man was dead, and left the house.

You know these people. They have a physical horror of death. Until the priest spoke, the room had been full of people. The words were hardly out of his mouth before it was empty. It was night now. They hurried down the dark steps and out into the street.

Angelo was away, Cristina had not come back—the simple woman servant who had nursed the sick man fled with the rest, and the body was left alone in the flickering light of the earthen oil lamp.

Five minutes later two men looked in cautiously and crept forward toward the bed. They were the one-eyed Neapolitan mason and his Sicilian companion. They knew what they wanted. In a moment they had dragged from under the bed a small but heavy iron-bound box, and long before any one thought of coming back to the dead man they had left the house and the village under cover of the darkness. It was easy enough, for Alario's house is the last toward the gorge which leads down here, and the thieves merely went out by the back door, got over the stone wall, and had nothing to risk after that except the possibility of meeting some belated countryman, which was very small indeed, since few of the people use that path. They had a mattock and shovel, and they made their way here without accident.

I am telling you this story as it must have happened, for, of course, there were no witnesses to this part of it. The men brought the box down by the gorge, intending to bury it until they should be able to come back and take it away in a boat. They must have been clever enough to guess that some of the money would be in paper notes, for they would otherwise have buried it on the beach in the wet sand, where it would have been much safer. But the paper would have rotted if they had been obliged to leave it there long, so they dug their hole down there, close to that boulder. Yes, just where the mound is now.

Cristina did not find the doctor in Scalea, for he had been sent for from a place up the valley, halfway to San Domenico. If she had found him, he would have come on his mule by the upper road, which is smoother but much longer. But Cristina took the short cut by the rocks, which passes about fifty feet above the mound, and goes round that corner. The men were digging when she passed, and she heard them at work. It would not have been like her to go by without finding out what the noise was, for she was never afraid of anything in her life, and, besides, the fishermen sometimes came ashore here at night to get a stone for an anchor or to gather sticks to make a little fire. The night was dark, and Cristina probably came close to the two men before she could see what they were doing. She knew them, of course, and they knew her, and understood instantly that they were in her power. There was only one thing to be done for their safety, and they did it. They knocked her on the head, they dug the hole deep, and they buried her quickly with the iron-bound chest. They must have understood that their only chance of escaping suspicion lay in getting back to the village before their absence was noticed, for they returned immediately, and were found half an hour later gossiping quietly with the man who was making Alario's coffin. He was a crony of theirs, and had been working at the repairs in the old man's house. So far as I have been able to make out, the only persons who were supposed to know where Alario kept his treasure were Angelo and the one woman servant I have mentioned. Angelo was away; it was the woman who discovered the theft.

It is easy enough to understand why no one else knew where the money was. The old man kept his door locked and the key in his pocket when he was out, and did not let the woman enter to clean the place unless he was there himself. The whole village knew that he had money somewhere, however, and the masons had probably discovered the whereabouts of the chest by climbing in at the window in his absence. If the old man had not been delirious until he lost consciousness, he would have been in frightful agony of mind for his riches. The faithful woman servant forgot their existence only for a few moments when she fled with the rest, overcome by the horror of death. Twenty minutes had not passed before she returned with the two hideous old hags who are always called in to prepare the dead for burial. Even then she had not at first the courage to go near the bed with them, but she made a pretense of dropping something, went down on her knees as if to find it, and looked under the bedstead. The walls of the room were newly whitewashed down to the floor, and she saw at a glance that the chest was gone. It had been there in the afternoon, it had therefore been stolen in the short interval since she had left the room.

There are no carabineers stationed in the village; there is not so much as a municipal watchman, for there is no municipality. There never was such a place, I believe. Scalea is supposed to look after it in some mysterious way, and it takes a couple of hours to get anybody from there. As the old woman had lived in the village all her life, it did not even occur to her to apply to any civil authority for help. She simply set up a howl and ran through the village in the dark, screaming out that her dead master's house had been robbed. Many of the people looked out, but at first no one seemed inclined to help her. Most of them, judging her by themselves, whispered to each other that she had probably stolen the money herself. The first man to move was the father of the girl whom Angelo was to marry; having collected his household, all of whom felt a personal interest in the wealth which was to have come into the family, he declared it to be his opinion that the chest had been stolen by the two journeyman masons who lodged in the house. He headed a search for them, which naturally began in Alario's house and ended in the carpenter's workshop, where the thieves were found discussing a measure of wine with the carpenter over the half-finished coffin, by the light of one earthen lamp filled with oil and tallow. The search party at once accused the delinquents of the crime, and threatened to lock them up in the cellar till the carabineers could be fetched from Scalea. The two men looked at each other for one moment, and then without the slightest hesitation they put out the single light, seized the unfinished coffin between them, and using it as a sort of battering ram, dashed upon their assailants in the dark. In a few moments they were beyond pursuit.

That is the end of the first part of the story. The treasure had disappeared, and as no trace of it could be found the people naturally supposed that the thieves had succeeded in carrying it off. The old man was buried, and when Angelo came back at last he had to borrow money to pay for the miserable funeral, and had some difficulty in doing so. He hardly needed to be told that in losing his inheritance he had lost his bride. In this part of the world marriages are made on strictly business principles, and if the promised cash is not forthcoming on the appointed day the bride or the bridegroom whose parents have failed to produce it may as well take themselves off, for there will be no wedding. Poor Angelo knew that well enough. His father had been possessed of hardly any land, and now that the hard cash which he had brought from South America was gone, there was nothing left but debts for the building materials that were to have been used for enlarging and improving the old house. Angelo was beggared, and the nice plump little creature who was to have been his turned up her nose at him in the most approved fashion. As for Cristina, it was several days before she was missed, for no one remembered that she had been sent to Scalea for the doctor, who had never come. She often disappeared in the same way for days together, when she could find a little work here and there at the distant farms among the hills. But when she did not come back at all, people began to wonder, and at last made up their minds that she had connived with the masons and had escaped with them.

I paused and emptied my glass.

"That sort of thing could not happen anywhere else," observed Holger, filling his everlasting pipe again. "It is wonderful what a natural charm there is about murder and sudden death in a romantic country like this. Deeds that would be simply brutal and disgusting anywhere else become dramatic and mysterious because this is Italy and we are living in a genuine tower of Charles V built against genuine Barbary pirates."

"There's something in that," I admitted. Holger is the most romantic man in the world inside of himself, but he always thinks it necessary to explain why he feels anything.

"I suppose they found the poor girl's body with the box," he said presently.

"As it seems to interest you," I answered, "I'll tell you the rest of the story."

The moon had risen high by this time; the outline of the Thing on the mound was clearer to our eyes than before.

The village very soon settled down to its small, dull life. No one missed old Alario, who had been away so much on his voyages to South America that he had never been a familiar figure in his native place. Angelo lived in the half-finished house, and because he had no money to pay the old woman servant she would not stay with him, but once in a long time she would come and wash a shirt for him for old acquaintance' sake. Besides the house, he had inherited a small patch of ground at some distance from the village; he tried to cultivate it, but he had no heart in the work, for he knew he could never pay the taxes on it and on the house, which would certainly be confiscated by the Government, or seized for the debt of the building material, which the man who had supplied it refused to take back.

Angelo was very unhappy. So long as his father had been alive and rich, every girl in the village had been in love with him; but that was all changed now. It had been pleasant to be admired and courted, and invited to drink wine by fathers who had girls to marry. It was hard to be stared at coldly, and sometimes laughed at because he had been robbed of his inheritance. He cooked his miserable meals for himself, and from being sad became melancholy and morose.

At twilight, when the day's work was done, instead of hanging about in the open space before the church with young fellows of his own age, he took to wandering in lonely places on the outskirts of the village till it was quite dark. Then he slunk home and went to bed to save the expense of a light. But in those lonely twilight hours he began to have strange waking dreams. He was not always alone, for often when he sat on the stump of a tree, where the narrow path turns down the gorge, he was sure that a woman came up noiselessly over the rough stones, as if her feet were bare; and she stood under a clump of chestnut trees only half a dozen yards down the path, and beckoned to him without speaking. Though she was in the shadow he knew that her lips were red, and that when they parted a little and smiled at him she showed two small sharp teeth. He knew this at first rather than saw it, and he knew that it was Cristina, and that she was dead. Yet he was not afraid; he only wondered whether it was a dream, for he thought that if he had been awake he should have been frightened.

Besides, the dead woman had red lips, and that could only happen in a dream. Whenever he went near the gorge after sunset she was already there waiting for him, or else she very soon appeared, and he began to be sure that she came a little nearer to him every day. At first he had only been sure of her blood-red mouth, but now each feature grew distinct, and the pale face looked at him with deep and hungry eyes.

It was the eyes that grew dim. Little by little he came to know that some day the dream would not end when he turned away to go home, but would lead him down the gorge out of which the vision rose. She was nearer now when she beckoned to him. Her cheeks were not livid like those of the dead, but pale with starvation, with the furious and unappeased physical hunger of her eyes that devoured him. They feasted on his soul and cast a spell over him, and at last they were close to his own and held them. He could not tell whether her breath was as hot as fire or as cold as ice; he could not tell whether her red lips burned his or froze them, or whether her five fingers on his wrists seared scorching scars or bit his flesh like frost; he could not tell whether he was awake or asleep, whether she was alive or dead, but he knew that she loved him, she alone of all creatures, earthly or unearthly, and her spell had power over him.

When the moon rose high that night the shadow of that Thing was not alone down there upon the mound.

Angelo awoke in the cool dawn, drenched with dew and chilled through flesh, and blood, and bone. He opened his eyes to the faint gray light, and saw the stars still shining overhead. He was very weak, and his heart was beating so slowly that he was almost like a man fainting. Slowly he turned his head on the mound, as on a pillow, but the other face was not there. Fear seized him suddenly, a fear unspeakable and unknown; he sprang to his feet and fled up the gorge, and he never looked behind him until he reached the door of the house on the outskirts of the village. Drearily he went to his work that day, and wearily the hours dragged themselves after the sun, till at last he touched the sea and sank, and the great sharp hills above Maratea turned purple against the dove-colored eastern sky.

Angelo shouldered his heavy hoe and left the field. He felt less tired now than in the morning when he had begun to work, but he promised himself that he would go home without lingering by the gorge, and eat the best supper he could get himself, and sleep all night in his bed like a Christian man. Not again would he be tempted down the narrow way by a shadow with red lips and icy breath; not again would he dream that dream of terror and delight. He was near the village now; it was half an hour since the sun had set, and the cracked church bell sent little discordant echoes across the rocks and ravines to tell all good people that the day was done. Angelo stood still a moment where the path forked, where it led toward the village on the left, and down to the gorge on the right, where a clump of chestnut trees overhung the narrow way. He stood still a minute, lifting his battered hat from his head and gazing at the fast-fading sea westward, and his lips moved as he silently repeated the familiar evening prayer. His lips moved, but the words that followed them in his brain lost their meaning and turned into others, and ended in a name that he spoke aloud—Cristina! With the name, the tension of his will relaxed suddenly, reality went out and the dream took him again and bore him on swiftly and surely like a man walking in his sleep, down, down, by the steep path in the gathering darkness. And as she glided beside him, Cristina whispered strange sweet things in his ear, which somehow, if he had been awake, he knew that he could not quite have understood; but now they were the most wonderful words he had ever heard in his life. And she kissed him also, but not upon his mouth. He felt her sharp kisses upon his white throat, and he knew that her lips were red. So the wild dream sped on through twilight and darkness and moonrise, and all the glory of the summer's night. But in the chilly dawn he lay as one half dead upon the mound down there, recalling and not recalling, drained of his blood, yet strangely longing to give those red lips more. Then came the fear, the awful nameless panic, the mortal horror that guards the confines of the world we see not, neither know of as we know of other things, but which we feel when its icy chill freezes our bones and stirs our hair with the touch of a ghostly hand. Once more Angelo sprang from the mound and fled up the gorge in the breaking day, but his step was less sure this time, and he panted for breath as he ran; and when he came to the bright spring of water that rises halfway up the hillside, he dropped upon his knees and hands and plunged his whole face in and drank as he had never drunk before—for it was the thirst of the wounded man who has lain bleeding all night long upon the battlefield.

She had him fast now, and he could not escape her, but would come to her every evening at dusk until she had drained him of his last drop of blood. It was in vain that when the day was done he tried to take another turning and to go home by a path that did not lead near the gorge. It was in vain that he made promises to himself each morning at dawn when he climbed the lonely way up from the shore to the village. It was all in vain, for when the sun sank burning into the sea, and the coolness of the evening stole out as from a hiding-place to delight the weary world, his feet turned toward the old way, and she was waiting for him in the shadow under the chestnut trees; and then all happened as before, and she fell to kissing his white throat even as she flitted lightly down the way, winding one arm about him. And as his blood failed, she grew more hungry and more thirsty every day, and every day when he awoke in the early dawn it was harder to rouse himself to the effort of climbing the steep path to the village; and when he went to his work his feet dragged painfully, and there was hardly strength in his arms to wield the heavy hoe. He scarcely spoke to any one now, but the people said he was "consuming himself" for love of the girl he was to have married when he lost his inheritance; and they laughed heartily at the thought, for this is not a very romantic country. At this time, Antonio, the man who stays here to look after the tower, returned from a visit to his people, who live near Salerno. He had been away all the time since before Alario's death and knew nothing of what had happened. He has told me that he came back late in the afternoon and shut himself up in the tower to eat and sleep, for he was very tired. It was past midnight when he awoke, and when he looked out the waning moon was rising over the shoulder of the hill. He looked out toward the mound, and he saw something, and he did not sleep again that night. When he went out again in the morning it was broad daylight, and there was nothing to be seen on the mound but loose stones and driven sand. Yet he did not go very near it; he went straight up the path to the village and directly to the house of the old priest.

"I have seen an evil thing this night," he said; "I have seen how the dead drink the blood of the living. And the blood is the life."

"Tell me what you have seen," said the priest in reply.

Antonio told him everything he had seen.

"You must bring your book and your holy water tonight," he added. "I will be here before sunset to go down with you, and if it pleases your reverence to sup with me while we wait, I will make ready."

"I will come," the priest answered, "for I have read in old books of these strange beings which are neither quick nor dead, and which lie ever fresh in their graves, stealing out in the dusk to taste life and blood."

Antonio cannot read, but he was glad to see that the priest understood the business; for, of course, the books must have instructed him as to the best means of quieting the half-living Thing forever.

So Antonio went away to his work, which consists largely in sitting on the shady side of the tower, when he is not perched upon a rock with a fishing line catching nothing. But on that day he went twice to look at the mound in the bright sunlight, and he searched round and round for some hole through which the being might get in and out; but he found none. When the sun began to sink and the air was cooler in the shadows, he went up to fetch the old priest, carrying a little wicker basket with him; and in this they placed a bottle of holy water, and the basin, and sprinkler, and the stole which the priest would need; and they came down and waited in the door of the tower till it should be dark. But while the light still lingered very gray and faint, they saw something moving, just there, two figures, a man's that walked, and a woman's that flitted beside him, and while her head lay on his shoulder she kissed his throat. The priest has told me that, too, and that his teeth chattered and he grasped Antonio's arm. The vision passed and disappeared into the shadow. Then Antonio got the leathern flask of strong liquor, which he kept for great occasions, and poured such a draught as made the old man feel almost young again; and he got the lantern, and his pick and shovel, and gave the priest his stole to put on and the holy water to carry, and they went out together toward the spot where the work was to be done. Antonio says that in spite of the rum his own knees shook together, and the priest stumbled over his Latin. For when they were yet a few yards from the mound the flickering light of the lantern fell upon Angelo's white face, unconscious as if in sleep, and on his upturned throat, over which a very thin red line of blood trickled down into his collar; and the flickering light of the lantern played upon another face that looked up from the feast—upon two deep, dead eyes that saw in spite of death—upon parted lips redder than life itself—upon two gleaming teeth on which glistened a rosy drop. Then the priest, good old man, shut his eyes tight and showered holy water before him, and his cracked voice rose almost to a scream; and then Antonio, who is no coward after all, raised his pick in one hand and the lantern in the other, as he sprang forward, not knowing what the end should be; and then he swears that he heard a woman's cry, and the Thing was gone, and Angelo lay alone on the mound unconscious, with the red line on his throat and the beads of deathly sweat on his cold forehead. They lifted him, half-dead as he was, and laid him on the ground close by! then Antonio went to work, and the priest helped him, though he was old and could not do much; and they dug deep, and at last Antonio, standing in the grave, stooped down with his lantern to see what he might see.

His hair used to be dark brown, with grizzled streaks about the temples; in less than a month from that day he was as gray as a badger. He was a miner when he was young, and most of these fellows have seen ugly sights now and then, when accidents have happened, but he had never seen what he saw that night—that Thing which is neither alive nor dead, that Thing that will abide neither above ground nor in the grave. Antonio had brought something with him which the priest had not noticed. He had made it that afternoon—a sharp stake shaped from a piece of tough old driftwood. He had it with him now, and he had his heavy pick, and he had taken the lantern down into the grave. I don't think any power on earth could make him speak of what happened then, and the old priest was too frightened to look in. He says he heard Antonio breathing like a wild beast, and moving as if he were fighting with something almost as strong as himself; and he heard an evil sound also, with blows, as of something violently driven through flesh and bone; and then the most awful sound of all—a woman's shriek, the unearthly scream of a woman neither dead nor alive, but buried deep for many days. And he, the poor old priest, could only rock himself as he knelt there in the sand, crying aloud his prayers and exorcisms to drown these dreadful sounds. Then suddenly a small iron-bound chest was thrown up and rolled over against the old man's knee, and in a moment more Antonio was beside him, his face as white as tallow in the flickering light of the lantern, shoveling the sand and pebbles into the grave with furious haste, and looking over the edge till the pit was half full; and the priest had said that there was much fresh blood on Antonio's hands and on his clothes.

I had come to the end of my story. Holger finished his wine and leaned back in his chair.

"So Angelo got his own again," he said. "Did he marry the prim and plump young person to whom he had been betrothed?"

"No; he had been badly frightened. He went to South America, and has not been heard of since."

"And that poor thing's body is there still, I suppose," said Holger. "Is it quite dead yet, I wonder?"

I wonder, too. But whether it is dead or alive, I should hardly care to see it, even in broad daylight.

Antonio is as gray as a badger, and he has never been quite the same man since that night.

AUGUST DERLETH
(1909–1971)

August Derleth was born on February 24, 1909, in Sauk City, Wisconsin, where he resided until his death on July 4, 1971. His first story, "Bat's Belfry," was published in Weird Tales when he was seventeen. Derleth was noted for his many novels with Wisconsin settings, including Bright Journey (1940). His most widely known and acclaimed written work is Prairie Saga, a series of novels depicting life in a Wisconsin community (modeled after Sauk City) from 1830 to the mid-twentieth century, including Still is the Summer Night (1937), Wind over Wisconsin (1938), and Restless is the River (1939). He also wrote four volumes of poetry about the region.

A mystery and science fiction writer and editor, Derleth is also known for his popularization of the work of H. P. Lovecraft through his publishing company Arkham House, which he founded in 1939. While publishing the works of such masters as Ray Bradbury, Robert Bloch, and Stanley McNail, he also wrote his own work in a variety of styles. Derleth was so prolific a writer, he used several pseudonyms to avoid betraying the number of stories that flowed from his pen. Derleth authored a series of murder mysteries featuring a detective, similar to Sherlock Holmes, named Solar Pons. He wrote 152 short stories and ten novels in an epic meant to rival Balzac's Human Comedy. Among Derleth's other writings are three short stories, "The Mask of Cthulhu" (1958), "The Trail of Cthulhu" (1962), and a collection called Tales of the Cthulhu Mythos (1969), all based on Lovecraft's Cthulhu Mythos, an invented horror folk mythology of primordial and evil godlike beings from an ancient world who still survive and practice their abominable rites in hidden corners of our world. He also edited a great many anthologies, both science fiction and horror, including Strange Ports of Call (1948) and Who Knocks? (1946).

"The Drifting Snow," included here, is a surprisingly poetic tale, very unlike the melodramatic and breathless Lovecraftian fiction that Derleth admired (and sometimes wrote). There is a delicate lyricism in his conception of a snow vampire who kills with tiny, deadly hands, which adds a particular chill to this effective variation on the theme of evil vampires versus endangered mortals.

THE DRIFTING SNOW

Aunt Mary's advancing footsteps halted suddenly, short of the table, and Clodetta turned to see what was keeping her. She was standing very rigidly, her eyes fixed upon the French windows just opposite the door through which she had entered, her cane held stiffly before her.

Clodetta shot a quick glance across the table toward her husband, whose attention had also been drawn to his aunt; his face vouchsafed her nothing. She turned again to find that the old lady had transferred her gaze to her, regarding her stonily and in silence. Clodetta felt uncomfortable.

"Who withdrew the curtains from the west windows?"

Clodetta flushed, remembering. "I did, Aunt. I'm sorry. I forgot about your not wanting them drawn away."

The old lady made an odd, grunting sound, shifting her gaze once again to the French windows. She made a barely perceptible movement, and Lisa ran forward from the shadow of the hall, where she had been regarding the two at table with stern disapproval. The servant went directly to the west windows and drew the curtains.

Aunt Mary came slowly to the table and took her place at its head. She put her cane against the side of her chair, pulled at the chain about her neck so that her lorgnette lay in her lap, and looked from Clodetta to her nephew, Ernest.

Then she fixed her gaze on the empty chair at the foot of the table, and spoke without seeming to see the two beside her.

"I told both of you that none of the curtains over the west windows was to be withdrawn after sundown, and you must have noticed that none of those windows has been for one instant uncovered at night. I took especial care to put you in rooms facing east, and the sitting-room is also in the east."

"I'm sure Clodetta didn't mean to go against your wishes, Aunt Mary," said Ernest abruptly.

"No, of course not, Aunt."

The old lady raised her eyebrows, and went on impassively. "I didn't think it wise to explain why I made such a request. I'm not going to explain. But I do want to say that there is a very definite danger in drawing away the curtains. Ernest has heard that before, but you, Clodetta, have not."

Clodetta shot a startled glance at her husband. The old lady caught it, and said, "It's all very well to believe that my mind's wandering or that I'm getting eccentric, but I shouldn't advise you to be satisfied with that."

A young man came suddenly into the room and made for the seat at the foot of the table, into which he flung himself with an almost inaudible greeting to the other three.

"Late again, Henry," said the old lady.

Henry mumbled something and began hurriedly to eat. The old lady sighed, and began presently to eat also, whereupon Clodetta and Ernest did likewise. The old servant, who had continued to linger behind Aunt Mary's chair, now withdrew, not without a scornful glance at Henry.

Clodetta looked up after a while and ventured to speak, "You aren't as isolated as I thought you might be up here, Aunt Mary."

"We aren't, my dear, what with telephones and cars and all. But only twenty years ago it was quite a different thing, I can tell you." She smiled reminiscently and looked at Ernest. "Your grandfather was living then, and many's the time he was snowbound with no way to let anybody know."

"Down in Chicago when they speak of 'up north' or the 'Wisconsin woods' it seems very far away," said Clodetta.

"Well, it *is* far away," put in Henry, abruptly. "And, Aunt, I hope you've made some provision in case we're locked in here for a day or two. It looks like snow outside, and the radio says a blizzard's coming."

The old lady grunted and looked at him. "Ha, Henry—you're overly concerned, it seems to me. I'm afraid you've been regretting this trip ever since you set foot in my house. If you're worrying about a snowstorm, I can have Sam drive you down to Wausau, and you can be in Chicago tomorrow."

"Of course not."

Silence fell, and presently the old lady called gently, "Lisa," and the servant came into the room to help her from her chair, though, as Clodetta had previously said to her husband, "She didn't need help."

From the doorway, Aunt Mary bade them all good-night, looking impressively formidable with her cane in one hand and her unopened lorgnette in the other, and vanished into the dusk of the hall, from which her receding footsteps sounded together with those of the servant, who was seldom seen away from her. These two were alone in the house most of the time, and only very brief periods when the old lady had up her nephew Ernest, "dear John's boy," or Henry, of whose father the old lady never spoke, helped to relieve the pleasant somnolence of their quiet lives. Sam, who usually slept in the garage, did not count.

Clodetta looked nervously at her husband, but it was Henry who said what was uppermost in their thoughts.

"I think she's losing her mind," he declared matter-of-factly. Cutting off Clodetta's protest on her lips, he got up and went into the sitting-room, from which came presently the strains of music from the radio.

Clodetta fingered her spoon idly and finally said, "I do think she is a little queer, Ernest."

Ernest smiled tolerantly. "No, I don't think so. I've an idea why she keeps the west windows covered. My grandfather died out there—he was overcome by the cold one night, and froze on the slope of the hill. I don't rightly know how it happened—I was away at the time. I suppose she doesn't like to be reminded of it."

"But where's the danger she spoke of, then?"

He shrugged. "Perhaps it lies in her—she might be affected and affect us in turn." He paused for an instant, and finally added, "I suppose she *does* seem a little strange to you—but she was like that as long as I can remember; next time you come, you'll be used to it."

Clodetta looked at her husband for a moment before replying. At last she said, "I don't think I like the house, Ernest."

"Oh, nonsense, darling." He started to get up, but Clodetta stopped him.

"Listen Ernest. I remembered perfectly well Aunt Mary's not wanting those curtains drawn away—but I just felt I had to do it. I didn't want to, but—*something made me do it.*" Her voice was unsteady.

"Why, Clodetta," he said, faintly alarmed. "Why didn't you tell me before?"

She shrugged. "Aunt Mary might have thought I'd gone wool-gathering."

"Well, it's nothing serious, but you've let it bother you a little and that isn't good for you. Forget it; think of something else. Come and listen to the radio."

They rose and moved toward the sitting-room together. At the door Henry met them. He stepped aside a little, saying, "I might have known we'd be marooned up here," and adding, as Clodetta began to protest, "We're going to be all right. There's a wind coming up and it's beginning to snow, and I know what that means." He passed them and went into the deserted dining-room, where he stood a moment looking at the too long table. Then he turned aside and went over to the French windows, from which he drew away the curtains and stood there peering out into the darkness. Ernest saw him standing at the window, and protested from the sitting-room.

"Aunt Mary doesn't like those windows uncovered, Henry."

Henry half turned and replied, "Well, *she* may think it's dangerous, but I can risk it."

Clodetta, who had been staring beyond Henry into the night through the French windows, said suddenly, "Why, there's someone out there!"

Henry looked quickly through the glass and replied, "No, that's the snow; it's coming down heavily, and the wind's drifting it this way and that." He dropped the curtains and came away from the windows.

Clodetta said uncertainly, "Why, I could have sworn I saw someone out there, walking past the window."

"I suppose it does look that way from here," offered Henry, who had come back into the sitting-room. "But personally, I think you've let Aunt Mary's eccentricities impress you too much."

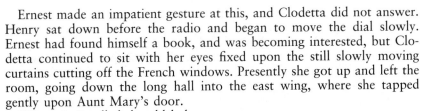

Ernest made an impatient gesture at this, and Clodetta did not answer. Henry sat down before the radio and began to move the dial slowly. Ernest had found himself a book, and was becoming interested, but Clodetta continued to sit with her eyes fixed upon the still slowly moving curtains cutting off the French windows. Presently she got up and left the room, going down the long hall into the east wing, where she tapped gently upon Aunt Mary's door.

"Come in," called the old lady.

Clodetta opened the door and stepped into the room where Aunt Mary sat in her dressing-robe, her dignity, in the shape of her lorgnette and cane, resting respectively on her bureau and in the corner. She looked surprisingly benign, as Clodetta at once confessed.

"Ha, thought I was an ogre in disguise, did you?" said the old lady, smiling in spite of herself. "I'm really not, you see, but I am a sort of bogy about the west windows, as you have seen."

"I wanted to tell you something about those windows, Aunt Mary," said Clodetta. She stopped suddenly. The expression on the old lady's face had given way to a curiously dismaying one. It was not anger, not distaste—it was a lurking suspense. Why, the old lady was afraid!

"What?" she asked Clodetta shortly.

"I was looking out—just for a moment or so—and I thought I saw someone out there."

"Of course, you didn't, Clodetta. Your imagination, perhaps, or the drifting snow."

"My imagination? Maybe. But there was no wind to drift the snow, though one has come up since."

"I've often been fooled that way, my dear. Sometimes I've gone out in the morning to look for footprints—there weren't any, ever. We're pretty far away from civilization in a snowstorm, despite our telephones and radios. Our nearest neighbor is at the foot of the long, sloping rise—over three miles away—and all wooded land between. There's no highway nearer than that."

"It was so clear, I could have sworn to it."

"Do you want to go out in the morning and look?" asked the old lady shortly.

"Of course not."

"Then you didn't see anything?"

It was half question, half demand. Clodetta said, "Oh, Aunt Mary, you're making an issue of it now."

"Did you or didn't you in your own mind see anything, Clodetta?"

"I guess I didn't, Aunt Mary."

"Very well. And now do you think we might talk about something more pleasant?"

"Why, I'm sure—I'm sorry, Aunt. I didn't know that Ernest's grandfather had died out there."

"Ha, he's told you that, has he? Well?"

"Yes, he said that was why you didn't like the slope after sunset—that you didn't like to be reminded of his death."

The old lady looked at Clodetta impassively. "Perhaps he'll never know how near right he was."

"What do you mean, Aunt Mary?"

"Nothing for you to know, my dear." She smiled again, her sternness dropping from her. "And now I think you'd better go, Clodetta; I'm tired."

Clodetta rose obediently and made for the door, where the old lady stopped her. "How's the weather?"

"It's snowing—hard, Henry says—and blowing."

The old lady's face showed her distaste at the news. "I don't like to hear that, not at all. Suppose someone should look down that slope to-night?" She was speaking to herself, having forgotten Clodetta at the door. Seeing her again abruptly, she said, "But you don't know, Clodetta. Goodnight."

Clodetta stood with her back against the closed door, wondering what the old lady could have meant. *But you don't know, Clodetta.* That was curious. For a moment or two the old lady had completely forgotten her.

She moved away from the door, and came upon Ernest just turning into the east wing.

"Oh, there you are," he said. "I wondered where you had gone."

"I was talking a bit with Aunt Mary."

"Henry's been at the west windows again—and now *he* thinks there's someone out there."

Clodetta stopped short. "Does he really think so?"

Ernest nodded gravely. "But the snow's drifting frightfully, and I can imagine how that suggestion of yours worked on his mind."

Clodetta turned and went back along the hall. "I'm going to tell Aunt Mary."

He started to protest, but to no avail, for she was already tapping on the old lady's door, and indeed opening the door and entering the room before he could frame an adequate protest.

"Aunt Mary," she said, "I didn't want to disturb you again, but Henry's been at the French windows in the dining-room, and he says he's seen someone out there."

The effect on the old lady was magical. "He's seen them!" she exclaimed. Then she was on her feet, coming rapidly over to Clodetta. "How long ago?" she demanded, seizing her almost roughly by the arms. "Tell me, quickly. How long ago did he see them?"

Clodetta's amazement kept her silent for a moment, but at last she spoke, feeling the old lady's keen eyes staring at her. "It was some time ago, Aunt Mary, after supper."

The old lady's hands relaxed, and with it her tension. "Oh," she said,

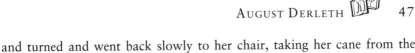

and turned and went back slowly to her chair, taking her cane from the corner where she had put it for the night.

"Then there *is* someone out there?" challenged Clodetta, when the old lady had reached her chair.

For a long time, it seemed to Clodetta, there was no answer. Then presently the old lady began to nod gently, and a barely audible "Yes" escaped her lips.

"Then we had better take them in, Aunt Mary."

The old lady looked at Clodetta earnestly for a moment; then she replied, her voice firm and low, her eyes fixed upon the wall beyond. "We can't take them in, Clodetta—because they're not alive."

At once Henry's words came flashing into Clodetta's memory—"She's losing her mind"—and her involuntary start betrayed her thought.

"I'm afraid I'm not mad, my dear—I hoped at first I might be, but I wasn't. I'm not, now. There was only one of them out there at first—the girl; Father is the other. Quite long ago, when I was young, my father did something which he regretted all his days. He had a too strong temper, and it maddened him. One night he found out that one of my brothers— Henry's father—had been very familiar with one of the servants, a very pretty girl, older than I was. He thought she was to blame, though she wasn't, and he didn't find it out until too late. He drove her from the house, then and there. Winter had not yet set in, but it was quite cold, and she had some five miles to go to her home. We begged Father not to send her away—though we didn't know what was wrong then—but he paid no attention to us. The girl had to go.

"Not long after she had gone, a biting wind came up, and close upon it a fierce storm. Father had already repented his hasty action, and sent some of the men to look for the girl. They didn't find her, but in the morning she was found frozen to death on the long slope of the hill to the west."

The old lady sighed, paused a moment, and went on. "Years later— she came back. She came in a snowstorm, as she went; but she had become a vampire. We all saw her. We were at supper table, and Father saw her first. The boys had already gone upstairs, and Father and the two of us girls, my sister and I, did not recognize her. She was just a dim shape floundering about in the drifting snow beyond the French windows. Father ran out to her, calling to us to send the boys after him. We never saw him alive again. In the morning we found him in the same spot where years before the girl had been found. He, too, had died of exposure.

"Then, a few years after—she returned with the snow, and she brought him along; he, too, had become a vampire. They stayed until the last snow, always trying to lure someone out there. After that, I knew, and had the windows covered during the winter nights, from sunset to dawn, because they never went beyond the west slope.

"Now you know, Clodetta."

Whatever Clodetta was going to say was cut short by running footsteps in the hall, a hasty rap, and Ernest's head appearing suddenly in the open doorway.

"Come on, you two," he said, almost gayly, "there *are* people out on the west slope—a girl and an old man—and Henry's gone out to fetch them in!"

Then, triumphant, he was off. Clodetta came to her feet, but the old lady was before her, passing her and almost running down the hall, calling loudly for Lisa, who presently appeared in nightcap and gown from her room.

"Call Sam, Lisa," said the old lady, "and send him to me in the dining-room."

She ran on into the dining-room, Clodetta close on her heels. The French windows were open, and Ernest stood on the snow-covered terrace beyond, calling his cousin. The old lady went directly over to him, even striding into the snow to his side, though the wind drove the snow against her with great force. The wooded western slope was lost in a snow-fog; the nearest trees were barely discernible.

"Where could they have gone?" Ernest said, turning to the old lady, whom he had thought to be Clodetta. Then, seeing that it was the old lady, he said, "Why, Aunt Mary—and so little on, too! You'll catch your death of cold."

"Never mind, Ernest," said the old lady. "I'm all right. I've had Sam get up to help you look for Henry—but I'm afraid you won't find him."

"He can't be far; he just now went out."

"He went before you saw where; he's far enough gone."

Sam came running into the blowing snow from the dining-room, muffled in a greatcoat. He was considerably older than Ernest, almost the old lady's age. He shot a questioning glance at her and asked, "Have they come again?"

Aunt Mary nodded. "You'll have to look for Henry. Ernest will help you. And remember, don't separate. And don't go far from the house."

Clodetta came with Ernest's overcoat, and together the two women stood there, watching them until they were swallowed up in the wall of driven snow. Then they turned slowly and went back into the house.

The old lady sank into a chair facing the windows. She was pale and drawn, and looked, as Clodetta said afterward, "as if she'd fallen together." For a long time she said nothing. Then, with a gentle little sigh, she turned to Clodetta and spoke.

"Now there'll be three of them out there."

Then, so suddenly that no one knew how it happened, Ernest and Sam appeared beyond the windows, and between them they dragged Henry. The old lady flew to open the windows, and the three of them, cloaked in snow, came into the room.

"We found him—but the cold's hit him pretty hard, I'm afraid," said Ernest.

The old lady sent Lisa for cold water, and Ernest ran to get himself other clothes. Clodetta went with him, and in their rooms told him what the old lady had related to her.

Ernest laughed. "I think you believed that, didn't you, Clodetta? Sam and Lisa do, I know, because Sam told me the story long ago. I think the shock of Grandfather's death was too much for all three of them."

"But the story of the girl, and then——"

"That part's true, I'm afraid. A nasty story, but it did happen."

"But those people Henry and I saw!" protested Clodetta weakly.

Ernest stood without movement. "That's so," he said, "I saw them, too. Then they're out there yet, and we'll have to find them!" He took up his overcoat again, and went from the room, Clodetta protesting in a shrill unnatural voice. The old lady met him at the door of the dining-room, having overheard Clodetta pleading with him.

"No, Ernest—you can't go out there again," she said. "There's no one there."

He pushed gently into the room and called to Sam, "Coming Sam? There're still two of them out there—we almost forgot them."

Sam looked at him strangely. "What do you mean?" he demanded roughly. He looked challengingly at the old lady, who shook her head.

"The girl and the old man, Sam. We've got to get them, too."

"Oh, *them*," said Sam. "They're dead!"

"Then I'll go out alone," said Ernest.

Henry came to his feet suddenly, looking dazed. He walked forward a few steps, his eyes traveling from one to the other of them, yet apparently not seeing them. He began to speak abruptly, in an unnatural child-like voice.

"*The snow,*" he murmured, "*the snow—the beautiful hands, so little, so lovely—her beautiful hands—and the snow, the beautiful, lovely snow, drifting and falling about her. . . .*"

He turned slowly and looked toward the French windows, the others following his gaze. Beyond was a wall of white, where the snow was drifting against the house. For a moment Henry stood quietly watching then suddenly a white figure came forward from the snow—a young girl, cloaked in long snow-whips, her glistening eyes strangely fascinating.

The old lady flung herself forward, her arms outstretched to cling to Henry, but she was too late. Henry had run toward the windows, had opened them, and even as Clodetta cried out, had vanished into the wall of snow beyond.

Then Ernest ran forward, but the old lady threw her arms around him and held him tightly, murmuring, "You shall not go! Henry is gone beyond our help!"

Clodetta came to help her, and Sam stood menacingly at the French windows, now closed against the wind and the sinister snow. So they held him, and would not let him go.

"And tomorrow," said the old lady in a harsh whisper, "we must go to their graves and stake them down. We should have gone before."

In the morning they found Henry's body crouched against the bole of an ancient oak, where two others had been found years before. There were almost obliterated marks of where something had dragged him, a long, uneven swath in the snow, and yet no footprints, only strange, hollowed places along the way, as if the wind had whirled the snow away, and only the wind.

But on his skin were signs of the snow vampire—the delicate small prints of a young girl's hands.

STEPHEN KING
(b. 1947)

The name Stephen King has become almost as much of an icon of horror fiction as that fictional creation, Dracula, himself. Born in Portland, Maine, King attended the University of Maine and he worked as a janitor, a laborer in a knitting mill, and a high school English teacher before beginning his career as a writer. Before he was fifty, King was in the record books as "the best selling horror writer in history . . . [with more than] seventy million copies of his books in print."*

King's first short story, "The Glass Floor," was published in Startling Mystery Stories *(1967). His first published novel,* Carrie: A Novel of a Girl with a Frightening Power *(1974), was made into a movie, as were most of his other novels, including* The Shining *(1977),* Firestarter *(1980),* Pet Semetary *(1983), and* Misery *(1987). King wrote four novels before* Carrie *that were later published under the pseudonym Richard Bachman:* Rage *(1977),* The Long Walk *(1979),* Roadwork *(1981), and* The Running Man *(1982). He has received numerous awards and honors:* Carrie *was one of* School Library Journal's *Best Books of 1975;* Salem's Lot *(1975),* The Stand *(1978),* Night Shift *(1978),* The Dead Zone *(1979),* The Mist *(1981), and* The Breathing Method *(1983) were all nominated for World Fantasy awards;* The Shining *was nominated for both the Hugo and the Nebula awards in 1978; and "Lunch at the Gotham Café" was nominated for the Bram Stoker Award for Best Novelette in 1996.*

There is no easy way to explain a phenomenon like King beyond pointing to the obvious: he is industrious, inventive, and a master of "the common touch" prose style. King has, by mythologizing frightening aspects of twentieth-century life, established a claim to greatness as a writer of horror fiction. In Danse Macabre *(1981), his Hugo Award-winning non-fiction work, he puts his goal as a writer directly: " . . . I will try to terrify the reader. If I cannot terrify him/her, I will try to horrify; and if I find I cannot horrify, I'll go for the gross-out. . . ."*

The influence of Bram Stoker's Dracula *on* Salem's Lot *is pronounced and is acknowledged by King. For example, the scene in which the vampirized body of Susan Norton is staked is an almost gesture-by-gesture replay of the staking of Lucy in Stoker's novel. There, Holmwood uses a three-foot-long oak stake and a coal-breaking hammer. In a witty and ingenious modernization of Stoker's scene, King has Ben Mears, who loves Susan, use a broken baseball bat and a Sears Roebuck hammer. The use of the homely implements in both works adds to the horror of the scene.*

*Jack Sullivan, ed. *The Penguin Encyclopedia of Horror and the Supernatural.*

Excerpt from
SALEM'S LOT

When he first heard the distant snapping of twigs, he crept behind the trunk of a large spruce and stood there, waiting to see who would show up. *They* couldn't come out in the daytime, but that didn't mean *they* couldn't get people who could; giving them money was one way, but it wasn't the only way. Mark had seen that guy Straker in town, and his eyes were like the eyes of a toad sunning itself on a rock. He looked like he could break a baby's arm and smile while he did it.

He touched the heavy shape of his father's target pistol in his jacket pocket. Bullets were no good against *them*—except maybe silver ones—but a shot between the eyes would punch that Straker's ticket, all right.

His eyes shifted downward momentarily to the roughly cylindrical shape propped against the tree, wrapped in an old piece of toweling. There was a woodpile behind his house, half a cord of yellow ash stove lengths which he and his father had cut with the McCulloch chain saw in July and August. Henry Petrie was methodical, and each length, Mark knew, would be within an inch of three feet, one way or the other. His father knew the proper length just as he knew that winter followed fall and that yellow ash would burn longer and cleaner in the living room fireplace.

His son, who knew other things, knew that ash was for men—things—like *him*. This morning, while his mother and father were out on their Sunday bird walk, he had taken one of the lengths and whacked one end into a rough point with his Boy Scout hatchet. It was rough, but it would serve.

He saw a flash of color and shrank back against the tree, peering around the rough bark with one eye. A moment later he got his first clear glimpse of the person climbing the hill. It was a girl. He felt a sense of relief mingled with disappointment. No henchman of the devil there; that was Mr. Norton's daughter.

His gaze sharpened again. She was carrying a stake of her own! As she drew closer, he felt an urge to laugh bitterly—a piece of snow fence, that's what she had. Two swings with an ordinary tool box hammer would split it right in two.

She was going to pass his tree on the right. As she drew closer, he began to slide carefully around his tree to the left, avoiding any small twigs that might pop and give him away. At last the synchronized little movement was done; her back was to him as she went up on the hill toward the break in the trees. She was going very carefully, he noted with

approval. That was good. In spite of the silly snow fence stake, she apparently had some idea of what she was getting into. Still, if she went much further, she was going to be in trouble. Straker was at home. Mark had been here since twelve-thirty, and he had seen Straker go out to the driveway and look down the road and then go back into the house. Mark had been trying to make up his mind on what to do himself when this girl had entered things, upsetting the equation.

He was pondering how to make his presence known to her without having her scream her head off when the motor of Straker's car roared into life. She jumped visibly, and at first he was afraid she was going to break and run, crashing through the woods and advertising her presence for a hundred miles. But then she hunkered down again, holding on to the ground like she was afraid it would fly away from her. She's got guts even if she is stupid, he thought approvingly.

Straker's car backed down the driveway—she would have a much better view from where she was; he could only see the Packard's black roof—hesitated for a moment, and then went off down the road toward town.

He decided they had to team up. Anything would be better than going up to that house alone. He had already sampled the poison atmosphere that enveloped it. He had felt it from a half a mile away, and it thickened as you got closer.

Now he ran lightly up the carpeted incline and put his hand on her shoulder. He felt her body tense, knew she was going to scream, and said, "Don't yell. It's all right. It's me."

She didn't scream. What escaped was a terrified exhalation of air. She turned around and looked at him, her face white. "W-Who's me?"

He sat down beside her. "My name is Mark Petrie. I know you; you're Sue Norton. My dad knows your dad."

"Petrie . . . ? Henry Petrie?"

"Yes, that's my father."

"What are you doing here?" Her eyes were moving continually over him, as if she hadn't been able to take in his actuality yet.

"The same thing you are. Only that stake won't work. It's too . . ." He groped for a word that had checked into his vocabulary through sight and definition but not by use. "It's too flimsy."

She looked down at her piece of snow fence and actually blushed. "Oh, that. Well, I found that in the woods and . . . and thought someone might fall over it, so I just—"

He cut her adult temporizing short impatiently: "You came to kill the vampire, didn't you?"

"Wherever did you get that idea? Vampires and things like that?"

He said somberly, "A vampire tried to get me last night. It almost did, too."

"That's absurd. A big boy like you should know better than to make up—"

"It was Danny Glick."

She recoiled, her eyes wincing as if he had thrown a mock punch instead of words. She groped out, found his arm, and held it. Their eyes locked. "Are you making this up, Mark?"

"No," he said.

"And you came here alone?" she asked when he had finished. "You believed it and came up here alone?"

"Believed it?" He looked at her, honestly puzzled. "Sure I believed it. I saw it, didn't I?"

There was no response to that, and suddenly she was ashamed of her instant doubt (no, doubt was too kind a word).

"How come you're here?"

She hesitated a moment and then said, "There are some men in town who suspect that there is a man in that house whom no one has seen. That he might be a . . . a . . . ." Still she could not say the word, but he nodded his understanding. Even on short acquaintance, he seemed quite an extraordinary little boy.

Abridging all that she might have added, she said simply, "So I came to look and find out."

He nodded at the stake. "And brought that to pound through him?"

"I don't know if I could do that."

"I could," he said calmly. "After what I saw last night. Danny was outside my window, holding on like a great big fly. And his teeth . . . ." He shook his head, dismissing the nightmare as a businessman might dismiss a bankrupt client.

"Do your parents know you're here?" she asked, knowing they must not.

"No," he said matter-of-factly. "Sunday is their nature day. They go on bird walks in the mornings and do other things in the afternoon. Sometimes I go and sometimes I don't. Today they went for a ride up the coast."

"You're quite a boy," she said.

"No, I'm not," he said, his composure unruffled by the praise. "But I'm going to get rid of *him*." He looked up at the house.

"Are you sure—"

"Sure I am. So're you. Can't you *feel* how bad he is? Doesn't that house make you afraid, just looking at it?"

"Yes," she said simply, giving in to him. His logic was the logic of nerve endings.

"How are we going to do it?" she asked, automatically giving over the leadership of the venture to him.

"Just go up there and break in," he said. "Find him, pound the stake— *my* stake—through his heart, and get out again. He's probably down cellar. They like dark places. Did you bring a flashlight?"

"No."

"Damn it, neither did I." He shuffled his sneakered feet aimlessly in the leaves for a moment. "Probably didn't bring a cross either, did you?"

"Yes, I did," Susan said. She pulled the link chain out of her blouse and showed him. He nodded and then pulled a chain out of his own shirt.

"I hope I can get this back before my folks come home." he said gloomily. "I crooked it from my mother's jewelry box. I'll catch hell if she finds out." He looked around. The shadows had lengthened even as they talked, and they both felt an impulse to delay and delay.

"When we find him, don't look in his eyes," Mark told her. "He can't move out of his coffin, not until dark, but he can still hook you with his eyes. Do you know anything religious by heart?"

They had started through the bushes between the woods and the unkempt lawn of the Marsten House.

"Well, the Lord's Prayer—"

"Sure, that's good. I know that one, too. We'll both say it while I pound the stake in."

He saw her expression, revolted and half flagging, and he took her hand and squeezed it. His self-possession was disconcerting. "Listen, we have to. I bet he's got half the town after last night. If we wait any longer, he'll have it all. It will go fast, now."

"After last night?"

"I dreamed it," Mark said. His voice was still calm, but his eyes were dark. "I dreamed of them going to houses and calling on phones and begging to be let in. Some people knew, way down deep they knew, but they let them in just the same. Because it was easier to do that than to think something so bad might be real."

"Just a dream," she said uneasily.

"I bet there's a lot of people lying around in bed today with the curtains closed or the shades drawn, wondering if they've got a cold or the flu or something. They feel all weak and fuzzy-headed. They don't want to eat. The idea of eating makes them want to puke."

"How do you know so much?"

"I read the monster magazines," he said, "and go to see the movies when I can. Usually I have to tell my mom I'm going to see Walt Disney. And you can't trust all of it. Sometimes they just make stuff up so the story will be bloodier."

As Mark had said, this close to the house it was just not possible to scoff. All the thought processes, the act of conversation itself, were overshadowed by a more fundamental voice that was screaming *danger! danger!* in words that were not words at all. Susan's heartbeat and respiration were up, yet her skin was cold with the capillary-dilating effect of adrenaline, which keeps the blood hiding deep in the body's wells during moments of stress. Her kidneys were tight and heavy. Her eyes seemed preternaturally sharp, taking in every splinter and paint flake on the side of the house. And all of this had been triggered by no external stimuli at all: no men with guns, no large and snarling dogs, no smell of fire. A deeper watchman than her five senses had been wakened after a long season of sleep. And there was no ignoring it.

She peered through a break in the lower shutters. "Why, they haven't done a thing to it," she said almost angrily. "It's a mess."

"Let me see. Boost me up."

She laced her fingers together so he could look through the broken slats and into the crumbling living room of the Marsten House. He saw a deserted, boxy parlor with a thick patina of dust on the floor (many footprints had been tracked through it), peeling wallpaper, two or three old easy chairs, a scarred table. There were cobwebs festooned in the room's upper corners, near the ceiling.

Before she could protest, he had rapped the hook-and-eye combination that held the shutter closed with the blunt end of his stake. The lock fell to the ground in two rusty pieces, and the shutters creaked outward an inch or two.

"Hey!" she protested. "You shouldn't—"

"What do you want to do? Ring the doorbell?"

He accordioned back the right-hand shutter and rapped one of the dusty, wavy panes of glass. It tinkled inward. The fear leaped up in her, hot and strong, making a coppery taste in her mouth.

He knocked the protruding shards of glass out of the pane he had broken, switched the stake to his other hand, then reached through and unlatched the window. It moaned slightly as he pushed it up, and then the way was open.

She let him down and they looked wordlessly at the window for a moment. Then Susan stepped forward, pushed on the splintery windowsill preparatory to boosting herself up. The fear in her was sickening with its greatness, settled in her belly like a horrid pregnancy.

She had always consciously or unconsciously formed fear into a simple equation: fears = unknown. And to solve the equation, one simply reduced the problem to simple algebraic terms, thus: unknown = creaky board (or whatever), creaky board = nothing to be afraid of. In the modern world all terrors could be gutted by simple use of the transitive axiom of equality. Some fears were justified, of course (you don't drive when you're too plowed to see, don't extend the hand of friendship to snarling dogs, don't go parking with boys you don't know—how did the old joke go? Screw or walk?), but until now she had not believed that some fears were larger than comprehension, apocalyptic and nearly paralyzing. This equation was insoluble. The act of moving forward at all became heroism.

She boosted herself with a smooth flex of muscles, swung one leg over the sill, then dropped to the dusty parlor floor and looked around. There

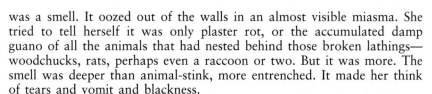

was a smell. It oozed out of the walls in an almost visible miasma. She tried to tell herself it was only plaster rot, or the accumulated damp guano of all the animals that had nested behind those broken lathings—woodchucks, rats, perhaps even a raccoon or two. But it was more. The smell was deeper than animal-stink, more entrenched. It made her think of tears and vomit and blackness.

"Hey," Mark called softly. His hands waved above the windowsill. "A little help."

She leaned out, caught him under the armpits, and dragged him up until he had caught a grip on the windowsill. Then he jackknifed himself in neatly. His sneakered feet thumped the carpet, and then the house was still again.

They found themselves listening to the silence, fascinated by it. There did not even seem to be the faint, high hum that comes in utter stillness, the sound of nerve endings idling in neutral. There was only a great dead soundlessness and the beat of blood in their own ears.

And yet they both knew, of course. They were not alone.

"Come on," he said. "Let's look around." He clutched the stake very tightly and for just a moment looked longingly back at the window.

She moved slowly toward the hall and he came after her. Just outside the door there was a small end table with a book on it. Mark picked it up.

"Hey," he said. "Do you know Latin?"

"A little, from high school."

"What's this mean?" He showed her the binding.

She sounded the words out, a frown creasing her forehead. Then she shook her head. "Don't know."

He opened the book at random, and flinched. There was a picture of a naked man holding a child's gutted body toward something you couldn't see. He put the book down, glad to let go of it—the stretched binding felt uncomfortably familiar under his hand—and they went down the hallway toward the kitchen together. The shadows were more prominent here. The sun had gotten around to the other side of the house.

"Do you smell it?" he asked.

"Yes."

"It's worse back here, isn't it?"

"Yes."

He was remembering the cold-pantry his mother had kept in the other house, and how one year three bushel baskets of tomatoes had gone bad down there in the dark. This smell was like that, like the smell of tomatoes decaying into putrescence.

Susan whispered: "God, I'm so scared."

His hand groped out, found hers, and they locked tightly.

The kitchen linoleum was old and gritty and pocked, worn black in front of the old porcelain-tub sink. A large, scarred table stood in the middle of the floor, and on it was a yellow plate, a knife and fork, and a scrap of raw hamburger.

The cellar door was standing ajar.

"That's where we have to go," he said.

"Oh," she said weakly.

The door was open just a crack, and the light did not penetrate at all. The tongue of darkness seemed to lick hungrily at the kitchen, waiting for night to come so it could swallow it whole. That quarter inch of darkness was hideous, unspeakable in its possibilities. She stood beside Mark, helpless and moveless.

Then he stepped forward and pulled the door open and stood for a moment, looking down. She saw a muscle jump beneath his jaw.

"I think—" he began, and she heard something behind her and turned, suddenly feeling slow, feeling too late. It was Straker. He was grinning.

Mark turned, saw, and tried to dive around him. Straker's fist crashed into his chin and he knew no more.

When Mark came to, he was being carried up a flight of stairs—not the cellar stairs, though. There was not that feeling of stone enclosure, and the air was not so fetid. He allowed his eyelids to unclose themselves a tiny fraction, letting his head still loll limply on his neck. A stair landing coming up . . . the second floor. He could see quite clearly. The sun was not down yet. Thin hope, then.

They gained the landing, and suddenly the arms holding him were gone. He thumped heavily onto the floor. Hitting his head.

"Do you not think I know when someone is playing the possum, young master?" Straker asked him. From the floor he seemed easily ten feet tall. His bald head glistened with a subdued elegance in the gathering gloom. Mark saw with growing terror that there was a coil of rope around his shoulder.

He grabbed for the pocket where the pistol had been.

Straker threw back his head and laughed. "I have taken the liberty of removing the gun, young master. Boys should not be allowed weapons they do not understand . . . any more than they should lead young ladies to houses where their commerce has not been invited."

"What did you do with Susan Norton?"

Straker smiled. "I have taken her where she wished to go, my boy. Into the cellar. Later, when the sun goes down, she will meet the man she came here to meet. You will meet him yourself, perhaps later tonight, perhaps tomorrow night. He may give you to the girl, of course . . . but I rather think he'll want to deal with you himself. The girl will have friends of her own, some of them perhaps meddlers like yourself."

Mark lashed out with both feet at Straker's crotch, and Straker sidestepped liquidly, like a dancer. At the same moment he kicked his own foot out, connecting squarely with Mark's kidneys.

Mark bit his lips and writhed on the floor.

Straker chuckled. "Come, young master. To your feet."

"I . . . I can't."

"Then crawl," Straker said contemptuously. He kicked again, this time striking the large muscle of the thigh. The pain was dreadful, but Mark clenched his feet together. He got to his knees, and then to his feet.

They progressed down the hall toward the door at the far end. The pain in his kidneys was subsiding to a dull ache. "What are you going to do with me?"

"Truss you like a spring turkey, young master. Later, after my Master holds intercourse with you, you will be set free."

"Like the others?"

Straker smiled.

As Mark pushed open the door and stepped into the room, something odd seemed to happen in his mind. The fear did not fall away from it, but it seemed to stop acting as a brake on his thoughts, jamming all productive signals. His thoughts began to flicker past with amazing speed, not in words or precisely in images, but in a kind of symbolic shorthand. He felt like a light bulb that has suddenly received a surge of power from no known source.

The room itself was utterly prosaic. The wallpaper hung in strips, show-ing the white plaster and sheet rock beneath. The floor was heavily dusted with time and plaster, but there was only one set of footprints in it, suggesting someone had come up once, looked around, and left again. There were two stacks of magazines, a cast-iron cot with no spring or mattress, and a small tin plate with a faded Currier & Ives design that had once blocked the stove hole in the chimney. The window was shut-tered, but enough light filtered dustily through the broken slats to make Mark think there might be an hour of daylight left. There was an aura of old nastiness about the room.

It took perhaps five seconds to open the door, see these things, and cross to the center of the room where Straker told him to stop. In that short period, his mind raced along three tracks and saw three possible outcomes to the situation he found himself in.

On one, he suddenly sprinted across the room toward the shuttered window and tried to crash through both glass and shutter like a Western movie hero, taking the drop to whatever lay below with blind hope. In one mental eye he saw himself crashing through only to fall onto a rusty pile of junked farm machinery, twitching away the last seconds of his life impaled on blunt harrow blades like a bug on a pin. In the other eye he saw himself crashing through the glass and into the shutter which trem-bled but did not break. He saw Straker pulling him back, his clothes torn, his body lacerated and bleeding in a dozen places.

On the second track, he saw Straker tie him up and leave. He saw himself trussed on the floor, saw the light fading, saw his struggles become

more frenzied (but just as useless), and heard, finally, the steady tread on the stairs of one who was a million times worse than Straker.

On the third track, he saw himself using a trick he had read about last summer in a book on Houdini. Houdini had been a famous magician who had escaped jail cells, chained boxes, bank vaults, steamer trunks thrown into rivers. He could get out of ropes, police handcuffs, and Chinese fingerpullers. And one of the things the book said he did was hold his breath and tighten his hands into fists when a volunteer from the audience was tying him up. You bulged your thighs and forearms and neck muscles, too. If your muscles were big, you had a little slack when you relaxed them. The trick then was to relax completely, and go at your escape slowly and surely, never letting panic hurry you up. Little by little, your body would give you sweat for grease, and that helped, too. The book made it sound very easy.

"Turn around," Straker said. "I am going to tie you up. While I tie you up, you will not move. If you move, I take this"—he cocked his thumb before Mark like a hitchhiker—"and pop your right eye out. Do you understand?"

Mark nodded. He took a deep breath, held it, and bunched all his muscles.

Straker threw his coil of rope over one of the beams.

"Lie down," he said.

Mark did.

He crossed Mark's hands behind his back and bound them tightly with the rope. He made a loop, slipped it around Mark's neck, and tied it in a hangman's knot. "You're made fast to the very beam my Master's friend and sponsor in this country hung himself from, young master. Are you flattered?"

Mark grunted, and Straker laughed. He passed the rope through Mark's crotch, and he groaned as Straker took up the slack with a brutal jerk.

He chuckled with monstrous good nature. "So your jewels hurt? They will not for long. You are going to lead an ascetic's life, my boy—a long, long life."

He banded the rope over Mark's taut thighs, made the knot tight, banded it again over his knees, and again over his ankles. Mark needed to breathe very badly now, but he held on stubbornly.

"You're trembling, young master," Straker said mockingly. "Your body is all in hard little knots. Your flesh is white—but it will be whiter! Yet you need not be so afraid. My Master has the capacity for kindness. He is much loved, right here in your own town. There is only a little sting, like the doctor's needle, and then sweetness. And later on you will be let free. You will go see your mother and father, yes? You will see them after they sleep."

He stood up and looked down at Mark benignly. "I will say good-by for a bit now, young master. Your lovely consort is to be made comfortable. When we meet again, you will like me better."

He left, slamming the door behind him. A key rattled in the lock. And as his feet descended the stairs, Mark let out his breath and relaxed his muscles with a great, whooping sigh.

The ropes holding him loosened—a little.

He lay moveless, collecting himself. His mind was still flying with that same unnatural, exhilarating speed. From his position, he looked across the swelled, uneven floor to the iron cot frame. He could see the wall beyond it. The wallpaper was peeled away from that section and lay beneath the cot frame like a discarded snakeskin. He focused on a small section of the wall and examined it closely. He flushed everything else from his mind. The book on Houdini said that concentration was all-important. No fear or taint of panic must be allowed in the mind. The body must be completely relaxed. And the escape must take place in the mind before a single finger did so much as twitch. Every step must exist concretely in the mind.

He looked at the wall, and minutes passed.

The wall was white and bumpy, like an old drive-in movie screen. Eventually, as his body relaxed to its greatest degree, he began to see himself projected there, a small boy wearing a blue T-shirt and Levi's jeans. The boy was on his side, arms pulled behind him, wrists nestling the small of the back above the buttocks. A noose looped around his neck, and any hard struggling would tighten that running slipknot inexorably until enough air was cut off to black out the brain.

He looked at the wall.

The figure there had begun to move cautiously, although he himself lay perfectly still. He watched all the movements of the simulacrum raptly. He had achieved a level of concentration necessary to the Indian fakirs and yogis, who are able to contemplate their toes or the tips of their noses for days, the state of certain mediums who levitate tables in a state of unconsciousness or extrude long tendrils of teleplasm from the nose, the mouth, the fingertips. His state was close to sublime. He did not think of Straker or the fading daylight. He no longer saw the gritty floor, the cot frame, or even the wall. He only saw the boy, a perfect figure which went through a tiny dance of carefully controlled muscles.

He looked at the wall.

And at last he began to move his wrists in half circles, toward each other. At the limit of each half circle, the thumb sides of his palms touched. No muscles moved but those in his lower forearms. He did not hurry. He looked at the wall.

As sweat rose through his pores, his wrists began to turn more freely. The half circles became three-quarters. At the limit of each, the backs of his hands pressed together. The loops holding them had loosened a tiny bit more.

He stopped.

After a moment had passed, he began to flex his thumbs against his palms and press his fingers together in a wriggling motion. His face was utterly expressionless, the plaster face of a department store dummy.

Five minutes passed. His hands were sweating freely now. The extreme level of his concentration had put him in partial control of his own sympathetic nervous system, another device of yogis and fakirs, and he had, unknowingly, gained some control over his body's involuntary functions. More sweat trickled from his pores than his careful movements could account for. His hands had become oily. Droplets fell from his forehead, darkening the white dust on the floor.

He began to move his arms in an up-and-down piston motion, using his biceps and back muscles now. The noose tightened a little, but he could feel one of the loops holding his hands beginning to drag lower on his right palm. It was sticking against the pad of the thumb now, and that was all. Excitement shot through him and he stopped at once until the emotion had passed away completely. When it had, he began again. Up-down. Up-down. Up-down. He gained an eighth of an inch at a time. And suddenly, shockingly, his right hand was free.

He left it where it was, flexing it. When he was sure it was limber, he eased the fingers under the loop holding the left wrist and tented them. The left hand slid free.

He brought both hands around and put them on the floor. He closed his eyes for a moment, The trick now was to not think he had it made. The trick now was to move with great deliberation.

Supporting himself with his left hand, he let his right roam over the bumps and valleys of the knot which secured the noose at his neck. He saw immediately that he would have to nearly choke himself to free it— and he was going to tighten the pressure on his testicles, which already throbbed dully.

He took a deep breath and began to work on the knot. The rope tightened by steady degrees, pressing into his neck and crotch. Prickles of coarse hemp dug into his throat like miniature tattoo needles. The knot defied him for what seemed an endless time. His vision began to fade under the onslaught of large black flowers that burst into soundless bloom before his eyes. He refused to hurry. He wiggled the knot steadily, and at last felt new slack in it. For a moment the pressure on his groin tightened unbearably, and then with a convulsive jerk, he threw the noose over his head and the pain lessened.

He sat up and hung his head over, breathing raggedly, cradling his wounded testicles in both hands. The sharp pain became a dull, pervading ache that made him feel nauseated.

When it began to abate a little, he looked over at the shuttered window. The light coming through the broken slats had faded to a dull ocher—it was almost sundown. And the door was locked.

He pulled the loose loop of rope over the beam, and set to work on the knots that held his legs. They were maddeningly tight, and his concentration had begun to slip away from him as reaction set in. He freed his thighs, the knees, and after a seemingly endless struggle, his ankles. He stood up weakly among the harmless loops of rope and staggered. He began to rub his thighs.

There was a noise from below: footsteps.

He looked up, panicky, nostrils dilating. He hobbled over to the window and tried to lift it. Nailed shut, with rusted tenpennies bent over the cheap wood of the half sill like staples.

The feet were coming up the stairs.

He wiped his mouth with his hand and stared wildly around the room. Two bundles of magazines. A small tin plate with a picture of an 1890s summer picnic on the back. The iron cot frame.

He went to it despairingly and pulled up one end. And some distant gods, perhaps seeing how much luck he had manufactured by himself, doled out a little of their own.

The steps had begun down the hall toward the door when he unscrewed the steel cot leg to its final thread and pulled it free.

When the door opened, Mark was standing behind it with the bed leg upraised, like a wooden Indian with a tomahawk.

"Young master, I've come to—"

He saw the empty coils of rope and froze for perhaps one full second in utter surprise. He was halfway through the door.

To Mark, things seemed to have slowed to the speed of a football maneuver seen in instant replay. He seemed to have minutes rather than bare seconds to aim at the one-quarter skull circumference visible beyond the edge of the door.

He brought the leg down with both hands, not as hard as he could—he sacrificed some force for better aim. It struck Straker just above the temple, as he started to turn to look behind the door. His eyes, open wide, squeezed shut in pain. Blood flew from the scalp wound in an amazing spray.

Straker's body recoiled and he stumbled backward into the room. His face was twisted into a terrifying grimace. He reached out and Mark hit him again. This time the pipe struck his bald skull just above the bulge of the forehead, and there was another gout of blood.

He went down bonelessly, his eyes rolling up in his head.

Mark skirted the body, looking at it with eyes that were bulging and wide. The end of the bed leg was painted with blood. It was darker than Technicolor movie blood. Looking at it made him feel sick, but looking at Straker made him feel nothing.

I killed him, he thought. And on the heels of that: *Good. Good.*

Straker's hand closed around his ankle.

Mark gasped and tried to pull his foot away. The hand held fast like a steel trap and now Straker was looking up at him, his eyes cold and bright through a dripping mask of blood. His lips were moving, but no sound came out. Mark pulled harder, to no avail. With a half groan, he began to hammer at Straker's clutching hand with the bed leg. Once, twice, three times, four. There was the awful pencil sound of snapping fingers. The hand loosened, and he pulled free with a yank that sent him stumbling out through the doorway and into the hall.

Straker's head had dropped to the floor again, but his mangled hand opened and closed on the air with tenebrous vitality, like the jerking of a dog's paws in dreams of cat-chasing.

The bed leg fell from his nerveless fingers and he backed away, trembling. Then panic took him and he turned and fled down the stairs, leaping two or three at a time on his numb legs, his hand skimming the splintered banister.

The front hall was shadow-struck, horribly dark.

He went into the kitchen, casting lunatic, shying glances at the open cellar door. The sun was going down in a blazing mullion of reds and yellows and purples.

Mark knew nothing of that, but he knew the vampire's time was imminent. To stay longer meant confrontation on top of confrontation; to go back down into that cellar and try to save Susan meant induction into the ranks of the Undead.

Yet he went to the cellar door and actually walked down the first three steps before his fear wrapped him in almost physical bonds and would allow him to go no further. He was weeping, and his body was trembling wildly, as if with ague.

"Susan!" he screamed. "Run!"

"M-Mark?" Her voice, sounding weak and dazed. "I can't see. It's dark—"

There was a sudden booming noise, like a hollow gunshot, followed by a profound and soulless chuckle.

Susan screamed . . . a sound that trailed away to a moan and then to silence.

Still he paused, on feather-feet that trembled to blow him away.

And from below came a friendly voice, amazingly like his father's: "Come down, my boy. I admire you."

The power in the voice alone was so great that he felt the fear ebbing from him, the feathers in his feet turning to lead. He actually began to grope down another step before he caught hold of himself—and the catching hold took all the ragged discipline he had left.

"Come down," the voice said, closer now. It held, beneath the friendly fatherliness, the smooth steel of command.

Mark shouted down: "I know your name! It's Barlow!"

And fled.

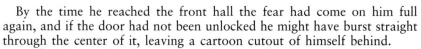

By the time he reached the front hall the fear had come on him full again, and if the door had not been unlocked he might have burst straight through the center of it, leaving a cartoon cutout of himself behind.

He fled down the driveway and then straight down the center of the Brooks Road toward town and dubious safety. Yet might not the king vampire come after him, even now?

He swerved off the road and made his way blunderingly through the woods, splashing through Taggart Stream and falling in a tangle of burdocks on the other side, and finally out into his own back yard.

He walked through the kitchen door and looked through the arch into the living room to where his mother, with worry written across her face in large letters, was talking into the telephone with the directory open on her lap.

She looked up and saw him, and relief spread across her face in a physical wave.

"—here he is—"

She set the phone into its cradle without waiting for a response and walked toward him. He saw with greater sorrow than she would have believed that she had been crying.

"Oh, Mark . . . where have you been?"

"He's home?" His father called from the den. His face, unseen, was filling with thunder.

"*Where have you been?*" She caught his shoulders and shook them.

"Out," he said wanly. "I fell down running home."

There was nothing else to say. The essential and defining characteristic of childhood is not the effortless merging of dream and reality, but only alienation. There are no words for childhood's dark turns and exhalations. A wise child recognizes it and submits to the necessary consequences. A child who counts the cost is a child no longer.

He added: "The time got away from me. It—"

Then his father, descending upon him.

Some time in the darkness before Monday's dawn.

Scratching at the window.

He came up from sleep with no pause, no intervening period of drowsiness or orientation. The insanities of sleep and waking had become remarkably similar.

The white face in the darkness outside the glass was Susan's.

"Mark . . . let me in."

He got out of bed. The floor was cold under his bare feet. He was shivering.

"Go away," he said tonelessly. He could see that she was still wearing the same blouse, the same slacks. I wonder if *her* folks are worried, he thought. If they've called the police.

"It's not so bad, Mark," she said, and her eyes were flat and obsidian. She smiled, showing her teeth, which shone in sharp relief below her pale gums. "It's ever so nice. Let me in, I'll show you. I'll kiss you, Mark. I'll kiss you all over like your mother never did."

"Go away," he repeated.

"One of us will get you sooner or later," she said. "There are lots more of us now. Let it be me, Mark. I'm . . . I'm hungry." She tried to smile, but it turned into a nightshade grimace that made his bones cold.

He held up his cross and pressed it against the window.

She hissed, as if scalded, and let go of the window frame. For a moment she hung suspended in air, her body becoming misty and indistinct. Then, gone. But not before he saw (or thought he saw) a look of desperate unhappiness on her face.

The night was still and silent again.

There are lots more of us now.

His thoughts turned to his parents, sleeping in thoughtless peril below him, and dread gripped his bowels.

Some men knew, she had said, or suspected.

Who?

The writer, of course. The one she dated. Mears, his name was. He lived at Eva's boardinghouse. Writers knew a lot. It would be him. And he would have to get to Mears before she did—

He stopped on his way back to bed.

If she hadn't already.

·······II·······
THE PSYCHOLOGICAL VAMPIRE

Unlike their bloodthirsty brethren, psychological vampires are more subtle in their depredations and far more difficult to detect. They may, however, be the one variety of "vampire" that almost everyone has encountered in real life. Who among us does not know at least one individual whose very presence drains all the life and energy from any occasion? Psychological vampires are not confined to the pages of fiction; the world has its share of dangerously needy people who, like Luella Miller, batten onto unsuspecting prey in all sorts of parasitic relationships.

Psychological vampire fiction is largely a twentieth-century phenomenon; one might argue that it is a uniquely post-Freudian genre. Certainly, as the century has progressed, the psychodynamics of behavior have occupied our culture. The first twentieth-century vampire novel is George Sylvester Viereck's *The House of the Vampire* (1907), in which a celebrated artist, Reginald Clarke, drains his friends of their creativity rather than their blood.

Because of their realistic nature, most psychological vampires in modern fiction probably lurk unexposed in the pages of mainstream fiction; note the inclusion in this section of stories by John Cheever and Joyce Carol Oates. Psychological vampirism, both as reality and metaphor, has been explored most thoroughly via the short story.

In all but one of the stories that follow, the vampire craves and steals energy, life energy or mind energy, or what used to be called "élan vital." In Oates's *Bellefleur*, the word "steal" perhaps overstates the case, because Oates's Veronica is fascinated by her vampire and is more than half willing to have him take whatever he wants, energy or blood. And in Algernon Blackwood's "The Transfer," we see two vampiric forces in collision; the one that is morally evil is engulfed. Other stories, not included here, such as " . . . To Feel Another's Woe" by Chet Williamson and "The Slug" by the late Karl Edward Wagner, even return to the theme of creative vampirism first explored decades ago in *The House of the Vampire*. Vampirism, as a fictional conceit, provides both writers and readers with a useful and astonishingly versatile tool for exploring the darker aspects of human relationships and psychology.

MARY E. WILKINS-FREEMAN
(1852–1930)

Born in Randolph, Massachusetts, the daughter of a carpenter, Mary E. Wilkins-Freeman was a schoolteacher who occasionally published books for extra income. She began her career writing children's poetry, and in 1882 published her first adult story, "The Beggar King." When she was nearly fifty she married Dr. Charles Freeman, an alcoholic who, eighteen years later, was committed to a state hospital for the insane.

Wilkins-Freeman was a sensitive writer of local color fiction (A New England Nun and Other Stories, 1891) and tales of the supernatural (The Wind in the Rosebush and Other Supernatural Ghost Stories, 1903); her prose is simple and lucid, cloaking an extraordinarily perceptive and complex intelligence.

She produced dozens of volumes of short stories and as many novels. Her works include Pembroke (1894), The Heart's Highway: A Romance of Virginia in the Seventeenth Century (1900), The Portion of Labor (1901), Six Trees (1903), and The Givers (1904), as well as an early collection of short fiction, titled A Humble Romance and Other Stories (1891).

The following story, "Luella Miller," presents us with an early example of psychological vampire fiction, in which we find the bland and innocent Luella Miller ingesting the well-being of those who care for her. The opening passage sets up the intimate ambiance of a village in which everyone knows everyone else by sight. We have Luella Miller, and we have the presence of evil in the village.

Luella seems "strange"—the way she sits, the way she walks—but that strangeness is hardly as horrifying as Luella's ability to swallow other people's energy. The horror is built up in such small increments that when the reader has finished the tale, one of Luella's earlier mild remarks, "I never made coffee in all my life," takes on all the portentousness of a death knell.

LUELLA MILLER

Close to the village street stood the one-story house in which Luella Miller, who had an evil name in the village, had dwelt. She had been dead for years, yet there were those in the village who, in spite of the clearer light which comes on a vantage-point from a long-past danger, half believed in the tale which they had heard from their childhood. In their hearts, although they scarcely would have owned it, was a survival of the wild horror and frenzied fear of their ancestors who had dwelt in the same age with Luella Miller. Young people even would stare with a shudder at the old house as they passed, and children never played around it as was their wont around an untenanted building. Not a window in the old Miller house was broken: the panes reflected the morning sunlight in patches of emerald and blue, and the latch of the sagging front door was never lifted, although no bolt secured it. Since Luella Miller had been carried out of it, the house had had no tenant except one friendless old soul who had no choice between that and the far-off shelter of the open sky. This old woman, who had survived her kindred and friends, lived in the house one week, then one morning no smoke came out of the chimney, and a body of neighbours, a score strong, entered and found her dead in her bed. There were dark whispers as to the cause of her death, and there were those who testified to an expression of fear so exalted that it showed forth the state of the departing soul upon the dead face. The old woman had been hale and hearty when she entered the house, and in seven days she was dead; it seemed that she had fallen a victim to some uncanny power. The minister talked in the pulpit with covert severity against the sin of superstition; still the brief prevailed. Not a soul in the village but would have chosen the almshouse rather than that dwelling. No vagrant, if he heard the tale, would seek shelter beneath that old roof, unhallowed by nearly half a century of superstitious fear.

There was only one person in the village who had actually known Luella Miller. That person was a woman well over eighty, but a marvel of vitality and unextinct youth. Straight as an arrow, with the spring of one recently let loose from the bow of life, she moved about the streets, and she always went to church, rain or shine. She had never married, and had lived alone for years in a house across the road from Luella Miller's.

This woman had none of the garrulousness of age, but never in all her life had she ever held her tongue for any will save her own, and she never spared the truth when she essayed to present it. She it was who bore testimony to the life, evil, though possibly wittingly or designedly so, of Luella Miller, and to her personal appearance. When this old woman spoke—and she had the gift of description, although her thoughts were clothed in the rude vernacular of her native village—one could seem to see Luella Miller as she had really looked. According to this woman, Lydia Anderson by name, Luella Miller had been a beauty of a type rather unusual in New England. She had been a slight, pliant sort of creature, as ready with a strong yielding to fate and as unbreakable as a willow. She had glimmering lengths of straight, fair hair, which she wore softly looped around a long, lovely face. She had blue eyes full of soft pleading, little slender, clinging hands, and a wonderful grace of motion and attitude.

"Luella Miller used to sit in a way nobody else could if they sat up and studied a week of Sundays," said Lydia Anderson, "and it was a sight to see her walk. If one of them willows over there on the edge of the brook could start up and get its roots free of the ground, and move off, it would go just the way Luella Miller used to. She had a green shot silk she used to wear, too, and a hat with green ribbon streamers, and a lace veil blowing across her face and out sideways, and a green ribbon flyin' from her waist. That was what she came out bride in when she married Erastus Miller. Her name before she was married was Hill. There was always a sight of "l's" in her name, married or single. Erastus Miller was good lookin', too, better lookin' than Luella. Sometimes I used to think that Luella wa'n't so handsome after all. Erastus just about worshiped her. I used to know him pretty well. He lived next door to me, and we went to school together. Folks used to say he was waitin' on me, but he wa'n't. I never thought he was except once or twice when he said things that some girls might have suspected meant somethin'. That was before Luella came here to teach the district school. It was funny how she came to get it, for folks said she hadn't any education, and that one of the big girls, Lottie Henderson, used to do all the teachin' for her, while she sat back and did embroidery work on a cambric pocket-handkerchief. Lottie Henderson was a real smart girl, a splendid scholar, and she just set her eyes by Luella, as all the girls did. Lottie would have made a real smart woman, but she died when Luella had been here about a year—just faded away and died: nobody knew what ailed her. She dragged herself to that schoolhouse and helped Luella teach till the very last minute. The committee all knew how Luella didn't do much of the work herself, but they winked at it. It wa'n't long after Lottie died that Erastus married her. I always thought he hurried it up because she wa'n't fit to teach. One of the big boys used to help her after Lottie died, but he hadn't much government, and the school didn't do very well, and Luella might have had to give it up, for the committee couldn't have shut their eyes to things much longer. The boy that helped her was a real honest, innocent sort of fellow, and he was a good scholar, too. Folks said he overstudied, and that was the reason he was took crazy the year after Luella married, but I don't know. And I don't know what made Erastus Miller go into consumption of the blood the year after he was married: consumption wa'n't in his family. He just grew weaker and weaker, and went almost bent double when he tried to wait on Luella, and he spoke feeble, like an old man. He worked terrible hard till the last trying to save up a little to leave Luella. I've seen him out in the worst storms on a wood-sled—he used to cut and sell wood—and he was hunched up on top lookin' more dead than alive. Once I couldn't stand it: I went over and helped him pitch some wood on the cart—I was always strong in my arms. I wouldn't stop for all he told me to, and I guess he was glad enough for the help. That was only a week before he died. He fell on the kitchen floor while he was gettin' breakfast. He always got the breakfast and let Luella lay abed. He did all the sweepin' and the washin' and the ironin' and most of the cookin'. He couldn't bear to have Luella lift her finger, and she let him do for her. She lived like a queen for all the work she did. She didn't even do her sewin'. She said it made her shoulder ache to sew, and poor Erastus's sister Lily used to do all her sewin'. She wa'n't able to, either; she was never strong in her back, but she did it beautifully. She had to, to suit Luella, she was so dreadful particular. I never saw anythin' like the fagottin' and hemstitchin' that Lily Miller did for Luella. She made all Luella's weddin' outfit, and that green silk dress, after Maria Babbit cut it. Maria she cut it for nothin', and she did a lot more cuttin' and fittin' for nothin' for Luella, too. Lily Miller went to live with Luella after Erastus died. She gave up her home, though she was real attached to it and wa'n't a mite afraid to stay alone. She rented it and she went to live with Luella right away after the funeral."

Then this old woman, Lydia Anderson, who remembered Luella Miller, would go on to relate the story of Lily Miller. It seemed that on the removal of Lily Miller to the house of her dead brother, to live with his widow, the village people first began to talk. This Lily Miller had been hardly past her first youth, and a most robust and blooming woman, rosy-cheeked, with curls of strong, black hair overshadowing round, candid temples and bright dark eyes. It was not six months after she had taken up her residence with her sister-in-law that her rosy color faded and her pretty curves became wan hollows. White shadows began to show in the black rings of her hair, and the light died out of her eyes, her features sharpened, and there were pathetic lines at her mouth, which yet wore always an expression of utter sweetness and even happiness. She was devoted to her sister; there was no doubt that she loved her with her whole heart, and was perfectly content in her service. It was her sole anxiety lest she should die and leave her alone.

"The way Lily Miller used to talk about Luella was enough to make you mad and enough to make you cry," said Lydia Anderson. "I've been in there sometimes toward the last when she was too feeble to cook and carried her some blanc-mange or custard—somethin' I thought she might relish and she'd thank me, and when I asked her how she was, say she felt better than she did yesterday, and asked me if I didn't think she looked better, dreadful pitiful, and say poor Luella had an awful time takin' care of her and doin' the work—she wa'n't strong enough to do anythin'—when all the time Luella wa'n't liftin' her finger and poor Lily didn't get any care except what the neighbours gave her, and Luella eat up everythin' that was carried in for Lily. I had it real straight that she did. Luella used to just sit and cry and do nothin'. She did act real fond of Lily, and she pined away considerable, too. There was those that thought she'd go into a decline herself. But after Lily died, her Aunt Abby Mixter came, and then Luella picked up and grew as fat and rosy as ever. But poor Aunt Abby begun to droop just the way Lily had, and I guess somebody wrote to her married daughter, Mrs. Sam Abbot, who lived in Barre, for she wrote her mother that she must leave right away and come and make her a visit, but Aunt Abby wouldn't go. I can see her now. She was a real good-lookin' woman, tall and large, with a big, square face and a high forehead that looked of itself kind of benevolent and good. She just tended out on Luella as if she had been a baby, and when her married daughter sent for her she wouldn't stir one inch. She'd always thought a lot of her daughter, too, but she said Luella needed her and her married daughter didn't. Her daughter kept writin' and writin', but it didn't do any good. Finally she came, and when she saw how bad her mother looked, she broke down and cried and all but went on her knees to have her come away. She spoke her mind out to Luella, too. She told her that she'd killed her husband and everybody that had anythin' to do with her, and she'd thank her to leave her mother alone. Luella went into hysterics, and Aunt Abby was so frightened that she called me after her daughter went. Mrs. Sam Abbot she went away fairly cryin' out loud in the buggy, the neighbours heard her, and well she might, for she never saw her mother again alive. I went in that night when Aunt Abby called for me, standin' in the door with her little green-checked shawl over her head. I can see her now. 'Do come over here, Miss Anderson,' she sung out, kind of gasping for breath. I didn't stop for anythin'. I put over as fast as I could, and when I got there, there was Luella laughin' and cryin' all together, and Aunt Abby trying to hush her, and all the time she herself was white as a sheet and shakin' so she could hardly stand. 'For the land sakes, Mrs. Mixter,' says I, 'you look worse than she does. You ain't fit to be up out of your bed.'

" 'Oh, there ain't anythin' the matter with me,' says she. Then she went on talkin' to Luella. 'There, there, don't, don't, poor little lamb,' says she. 'Aunt Abby is here. She ain't goin' away and leave you. Don't, poor little lamb.'

" 'Do leave her with me, Mrs. Mixter, and you get back to bed,' says I, for Aunt Abby had been layin' down considerable lately, though somehow she contrived to do the work.

" 'I'm well enough,' says she. 'Don't you think she had better have the doctor, Miss Anderson?'

" 'The doctor,' says I, 'I think *you* had better have the doctor. I think you need him much worse than some folks I could mention.' And I looked right straight at Luella Miller laughin' and cryin' and goin' on as if she was the center of all creation. All the time she was actin' so—seemed as if she was too sick to sense anythin'—she was keepin' a sharp lookout as to how we took it out of the corner of one eye. I see her. You could never cheat me about Luella Miller. Finally I got real mad and I run home and I got a bottle of valerian I had, and I poured some boilin' hot water on a handful of catnip, and I mixed up that catnip tea with most half a wineglass of valerian, and I went with it over to Luella's. I marched right up to Luella, a-holdin' out of that cup, all smokin'. 'Now,' says I, 'Luella Miller, *you swaller this!*'

" 'What is—what is it, oh, what is it?' she sort of screeches out. Then she goes off a-laughin' enough to kill.

" 'Poor lamb, poor little lamb,' says Aunt Abby, standin' over her, all kind of tottery, and tryin' to bathe her head with camphor.

" '*You swaller this right down,*' says I. And I didn't waste any ceremony. I just took hold of Luella Miller's chin and I tipped her head back, and I caught her mouth open with laughin', and I clapped that cup to her lips and I fairly hollered at her: 'Swaller, swaller, swaller!' and she gulped it right down. She had to, and I guess it did her good. Anyhow, she stopped cryin' and laughin' and let me put her to bed, and she went to sleep like a baby inside of half an hour. That was more than poor Aunt Abby did. She lay awake all that night and I stayed with her, though she tried not to have me; said she wa'n't sick enough for watchers. But I stayed, and I made some good cornmeal gruel and I fed her a teaspoon every little while all night long. It seemed to me as if she was jest dyin' from bein' all wore out. In the mornin' as soon as it was light I run over to the Bisbees and sent Johnny Bisbee for the doctor. I told him to tell the doctor to hurry, and he come pretty quick. Poor Aunt Abby didn't seem to know much of anythin' when he got there. You couldn't hardly tell she breathed, she was so used up. When the doctor had gone, Luella came into the room lookin' like a baby in her ruffled nightgown. I can see her now. Her eyes were as blue and her face all pink and white like a blossom, and she looked at Aunt Abby in the bed sort of innocent and surprised. 'Why,' says she, 'Aunt Abby ain't got up yet?'

" 'No, she ain't,' says I, pretty short.

" 'I thought I didn't smell the coffee,' says Luella.

" 'Coffee,' says I. 'I guess if you have coffee this mornin' you'll make it yourself."

" 'I never made the coffee in all my life,' says she, dreadful astonished. 'Erastus always made the coffee as long as he lived, and then Lily she made it, and then Aunt Abby made it. I don't believe I *can* make the coffee, Miss Anderson.'

" 'You can make it or go without, jest as you please,' says I.

" 'Ain't Aunt Abby goin' to get up?' says she.

" 'I guess she won't get up,' says I, 'sick as she is.' I was gettin' madder and madder. There was somethin' about that little pink-and-white thing standin' there and talkin' about coffee, when she had killed so many better folks than she was, and had jest killed another, that made me feel 'most as if I wished somebody would up and kill her before she had a chance to do any more harm.

" 'Is Aunt Abby sick?' says Luella, as if she was sort of aggrieved and injured.

" 'Yes,' says I, 'she's sick, and she's goin' to die, and then you'll be left alone, and you'll have to do for yourself and wait on yourself, or do without things.' I don't know but I was sort of hard, but it was the truth, and if I was any harder than Luella Miller had been I'll give up. I ain't never been sorry that I said it. Well, Luella, she up and had hysterics again at that, and I jest let her have 'em. All I did was to bundle her into the room on the other side of the entry where Aunt Abby couldn't hear her, if she wa'n't past it—I don't know but she was—and set her down hard in a chair and told her not to come back into the other room, and she minded. She had her hysterics in there till she got tired. When she found out that nobody was comin' to coddle her and do for her she stopped. At least I suppose she did. I had all I could do with poor Aunt Abby tryin' to keep the breath of life in her. The doctor had told me that she was dreadful low, and give me some very strong medicine to give to her in drops real often, and told me real particular about the nourishment. Well, I did as he told me real faithful till she wa'n't able to swaller any longer. Then I had her daughter sent for. I had begun to realize that she wouldn't last any time at all. I hadn't realized it before, though I spoke to Luella the way I did. The doctor he came, and Mrs. Sam Abbot, but when she got there it was too late; her mother was dead. Aunt Abby's daughter just give one look at her mother layin' there, then she turned sort of sharp and sudden and looked at me.

" 'Where is she?' says she, and I knew she meant Luella.

" 'She's out in the kitchen,' says I. 'She's too nervous to see folks die. She's afraid it will make her sick.'

"The Doctor he speaks up then. He was a young man. Old Doctor Park had died the year before, and this was a young fellow just out of college. 'Mrs. Miller is not strong,' says he, kind of severe, 'and she is quite right in not agitating herself.'

" 'You are another, young man; she's got her pretty claw on you,' thinks I, but I didn't say anythin' to him. I just said over to Mrs. Sam Abbot that Luella was in the kitchen, and Mrs. Sam Abbot she went out there, and I went, too, and I never heard anythin' like the way she talked to Luella Miller. I felt pretty hard to Luella myself, but this was more than I ever would have dared to say. Luella she was too scared to go into hysterics. She jest flopped. She seemed to jest shrink away to nothin' in that kitchen chair, with Mrs. Sam Abbot standin' over her and talkin' and tellin' her the truth. I guess the truth was most too much for her and no mistake, because Luella presently actually did faint away, and there wa'n't any sham about it, the way I always suspected there was about them hysterics. She fainted dead away and we had to lay her flat on the floor, and the Doctor he came runnin' out and he said somethin' about a weak heart dreadful fierce to Mrs. Sam Abbot, but she wa'n't a mite scared. She faced him jest as white as even Luella was layin' there lookin' like death and the Doctor feelin' of her pulse.

" 'Weak heart,' says she, 'weak heart; weak fiddlesticks! There ain't nothin' weak about that woman. She's got strength enough to hang onto other folks till she kills 'em. Weak? It was my poor mother that was weak: this woman killed her as sure as if she had taken a knife to her.'

"But the Doctor he didn't pay much attention. He was bendin' over Luella layin' there with her yellow hair all streamin' and her pretty pink-and-white face all pale, and her blue eyes like stars gone out, and he was holdin' onto her hand and smoothin' her forehead, and tellin' me to get the brandy in Aunt Abby's room, and I was sure as I wanted to be that Luella had got somebody else to hang onto, now Aunt Abby was gone, and I thought of poor Erastus Miller, and I sort of pitied the poor young Doctor, led away by a pretty face, and I made up my mind I'd see what I could do.

"I waited till Aunt Abby had been dead and buried about a month, and the Doctor was goin' to see Luella steady and folks were beginnin' to talk; then one evenin', when I knew the Doctor had been called out of town and wouldn't be around, I went over to Luella's. I found her all dressed up in a blue muslin with white polka dots on it, and her hair curled jest as pretty, and there wa'n't a young girl in the place could compare with her. There was somethin' about Luella Miller seemed to draw the heart right out of you, but she didn't draw it out of *me*. She was settin' rocking in the chair by her sittin'-room window, and Maria Brown had gone home. Maria Brown had been in to help her, or rather to do the work, for Luella wa'n't helped when she didn't do anythin'. Maria Brown was real capable and she didn't have any ties; she wa'n't married, and lived alone, so she'd offered. I couldn't see why she should do the work any more than Luella; she wa'n't any too strong; but she seemed to think she could and Luella seemed to think so, too, so she went over and did all the work—washed, and ironed, and baked, while Luella sat and rocked. Maria didn't live long afterward. She began to fade away just the same fashion the others had. Well, she was warned, but she acted real mad when folks said anythin': said Luella was a poor, abused woman, too delicate to help herself, and they'd ought to be ashamed, and if she died helpin' them that couldn't help themselves she would—and she did.

" 'I s'pose Maria has gone home,' says I to Luella, when I had gone in and sat down opposite her.

" 'Yes, Maria went half an hour ago, after she had got supper and washed the dishes,' says Luella, in her pretty way.

" 'I suppose she has got a lot of work to do in her own house tonight,' says I, kind of bitter, but that was all thrown away on Luella Miller. It seemed to her right that other folks that wa'n't any better able than she was herself should wait on her, and she couldn't get it through her head that anybody should think it *wa'n't* right.

" 'Yes,' says Luella, real sweet and pretty, 'yes, she said she had to do her washin' tonight. She has let it go for a fortnight along of comin' over here.'

" 'Why don't she stay home and do her washin' instead of comin' over here and doin' *your* work, when you are just as well able, and enough sight more so, than she is to do it?' says I.

"Then Luella she looked at me like a baby who has a rattle shook at it. She sort of laughed as innocent as you please. 'Oh, I can't do the work myself, Miss Anderson,' says she. 'I never did. Maria *has* to do it.'

"Then I spoke out: 'Has to do it!' says I. 'Has to do it! She don't have to do it, either. Maria Brown has her own home and enough to live on. She ain't beholden to you to come over here and slave for you and kill herself.'

"Luella she jest set and stared at me for all the world like a doll-baby that was so abused that it was comin' to life.

" 'Yes,' says I, 'she's killin' herself. She's goin' to die just the way Erastus did, and Lily, and your Aunt Abby. You're killin' her jest as you did them. I don't know what there is about you, but you seem to bring a curse,' says I. 'You kill everybody that is fool enough to care anythin' about you and do for you.'

"She stared at me and she was pretty pale.

" 'And Maria ain't the only one you're goin' to kill,' says I. 'You're goin' to kill Doctor Malcom before you're done with him.'

"Then a red color came flamin' all over her face. 'I ain't goin' to kill him, either,' says she, and she began to cry.

" 'Yes, you *be!*' says I. Then I spoke as I had never spoke before. You see, I felt it on account of Erastus. I told her that she hadn't any business to think of another man after she'd been married to one that had died for her: that she was a dreadful woman; and she was, that's true enough, but sometimes I have wondered lately if she knew it—if she wa'n't like a baby with scissors in its hand cuttin' everybody without knowin' what it was doin'.

"Luella she kept gettin' paler and paler, and she never took her eyes off my face. There was somethin' awful about the way she looked at me and never spoke one word. After awhile I quit talkin' and I went home. I watched that night, but her lamp went out before nine o'clock, and when Doctor Malcom came drivin' past and sort of slowed up he see there wa'n't any light and he drove along. I saw her sort of shy out of meetin' the next Sunday, too, so he shouldn't go home with her, and I begun to think mebbe she did have some conscience after all. It was only a week after that that Maria Brown died—sort of sudden at the last, though everybody had seen it was comin'. Well, then there was a good deal of feelin' and pretty dark whispers. Folks said the days of witchcraft had come again, and they were pretty shy of Luella. She acted sort of offish to the Doctor and he didn't go there, and there wa'n't anybody to do anythin' for her. I don't know how she *did* get along. I wouldn't go in there and offer to help her—not because I was afraid of dyin' like the rest but I thought she was just as well able to do her own work as I was to do it for her, and I thought it was about time that she did it and stopped killin' other folks. But it wa'n't very long before folks began to say that Luella herself was goin' into a decline jest the way her husband, and Lily, and Aunt Abby and the others had, and I saw myself that she looked pretty bad. I used to see her goin' past from the store with a bundle as if she could hardly crawl, but I remembered how Erastus used to wait and 'tend when he couldn't hardly put one foot before the other, and I didn't go out to help her.

"But at last one afternoon I saw the Doctor come drivin' up like mad with his medicine chest, and Mrs. Babbit came in after supper and said that Luella was real sick.

" 'I'd offer to go in and nurse her,' says she, 'but I've got my children to consider, and mebbe it ain't true what they say, but it's queer how folks that have done for her have died.'

"I didn't say anythin', but I considered how she had been Erastus's wife and how he had set his eyes by her, and I made up my mind to go in the next mornin', unless she was better, and see what I could do; but the next mornin' I see her at the window, and pretty soon she came steppin' out as spry as you please, and a little while afterward Mrs. Babbit came in and told me that the Doctor had got a girl from out of town, a Sarah Jones, to come there, and she said she was pretty sure that the Doctor was goin' to marry Luella.

"I saw him kiss her in the door that night myself, and I knew it was true. The woman came that afternoon, and the way she flew around was a caution. I don't believe Luella had swept since Maria died. She swept and dusted, and washed and ironed; wet clothes and dusters and carpets were flyin' over there all day, and every time Luella set her foot out when the Doctor wa'n't there there was that Sarah Jones helpin' of her up and down the steps, as if she hadn't learned to walk.

"Well, everybody knew that Luella and the Doctor were goin' to be married, but it wa'n't long before they began to talk about his lookin' so poorly, jest as they had about the others; and they talked about Sarah Jones, too.

"Well, the Doctor did die, and he wanted to be married first, so as to leave what little he had to Luella, but he died before the minister could get there, and Sarah Jones died a week afterward.

"Well, that wound up everything for Luella Miller. Not another soul in the whole town would lift a finger for her. There got to be a sort of panic. Then she began to droop in good earnest. She used to have to go to the store herself, for Mrs. Babbit was afraid to let Tommy go for her, and I've seen her goin' past and stoppin' every two or three steps to rest. Well, I stood it as long as I could, but one day I see her comin' with her arms full and stoppin' to lean against the Babbit fence, and I run out and took her bundles and carried them to her house. Then I went home and never spoke one word to her though she called after me dreadful kind of pitiful. Well, that night I was taken sick with a chill, and I was sick as I wanted to be for two weeks. Mrs. Babbit had seen me run out to help Luella and she came in and told me I was goin' to die on account of it. I didn't know whether I was or not, but I considered I had done right by Erastus's wife.

"That last two weeks Luella she had a dreadful hard time, I guess. She was pretty sick, and as near as I could make out nobody dared go near her. I don't know as she was really needin' anythin' very much, for there was enough to eat in her house and it was warm weather, and she made out to cook a little flour gruel every day, I know, but I guess she had a hard time, she that had been so petted and done for all her life.

"When I got so I could go out, I went over there one morning. Mrs. Babbit had just come in to say she hadn't seen any smoke and she didn't know but what it was somebody's duty to go in, but she couldn't help thinkin' of her children, and I got right up, though I hadn't been out of the house for two weeks, and I went in there, and Luella she was layin' on the bed, and she was dyin'.

"She lasted all that day and into the night. But I sat there after the new doctor had gone away. Nobody else dared to go there. It was about midnight that I left her for a minute to run home and get some medicine I had been takin', for I begun to feel rather bad.

"It was a full moon that night, and just as I started out of my door to cross the street back to Luella's, I stopped short, for I saw something."

Lydia Anderson at this juncture always said with a certain defiance that she did not expect to be believed, and then proceeded in a hushed voice:

"I saw what I saw, and I know I saw it, and I will swear on my death bed that I saw it. I saw Luella Miller and Erastus Miller, and Lily, and Aunt Abby, and Maria, and the Doctor, and Sarah, all goin' out her door, and all but Luella shone white in the moonlight, and they were all helpin' her along till she seemed to fairly fly in the midst of them. Then it all disappeared. I stood a minute with my heart poundin', then I went over there. I thought of goin' for Mrs. Babbit, but I thought she'd be afraid. So I went alone, though I knew what had happened. Luella was layin' real peaceful, dead on her bed."

This was the story that the old woman, Lydia Anderson, told, but the sequel was told by the people who survived her, and this is the tale which has become folklore in the village.

Lydia Anderson died when she was eighty-seven. She had continued wonderfully hale and hearty for one of her years until about two weeks before her death.

One bright moonlight evening she was sitting beside a window in her parlor when she made a sudden exclamation, and was out of the house and across the street before the neighbor who was taking care of her could stop her. She followed as fast as possible and found Lydia Anderson stretched on the ground before the door of Luella Miller's deserted house, and she was quite dead.

The next night there was a red gleam of fire athwart the moonlight and the old house of Luella Miller was burned to the ground. Nothing is now left of it except a few old cellar stones and a lilac bush, and in summer a helpless trail of morning glories among the weeds, which might be considered emblematic of Luella herself.

ALGERNON BLACKWOOD
(1869–1951)

Born into a distinguished family in England, Algernon Blackwood spent a poverty-stricken young manhood in Canada. After working a few odd jobs there and in New York, he returned to England in 1899.

Blackwood's first book of short stories, The Empty House, was published in 1906. The following year The Listener was published, which contains his best-known work, "The Willows." He also penned the novels Jimbo (1909), The Centaur (1911), and A Prisoner in Fairyland (1913). His other collections of short stories include Pan's Garden (1912), The Dance of Death (1927), John Silence (1908), and Tales of the Uncanny and Supernatural (1949).

Blackwood believed in the supernatural. He was only one of a number of successful authors belonging to the Order of the Golden Dawn, an occult society created in 1888 by Samuel Lidell MacGregor Mathers and whose most infamous member was Aleister Crowley, a well-known occultist whose scandalous reputation persists to this day. Members of this group produced much of the United Kingdom's horror fiction of the time (one report lists Bram Stoker as a member).

Blackwood's supernatural fiction often focuses on outdoor scenes. He was a believer in the unseen powers that reside in people and places, and made his short stories turn on that belief, as in "The Man Whom the Trees Loved" (1912) in which he writes, "We must believe that in plants there exists a faint copy of what we know as consciousness in ourselves." In other tales, islands, meadows, and rivers seem to remember the events that have taken place in or near them. One such tale is the remarkable "The Willows," in which a clump of willows on an island in a river are the malevolent force. Another, equally terrifying, is "The Doll" (1946) in which the doll is an agent of vengeance.

"The Transfer" could well fit into more than one of the categories identified in this anthology, for example that of Non-Human Vampire. It is placed here because the two forces that clash are both vampiric, although it is psychic energy, not blood, that is engulfed in the battle between them. This struggle of avidities ends, to the delight of the reader, in the triumph of poetic justice.

THE TRANSFER

The child began to cry in the early afternoon—about three o'clock, to be exact. I remember the hour, because I had been listening with secret relief to the sound of the departing carriage. Those wheels fading into the distance down the gravel drive with Mrs. Frene, and her daughter Gladys to whom I was governess, meant for me some hours' welcome rest, and the June day was oppressively hot. Moreover, there was this excitement in the little country household that had told upon us all, but especially upon myself. This excitement, running delicately behind all the events of the morning, was due to some mystery, and the mystery was of course kept concealed from the governess. I had exhausted myself with guessing and keeping on the watch. For some deep and unexplained anxiety possessed me, so that I kept thinking of my sister's dictum that I was really much too sensitive to make a good governess, and that I should have done far better as a professional clairvoyant.

Mr. Frene, senior, "Uncle Frank," was expected for an unusual visit from town about tea-time. That I knew. I also knew that his visit was concerned somehow with the future welfare of little Jamie, Gladys' seven-year-old brother. More than this, indeed, I never knew, and this missing link makes my story in a fashion incoherent—an important bit of the strange puzzle left out. I only gathered that the visit of Uncle Frank was of a condescending nature, that Jamie was told he must be upon his very best behavior to make a good impression, and that Jamie, who had never seen his uncle, dreaded him horribly already in advance. Then, trailing thinly through the dying crunch of the carriage wheels this sultry afternoon, I heard the curious little wail of the child's crying, with the effect, wholly unaccountable, that every nerve in my body shot its bolt electrically, bringing me to my feet with a tingling of unequivocal alarm. Positively, the water ran into my eyes. I recalled his white distress that morning when told that Uncle Frank was motoring down for tea and that he was to be "very nice indeed" to him. It had gone into me like a knife. All through the day, indeed, had run this nightmare quality of terror and vision.

"The man with the 'normous face?" he had asked in a little voice of awe, and then gone speechless from the room in tears that no amount of soothing management could calm. That was all I saw; and what he meant by "the 'normous face" gave me only a sense of vague presentiment. But it came as anticlimax somehow—a sudden revelation of the mystery and excitement that pulsed beneath the quiet of the stifling summer day. I feared for him. For of all that commonplace household I loved Jamie best, though professionally I had nothing to do with him. He was a high-strung, ultra-sensitive child, and it seemed to me that no one understood him, least of all his honest, tender-hearted parents; so that his little wailing voice brought me from my bed to the window in a moment like a call for help.

The haze of June lay over that big garden like a blanket; the wonderful flowers, which were Mr. Frene's delight, hung motionless; the lawns, so soft and thick, cushioned all other sounds; only the limes and huge clumps of guelder roses hummed with bees. Through this muted atmosphere of heat and haze the sound of the child's crying floated faintly to my ears—from a distance. Indeed, I wonder now that I heard it at all, for the next moment I saw him down beyond the garden, standing in his white sailor suit alone, two hundred yards away. He was down by the ugly patch where nothing grew—the Forbidden Corner. A faintness then came over me at once, a faintness as of death, when I saw him *there* of all places—where he never was allowed to go, and where, moreover, he was usually too terrified to go. To see him standing solitary in that singular spot, above all to hear him crying there, bereft me momentarily of the power to act. Then, before I could recover my composure sufficiently to call him in, Mr. Frene came round the corner from the Lower Farm with the dogs, and, seeing his son, performed that office for me. In his loud, good-natured, hearty voice he called him, and Jamie turned and ran as though some spell had broken just in time—ran into the open arms of his fond but uncomprehending father, who carried him indoors on his shoulder, while asking "what all this hubbub was about?" And, at their heels, the tailless sheep dogs followed, barking loudly, and performing what Jamie called their "Gravel Dance," because they ploughed up the moist, rolled gravel with their feet.

I stepped back swiftly from the window lest I should be seen. Had I witnessed the saving of the child from fire or drowning the relief could hardly have been greater. Only Mr. Frene, I felt sure, would not say and do the right thing quite. He would protect the boy from his own vain imaginings, yet not with the explanation that could really heal. They disappeared behind the rose trees, making for the house. I saw no more till later, when Mr. Frene, senior, arrived.

To describe the ugly patch as "singular" is hard to justify, perhaps, yet some such word is what the entire family sought, though never—oh, never!—used. To Jamie and myself, though equally we never mentioned it, that treeless, flowerless spot was more than singular. It stood at the far end of the magnificent rose garden, a bald, sore place, where the black earth showed uglily in winter, almost like a piece of dangerous bog, and in summer baked and cracked with fissures where green lizards shot their fire in passing. In contrast to the rich luxuriance of death amid life, a center of disease that cried for healing lest it spread. But it never did spread. Behind it stood the thick wood of silver birches and, glimmering beyond, the orchard meadow, where the lambs played.

The gardeners had a very simple explanation of its barrenness—that the water all drained off it owing to the lie of the slopes immediately about it, holding no remnant to keep the soil alive. I cannot say. It was Jamie—Jamie who felt its spell and haunted it, who spent whole hours there, even while afraid, and for whom it was finally labeled "strictly out of bounds" because it stimulated his already big imagination, not wisely but too darkly—it was Jamie who buried ogres there and heard it crying in an earthly voice, swore that it shook its surface sometimes while he watched it, and secretly gave it food in the form of birds or mice or rabbits he found dead upon his wonderings. And it was Jamie who put so extraordinarily into words the *feeling* that the horrid spot had given me from the moment I first saw it.

"It's bad, Miss Gould," he told me.

"But, Jamie, nothing in Nature is bad—exactly; only different from the rest sometimes."

"Miss Gould, if you please, then it's empty. It's not fed. It's dying because it can't get the food it wants."

And when I stared into the little pale face where the eyes shone so dark and wonderful, seeking within myself for the right thing to say to him, he added, with an emphasis and conviction that made me suddenly turn cold: "Miss Gould"—he always used my name like this in all his sentences—"it's hungry, don't you see? But *I* know what would make it feel all right."

Only the conviction of an earnest child, perhaps, could have made so outrageous a suggestion worth listening to for an instant; but for me, who felt that things an imaginative child believed were important, it came with a vast disquieting shock of reality. Jamie, in this exaggerated way, had caught at the edge of a shocking fact—a hint of dark, undiscovered truth that leaped into that sensitive imagination. Why there lay horror in the words I cannot say, but I think some power of darkness trooped across the suggestion of that sentence at the end, "I know what would make it feel all right." I remember that I shrank from asking explanation. Small groups of other words, veiled fortunately by his silence, gave life to an unspeakable possibility that hitherto had lain at the back of my own consciousness. The way it sprang to life proves, I think, that my mind already contained it. The blood rushed from my heart as I listened. I remember that my knees shook. Jamie's idea was—had been all along—my own as well.

And now, as I lay down on my bed and thought about it all, I understood why the coming of his uncle involved somehow an experience that wrapped terror at its heart. With a sense of nightmare certainty that left me too weak to resist the preposterous idea, too shocked, indeed, to argue or reason it away, this certainty came with its full, black blast of conviction; and the only way I can put it into words, since nightmare horror really is not properly tellable at all, seems this: that there *was* something missing in that dying patch of garden; something lacking that it ever searched for; something, once found and taken, that would turn it rich and living as the rest; more—that there *was* some living person who could do this for it. Mr. Frene, senior, in a word, "Uncle Frank," was this person who out of his abundant life could supply the lack—unwittingly.

For this connection between the dying, empty patch and the person of this vigorous, wealthy, and successful man had already lodged itself in my subconsciousness before I was aware of it. Clearly it must have lain there all along, though hidden. Jamie's words, his sudden pallor, his vibrating emotion of fearful anticipation had developed the plate, but it was his weeping alone there in the Forbidden Corner that had printed it. The photograph shone framed before me in the air. I hid my eyes. But for the redness—the charm of my face goes to pieces unless my eyes are clear—I could have cried. Jamie's words that morning about the " 'normous face" came back upon me like a battering ram.

Mr. Frene, senior, had been so frequently the subject of conversation in the family since I came, I had so often heard him discussed, and had then read so much about him in the papers—his energy, his philanthropy, his success with everything he laid his hand to—that a picture of the man had grown complete within me. I knew him as he was—within; or, as my sister would have said—clairvoyantly. And the only time I saw him (when I took Gladys to a meeting where he was chairman, and later *felt* his atmosphere and presence while for a moment he patronizingly spoke with her) had justified the portrait I had drawn. The rest, you may say, was a woman's wild imagining; but I think rather it was that kind of divining intuition which women share with children. If souls could be made visible, I would stake my life upon the truth and accuracy of my portrait.

For this Mr. Frene was a man who drooped alone, but grew vital in a crowd—because he used their vitality. He was a supreme, unconscious artist in the science of taking the fruits of others' work and living—for his own advantage. He vampired, unknowingly no doubt, every one with whom he came in contact; left them exhausted, tired, listless. Others fed him, so that while in a full room he shone, alone by himself and with no life to draw upon he languished and declined. In the man's immediate neighborhood you felt his presence draining you; he took your ideas, your strength, your very words, and later used them for his own benefit and aggrandizement. Not evilly, of course; the man was good enough; but you felt that he was dangerous owing to the facile way he absorbed into himself all loose vitality that was to be had. His eyes and voice and presence devitalized you. Life, it seemed, not highly organized enough to resist, must shrink from his too near approach and hide away for fear of being appropriated, for fear, that is, of—death.

Jamie, unknowingly, put in the finishing touch to my unconscious portrait. The man carried about with him some silent, compelling trick of drawing out all your reserves—then swiftly pocketing them. At first you would be conscious of taut resistance; this would slowly shade off into weariness; the will would become flaccid; then you either moved away or yielded—agreed to all he said with a sense of weakness pressing ever closer upon the edges of collapse. With a male antagonist it might be different, but even then the effort of resistance would generate force that *he* absorbed and not the other. He never gave out. Some instinct taught him how to protect himself from that. To human beings, I mean, he never gave out. This time it was a very different matter. He had no more chance than a fly before the wheels of a huge—what Jamie used to call—"attraction" engine.

So this was how I saw him—a great human sponge, crammed and soaked with the life, or proceeds of life, absorbed from others—stolen. My idea of a human vampire was satisfied. He went about carrying these accumulations of the life of others. In this sense his "life" was not really his own. For the same reason, I think, it was not so fully under his control as he imagined.

And in another hour this man would be here. I went to the window. My eye wandered to the empty patch, dull black there amid the rich luxuriance of the garden flowers. It struck me as a hideous bit of emptiness yawning to be filled and nourished. The idea of Jamie playing round its bare edge was loathsome. I watched the big summer clouds above, the stillness of the afternoon, the haze. The silence of the over-heated garden was oppressive. I had never felt a day so stifling, motionless. It lay there waiting. The household, too, was waiting—waiting for the coming of Mr. Frene from London in his big motor-car.

And I shall never forget the sensation of icy shrinking and distress with which I heard the rumble of the car. He had arrived. Tea was all ready on the lawn beneath the lime trees, and Mrs. Frene and Gladys, back from their drive, were sitting in wicker chairs. Mr. Frene, junior, was in the hall to meet his brother, but Jamie, as I learned afterward, had shown such hysterical alarm, offered such bold resistance, that it had been deemed wiser to keep him in his room. Perhaps, after all, his presence might not be necessary. The visit clearly had to do with something on the uglier side of life—money, settlements, or what not; I never knew exactly; only that his parents were anxious, and that Uncle Frank had to be propitiated. It does not matter. That has nothing to do with the affair. What has to do with it—or I should not be telling the story—is that Mrs. Frene sent for me to come down "in my nice white dress, if I didn't mind," and that I was terrified, yet pleased, because it meant that a pretty face would be considered a welcome addition to the visitor's landscape. Also, most odd it was, I felt my presence was somehow inevitable, that in some way it was intended that I should witness what I did witness. And the instant I came upon the lawn—I hesitate to set it down, it sounds so foolish, disconnected—I could have sworn, as my eyes met his, that a kind of sudden darkness came, taking the summer brilliance out of everything, and that it was caused by troops of small black horses that raced about us from his person—to attack.

After a first momentary approving glance he took no further notice of me. The tea and talk went smoothly; I helped to pass the plates and cups, filling in pauses with little undertalk to Gladys. Jamie was never mentioned. Outwardly all seemed well, but inwardly everything was awful—skirting the edge of things unspeakable, and so charged with danger that I could not keep my voice from trembling when I spoke.

I watched his hard, bleak face; I noticed how thin he was, and the curious, oily brightness of his steady eyes. They did not glitter, but they drew you with a sort of soft, creamy shine like Eastern eyes. And everything he said or did announced what I may dare to call the *suction* of his presence. His nature achieved this result automatically. He dominated us all, yet so gently that until it was accomplished no one noticed it.

Before five minutes had passed, however, I was aware of one thing only. My mind focused exclusively upon it, and so vividly that I marveled the others did not scream, or run, or do something violent to prevent it. And it was this; that, separated merely by some dozen yards or so, this man, vibrating with the acquired vitality of others, stood within easy reach of that spot of yawning emptiness, waiting and eager to be filled. Earth scented her prey.

These two active "centers" were within fighting distance; he so thin, so hard, so keen, yet really spreading large with the loose "surround" of others' life he had appropriated, so practiced and triumphant; that other so patient, deep, with so mighty a draw of the whole earth behind it, and—ugh!—so obviously aware that its opportunity at last had come.

I saw it all as plainly as though I watched two great animals prepare for battle, both unconsciously; yet in some inexplicable way I saw it, of course, within me, and not externally. The conflict would be hideously unequal. Each side had already sent out emissaries, how long before I could not tell, for the first evidence *he* gave that something was going wrong with him was when his voice grew suddenly confused, he missed his words, and his lips trembled a moment and turned flabby. The next second his face betrayed that singular and horrid change, growing somehow loose about the bones of the cheek, and larger, so that I remembered Jamie's miserable phrase. The emissaries of the two kingdoms, the human and the vegetable, had met, I make it out, in that very second. For the first time in his long career of battening on others, Mr. Frene found himself pitted against a vaster kingdom than he knew and, so finding, shook inwardly in that little part that was his definite actual self. He felt the huge disaster coming.

"Yes, John," he was saying, in his drawling, self-congratulating voice, "Sir George gave me that car—gave it to me as a present. Wasn't it char—?"

and then broke off abruptly, stammered, drew breath, stood up, and looked uneasily about him. For a second there was a gaping pause. It was like the click which starts some huge machinery moving—that instant's pause before it actually starts. The whole thing, indeed, then went with the rapidity of machinery running down and beyond control. I thought of a giant dynamo working silently and invisible.

"What's that?" he cried, in a soft voice charged with alarm. "What's that horrid place? And someone's crying there—who is it?"

He pointed to the empty patch. Then, before anyone could answer, he started across the lawn toward it, going every minute faster. Before anyone could move he stood upon the edge. He leaned over—peering down into it.

It seemed a few hours passed, but really they were seconds, for time is measured by the quality and not the quantity of sensations it contains. I saw it all with merciless, photographic detail, sharply etched amid the general confusion. Each side was intensely active, but only one side, the human, exerted *all* its force—in resistance. The other merely stretched out a feeler, as it were, from its vast, potential strength; no more was necessary. It was such a soft and easy victory. Oh, it was rather pitiful! There was no bluster or great effort, on one side at least. Close by his side I witnessed it, for I, it seemed, alone had moved and followed him. No one else stirred, though Mrs. Frene clattered noisily with the cups, making some sudden impulsive gesture with her hands, and Gladys, I remember, gave a cry—it was like a little scream—"Oh, mother, it's the heat, isn't it?" Mr. Frene, her father, was speechless, pale as ashes.

But the instant I reached his side, it became clear what had drawn me there thus instinctively. Upon the other side, among the silver birches, stood little Jamie. He was watching. I experienced—for him—one of those moments that shake the heart; a liquid fear ran all over me, the more effective because unintelligible really. Yet I felt that if I could know all, and what lay actually behind, my fear would be more than justified; that the thing *was* awful, full of awe.

And then it happened—a truly wicked sight—like watching a universe in action, yet all contained within a small square foot of space. I think he understood vaguely that if someone could only take his place he might be saved, and that was why, discerning instinctively the easiest substitute within reach, he saw the child and called aloud to him across the empty patch, "James, my boy, come here!"

His voice was like a thin report, but somehow flat and lifeless, as when a rifle misses fire, sharp, yet weak; it had no "crack" in it. It was really supplication. And, with amazement, I heard my own ring out imperious and strong, though I was not conscious of saying it, "Jamie, don't move. Stay where you are!" But Jamie, the little child, obeyed neither of us. Moving up nearer to the edge, he stood there—laughing! I heard that laughter, but could have sworn it did not come from him. The empty, yawning patch gave out that sound.

Mr. Frene turned sideways, throwing up his arms. I saw his hard, bleak face grow somehow wider, spread through the air, and downward. A similar thing, I saw, was happening at the same time to his entire person, for it drew out into the atmosphere in a stream of movement. The face for a second made me think of those toys of green india rubber that children pull. It grew enormous. But this was an external impression only. What actually happened, I clearly understood, was that all this vitality and life he had transferred from others to himself for years was now in turn being taken from him and transferred—elsewhere.

One moment on the edge he wobbled horribly, then with that queer sideways motion, rapid yet ungainly, he stepped forward into the middle of the patch and fell heavily upon his face. His eyes, as he dropped, faded shockingly, and across the countenance was written plainly what I can only call an expression of destruction. He looked utterly destroyed. I caught a sound—from Jamie?—but this time not of laughter. It was like a gulp; it was deep and muffled and it dipped away into the earth. Again I thought of a troop of small black horses galloping away down a subterranean passage beneath my feet—plunging into the depths—their tramping growing fainter and fainter into buried distance. In my nostrils was a pungent smell of earth.

And then—all passed. I came back into myself. Mr. Frene, junior, was lifting his brother's head from the lawn where he had fallen from the heat, close beside the tea table. He had never really moved from there. And Jamie, I learned afterward, had been the whole time asleep upon his bed upstairs, worn out with his crying and unreasoning alarm. Gladys came running out with cold water, sponge and towel, brandy too—all kinds of things. "Mother, it *was* the heat, wasn't it?" I head her whisper, but I did not catch Mrs. Frene's reply. From her face it struck me that she was bordering on collapse herself. Then the butler followed, and they just picked him up and carried him into the house. He recovered even before the doctor came.

But the queer thing to me is that I was convinced the others all had seen what I saw, only that no one said a word about it; and to this day no one *has* said a word. And that was, perhaps, the most horrid part of all.

From that day to this I have scarcely heard a mention of Mr. Frene, senior. It seemed as if he dropped suddenly out of life. The papers never mentioned him. His activities ceased, as it were. His afterlife, at any rate, became singularly ineffective. Certainly he achieved nothing worth public mention. But it may be only that, having left the employ of Mrs. Frene, there was no particular occasion for me to hear anything.

The afterlife of that empty patch of garden, however, was quite otherwise. Nothing, so far as I know, was done to it by gardeners, or in the way of draining it or bringing in new earth, but even before I left in the following summer it had changed. It lay untouched, full of great, luscious, driving weeds and creepers, very strong, full-fed, and bursting thick with life.

FRITZ LEIBER
(1910–1992)

Fritz Leiber was born in Chicago, the son of a Shakespearean actor. He attended the University of Chicago, including a year at the theological seminary. His subsequent career spanned stints as an editor and as a drama teacher. Leiber became interested in writing through correspondence with a college friend, Harry Fischer, with whom he would later collaborate on many short stories.

Leiber was, like so many of his pulp-fiction contemporaries, an endlessly prolific writer. In his early career he published stories in both Weird Tales and Unknown, edited by John W. Campbell, who encouraged his work. Leiber's first story, "Two Sought Adventure," introduced Gray Mouser and Fahfrd, two characters around whom Leiber would, for a half century, base a series of adventures.

Collections of Leiber's short stories include The Ghost Light (1984), The World of Fritz Leiber (1976), and The Leiber Chronicles (1990). Leiber was the winner of every major American accolade in the field of science fiction and fantasy, including six Hugo awards, four Nebula awards, the Bram Stoker Life-Achievement Award, the World Fantasy Convention's Grandmaster Award, and a score of others.

Throughout his works, such as The Conjure Wife, Leiber explores a fascination with and contempt for women. This successful early novel is based on the enduring notion that women retain mystical powers which men have lost. In "The Snow Women" (1970) Leiber again has witches as rulers of their bleak domain.

"The Girl with the Hungry Eyes," included here, follows a similar theme. The battle of the sexes is implicit in the tale, as is an endemic male fear of women. In it, Leiber's photographer-narrator meets "La Belle Dame Sans Merci," a woman who is enticingly sexy, mysterious, and deadly. Prompted by an inexplicable, salubrious fear, he escapes to tell about it.

THE GIRL WITH
THE HUNGRY EYES

All right, I'll tell you why the Girl gives me the creeps. Why I can't stand to go downtown and see the mob slavering up at her on the tower, with that pop bottle or pack of cigarettes or whatever it is beside her. Why I hate to look at magazines any more because I know she'll turn up somewhere in a brassiere or a bubble bath. Why I don't like to think of millions of Americans drinking in that poisonous half-smile. It's quite a story—more story than you're expecting.

No, I haven't suddenly developed any long-haired indignation at the evils of advertising and the national glamour-girl complex. That'd be a laugh for a man in my racket, wouldn't it? Though I think you'll agree there's something a little perverted about trying to capitalize on sex that way. But it's okay with me. And I know we've had the Face and the Body and the Look and what not else, so why shouldn't someone come along who sums it all up so completely, that we have to call her the Girl and blazon her on all the billboards from Times Square to Telegraph Hill?

But the Girl isn't like any of the others. She's unnatural. She's morbid. She's unholy.

Oh it's 1948, is it, and the sort of thing I'm hinting at went out with witchcraft? But you see I'm not altogether sure myself what I'm hinting at, beyond a certain point. There are vampires and vampires, and not all of them suck blood.

And there were the murders, if they were murders.

Besides, let me ask you this. Why, when America is obsessed with the Girl, don't we find out more about her? Why doesn't she rate a *Time* cover with a droll biography inside? Why hasn't there been a feature in *Life* or the *Post*? A Profile in *The New Yorker*? Why hasn't *Charm* or *Mademoiselle* done her career saga? Not ready for it? Nuts!

Why haven't the movies snapped her up? Why hasn't she been on *Information, Please*? Why don't we see her kissing candidates at political rallies? Why isn't she chosen queen of some sort of junk or other at a convention?

Why don't we read about her tastes and hobbies, her views of the Russian situation? Why haven't the columnists interviewed her in a kimono on the top floor of the tallest hotel in Manhattan, and told us who her boyfriends are?

Finally—and this is the real killer—why hasn't she ever been drawn or painted?

Oh, no she hasn't. If you knew anything about commercial art you'd know that. Every blessed one of those pictures was worked up from a photograph. Expertly? Of course. They've got the top artists on it. But that's how it's done.

And now I'll tell you the *why* of all that. It's because from the top to the bottom of the whole world of advertising, news, and business, there isn't a solitary soul who knows where the Girl came from, where she lives, what she does, who she is, even what her name is.

You heard me. What's more, not a single solitary soul ever *sees* her—except one poor damned photographer, who's making more money off her than he ever hoped to in his life and who's scared and miserable as hell every minute of the day.

No, I haven't the faintest idea who he is or where he has his studio. But I know there has to be such a man and I'm morally certain he feels just like I *said*.

Yes, I might be able to find her, if I tried. I'm not sure though—by now she probably has other safeguards. Besides, I don't want to.

Oh, I'm off my rocker, am I? That sort of thing can't happen in this Year of our Atom 1948? People can't keep out of sight that way, not even Garbo?

Well I happen to know they can, because last year I was that poor damned photographer I was telling you about. Yes, last year, in 1947, when the Girl made her first poisonous splash right here in this big little city of ours.

Yes, I knew you weren't here last year and you don't know about it. Even the Girl had to start small. But if you hunted through the files of the local newspapers, you'd find some ads, and I might be able to locate you some of the old displays—I think Lovelybelt is still using one of them. I used to have a mountain of photos myself, until I burned them.

Yes, I made my cut off her. Nothing like what that other photographer must be making, but enough so it still bought this whiskey. She was funny about money. I'll tell you about that.

But first picture me in 1947. I had a fourth-floor studio in that rathole the Hauser Building, catty-corner from Ardleigh Park.

I'd been working at the Marsh-Mason studios until I'd got my bellyful of it and decided to start in for myself. The Hauser Building was crummy—I'll never forget how the stairs creaked—but it was cheap and there was a skylight.

Business was lousy. I kept making the rounds of all the advertisers and agencies, and some of them didn't object to me too much personally, but my stuff never clicked. I was pretty near broke. I was behind on my rent. Hell, I didn't even have enough money to have a girl.

It was one of those dark gray afternoons. The building was awfully quiet—even with the storage they can't half rent the Hauser. I'd just finished developing some pix I was doing on speculation for Lovelybelt

Girdles and Buford's Pool and Playground—the last a faked-up beach scene. My model had left. A Miss Leon. She was a civics teacher at one of the high schools and modeled for me on the side, just lately on speculation too. After one look at the prints, I decided that Miss Leon probably wasn't just what Lovelybelt was looking for—or my photography either. I was about to call it a day.

And then the street door slammed four storeys down and there were steps on the stairs and she came in.

She was wearing a cheap, shiny black dress. Black pumps. No stockings. And except that she had a gray cloth coat over one of them, those skinny arms of hers were bare. Her arms are pretty skinny, you know, or can you see things like that any more?

And then the thin neck, the slightly gaunt, almost prim face, the tumbling mass of dark hair, and looking out from under it the hungriest eyes in the world.

That's the real reason she's plastered all over the country today, you know—those eyes. Nothing vulgar, but just the same they're looking at you with a hunger that's all sex and something more than sex. That's what everybody's been looking for since the Year One—something a little more than sex.

Well, boys, there I was, along with the Girl, in an office that was getting shadowy, in a nearly empty building. A situation that a million male Americans have undoubtedly pictured to themselves with various lush details. How was I feeling? Scared.

I know sex can be frightening. That cold, heart-thumping when you're alone with a girl and feel you're going to touch her. But if it was sex this time, it was overlaid with something else.

At least I wasn't thinking about sex.

I remember that I took a backward step and that my hand jerked so that the photos I was looking at sailed to the floor.

There was the faintest dizzy feeling like something was being drawn out of me. Just a little bit.

That was all. Then she opened her mouth and everything was back to normal for a while.

"I see you're a photographer, mister," she said. "Could you use a model?"

Her voice wasn't very cultivated.

"I doubt it," I told her, picking up the pix. You see, I wasn't impressed. The commercial possibilities of her eyes hadn't registered on me yet, by a long shot. "What have you done?"

Well she gave me a vague sort of story and I began to check her knowledge of model agencies and studios and rates and what not and pretty soon I said to her, "Look here, you never modeled for a photographer in your life. You just walked in here cold."

Well, she admitted that was more or less so.

All along through our talk I got the idea she was feeling her way, like someone in a strange place. Not that she was uncertain of herself, or of me, but just of the general situation.

"And you think anyone can model?" I asked her pityingly.

"Sure," she said.

"Look," I said, "a photographer can waste a dozen negatives trying to get one halfway human photo of an average woman. How many do you think he'd have to waste before he got a real catchy, glamorous pix of her?"

"I think I could do it," she said.

Well, I should have kicked her out right then. Maybe I admired the cool way she stuck to her dumb little guns. Maybe I was touched by her underfed look. More likely I was feeling mean on account of the way my pix had been snubbed by everybody and I wanted to take it out on her by showing her up.

"Okay, I'm going to put you on the spot," I told her. "I'm going to try a couple of shots of you. Understand, it's strictly on spec. If somebody should ever want to use a photo of you, which is about one chance in two million, I'll pay you regular rates for your time. Not otherwise."

She gave me a smile. The first. "That's swell by me," she said.

Well, I took three or four shots, close-ups of her face since I didn't fancy her cheap dress, and at least she stood up to my sarcasm. Then I remembered I still had the Lovelybelt stuff and I guess the meanness was still working in me because I handed her a girdle and told her to go behind the screen and get into it and she did, without getting flustered as I'd expected, and since we'd gone that far I figured we might as well shoot the beach scene to round it out, and that was that.

All this time I wasn't feeling anything particular in one way or the other except every once in a while I'd get one of those faint dizzy flashes and wonder if there was something wrong with my stomach or if I could have been a bit careless with my chemicals.

Still, you know, I think the uneasiness was in me all the while.

I tossed her a card and pencil. "Write your name and address and phone," I told her and made for the darkroom.

A little later she walked out. I didn't call any good-byes. I was irked because she hadn't fussed around or seemed anxious about her poses, or even thanked me, except for that one smile.

I finished developing the negatives, made some prints, glanced at them, decided they weren't a great deal worse than Miss Leon. On an impulse I slipped them in with the pix I was going to take on the rounds next morning.

By now I'd worked long enough so I was a bit fagged and nervous, but I didn't dare waste enough money on liquor to help that. I wasn't very hungry. I think I went to a cheap movie.

I didn't think of the Girl at all, except maybe to wonder faintly why in my present womanless state I hadn't made a pass at her. She had seemed to belong to a, well, distinctly more approachable social stratum than Miss Leon. But then of course there were all sorts of arguable reasons for my not doing that.

Next morning I made the rounds. My first step was Munsch's Brewery. They were looking for a "Munsch Girl." Papa Munsch had a sort of affection for me, though he razzed my photography. He had a good natural judgment about that, too. Fifty years ago he might have been one of the shoestring boys who made Hollywood.

Right now he was out in the plant pursuing his favorite occupation. He put down the beaded can, smacked his lips, gabbled something technical to someone about hops, wiped his fat hands on the big apron he was wearing, and grabbed my thin stack of pix.

He was about halfway through, making noises with his tongue and teeth, when he came to her. I kicked myself for even having stuck her in.

"That's her," he said. "The photography's not so hot, but that's the girl."

It was all decided. I wondered now why Papa Munsch sensed what the girl had right away, while I didn't. I think it was because I saw her first in the flesh, if that's the right word.

At the time I just felt faint.

"Who is she?" he asked.

"One of my new models." I tried to make it casual.

"Bring her out tomorrow morning," he told me. "And your stuff. We'll photograph her here. I want to show you.

"Here, don't look so sick," he added. "Have some beer."

Well I went away telling myself it was just a fluke, so that she'd probably blow it tomorrow with her inexperience, and so on.

Just the same, when I reverently laid my next stack of pix on Mr. Fitch, of Lovelybelt's rose-colored blotter, I had hers on top.

Mr. Fitch went through the motions of being an art critic. He leaned over backward, squinted his eyes, waved his long fingers, and said, "Hmmm. What do you think, Miss Willow? Here, in this light. Of course the photograph doesn't show the bias cut. And perhaps we should use the Lovelybelt Imp instead of the Angel. Still, the girl. . . . Come over here, Binns." More finger-waving. "I want a married man's reaction."

He couldn't hide the fact that he was hooked.

Exactly the same thing happened at Buford's Pool and Playground, except that Da Costa didn't need a married man's say-so.

"Hot stuff," he said, sucking his lips. "Oh, boy, you photographers!"

I hot-footed it back to the office and grabbed up the card I'd given to her to put down her name and address.

It was blank.

I don't mind telling you that the next five minutes were about the worst

I ever went through, in an ordinary way. When next morning rolled around and I still hadn't got hold of her, I had to start stalling.

"She's sick," I told Papa Munsch over the phone.

"She's at a hospital?" he asked me.

"Nothing that serious," I told him.

"Get her out here then. What's a little headache?"

"Sorry, I can't."

Papa Munsch got suspicious. "You really got this girl?"

"Of course I have."

"Well, I don't know. I'd think it was some New York model, except I recognized your lousy photography."

I laughed.

"Well look, you get her here tomorrow morning, you hear?"

"I'll try."

"Try nothing. You get her out here."

He didn't know half of what I tried. I went around to all the model and employment agencies. I did some slick detective work at the photographic and art studios. I used up some of my last dimes putting advertisements in all three papers. I looked at high school yearbooks and at employee photos in local house organs. I went to restaurants and drugstores, looking for waitresses, and to dime stores and department stores, looking at clerks. I watched the crowds coming out of movie theaters. I roamed the streets.

Evenings I spent quite a bit of time along Pick-up Row. Somehow that seemed the right place.

The fifth afternoon I knew I was licked. Papa Munsch's deadline—he'd given me several, but this was it—was due to run out at six o'clock. Mr. Fitch had already canceled.

I was at the studio window, looking out at Ardleigh Park.

She walked in.

I'd gone over this moment so often in my mind that I had no trouble putting on my act. Even the faint dizzy feeling didn't throw me off.

"Hello," I said, hardly looking at her.

"Hello," she said.

"Not discouraged yet?'

"No." It didn't sound uneasy or defiant. It was just a statement.

I snapped a look at my watch, and got up and said curtly, "Look here, I'm going to give you a chance. There's a client of mine looking for a girl your general type. If you do a real good job you may break into the modeling business.

"We can see him this afternoon if we hurry," I said. I picked up my stuff. "Come on. And next time, if you expect favors, don't forget to leave your phone number."

"Uh, uh," she said, not moving.

"What do you mean?" I said.

"I'm not going to see any client of yours."

"The hell you aren't," I said. "You little nut, I'm giving you a break."

She shook her head slowly. "You're not fooling me, baby, you're not fooling me at all. They *want* me." And she gave me the second smile.

At the time I thought she must have seen my newspaper ad. Now I'm not so sure.

"And now I'll tell you how we're going to work," she went on. "You aren't going to have my name or address or phone number. Nobody is. And we're going to do all the pictures right here. Just you and me."

You can imagine the roar I raised at that. I was everything—angry, sarcastic, patiently explanatory, off my nut, threatening, pleading.

I would have slapped her face off, except it was photographic capital.

In the end all I could do was phone Papa Munsch and tell him her conditions. I knew I didn't have a chance, but I had to take it.

He gave me a really angry bawling out, said "no" several times and hung up.

It didn't faze her. "We'll start shooting at ten o'clock tomorrow," she said.

It was just like her, using that corny line from the movie magazines.

About midnight Papa Munsch called me up.

"I don't know what insane asylum you're renting this girl from," he said, "but I'll take her. Come around tomorrow morning and I'll try to get it through your head just how I want the pictures. And I'm glad I got you out of bed!"

After that it was a breeze. Even Mr. Fitch reconsidered and after taking two days to tell me it was quite impossible, he accepted the conditions too.

Of course you're all under the spell of the Girl, so you can't understand how much self-sacrifice it represented on Mr. Fitch's part when he agreed to forgo supervising the photography of my model in the Lovelybelt Imp or Vixen or whatever it was we finally used.

Next morning she turned up on time according to her schedule, and we went to work. I'll say one thing for her, she never got tired and she never kicked at the way I fussed over shots. I got along okay except I still had the feeling of something being shoved away gently. Maybe you've felt it just a little, looking at her picture.

When we finished I found out there were still more rules. It was about the middle of the afternoon. I started down with her to get a sandwich and coffee.

"Uh uh," she said, "I'm going down alone. And look, baby, if you ever try to follow me, if you ever so much as stick your head out that window when I go, you can hire yourself another model."

You can imagine how all this crazy stuff strained my temper—and my imagination. I remember opening the window after she was gone—I waited a few minutes first—and standing there getting some fresh air and trying to figure out what could be back of it, whether she was hiding from the police, or was somebody's ruined daughter, or maybe had got the idea it was smart to be temperamental, or more likely Papa Munsch was right and she was partly nuts.

But I had my pix to finish up.

Looking back it's amazing to think how fast her magic began to take hold of the city after that. Remembering what came after I'm frightened of what's happening to the whole country—and maybe the world. Yesterday I read something in *Time* about the Girl's picture turning up on billboards in Egypt.

The rest of my story will help show you why I'm frightened in that big general way. But I have a theory, too, that helps explain, though it's one of those things that's beyond that "certain point." It's about the Girl. I'll give it to you in a few words.

You know how modern advertising gets everybody's mind set in the same direction, wanting the same things, imagining the same things. And you know the psychologists aren't so skeptical of telepathy as they used to be.

Add up the two ideas. Suppose the identical desires of millions of people focused on one telepathic person. Say a girl. Shaped her in their image.

Imagine her knowing the hiddenmost hungers of millions of men. Imagine her seeing deeper into those hungers than the people that had them, seeing the hatred and the wish for death behind the lust. Imagine her shaping herself in that complete imagine, keeping herself as aloof as marble. Yet imagine the hunger she might feel in answer to their hunger.

But that's getting a long way from the facts of my story. And some of those facts are darn solid. Like money. We made money.

That was the funny thing I was going to tell you. I was afraid the Girl was going to hold me up. She really had me over a barrel, you know.

But she didn't ask for anything but the regular rates. Later on I insisted on pushing more money at her, a whole lot. But she always took it with that same contemptuous look, as if she were going to toss it down the first drain when she got outside.

Maybe she did.

At any rate, I had money. For the first time in months I had money enough to get drunk, buy new clothes, take taxicabs. I could make a play for any girl I wanted to. I only had to pick.

And so of course I had to go and pick—

But first let me tell you about Papa Munsch.

Papa Munsch wasn't the first of the boys to try to meet my model but I think he was the first to really go soft on her. I could watch the change in his eyes as he looked at her pictures. They began to get sentimental, reverent. Mama Munsch had been dead for two years.

He was smart about the way he planned it. He got me to drop some information which told him when she came to work, and then one morning he came pounding up the stairs a few minutes before.

"I've got to see her, Dave," he told me.

I argued with him, I kidded him. I explained he didn't know just how serious she was about her crazy ideas. I pointed out he was cutting both our throats. I even amazed myself by bawling him out.

He didn't take any of it in his usual way. He just kept repeating, "But, Dave, I've got to see her."

The street door slammed.

"That's her," I said, lowering my voice. "You've got to get out."

He wouldn't, so I shoved him in the darkroom. "And keep quiet," I whispered. "I'll tell her I can't work today."

I knew he'd try to look at her and probably come busting in, but there wasn't anything else I could do.

The footsteps came to the fourth floor. But she never showed at the door. I got uneasy.

"Get that bum out of there!" she yelled suddenly from beyond the door. Not very loud, but in her commonest voice.

"I'm going up to the next landing," she said, "and if that fat-bellied bum doesn't march straight down to the street, he'll never get another pix of me except spitting in his lousy beer."

Papa Munsch came out of the darkroom. He was white. He didn't look at me as he went out. He never looked at her pictures in front of me again.

That was Papa Munsch. Now it's me I'm telling about. I talked about the subject with her, I hinted, eventually I made my pass.

She lifted my hand off her as if it were a damp rag.

"Nix, baby," she said. "This is working time."

"But afterward . . ." I pressed.

"The rules still hold." And I got what I think was the fifth smile.

It's hard to believe, but she never budged an inch from that crazy line. I mustn't make a pass at her in the office, because our work was very important and she loved it and there mustn't be any distractions. And I couldn't see her anywhere else, because if I tried to, I'd never snap another picture of her—and all this with more money coming in all the time and me never so stupid as to think my photography had anything to do with it.

Of course I wouldn't have been human if I hadn't made more passes. But they always got the wet-rag treatment and there weren't any more smiles.

I changed. I went sort of crazy and light-headed—only sometimes I felt my head was going to burst. And I started to talk to her all the time. About myself.

It was like being in a constant delirium that never interfered with business. I didn't pay attention to the dizzy feeling. It seemed natural.

I'd walk around and for a moment the reflector would look like a sheet of white-hot steel, or the shadows would seem like armies of moths, or the camera would be a big black coal car. But the next instant they'd come all right again.

I think sometimes I was scared to death of her. She'd seem the strangest, horriblest person in the world. But other times . . .

And I talked. It didn't matter what I was doing—lighting her, posing her, fussing with props, snapping my pix—or where she was—on the platform, behind the screen, relaxing with a magazine—I kept up a steady gab.

I told her everything I knew about myself. I told her about my first girl. I told her about my brother Bob's bicycle. I told her about running away on a freight and the licking Pa gave me when I came home. I told her about shipping to South America and the blue sky at night. I told her about Betty. I told her about my mother dying of cancer. I told her about being beaten up in a fight in an alley behind a bar. I told her about Mildred. I told her about the first picture I ever sold. I told her how Chicago looked from a sailboat. I told her about the longest drunk I was ever on. I told her about Marsh-Mason. I told her about Gwen. I told her about how I met Papa Munsch. I told her about hunting her. I told her about how I felt now.

She never paid the slightest attention to what I said. I couldn't even tell if she heard me.

It was when we were getting our first nibble from national advertisers that I decided to follow her when she went home.

Wait, I can place it better than that. Something you'll remember from the out-of-town papers—those maybe-murders I mentioned. I think there were six.

I say "maybe" because the police could never be sure they weren't heart attacks. But there's bound to be suspicion when heart attacks happen to people whose hearts have been okay, and always at night when they're alone and away from home and there's a question of what they were doing.

The six deaths created one of those "mystery poisoner" scares. And afterward there was a feeling that they hadn't really stopped, but were being continued in a less suspicious way.

That's one of the things that scares me now.

But at that time my only feeling was relief that I'd decided to follow her.

I made her work until dark one afternoon. I didn't need any excuses, we were snowed under with orders. I waited until the street door slammed, then I ran down. I was wearing rubber-soled shoes. I'd slipped on a dark coat she'd never seen me in, and a dark hat.

I stood in the doorway until I spotted her. She was walking by Ardleigh Park toward the heart of town. It was one of those warm fall nights. I followed her on the other side of the street. My idea for tonight was just to find out where she lived. That would give me a hold on her.

She stopped in front of a display window of Everly's department store, standing back from the glow. She stood there looking in.

I remembered we'd done a big photograph of her for Everly's, to make a flat model for a lingerie display. That was what she was looking at.

At that time it seemed all right to me that she should adore herself, if that was what she was doing.

When people passed she'd turn away a little or drift back farther into the shadows.

Then a man came by alone. I couldn't see his face very well, but he looked middle-aged. He stopped and stood looking in the window.

She came out of the shadows and stepped up beside him.

How would you boys feel if you were looking at a poster of the Girl and suddenly she was there beside you, her arm linked with yours?

This fellow's reaction showed plain as day. A crazy dream had come to life for him.

They talked for a moment. Then he waved a taxi to the curb. They got in and drove off.

I got drunk that night. It was almost as if she'd known I was following her and had picked that way to hurt me. Maybe she had. Maybe this was the finish.

But the next morning she turned up at the usual time and I was back in the delirium, only now with some new angles added.

That night when I followed her she picked a spot under a street lamp, opposite one of the Munsch Girl billboards.

Now it frightens me to think of her lurking that way.

After about twenty minutes a convertible slowed down going past her, backed up, swung in to the curb.

I was closer this time. I got a good look at the fellow's face. He was a little younger, about my age.

Next morning the same face looked up at me from the front page of the paper. The convertible had been found parked on a side street. He had been in it. As in the other maybe-murders, the cause of death was uncertain.

All kinds of thoughts were spinning in my head that day, but there were only two things I knew for sure. That I'd got the first real offer from a national advertiser, and that I was going to take the Girl's arm and walk down the stairs with her when we quit work.

She didn't seem surprised. "You know what you're doing?" she said.

"I know."

She smiled. "I was wondering when you'd get around to it."

I began to feel good. I was kissing everything good-bye, but I had my arm around hers.

It was another of those warm fall evenings. We cut across into Ardleigh Park. It was dark there, but all around the sky was a sallow pink from the advertising signs.

We walked for a long time in the park. She didn't say anything and she didn't look at me, but I could see her lips twitching and after a while her hand tightened on my arm.

We stopped. We'd been walking across the grass. She dropped down and pulled me after her. She put her hands on my shoulders. I was looking down at her face. It was the faintest sallow pink from the glow in the sky. The hungry eyes were dark smudges.

I was fumbling with her blouse. She took my hand away, not like she had in the studio. "I don't want that," she said.

First I'll tell you what I did afterward. Then I'll tell you why I did it. Then I'll tell you what she said.

What I did was run away. I don't remember all of that because I was dizzy, and the pink sky was swinging against the dark trees. But after a while I staggered into the lights of the street. The next day I closed up the studio. The telephone was ringing when I locked the door and there were unopened letters on the floor. I never saw the Girl again in the flesh, if that's the right word.

I did it because I didn't want to die. I didn't want the life drawn out of me. There are vampires and vampires, and the ones that suck blood aren't the worst. If it hadn't been for the warning of those dizzy flashes, and Papa Munsch and the face in the morning paper, I'd have gone the way the others did. But I realized what I was up against while there was still time to tear myself away. I realized that wherever she came from, whatever shaped her, she's the quintessence of the horror behind the bright billboard. She's the smile that tricks you into throwing away your money and your life. She's the eyes that lead you on and on, and then show you death. She's the creature you give everything for and never really get. She's the being that takes everything you've got and gives nothing in return. When you yearn toward her face on the billboards, remember that. She's the lure. She's the bait. She's the Girl.

And this is what she said, "I want you. I want your high spots. I want everything that's made you happy and everything that's hurt you bad. I want your first girl. I want that shiny bicycle. I want that licking. I want that pinhole camera. I want Betty's legs. I want the blue sky filled with stars. I want your mother's death. I want your blood on the cobblestones. I want Mildred's mouth. I want the first picture you sold. I want the lights of Chicago. I want the gin. I want Gwen's hands. I want your wanting me. I want your life. Feed me, baby, feed me."

JOHN CHEEVER
(1912–1982)

John Cheever was born in Quincy, Massachusetts, and got his early education at the Thayer Academy in South Braintree, Massachusetts. He was expelled at the age of seventeen, which may account for the particular view he has of the culture of conformity that shaped him. He is reported to have begun writing at the age of ten or eleven.

Though he wrote novels, including The Wapshot Chronicle (1957), The Wapshot Scandal (1964), and Bullet Park (1969), he is considered a master of the short story. He received the Benjamin Franklin Short Story Award in 1954, an O. Henry Award in 1955, and an award from the National Institute of Arts and Letters. He was a regular contributor of short fiction to The New Yorker for many years, and his collection, The Short Stories of John Cheever (1978) won the Pulitzer Prize for Fiction in 1979.

"Torch Song" provides an interesting comparison with Mary E. Wilkins-Freeman's "Luella Miller." Wilkins-Freeman's tale is set in a village, while Cheever's takes place in New York City, urban to the core. And yet, Luella Miller and sweet-voiced Joan Harris are sisters under the skin.

While Cheever's story has a psychological vampire at its center, there is more to this tale. In it, Cheever displays an ear for suburban chit chat and a keen understanding of people who flatter themselves that they are leading lives of quiet desperation. Cheever offers us a glimpse into the lives of people who long ago accepted their own inability to disturb the universe.

TORCH SONG

After Jack Lorey had known Joan Harris in New York for a few years, he began to think of her as the Widow. She always wore black, and he was always given the feeling, by a curious disorder in her apartment, that the undertakers had just left. This impression did not stem from malice on his part, for he was fond of Joan. They came from the same city in Ohio and had reached New York at about the same time in the middle thirties. They were the same age, and during their first summer in the city they used to meet after work and drink Martinis in places like the Brevoort and Charles', and have dinner and play checkers at the Lafayette.

Joan went to a school for models when she settled in the city, but it turned out that she photographed badly, so after spending six weeks learning how to walk with a book on her head she got a job as a hostess in a Longchamps. For the rest of the summer she stood by the hatrack, bathed in an intense pink light and the string music of heartbreak, swinging her mane of dark hair and her black skirt as she moved forward to greet the customers. She was then a big, handsome girl with a wonderful voice, and her face, her whole presence, always seemed infused with a gentle and healthy pleasure at her surroundings, whatever they were. She was innocently and incorrigibly convivial, and would get out of bed and dress at three in the morning if someone called her and asked her to come out for a drink, as Jack often did. In the fall, she got some kind of freshman executive job in a department store. They saw less and less of each other and then for quite a while stopped seeing each other altogether. Jack was living with a girl he had met at a party, and it never occurred to him to wonder what had become of Joan.

Jack's girl had some friends in Pennsylvania, and in the spring and summer of his second year in town he often went there with her for weekends. All of this—the shared apartment in the Village, the illicit relationship, the Friday-night train to a country house—was what he had imagined life in New York to be, and he was intensely happy. He was returning to New York with his girl one Sunday night on the Lehigh line. It was one of those trains that move slowly across the face of New Jersey, bringing back to the city hundreds of people, like the victims of an immense and strenuous picnic, whose faces are blazing and whose muscles are lame. Jack and his girl, like most of the other passengers, were overburdened with vegetables and flowers. When the train stopped in Pennsylvania Station, they moved with the crowd along the platform, toward the escalator. As they were passing the wide, lighted windows of the diner,

Jack turned his head and saw Joan. It was the first time he had seen her since Thanksgiving, or since Christmas. He couldn't remember.

Joan was with a man who had obviously passed out. His head was in his arms on the table, and an overturned highball glass was near one of his elbows. Joan was shaking his shoulders gently and speaking to him. She seemed to be vaguely troubled, vaguely amused. The waiters had cleared off all the other tables and were standing around Joan, waiting for her to resurrect her escort. It troubled Jack to see in these straits a girl who reminded him of the trees and the lawns of his home town, but there was nothing he could do to help. Joan continued to shake the man's shoulders, and the crowd pressed Jack past one after another of the diner's windows, past the malodorous kitchen, and up the escalator.

He saw Joan, later that summer, when he was having dinner in a Village restaurant. He was with a new girl, a Southerner. There were many Southern girls in the city that year. Jack and his belle had wandered into the restaurant because it was convenient, but the food was terrible and the place was lighted with candles. Halfway through dinner, Jack noticed Joan on the other side of the room, and when he had finished eating, he crossed the room and spoke to her. She was with a tall man who was wearing a monocle. He stood, bowed stiffly from the waist, and said to Jack, "We are very pleased to meet you." Then he excused himself and headed for the toilet. "He's a count, he's a Swedish count," Joan said. "He's on the radio, Friday afternoons at four-fifteen. Isn't it exciting?" She seemed to be delighted with the count and the terrible restaurant.

Sometime the next winter, Jack moved from the Village to an apartment in the East Thirties. He was crossing Park Avenue one cold morning on his way to the office when he noticed, in the crowd, a woman he had met a few times at Joan's apartment. He spoke to her and asked about his friend. "Haven't you heard?" she said. She pulled a long face. "Perhaps I'd better tell you. Perhaps you can help." She and Jack had breakfast in a drugstore on Madison Avenue and she unburdened herself of the story.

The count had a program called "The Song of the Fiords," or something like that, and he sang Swedish folk songs. Everyone suspected him of being a fake, but that didn't bother Joan. He had met her at a party and, sensing a soft touch, had moved in with her the following night. About a week later, he complained of pains in his back and said he must have some morphine. Then he needed morphine all the time. If he didn't get morphine, he was abusive and violent. Joan began to deal with those doctors and druggists who peddle dope, and when they wouldn't supply her, she went down to the bottom of the city. Her friends were afraid she would be found some morning stuffed in a drain. She got pregnant. She had an abortion. The count left her and moved to a flea bag near Times Square, but she was so impressed by then with his helplessness, so afraid that he would die without her, that she followed him there and shared his room and continued to buy his narcotics. He abandoned her again, and Joan waited a week for him to return before she went back to her place and her friends in the Village.

It shocked Jack to think of the innocent girl from Ohio having lived with a brutal dope addict and traded with criminals, and when he got to his office that morning, he telephoned her and made a date for dinner that night. He met her at Charles'. When she came into the bar, she seemed as wholesome and calm as ever. Her voice was sweet, and reminded him of elms, of lawns, of those glass arrangements that used to be hung from porch ceilings to tinkle in the summer wind. She told him about the count. She spoke of him charitably and with no trace of bitterness, as if her voice, her disposition, were incapable of registering anything beyond simple affection and pleasure. Her walk, when she moved ahead of him toward their table, was light and graceful. She ate a large dinner and talked enthusiastically about her job. They went to a movie and said goodbye in front of her apartment house.

That winter, Jack met a girl he decided to marry. Their engagement was announced in January and they planned to marry in July. In the spring, he received, in his office mail, an invitation to cocktails at Joan's. It was for a Saturday when his fiancée was going to Massachusetts to visit her parents, and when the time came and he had nothing better to do, he took a bus to the Village. Joan had the same apartment. It was a walk-up. You rang the bell above the mailbox in the vestibule and were answered with a death rattle in the lock. Joan lived on the third floor. Her calling card was in a slot in the mailbox, and above her name was written the name Hugh Bascomb.

Jack climbed the two flights of carpeted stairs, and when he reached Joan's apartment, she was standing by the open door in a black dress. After she greeted Jack, she took his arm and guided him across the room. "I want you to meet Hugh, Jack," she said.

Hugh was big man with a red face and pale-blue eyes. His manner was courtly and his eyes were inflamed with drink. Jack talked with him for a little while and then went over to speak to someone he knew, who was standing by the mantelpiece. He noticed then, for the first time, the indescribable disorder of Joan's apartment. The books were in their shelves and the furniture was reasonably good, but the place was all wrong, somehow. It was as if things had been put in place without thought or real interest, and for the first time, too, he had the impression that there had been a death there recently.

As Jack moved around the room, he felt that he had met the ten or twelve guests at other parties. There was a woman executive with a fancy hat, a man who could imitate Roosevelt, a grim couple whose play was in rehearsal, and a newspaperman who kept turning on the radio for news of the Spanish Civil War. Jack drank Martinis and talked with the woman in the fancy hat. He looked out of the window at the back yards and the ailanthus trees and heard, in the distance, thunder exploding off the cliffs of the Hudson.

Hugh Bascomb got very drunk. He began to spill liquor, as if drinking, for him, were a kind of jolly slaughter and he enjoyed the bloodshed and the mess. He spilled whiskey from a bottle. He spilled a drink on his shirt and then tipped over someone else's drink. The party was not quiet, but Hugh's hoarse voice began to dominate the others. He attacked a photographer who was sitting in a corner explaining camera techniques to a homely woman. "What did you come to the party for if all you wanted to do was to sit there and stare at your shoes?" Hugh shouted. "What did you come for? Why didn't you stay at home?"

The photographer didn't know what to say. He was not staring at his shoes. Joan moved lightly to Hugh's side. "Please don't get into a fight now, darling," she said. "Not this afternoon."

"Shut up," he said. "Let me alone. Mind your own business." He lost his balance, and in struggling to steady himself he tipped over a lamp.

"Oh, your lovely lamp, Joan," a woman sighed.

"Lamps!" Hugh roared. He threw his arms into the air and worked them around his head as if he were bludgeoning himself. "Lamps. Glasses. Cigarette boxes. Dishes. They're killing me. They're killing me, for Christ's sake. Let's all go up to the mountains and hunt and fish and live like men, for Christ's sake."

People were scattering as if a rain had begun to fall in the room. It had, as a matter of fact, begun to rain outside. Someone offered Jack a ride uptown, and he jumped at the chance. Joan stood at the door, saying goodbye to her routed friends. Her voice remained soft, and her manner, unlike that of those Christian women who in the face of disaster can summon new and formidable sources of composure, seemed genuinely simple. She appeared to be oblivious of the raging drunk at her back, who was pacing up and down, grinding glass into the rug, and haranguing one of the survivors of the party with a story of how he, Hugh, had once gone without food for three weeks.

In July, Jack was married in an orchard in Duxbury, and he and his wife went to West Chop for a few weeks. When they returned to town, their apartment was cluttered with presents, including a dozen after-dinner coffee cups from Joan. His wife sent her the required note, but they did nothing else.

Late in the summer, Joan telephoned Jack at his office and asked if he wouldn't bring his wife to see her; she named an evening the following week. He felt guilty about not having called her, and accepted the invitation. This made his wife angry. She was an ambitious girl who liked a social life that offered rewards, and she went unwillingly to Joan's Village apartment with him.

Written above Joan's name on the mailbox was the name Franz Denzel.

Jack and his wife climbed the stairs and were met by Joan at the open door. They went into her apartment and found themselves among a group of people for whom Jack, at least, was unable to find any bearings.

Franz Denzel was a middle-aged German. His face was pinched with bitterness or illness. He greeted Jack and his wife with that elaborate and clever politeness that is intended to make guests feel that they have come too early or too late. He insisted sharply upon Jack's sitting in the chair in which he himself had been sitting, and then went and sat on a radiator. There were five other Germans sitting around the room, drinking coffee. In a corner was another American couple, who looked uncomfortable. Joan passed Jack and his wife small cups of coffee with whipped cream. "These cups belonged to Franz's mother," she said. "Aren't they lovely? They were the only things he took from Germany when he escaped from the Nazis."

Franz turned to Jack and said, "Perhaps you will give us your opinion on the American educational system. That is what we were discussing when you arrived."

Before Jack could speak, one of the German guests opened an attack on the American educational system. The other Germans joined in, and went on from there to describe every vulgarity that had impressed them in American life and to contrast German and American culture generally. Where, they asked one another passionately, could you find in America anything like the Mitropa dining cars, the Black Forest, the pictures in Munich, the music in Bayreuth? Franz and his friends began speaking in German. Neither Jack nor his wife nor Joan could understand German, and the other American couple had not opened their mouths since they were introduced. Joan went happily around the room, filling everyone's cup with coffee, as if the music of a foreign language were enough to make an evening for her.

Jack drank five cups of coffee. He was desperately uncomfortable. Joan went into the kitchen while the Germans were laughing at their German jokes, and he hoped she would return with some drinks, but when she came back, it was with a tray of ice cream and mulberries.

"Isn't this pleasant?" Franz asked, speaking in English again.

Joan collected the coffee cups, and as she was about to take them back to the kitchen, Franz stopped her.

"Isn't one of those cups chipped?"

"No, darling," Joan said. "I never let the maid touch them. I wash them myself."

"What's that?" he asked, pointing at the rim of one of the cups.

"That's the cup that's always been chipped, darling. It was chipped when you unpacked it. You noticed it then."

"These things were prefect when they arrived in this country," he said.

Joan went into the kitchen and he followed her.

Jack tried to make conversation with the Germans. From the kitchen there was the sound of a blow and a cry. Franz returned and began to eat his mulberries greedily. Joan came back with her dish of ice cream. Her voice was gentle. Her tears, if she had been crying, had dried as quickly as the tears of a child. Jack and his wife finished their ice cream and made their escape. The wasted and unnerving evening enraged Jack's wife, and he supposed that he would never see Joan again.

Jack's wife got pregnant early in the fall, and she seized on all the prerogatives of an expectant mother. She took long naps, ate canned peaches in the middle of the night, and talked about the rudimentary kidney. She chose to see only other couples who were expecting children, and the parties that she and Jack gave were temperate. The baby, a boy, was born in May, and Jack was very proud and happy. The first party he and his wife went to after her convalescence was the wedding of a girl whose family Jack had known in Ohio.

The wedding was at St. James's, and afterward there was a big reception at the River Club. There was an orchestra dressed like Hungarians, and a lot of champagne and Scotch. Toward the end of the afternoon, Jack was walking down a dim corridor when he heard Joan's voice. "Please don't, darling," she was saying. "You'll break my arm. *Please* don't, darling." She was being pressed against the wall by a man who seemed to be twisting her arm. As soon as they saw Jack, the struggle stopped. All three of them were intensely embarrassed. Joan's face was wet and she made an effort to smile through her tears at Jack. He said hello and went on without stopping. When he returned, she and the man had disappeared.

When Jack's son was less than two years old, his wife flew with the baby to Nevada to get a divorce. Jack gave her the apartment and all its furnishings and took a room in a hotel near Grand Central. His wife got her decree in due course, and the story was in the newspapers. Jack had a telephone call from Joan a few days later.

"I'm awfully sorry to hear about your divorce, Jack," she said. "She seemed like *such* a nice girl. But that wasn't what I called you about. I want your help, and I wondered if you could come down to my place tonight around six. It's something I don't want to talk about over the phone."

He went obediently to the Village that night and climbed the stairs. Her apartment was a mess. The pictures and the curtains were down and the books were in boxes. "You moving, Joan?" he asked.

"That's what I wanted to see you about, Jack. First, I'll give you a drink." She made two Old-Fashioneds. "I'm being evicted, Jack," she said. "I'm being evicted because I'm an immoral woman. The couple who have the apartment downstairs—they're charming people, I've always thought— have told the real-estate agent that I'm a drunk and a prostitute and all kinds of things. Isn't that fantastic? This real-estate agent has always been so nice to me that I didn't think he'd believe them, but he's canceled my lease, and if I make any trouble, he's threatened to take the matter up with the store, and I don't want to lose my job. This nice real-estate agent won't even talk with me any more. When I go over to the office, the receptionist leers at me as if I were some kind of dreadful woman. Of course, there have been a lot of men here and we sometimes are noisy, but I can't be expected to go to bed at ten every night. Can I? Well, the agent who manages this building has apparently told all the other agents in the neighborhood that I'm an immoral and drunken woman, and none of them will give me an apartment. I went in to talk with one man—he seemed to be such a nice old gentleman—and he made me an indecent proposal. Isn't it fantastic? I have to be out of here on Thursday and I'm literally being turned out into the street."

Joan seemed as serene and innocent as ever while she described this scourge of agents and neighbors. Jack listened carefully for some sign of indignation or bitterness or even urgency in her recital, but there was none. He was reminded of a torch song, of one of those forlorn and touching ballads that had been sung neither for him nor for her but for their older brothers and sisters by Marion Harris. Joan seemed to be singing her wrongs.

"They've made my life miserable," she went on quietly. "If I keep the radio on after ten o'clock, they telephone the agent in the morning and tell him I had some kind of orgy here. One night when Philip—I don't think you've met Philip; he's in the Royal Air Force; he's gone back to England—one night when Philip and some other people were here, they called the police. The police came bursting in the door and talked to me as if I were I don't know what and then looked in the bedroom. If they think there's a man up here after midnight, they call me on the telephone and say all kinds of disgusting things. Of course, I can put my furniture into storage and go to a hotel, I guess. I guess a hotel will take a woman with my kind of reputation, but I thought perhaps you might know of an apartment. I thought—"

It angered Jack to think of this big, splendid girl's being persecuted by her neighbors, and he said he would do what he could. He asked her to have dinner with him, but she said she was busy.

Having nothing better to do, Jack decided to walk uptown to his hotel. It was a hot night. The sky was overcast. On his way, he saw a parade in a dark side street of Broadway near Madison Square. All the buildings in the neighborhood were dark. It was so dark that he could not see the placards the marchers carried until he came to a street light. Their signs urged the entry of the United States into the war, and each platoon represented a nation that had been subjugated by the Axis powers. They marched up Broadway, as he watched, to no music, to no sound but their own steps on the rough cobbles. It was for the most part an army of elderly men and women—Poles, Norwegians, Danes, Jews, Chinese. A few idle people like himself lined the sidewalks, and the marchers passed between them with all the self-consciousness of enemy prisoners. There were children among them dressed in the costumes in which they had, for the newsreels, presented the Mayor with a package of tea, a petition, a protest, a constitution, a check, or a pair of tickets. They hobbled through the darkness of the loft neighborhood like a mortified and destroyed people, toward Greeley Square.

In the morning, Jack put the problem of finding an apartment for Joan up to his secretary. She started phoning real estate agents, and by afternoon she had found a couple of available apartments in the West Twenties. Joan called Jack the next day to say that she had taken one of the apartments and to thank him.

Jack didn't see Joan again until the following summer. It was a Sunday evening; he had left a cocktail party in a Washington Square apartment and had decided to walk a few blocks up Fifth Avenue before he took a bus. As he was passing the Brevoort, Joan called to him. She was with a man at one of the tables on the sidewalk. She looked cool and fresh, and the man appeared to be respectable. His name, it turned out, was Pete Bristol. He invited Jack to sit down and join in a celebration. Germany had invaded Russia that weekend, and Joan and Pete were drinking champagne to celebrate Russia's changed position in the war. The three of them drank champagne until it got dark. They had dinner and drank champagne with their dinner. They drank more champagne afterward and then went over to the Lafayette and then to two or three other places. Joan had always been tireless in her gentle way. She hated to see the night end, and it was after three o'clock when Jack stumbled into his apartment. The following morning he woke up haggard and sick, and with no recollection of the last hour or so of the previous evening. His suit was soiled and he had lost his hat. He didn't get to his office until eleven. Joan had already called him twice, and she called him again soon after he got in. There was no hoarseness at all in her voice. She said that she had to see him, and he agreed to meet her for lunch in a seafood restaurant in the Fifties.

He was standing at the bar when she breezed in, looking as though she had taken no part in that calamitous night. The advice she wanted concerned selling her jewelry. Her grandmother had left her some jewelry, and she wanted to raise money on it but didn't know where to go. She took some rings and bracelets out of her purse and showed them to Jack. He said that he didn't know anything about jewelry but that he could lend her some money. "Oh, I couldn't borrow money from you, Jack," she said. "You see, I want to get the money for Pete. I want to help him. He wants to open an advertising agency, and he needs quite a lot to begin with." Jack didn't press her to accept his offer of a loan after that, and the project wasn't mentioned again during lunch.

He next heard about Joan from a young doctor who was a friend of theirs. "Have you seen Joan recently?" the doctor asked Jack one evening when they were having dinner together. He said no. "I gave her a checkup last week," the doctor said, "and while she's been through enough to kill the average mortal—and you'll never know what she's been through—she still has the constitution of a virtuous and healthy woman. Did you hear about the last one? She sold her jewelry to put him into some kind of business, and as soon as he got the money, he left her for another girl, who had a car—a convertible."

Jack was drafted into the Army in the spring of 1942. He was kept at Fort Dix for nearly a month, and during this time he came to New York in the evening whenever he could get permission. Those nights had for him the intense keenness of a reprieve, a sensation that was heightened by the fact that on the train in from Trenton women would often press upon him dog-eared copies of *Life* and half-eaten boxes of candy, as though the brown clothes he wore were surely cerements. He telephoned Joan from Pennsylvania Station one night. "Come right over, Jack," she said. "Come right over. I want you to met Ralph."

She was living in that place in the West Twenties that Jack had found for her. The neighborhood was a slum. Ash cans stood in front of her house, and an old woman was there picking out bits of refuse and garbage and stuffing them into a perambulator. The house in which Joan's apartment was located was shabby, but the apartment itself seemed familiar. The furniture was the same. Joan was the same big, easygoing girl. "I'm so glad you called me," she said. "It's so good to see you. I'll make you a drink. I was having one myself. Ralph ought to be here by now. He promised to take me to dinner." Jack offered to take her to Cavanagh's, but she said that Ralph might come while she was out. "If he doesn't come by nine, I'm going to make myself a sandwich. I'm not really hungry."

Jack talked about the Army. She talked about the store. She had been working in the same place for—how long was it? He didn't know. He had never seen her at her desk and he couldn't imagine what she did. "I'm terribly sorry Ralph isn't here," she said. "I'm sure you'd like him. He's not a young man. He's a heart specialist who loves to play the viola." She turned on some lights, for the summer sky had got dark. "He has this dreadful wife on Riverside Drive and four ungrateful children. He—"

The noise of an air-raid siren, lugubrious and seeming to spring from pain, as if all the misery and indecision in the city had been given a voice, cut her off. Other sirens, in distant neighborhoods, sounded, until the dark air was full of their noise. "Let me fix you another drink before I have to turn out the lights," Joan said, and took his glass. She brought the drink back to him and snapped off the lights. They went to the windows, and, as children watch a thunderstorm, they watched the city darken. All the lights nearby went out but one. Air-raid wardens had begun to sound their whistles in the street. From a distant yard came a hoarse shriek of anger. "Put our your lights, you Fascists!" a woman screamed. "Put out your lights, you Nazi Fascist Germans. Turn out your lights. Turn out your lights." The last light went off. They went away from the window and sat in the lightless room.

In the darkness, Joan began to talk about her departed lovers, and from what she said Jack gathered that they had all had a hard time. Nils, the suspect count, was dead. Hugh Bascomb, the drunk, had joined the Merchant Marine and was missing in the North Atlantic. Franz, the German, had taken poison the night the Nazis bombed Warsaw. "We listened to the news on the radio," Joan said, "and then he went back to his hotel and took poison. The maid found him dead in the bathroom the next morning." When Jack asked her about the one who was going to open an advertising agency, she seemed at first to have forgotten him. "Oh, Pete," she said after a pause. "Well, he was always very sick, you know. He was supposed to go to Saranac, but he kept putting it off and putting it off and—" She stopped talking when she heard steps on the stairs, hoping, he supposed, that it was Ralph, but whoever it was turned at the landing and continued to the top of the house. "I wish Ralph would come," she said, with a sigh. "I want you to meet him." Jack asked her again to go out, but she refused, and when the all-clear sounded, he said goodbye.

Jack was shipped from Dix to an infantry training camp in the Carolinas and from there to an infantry division stationed in Georgia. He had been in Georgia three months when he married a girl from the Augusta boarding-house aristocracy. A year or so later, he crossed the continent in a day coach and thought sententiously that the last he might see of the country he loved was the desert towns like Barstow, that the last he might hear of it was the ringing of the trolleys on the Bay Bridge. He was sent into the Pacific and returned to the United States twenty months later, uninjured and apparently unchanged. As soon as he received his furlough, he went to Augusta. He presented his wife with the souvenirs he had brought from the islands, quarreled violently with her and all her family, and, after making arrangements for her to get an Arkansas divorce, left for New York.

Jack was discharged from the Army at a camp in the East a few months later. He took a vacation and then went back to the job he had left in 1942. He seemed to have picked up his life at approximately the moment when it had been interrupted by the war. In time, everything came to look and feel the same. He saw most of his old friends. Only two of the men he knew had been killed in the war. He didn't call Joan, but he met her one winter afternoon on a crosstown bus.

Her fresh face, her black clothes, and her soft voice instantly destroyed the sense—if he had ever had such a sense—that anything had changed or intervened since their last meeting, three or four years ago. She asked him up for cocktails and he went to her apartment the next Saturday afternoon. Her room and her guests reminded him of the parties she had given when she had first come to New York. There was a woman with a fancy hat, an elderly doctor, and a man who stayed close to the radio, listening for news from the Balkans. Jack wondered which of the men belonged to Joan and decided on an Englishman who kept coughing into a handkerchief that he pulled out of his sleeve. Jack was right. "Isn't Stephen brilliant?" Joan asked him a little later, when they were alone in a corner. "He knows more about the Polynesians than anyone else in the world."

Jack had returned not only to his old job but to his old salary. Since living costs had doubled and since he was paying alimony to two wives, he had to draw on his savings. He took another job, which promised more money, but it didn't last long and he found himself out of work. This didn't bother him at all. He still had money in the bank, and anyhow it was easy to borrow from friends. His indifference was the consequence not of lassitude or despair but rather of an excess of hope. He had the feeling that he had only recently come to New York from Ohio. The sense that he was very young and that the best years of his life still lay before him was an illusion that he could not seem to escape. There was all the time in the world. He was living in hotels then, moving from one to another every five days.

In the spring, Jack moved to a furnished room in the badlands west of Central Park. He was running out of money. Then, when he began to feel that a job was a desperate necessity, he got sick. At first, he seemed to have only a bad cold, but he was unable to shake it and he began to run a fever and to cough blood. The fever kept him drowsy most of the time, but he roused himself occasionally and went out to a cafeteria for a meal. He felt sure that none of his friends knew where he was, and he was glad of this. He hadn't counted on Joan.

Late one morning, he heard her speaking in the hall with his landlady. A few moments later, she knocked on his door. He was lying on the bed in a pair of pants and a soiled pajama top, and he didn't answer. She knocked again and walked in. "I've been looking everywhere for you, Jack," she said. She spoke softly. "When I found out that you were in a place like this I thought you must be broke or sick. I stopped at the bank and got some money, in case you're broke. I've brought you some Scotch. I thought a little drink wouldn't do you any harm. Want a little drink?"

Joan's dress was black. Her voice was low and serene. She sat in a chair beside his bed as if she had been coming there every day to nurse him. Her features had coarsened, he thought, but there were still very few lines in her face. She was heavier. She was nearly fat. She was wearing black cotton gloves. She got two glasses and poured Scotch into them. He drank his whiskey greedily. "I didn't get to bed until three last night," she said. Her voice had once before reminded him of a gentle and despairing song, but now, perhaps because he was sick, her mildness, the mourning she wore, her stealthy grace, made him uneasy. "It was one of those nights," she said. "We went to the theatre. Afterward, someone asked us up to his place. I don't know who he was. It was one of those places. They're so strange. There were some meat-eating plants and a collection of Chinese snuff bottles. Why do people collect Chinese snuff bottles? We all autographed a lampshade, as I remember, but I can't remember much."

Jack tried to sit up in bed, as if there were some need to defend himself, and then fell back again, against the pillows. "How did you find me, Joan?" he asked.

"It was simple," she said. "I called that hotel. The one you were staying in. They gave me this address. My secretary got the telephone number. Have another little drink."

"You know, you've never come to a place of mine before—never," he said. "Why did you come now?"

"Why did I come, darling?" she asked. "What a question! I've known you for thirty years. You're the oldest friend I have in New York. Remember that night in the Village when it snowed and we stayed up until morning and drank whiskey sours for breakfast? That doesn't seem like twelve years ago. And that night—"

"I don't like to have you see me in a place like this," he said earnestly. He touched his face and felt his beard.

"And all the people who used to imitate Roosevelt," she said, as if she had not heard him, as if she were deaf. "And that place on Staten Island where we all used to go for dinner when Henry had a car. Poor Henry. He bought a place in Connecticut and went out there by himself one weekend. He fell asleep with a lighted cigarette and the house, the barn, everything burned. Ethel took the children out to California." She poured more Scotch into his glass and handed it to him. She lighted a cigarette and put it between his lips. The intimacy of this gesture, which made it seem not only as if he were deathly ill but as if he were her lover, troubled him.

"As soon as I'm better," he said, "I'll take a room at a good hotel. I'll call you then. It was nice of you to come."

"Oh, don't be ashamed of this room, Jack," she said. "Rooms never bother me. It doesn't seem to matter to me where I am. Stanley had a filthy room in Chelsea. At least, other people told me it was filthy. I never noticed it. Rats used to eat the food I brought him. He used to have to hang the food from the ceiling, from the light chain."

"I'll call you as soon as I'm better," Jack said. "I think I can sleep now if I'm left alone. I seem to need a lot of sleep."

"You really *are* sick, darling," she said. "You must have a fever." She sat on the edge of his bed and put a hand on his forehead.

"How is that Englishman, Joan?" he asked. "Do you still see him?"

"What Englishman?" she said.

"You know. I met him at your house. He kept a handkerchief up his sleeve. He coughed all the time. You know the one I mean."

"You must be thinking of someone else," she said. "I haven't had an Englishman at my place since the war. Of course, I can't remember everyone." She turned and, taking one of his hands, linked her fingers in his.

"He's dead, isn't he?" Jack said. "That Englishman's dead." He pushed her off the bed, and got up himself. "Get out," he said.

"You're sick, darling," she said. "I can't leave you alone here."

"Get out," he said again, and when she didn't move, he shouted, "What kind of an obscenity are you that you can smell sickness and death the way you do?"

"You poor darling."

"Does it make you feel young to watch the dying?" he shouted. "Is that the lewdness that keeps you young? Is that why you dress like a crow? Oh, I know there's nothing I can say that will hurt you. I know there's nothing filthy or corrupt or depraved or brutish or base that the others haven't tried, but this time you're wrong. I'm not ready. My life isn't ending. My life's beginning. There are wonderful years ahead of me. There are, there are wonderful, wonderful, wonderful years ahead of me, and when they're over, when it's time, then I'll call you. Then, as an old friend, I'll call you and give you whatever dirty pleasure you take in watching the dying, but until then, you and your ugly and misshapen forms will leave me alone."

She finished her drink and looked at her watch. "I guess I'd better show up at the office," she said. "I'll see you later. I'll come back tonight. You'll feel better then, you poor darling." She closed the door after her, and he heard her light step on the stairs.

Jack emptied the whiskey bottle into the sink. He began to dress. He stuffed his dirty clothes into a bag. He was trembling and crying with sickness and fear. He could see the blue sky from his window, and in his fear it seemed miraculous that the sky should be blue, that the white clouds should remind him of snow, that from the sidewalk he could hear the shrill voices of children shrieking, "I'm the king of the mountain, I'm the king of the mountain, I'm the king of the mountain." He emptied the ashtray containing his nail parings and cigarette butts into the toilet, and swept the floor with a shirt, so that there would be no trace of his life, of his body, when that lewd and searching shape of death came there to find him in the evening.

JOYCE CAROL OATES
(b. 1938)

Born in Lockport, New York, Joyce Carol Oates studied at Syracuse University and the University of Wisconsin. Oates, a highly prolific writer known especially for her themes of violence and evil in modern society, has received numerous O. Henry awards for her short stories. She has described her vision as "of a highly complex America populated with presumably ordinary families who experience common yet intense emotions and relationships and who frequently encounter violence."

Oates, having previously taught at the University of Detroit from 1961 to 1967 and the University of Windsor, Ontario, Canada, from 1967 to 1978, is currently the Roger S. Berlind Distinguished Professor of the Humanities at Princeton University. Her first collection of short stories, By the North Gate, *was published in 1963 and her first novel,* With Shuddering Fall, *in 1964. Her other novels include* A Garden of Earthly Delights *(1967),* Expensive People *(1968),* Do With Me What You Will *(1973), and* Them *(1969), for which she won the National Book Award in 1970. She has also published under the pseudonym Rosamond Smith (*Lives of the Twins *[1987] and* Snake Eyes *[1992]). Oates has recently explored the horror genre with* Haunted: Tales of the Grotesque *(1994) and* Zombie *(1995).*

Bellefleur *includes in its intricate narrative line an ongoing dialogue about the existence or non-existence of God. In this excerpt, Oates exploits the sensuality implicit in the vampire's embrace. Norst, the vampire count, has all the romantic, fear-inspiring characteristics of the dynamic, dark, and handsome stranger whose "voice was liquid and sensuous . . . ," who spoke of "rapture" and of "passion." Above all, what our heroine Veronica finds exciting about Norst is the impossibility of knowing him truly.*

Eros and lassitude, death and dreams, and love—in Veronica and Norst we get a distillation of all the hints about sex and passion that are the usually-not-acknowledged aura of the vampire in fiction and film. Bellefleur *gives us one hot, meaty, sweaty, and erotic paroxysm of love after another.*

Excerpt from
BELLEFLEUR

Because of a vow she had made as a young woman in her
twenties, many years ago, after the second, or possibly the third, of her
fiancés died (and one of the fiancés was a handsome thirty-year-old naval
officer whose father owned a string of textile mills in the Mohawk Valley)
great-aunt Veronica never emerged from her suite of rooms before sunset,
and never wore anything but black. "Anyone as unhappy as I should hide
away from the sun," she said. It was thought that she had imagined
herself a beauty at one time—and perhaps she *had* been a beauty—and
now she was in mourning not only for the two or three men who might
have saved her from a perpetual virginity, but for her own youthful self:
for the girlhood that must have seemed at one time inviolable, but which
gradually eroded until nothing remained of it but the stubborn chaste
irrelevant vow she had made, evidently before witnesses: "Anyone as unhappy as I should remain hidden away from people, so as not to upset
them," she said boldly. "Ah, I *am* accursed!"

Because of the vow Germaine rarely saw her great-aunt, and then only
in the winter months when the sun set early and Germaine's bedtime
wasn't until well after dark. The surprise of great-aunt Veronica was her
ordinariness: if the children hadn't known of her unhappy loves and her
curious penitential vows they would have thought her far less interesting
than their grandparents, and certainly far less interesting than their temperamental great-grandmother Elvira (shortly to become, at the age of
101, a bride again). Great-aunt Veronica was a plump, full-hipped and
full-breasted woman of moderate height, with a placid sheep's face, small-
ish hazel eyes with innumerable blue tucks and pleats about them, a
mouth that might have been charming except for its complacent set, and
a fairly smooth, unlined skin that varied extremely in tone: sometimes it
was quite pale, at other times mottled and flushed, especially about the
cheeks, and at other times, still, it was ruddy, coarse, and heated, almost
brick-red, as if she had been exercising violently in the sun. (Though of
course she never exercised. It seemed to tire the poor woman even to
walk *downstairs*, which she did with an air of listlessness that not even
the promise of excellent claret and excellent food could dispel.)

Absolutely unexceptional were her pastimes: she did needlepoint, like
the other old women, but would never have had the stamina or the imagination to create works of art like aunt Matilde; she played gin rummy
from time to time, for modest stakes; she gossiped about relatives and

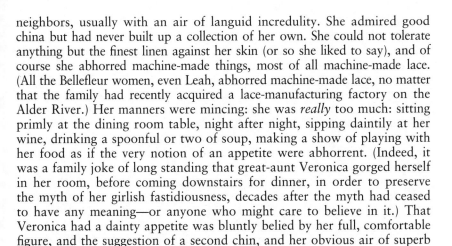

neighbors, usually with an air of languid incredulity. She admired good china but had never built up a collection of her own. She could not tolerate anything but the finest linen against her skin (or so she liked to say), and of course she abhorred machine-made things, most of all machine-made lace. (All the Bellefleur women, even Leah, abhorred machine-made lace, no matter that the family had recently acquired a lace-manufacturing factory on the Alder River.) Her manners were mincing: she was *really* too much: sitting primly at the dining room table, night after night, sipping daintily at her wine, drinking a spoonful or two of soup, making a show of playing with her food as if the very notion of an appetite were abhorrent. (Indeed, it was a family joke of long standing that great-aunt Veronica gorged herself in her room, before coming downstairs for dinner, in order to preserve the myth of her girlish fastidiousness, decades after the myth had ceased to have any meaning—or anyone who might care to believe in it.) That Veronica had a dainty appetite was bluntly belied by her full, comfortable figure, and the suggestion of a second chin, and her obvious air of superb health. For a woman of her age—! people were always remarking, in wonderment. Though no one knew exactly how old she was. Bromwell had once calculated that she must be much older than grandmother Cornelia, which would have made her more than seventy, but everyone laughed him out of the room—one of the few instances in which the child was demonstrably mistaken. For great-aunt Veronica looked, even at her most torpid, no more than fifty; at her freshest she might have been as young as forty. Her small undistinguished eyes sometimes shone with an inexplicable emotion that might have been a pleasure in her own enigmatic being.

Upon occasion she wore open-necked gowns, which exposed her pale, rather lardish skin, and the beautiful dark-heart-shaped stone she wore about her neck on a thin gold chain. Asked about the stone she always gazed down upon it sorrowfully, and touched it, and said after a long painful moment that it was a bloodstone—a gift from the first man she had ever loved—the only man (she saw this now, so many decades after) she had ever loved. A deep green stone, flecked with red jasper, glowing and fading with variations in light, pulling heavily on the thin chain: a stone heart the size of a child's heart. *Is* it beautiful, *do* you think it's beautiful? she would ask, frowning, peering down at it so that her small pudgy chin creased against her chest. She couldn't, she declared, judge any longer, herself. For it had been so many, many years since Count Ragnar Norst had given her the bloodstone.

But of course it was beautiful, people said. If one liked bloodstones.

Norst introduced himself to Veronica Bellefleur at a charity ball in Manhattan, attended, it was said, by many persons of questionable background. Though Veronica, then a comely young woman of twenty-four who wore her red-blond hair braided and wound about her head like a crown, and who distinguished herself by her high tinkling spontaneous laughter, had, of course, a chaperone, and would not ordinarily have countenanced a stranger's approach—let alone a stranger's daring in actually taking her hand and raising it to his lips!—there was from the very first something so peremptory and at the same time so artless about his manner that she could not assert herself against it. In handsome though rather dated formal attire, with a very dark goatee and gleaming dark curls on either side of his forehead, Count Ragnar Norst identified himself ambiguously as the youngest son in a family of merchants who owned a shipping line that spanned the globe, doing trade in New Guinea and Patagonia and the Ivory Coast, and as a diplomatic attaché whose embassy was, of course, in Washington, and as a "poet-adventurer" whose only desire was to live each day to the fullest. Veronica's confused impression of Norst upon that occasion was a positive but troubled one—he *was* attractive, but how intensely, how *queerly,* he had smiled at her! And with what unwelcome intimacy he had kissed her hand, as if they were old, intimate friends. . . .

Yet she dreamt of him almost at once. So that when he reappeared in her life some weeks later, at a crowded reception at the home of Senator Payne, not far from Bellefleur Manor, she greeted him with an unthinking vivacity—actually held her hand out to him, as if they *were* old friends. It was not until he seized the hand and raised it to his warm lips and bowed over it that Veronica realized the audacity of her behavior, but by then it was too late, for Norst was chattering to her about any number of things—the weather, the beautiful mountain scenery, the "'rustic" lakeside cottage he had rented for the summer at Lake Ayernus (about twelve miles south of Lake Noir), his hopes for seeing her as frequently as possible. Veronica laughed her high scandalized laugh, and blushed, but Norst took no heed: he thought her, in his own words, "dreadfully charming." And so very American.

It soon came about that Norst was visiting Veronica at the castle, driving over for luncheon or high tea in his extraordinary black car—a Lancia Lambda, it was, a saloon model that stood high off the ground on wooden-spoked wheels, comfortably roomy enough so that Veronica's wide-brimmed hats were not in the slightest disturbed as she climbed in. He drove her along the Nautauga River, and down through the picturesque rolling countryside to Lake Avernus, which, already in those days, was beginning to be known as a resort area for well-to-do Manhattanites who hadn't the interest or the wealth to acquire a genuine Chautauqua camp of the sort Raphael Bellefleur had built on the northern shore of Lake Noir. On those long leisurely drives—which poor Veronica was to remember the rest of her life—the couple talked of innumerable casual things, laughing frequently (for surely, from the start, they were half in love), and though Norst questioned Veronica closely about *her* life, her daily life, as if every detail about her delighted him, he was conspicuously

evasive in speaking of his own life: he had "duties" in regard to his family's shipping line which called him to New York often, he had "duties" in regard to the Swedish Embassy in Washington which called him there, often, and the rest of the time, well, the rest of the time was given over to . . . to his obligations to himself.

"For we have a grave responsibility, do we not, my dear Miss Bellefleur," he would say, squeezing her hand in excitement, "a responsibility entrusted to us at birth: the need, the *command* to fulfill ourselves, to develop our souls to their utmost? For this we need not only time and cunning, but courage, even audacity . . . and the sympathy of kindred souls."

Veronica was capable of intelligent skepticism in regard to innumerable domestic matters (dressmaker's and haberdashers' promises, for instance), and as a child of thirteen she had insolently repudiated the "God" of Unitarianism (for Veronica's branch of the family was solemnly experimenting with forms of Christianity they considered rational, since the irrational forms were too embarrassing altogether); she was *not* a stupid young woman; and yet, in Norst's charismatic presence, she seemed to lose all her powers of judgment, and allowed his words to wash over her. . . . His voice was liquid and sensuous, the first genuinely *charming,* even *seductive,* voice the unfortunate young woman had ever experienced. Ah, it hardly mattered what he said! It hardly mattered: gossip about mutual acquaintances at Lake Avernus, gossip about state and federal politics, praise for the Bellefleur estate and farm, fulsome flattery directed toward Veronica herself (who, in the flush of giddiness attending her "love" for the count, was undeniably beautiful, and not at all innocent of the effect of her cruel wasp-waisted corsets on the snug-fitting silk gowns she wore). Veronica gazed upon Norst with a girlish fascination she did not even try to hide, and murmured in agreement, yes, yes, whatever he said, it *sounded so* utterly plausible.

It was a most unorthodox courtship. Norst would disappear suddenly, leaving behind only a few scribbled words of apology (but never of explanation) with a manservant; and then he would reappear, a day or twelve days later, never doubting but that Veronica would see him—as if she hadn't innumerable suitors who treated her more considerately. As if she hadn't, Veronica's parents and brother chided her, any *pride.* But there was Ragnar Norst in his aristocratic car, which gleamed like a hearse, and gave off a scent (which in time became quite sweet, in Veronica's opinion) of wax polish, leather, finely-veneered wood, and something mustily damp, like a bog made rich by centuries of decay. At all times he wore impeccably formal attire—frock coats, handsome silk cravats, dazzling-white cuffs with pearl, gold, onyx, and bloodstone cuff links, starched collars, plissé shirts—and his pomaded hair with its twin curls was always perfect. Perhaps his skin was too swarthy, and his black eyes *too* black, and his mood too unpredictable (for if, one day, he was ebullient, gay, chattersome, and exhilarated, the next day he might be apathetic, or irritable, or melancholy, or so serious in his talk to Veronica of "the need to fulfill one's destiny" that the young woman turned aside in distress) . . . and in any case, as the Bellefleurs were beginning to say, more and more emphatically, there was something not altogether *clear* about him. Were the Norsts, indeed, an "ancient" Swedish family? Did they own a shipping line? But *which* shipping line? Was a Norst associated with the Swedish Embassy under his own name, or under an incognito? Was "Norst" itself an incognito? It is quite possible, Veronica's brother Aaron said, even granting the man (which I don't) his identity, that he is involved in espionage of some sort. . . . It hasn't been our habit, after all, to trust foreigners.

Veronica tearfully agreed; yet, once in Norst's presence, she forgot everything. He was so *manly*. He could entertain her for hours with Swedish folksongs played on a curious little instrument that resembled a zither, and produced a keening and yet lulling, almost soporific, sound, a "music" so intimate that it played along her nerves and pulses, and left her quite drained. He told her of his many travels—to Patagonia, to the African interior, to Egypt, Mesopotamia, Jordan, India, New Guinea, Styria, the land of Ganz—and began to intimate, more and more explicitly, that she would soon accompany him, if she wished. And then he addressed her as no other man had ever addressed her, seizing her limp hand and raising it to his lips, kissing it passionately: murmuring shamelessly of "love" and "kindred souls" and "mutual destiny" and the need for lovers to "surrender" themselves completely to one another. He called her "dearest," "my dear Veronica," "my dear beautiful Veronica," and did not seem to notice her discomfort; he spoke in a tremulous voice of "rapture" and "passion"—that "unexplored country" which a "virgin like yourself" must one day traverse, but only in the company of a lover who had opened himself completely to her. There must be, he cautioned, no secrets between lovers—absolutely no corners or recesses of the soul kept in darkness—otherwise the raptures of love will be merely physical, and short-lived, and if the lovers *die* into each other they will *die* literally, and not be resurrected—did she understand? Ah, it was imperative that she understand! And he embraced her, fairly shuddering with emotion; and poor Veronica nearly fainted. (For no man had ever spoken to her like this, nor had anyone so abruptly, and so passionately, taken her in his arms.)

"But you shouldn't! That isn't nice! Oh—that isn't nice!" Veronica gasped. And, like a frightened child, she burst into peals of laughter. "That isn't—*nice*—"

That night she retired early, her head reeling as if she had drunk too much wine, and she was hardly conscious of pulling the bedcovers up before she slipped—sank—was pulled into—sleep. And in the morning she found the heart-shaped bloodstone on the pillow beside her!—simply lying on the pillow beside her. (She knew at once, of course, that it was

a gift of Norst's, for two or three days earlier, as they dined in the Avernus Inn overlooking the magnificent lake, she had made a fuss over his cuff links—she'd never seen so richly dark a stone before, and found its scintillating depths quite fascinating. The family jewels she had inherited—a single sapphire, some modest-carated diamonds, a handful of opals, garnets, pearls—struck her suddenly as uninteresting. Norst's bloodstone cuff links might very well be, as he insisted gaily, inexpensive, even commonplace, but they exerted a fascination upon Veronica, who found it difficult to take her eyes off them during the meal.) And now—what a surprise! For several minutes she lay without moving, staring at the large stone, which was both green and red, and layered with darkness: *could* such a beautiful object be, indeed, commonplace?

He had gotten Veronica's maid to tiptoe into her room and lay the stone beside her, of course, and though the girl denied it—for her mistress was not so flummoxed by passion as to fail to wonder at the propriety of Norst's tipping (or bribing) a domestic servant—Veronica knew that this was the case: an audacious gesture, of which her family would angrily disapprove, but one which (ah, she couldn't help herself!) quite charmed her.

She slipped the bloodstone on a gold chain, and wore it about her neck that very day.

The more frequently Veronica saw Ragnar Norst, the less she felt she knew of him; it frightened her, and excited her, to realize that she would never *know* him at all. For one thing, his moods were so capricious. . . . He could start off on a walk with her in excellent high spirits, obviously filled to the brim with energy; fifteen minutes later he would be suddenly weary, and ask if Veronica wouldn't mind sitting on a bench for a while, and simply gazing, without speaking, at the landscape. Or perhaps he was sweetly melancholy, and kept staring mournfully into her eyes, as if he were yearning, starving, for something, for *her* . . . and then again, a few minutes later, he would be telling one of his lengthy, convoluted folktales, set in Sweden or Denmark or Norway, punctuated with bursts of laughter (for some of the tales, though sanctified tradition, struck the blushing young woman as distinctly ribald—not really suited for her ears). He was at all times unusually perceptive, however; she felt that he was *seeing* and *hearing* and *thinking* with an almost preternatural clarity. At one unfortunate luncheon, high on the terrace in the walled garden, Veronica's brother Aaron—a 230-pounder with an exaggerated sense of his own powers of ratiocination, far more suited for hunting than for civilized discourse—began to interrogate Norst almost rudely about his background ("Ah, you claim there is *Persian* blood on your mother's side of the family?—indeed? And on your father's side, what sort of blood, do you think—?"), and it was quite remarkable to witness Norst's transformation: he seemed immediately to sense that a direct confrontation with this brute would be not only disastrous, but distasteful, and so he replied to Aaron's questions in a courteous, even humble manner, readily admitting when necessary that he *couldn't* altogether explain certain . . . certain discrepancies . . . no, he regretted that he *couldn't* account for . . . not altogether . . . not at the present time. Veronica had never witnessed a performance of such exquisite subtlety and tact; she gazed upon him adoringly, and did not even trouble to be angry with her boorish brother (he was five years her senior, and imagined that he knew more than she, and that a great deal of what he knew had to do with *her*), even though his questioning had brought droplets of perspiration to Norst's forehead.

And then, afterward, it struck her—Persian blood! But how marvelous! How enchanting! *Persian* blood: which accounted for his swarthy skin and his dark mesmerizing eyes. Little as she knew about Swedes she knew even less about Persians and found the combination totally enchanting. . . .

"That 'Count' is an impostor," Aaron said. "He doesn't even trouble himself to lie intelligently to us."

"Oh, what do you know!" Veronica laughed, waving him away. "You don't know Ragnar at all."

(Later it was revealed that Aaron had spoken with Senator Payne, and with two or three acquaintances in Washington, to see if Norst's visa couldn't be canceled—if Norst couldn't be, with a minimum of legal squabbling, simply deported back to Europe. But he must have had friends in high positions, or at any rate friends whose authority was greater than that of Aaron's contacts, for nothing came of the move; and when Ragnar Norst returned to Europe he did so solely at his own wish.)

And so Veronica Bellefleur fell in love with the mysterious Ragnar Norst, though she was not conscious of "falling in love" but only of becoming more and more obsessed with him—with the thought, the aura, of him, which pursued her in the unlikeliest of places, and was liable to call forth a blush to her cheeks at the least appropriate of times. Even before her illness she was susceptible to odd lethargic reveries during which his image haunted her; she would give her head a shake, as if to cast herself free of his spell. A warm lulling erotic daze overcame her. She sighed often, and her words trailed off into silence, quite maddening Aaron, who knew, no matter how she denied it, that she was in love with the count. "But that man is an impostor," Aaron said angrily. "Just as I'm sure that stone of yours, if you allowed me to have it examined, would prove to be a fake—!"

"You don't know Ragnar in the slightest," Veronica said, shivering.

Yet she herself was often disturbed by him. He insisted they meet in the evening, in clandestine places (in the boathouse; beside Bloody Run; at the very rear of the walled garden, where there was a little grove of evergreens in which, by day, the children sometimes played) no matter how such situations compromised her; he insisted upon speaking "frankly" no matter how his words distressed her. Once he seized both her hands in his and murmured in a voice that shook with emotion, "Someday, my dearest Veronica, this masquerade will end—someday you will be mine—my most precious possession—and I will be yours—and you will know then the reality of—of—of the passion which nearly suffocates me—" And indeed his breath became so labored it was nearly a sob, and his eyes glowed with an unspeakable lust, and after a terrible moment during which he stared into her eyes almost angrily he turned aside, throwing himself back against a railing, his arm upraised as if to shield himself from the sight of her. His chest rose and fell so violently that Veronica wondered for a terrible moment if he were having a seizure of some kind.

For several minutes afterward Norst remained leaning against the railing, his heavy-lidded eyes closed, as if he were suddenly drained of all strength. And afterward, escorting her back to the manor house, he said very little, and walked feebly, like an aged man; in parting he did no more than murmur a gentle, melancholy goodbye, and failed even to lift his gaze to hers. "But Ragnar," Veronica asked, bold with desperation, "are you angry with me?—why have you turned away from me?" Still he did not look her in the face. He sighed, and said in a weary voice, "My dear, perhaps it would be for the best—for *you,* I am thinking only of *you*—if we never met again."

That night she dreamt of him once again, far more vividly; she saw him more vividly, it seemed, than she had seen him in the flesh. He seized both her hands and squeezed them so hard she cried out in pain and surprise, and then he pulled her to him, to his breast, and closed her in his strong arms. She would have fainted, she would have fallen, had he not held her so tight. . . . He kissed her full on the lips, and then buried his face in her neck, and then, while the swooning girl tried with feeble hands to prevent him, he tore open her bodice and began to kiss her breasts, all the while holding her still, and murmuring lulling commanding words of love. It excited him all the more, that she was wearing the bloodstone around her neck (for indeed Veronica was wearing it in bed, beneath her nightgown). You must stop, Ragnar, she whispered, her face crimson with shame, you must stop, you must *stop*—

By day she only half-recalled her tempestuous dreams, though she was still under their spell. Strange emotions washed over her, and left her so drained of energy that her mother asked more than once if she were ill: she was by turns fearful, and disgusted, and wildly exhilarated, and ashamed, and defiant, and impatient (for when, *when,* would he see her again?—he'd left word with a servant that the embassy in Washington had called him), and delighted as a child (for she was certain he *would* see her again). Sometimes she ate ravenously, but most of the time she had no appetite at all—she simply sat at the dining room table, oblivious of the others, staring into space, sighing, her head aswim with languorous wraithlike images of her lover.

You must stop, Ragnar, a voice rose shrilly, you must, you must, you *must* stop before it's too late. . . .

*   *   *

And then a tragic accident befell poor Aaron, and it was Ragnar Norst himself who comforted the stricken young woman.

Unwisely, against his father's reiterated wishes, Aaron went out hunting alone in the woods above Bloody Run, accompanied only by one of his dogs. While crossing a white-water stream he evidently lost his footing, fell, and was carried hundreds of yards downstream, over a seven-foot falls, to his death in a swirling shallow rapids in which rocks and logs lay in manic profusion. The poor young man's throat was slashed by a protruding branch, and it was estimated that he must have bled to death, mercifully, in a matter of minutes. By the time the search party discovered him (he had been missing then two days) his body, so large, once so intimidating, was bled white, trapped in a tight little cove of froth-covered rocks and logs.

(Neither the dog nor the shotgun was ever recovered, which added to the mystery of the death.)

The stricken Veronica wept and wept, as much for the senselessness of Aaron's death as for the death itself: for to her there was no mystery, there was only the fact that she would never see Aaron again, never exchange words with him again. . . . No matter how they had quarreled they had loved each other very much.

How ugly that death was, and how *pointless!* If the headstrong young man had only listened to his father's words . . . No, Veronica could not bear it; she *would* not bear it. She wept for days on end and would allow no one to comfort her.

Until Ragnar Norst returned.

One morning he drove up the graveled lane in the stately black car (whose engine was overheated), and insisted that he be allowed to see Miss Veronica: for he had learned, in Washington, of Aaron's death, and he knew at once that Veronica must be comforted if she was to survive the crisis. She was so exquisite, so sensitive, the horror of a brute acciden-tal death might undermine her health. . . .

The very sight of Norst enlivened her. But she took care, being a discreet young woman, to hide her feelings; and, indeed, a moment later, the memory of her brother's death swept over her once again, and she suc-cumbed to a fresh attack of weeping. So Norst took her aside, and walked with her along the lake, at first saying nothing at all, and even urging her to cry; and then, when it seemed to him that she was somewhat stronger, he began to query her about death. About, that is, her fear of death.

Was it death itself that terrified her . . . or the accidental nature of that particular death? Was it *death* that so alarmed, or the fact that she would not (or so she assumed) ever see her brother again?

Above the choppy dark waters of Lake Noir they paused, to listen to

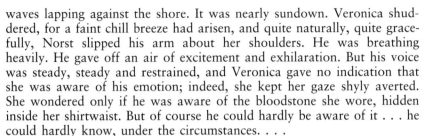

waves lapping against the shore. It was nearly sundown. Veronica shuddered, for a faint chill breeze had arisen, and quite naturally, quite gracefully, Norst slipped his arm about her shoulders. He was breathing heavily. He gave off an air of excitement and exhilaration. But his voice was steady, steady and restrained, and Veronica gave no indication that she was aware of his emotion; indeed, she kept her gaze shyly averted. She wondered only if he was aware of the bloodstone she wore, hidden inside her shirtwaist. But of course he could hardly be aware of it . . . he could hardly know, under the circumstances. . . .

His arm tightened about her slender shoulders and he brought his mouth close to her ear. In a gentle, trembling voice he began to speak of death: death and love: death and love and lovers: and how, by the sacrament of death, lovers are united, and their profane love redeemed. Veronica's heart beat so powerfully she could barely concentrate on his words. She was aware of his nearness, his almost overwhelming nearness; she was terrified that he would kiss her, as he had in her dreams, and abuse her, ignoring her astonished cries. . . . "Veronica, my dearest," he said, cupping her chin in his hand, turning her face so that he might look into her eyes, "you must know that lovers who die together transcend the physical nature of the human condition . . . the tedious physical nature of the human condition. . . . You must know that a pure spiritual love redeems the grossness of the flesh. . . . So long as I am beside you, to guide you, to protect you, there is nothing to fear . . . nothing, nothing to fear . . . in this world or the next. I would *never* allow you to suffer, my dear girl, do you understand? . . . do you trust me?"

Her eyelids were suddenly heavy; she was nearly overcome by a sense of lassitude, vaguely erotic, that very much resembled the lassitude of her most secret dreams. Norst's voice was gentle, soothing, rhythmic as the waves of Lake Noir, beating against her, washing over her. . . . Ah, she could not have protested *had* he attempted to kiss her!

But he was speaking, still, of love. Of lovers who would "eagerly" die for each other. "I for you, my dear sweet girl, and you for me—if you love me—and by that we are redeemed. It is so simple, and yet so profound! Do you see? Do you understand? Your brother's death offended you because it was an animal's death—brute, senseless, accidental, unshared—and with your sensitivity you crave meaning, and beauty, and a spiritual transcendence. You crave redemption, as I do. For by death in one another's arms, my love, we *are* redeemed . . . and all else is unadorned *unimagined* folly, from which you are perfectly justified to turn aside in horror. Do you understand, my love? Ah, but you will—you *will*. Only have faith in me, my dearest Veronica."

Faintly she murmured that she did not understand. And she felt so suddenly exhausted, she must lay her head against his shoulder.

"Life and death both, if unadorned by love," Norst continued, in a rapid, low, excited voice, "are ignominious . . . mere folly . . . mere accident. They are indistinguishable when not enhanced by passion. For ordinary people, as you must have seen by now, are little more than aphids . . . rats . . . brute unthinking animals . . . quite beneath our contempt, really . . . unless of course they frustrate us . . . in which case they must be taken into account . . . taken into account and dealt with . . . ugly as that might seem. Do you see, my dear? Yes? No? You must trust me, and all will become clear. You must have faith in me, Veronica, for you know, don't you, that I love you, and that I have sworn to have you . . . from a time long past . . . a time you cannot remember and I, I can but dimly recall. . . . As for ordinary people, my dear, you must give them no thought . . . you will one day learn to deal with them as I do, only out of necessity . . . I will guide you, I will protect you, if only you will have faith. . . . And you *must* not fear death, for the death of lovers, dying into love, being born again through love, has nothing of the crudity of ordinary death about it: do you understand?"

She understood. Yet of course she did not understand. But her head was so heavy, her eyelids burned with the need to close, if only he would embrace her, if only he would whisper to her the words she so fervently wished to hear. . . . He had declared his love for her; she had heard it; she *had* heard it; yet he had not, yet, declared his wish to marry her; he had said nothing about speaking to her father, or . . .

Suddenly he drew away from her. He was quite agitated, and rubbed both hands vigorously against his eyes. "My dear Veronica," he said, in a different voice, "I must get you back home. What can I be thinking of, keeping you out here in this cold wind—!"

She opened her eyes wide in disbelief.

"I *must* get you home, you poor girl," Norst murmured.

That night Veronica felt feverish, and despite the drop in temperature she left her French doors open. And she experienced a dream that was by far the most alarming, and the most curiously exhilarating, of any dream she had yet experienced.

She was, and yet she was not, unconscious. She slept, but at the same time was quite aware of her bed, her surroundings, and the fact that she lay asleep, her long thick hair loose on her pillow, the bloodstone exposed on her breast. I am asleep, she thought clearly, as if her spirit floated above her body, how strange, how wonderful, I am lying there asleep and my lover is shortly to come to me, and no one will know. . . .

Almost at once Norst did appear. He must have climbed over the balcony railing, for a moment later he stood before the window, dressed as usual in his frock coat, his white shirt glaringly white in the darkness, his goatee and the savage little curls on either side of his forehead vividly defined. He was silent. He was expressionless. Somewhat taller than his daylight self—Veronica, paralyzed, unable even to make her eyelids flutter, estimated that he must be nearly seven feet tall—he stood for a long moment without moving, simply gazing upon her with an expression of—was it infinite longing, infinite sorrow?—was it yearning?—love?

Ragnar, she tried to whisper. My dear. My bridegroom.

She would have opened her arms to him, but she could not move; she lay paralyzed beneath the covers. Asleep and yet fully awake: conscious of her wild accelerated heartbeat and of *his* heartbeat as well. Ragnar, she whispered. I love you as I have never loved any other man. . . .

Then he was close beside her bed, without having seemed to move.

He was close beside her bed, stooping over her, and she tried to raise her arms to him—ah, how she wanted to slide her arms about his neck!—how she wanted to pull him to her! But she could not move, she could do no more than draw in her breath sharply as he stooped to kiss her. She saw his dark moist eyes drawing near, she saw his mouth, his parted lips, and felt his breath—his warm, ragged, rather meaty breath—she smelled his breath which was dank, and somewhat fetid—it put her dizzily in mind of the farm—the farm laborers hauling carcasses—hogs strung up by their hind legs—blood gushing from their slashed throats, into enormous tubs— She drew in his breath, which was sour with something dried and stale and old, very old, and in a swoon she began to laugh, every part of her was being tickled, tickled to delirium, to a delicious frantic delirium, and she did not mind his breath, she did not mind it at all, or his agitation, his impatience, his roughness, the grinding of his teeth against hers in a harsh kiss—she did not mind at all—not at all—she wanted to shout, and pound at him with her fists—she wanted to scream—to throw herself about the bed—to kick off the covers, which so exasperatingly pressed upon her—and she was so hot—slick with perspiration—she could smell her own body, her bodily heat—it was shameful, and yet delicious—it made her want to snort with laughter—it made her want to grab hold of her lover—seize him by the hair, by the hair, and pummel him, and press his head against her, his face against her breasts—like that—yes, exactly like that—she could not bear it, what he was doing to her—his lips, his tongue, his sudden hard teeth—she could not bear it—she would scream, she would go mad, snorting, shouting, tearing at him with her nails—My lover, my bridegroom, she would scream, my husband, my *soul*—

As the days and weeks passed, and Veronica sank ever more deeply into a state of languid, sweet melancholy, it was commonly believed that the shock of Aaron's death had plunged her into a "black mood" and that she would, in time, emerge from it. Yet Veronica rarely thought of her brother. Her imagination dwelt almost exclusively upon Ragnar Norst. Throughout the long, tiresome day she yearned for the night, when Norst came to her, unfailingly, and gathered her up passionately in his arms, and made her his bride. There was no need for him to speak of love any longer; what happened between them went beyond love. Indeed, the trivial

notion of love—and marriage as well—now struck Veronica as uninteresting. That she had once hoped Ragnar Norst would ask her father for permission to marry her—! That she had once imagined him an ordinary man, and herself an ordinary woman—! Well, she had been a very innocent girl at the time.

Strange, wasn't it, people said, that the count had disappeared so suddenly. Evidently he had returned to Europe . . . ? And when would he return, had he said . . . ?

Veronica paid no attention. She knew that people whispered behind her back, wondering if she was unhappy; wondering if there was any sort of "understanding" between them. Would there be a marriage? Would there be a scandal? It did not trouble Veronica in the slightest, that her lover had left the country: for in her sleep he was magnificently present, and nothing else mattered.

During the day Veronica drifted about idly, thinking certain forbidden thoughts, recalling certain sharp, piercing, indefinable pleasures. She sang tuneless little songs under her breath, reminiscent of the songs Norst had sung. She tired easily, and liked to lie on a chaise longe wrapped in a shawl, gazing dreamily out toward the lake, watching the lakeshore drive. Sometimes Norst appeared to her though it wasn't night: she would blink, and see him standing there a few feet away, gazing at her with that shameless raw hunger, that embarrassing intensity she had not understood at the start. Graciously, languidly, she would lift her hand to him, and he would lean forward to raise it to his greedy lips . . . and then some clumsy heavy-footed fool of a servant would enter the room, and Norst would vanish.

"Oh, I hate you!" Veronica sometimes cried. "Why don't you all leave me alone!"

They began to worry about her. She was so listless, so pale, the color had gone out of her face and she looked positively waxen (though more beautiful than ever, Veronica thought, why don't you admit it—Ragnar's love has made me more beautiful than ever); she had no appetite for anything more than toast and fruit juice and an occasional pastry; she was absentminded, often didn't hear people speaking to her, seemed asleep with her eyes open, was obviously lost in grief for her poor dead brother. . . . Even when the doctor was examining her, listening to her heart with his silly instrument, she was daydreaming about her lover (who had appeared to her the night before, and who had promised to return the following night) and could not answer the questions put to her. She would have liked to explain: Her soul was swooning downward, gently downward, she was not at all unhappy, she was certainly not in mourning (in mourning for whom?—her boorish headstrong brother who had died such an ugly death?), everything was unfolding as it must, according to the destiny fate had determined for her. She would not resist, would not want to resist; nor did she want anyone else to interfere. Sometimes during the daylight hours she caught sight of a thin crescent moon, half-invisible in the pale sky, and the sight of it pierced her breast like her lover's kiss. She would lie down, suddenly dizzy, and let her head drop heavily back, and her eyes roll white in her skull. . . .

How sweet it was, this utterly unresisting melancholy: this sense of a downward spiral which was both the pathway her soul took, and her soul itself. The air grew heavy; it exerted pressure upon her; sometimes she found breathing difficult, and held her lungs still and empty for long moments at a time. She would have liked to explain to the nurse who now sat at the foot of her bed, or slept on a cot of her own just outside her door, that she was not at all unhappy. Others might be unhappy that she was leaving them but they were simply jealous, ignorant people who didn't understand her. They couldn't know how deeply she was loved, for instance; how Norst valued her; how he had promised to protect her.

There were times, however, when her dreams were confused and unpleasant, and Norst did not appear; or, if he did appear, his aspect was so greatly changed she could not recognize him. (Once he came in the shape of a gigantic yellow-eyed owl with ferocious ear tufts; another time he appeared in the shape of a monstrous stunted dwarf with a hump between his shoulder blades; still another time he was a tall, slender, eerily beautiful girl with Oriental eyes and a slow, sensuous smile—a smile Veronica could not bear to gaze upon, it was so knowing, so obscene.) On and on the dreams went, tumbling her about mercilessly, mocking her pleas for tenderness, for love, for her husband's embrace. When she woke from one of these dreams, often in the middle of the night, she would force herself to sit up, her head aching violently, and a flame of panic would touch her—for wasn't she seriously ill, wasn't she perhaps dying, couldn't something be done to stop the downward spiral of her soul? . . . Once, she heard her nurse groaning, thrashing about in the midst of her own nightmare.

And then two things happened: the nurse (an attractive woman in her mid-thirties who had been born in the village, and had trained in the Falls) grew gravely ill with a blood disorder, and Veronica herself, already weakened and anemic, caught a cold that passed into bronchitis and then into pneumonia in a matter of days. So she was hospitalized, and lapsed into a sort of stupor, during which busy dream-wraiths took care of her. They took excellent care of her: providing her with fresh, strong blood, and feeding her through tubes, so that she could not protest, and was thereby saved. In fact there was no question of dying, with so much skillful, professional activity on all sides; and in a week or two Veronica was not only fully conscious but even hungry. One of the Bellefleur maids shampooed her hair, which was still luxurious and beautiful; and she too was beautiful despite her pallor and the hollows around her eyes. One day she said, "I'm hungry," in a child's affronted voice, "I want to eat,

I'm hungry, and I'm bored with lying here in bed. . . . I can't stand it a minute longer!"

So she was saved. Her lungs were well; the bouts of dizziness had vanished; her color was back. Upon admission to the hospital her doctors had discovered, high on her left breast, a curious fresh scratch or bite, that looked at the same time as if it were fairly old, which must have been made by one of the Bellefleur cats, hugged unwisely against Veronica's bosom. (For though the Bellefleurs had not nearly so many cats and kittens in those days, as they did in Germaine's time, there were at least six or ten of them in the household, and any one of them might have been responsible for Veronica's tiny wound.) Veronica herself knew nothing about it: she belonged to that generation of women who rarely, and then only reluctantly, gazed upon their naked bodies, and so it was a considerable surprise for her to learn that there was, on her breast, an odd little scratch or bite that had become mildly inflamed. Of course it was a very *minor* affair, her doctors assured her, and had nothing to do with her serious problems of anemia and pneumonia.

Indirectly she learned, to her astonishment and grief, that her nurse had died—the poor woman had died of acute anemia only a few days after having left Bellefleur Manor. Most extraordinary was the fact that, according to the woman's family, she had been in perfect health until she went into the employ of the Bellefleurs; she had *never*, they claimed, been anemic at all.

But Veronica had not died.

Now the disturbing, tumultuous dreams were over. A part of her life was over. She slept deeply and profoundly, safe in her hospital room, and when she woke in the morning she woke completely, well rested, elated, wanting at once to be on her feet. She was ecstatic with good health. In her luxurious cashmere robe she walked about the hospital wing, attended by her personal maid, and of course everyone fell in love with her: for she was radiant as an angel, and that long red-blond hair that fell loose on her shoulders—! She was merry and prankish as a child, she told silly little jokes, she even toyed, for a day or two, with the idea of becoming a nurse. How charming she would look, in her prim white uniform. . . . And then, perhaps, she would marry a doctor. And the two of them would be on the side of life.

Yes, that was it: she wanted to be *on the side of life.*

She was very happy, and begged to be discharged from the hospital, but her family was cautious (for, after all, Veronica's nurse *had* died—and she *had* seemed to be in good health), and her doctors wanted to keep her under observation for another several days. For there was something about her case that perplexed them.

"But I want to go home now," she said, pouting. "I'm *bored* with doing nothing, I hate being an invalid, having people look at me in that condescending pitying way. . . ."

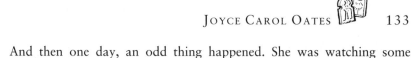
And then one day, an odd thing happened. She was watching some teenaged boys playing football in a field adjacent to the hospital grounds, and though she wanted to admire them, and to applaud their physical dexterity and stamina, she found herself becoming increasingly depressed. They were so energetic, so vulgar . . . so filled with life. . . . Like aphids or rats. . . . There was no subtlety to them, no meaning; no beauty. She turned away in disgust.

She turned away, and began to weep uncontrollably. What had she lost! What had gone out of her life, when they had "saved" her here in the hospital! Her thin cheeks were growing rounded again and her dead-white skin was turning rosy but the mirror's image did not please her; she saw that it was uninteresting, banal, really quite vulgar. *She* was uninteresting now, and her lover, if he returned, if he ever happened to gaze upon her, would be sadly disappointed.

(But her lover: who was he? She could not clearly recall him. *Ragnar Norst*. But who was that, what did he mean to her? Where had he gone? The dreams had vanished, and Ragnar Norst had vanished, and something so profound had gone out of her life that she halfway felt, despite her heartiness, her relentless normality, that it was her very soul that had been taken from her. The hospital had seen to that: it had "saved" her.)

Still, she was grateful to be alive. And of course the family was delighted to have her back again. They thought, still, that she had succumbed to a severe black mood as a consequence of Aaron's death, and she could not tell them otherwise.

Yes, Veronica thought, a dozen times a day, I *am* grateful to be alive.

And then one afternoon as she was being driven to the Falls for tea with an elderly aunt, she saw the Lancia Lambda approaching—saw it appear around a turn in the road, blankly regal, imperious, bearing down upon her with the authority of an image out of a dream. She immediately rapped on the glass partition and told the chauffeur to stop.

So Norst braked, and stopped his car, and came over to see her. He was wearing white. His hair and goatee and eyes were as black as ever, and his smile rather more hesitant than she recalled. Her lover? Her husband? This stranger? . . . He had heard, he said in a nervous murmur, of her illness. Evidently she had been hospitalized, and had been *very* ill. As soon as he returned from Sweden he had come up to see her, and had taken rooms at the Lake Avernus Inn. What a delight it was to see her, like this, so suddenly, with no warning—to see her looking so supremely healthy, and as beautiful as ever—

He broke off, and took her hand, squeezing it hard. A flame seemed to pass over his vision. He trembled, his breathing grew rapid and shallow, she felt, keenly, the near-paroxysm of his desire for her, and in that instant she knew that she loved him, and had loved him all along. He managed to disguise his agitation by playfully pulling her glove down an inch or two, and kissing the back of her hand; but even this gesture became a passionate one. Exclaiming, Veronica snatched her hand away.

They stared at each other for several minutes, in silence. She saw that he was indeed the man who had come to her in her dreams—and that he fully recognized her as well. But what was there to *say?* He was staying at Lake Avernus, a mere twelve miles away; naturally they would see each other; they would, perhaps, resume their daylight courtship. It was harmless, and it gave them something to do during the long daylight hours. Norst was asking about her family, and about her health; and about her nights. Did she sleep well, now? Did she wake fully rested? And would she, just for tonight, wear the bloodstone to bed? . . . and leave the window of her room open? Just for tonight, he said.

She laughed, her face burning, and fully meant to say no; but somehow she did not say no.

She was gazing with a bemused smile at the teethmarks on the back of her hand, which were filling in slowly with blood.

·······III·······
THE SCIENCE FICTION VAMPIRE

Vampires were born of myth and superstition, but our modern age demands more rational explanations. It is no longer enough to blame vampirism on supernatural curses and demonic possession. A more skeptical, secular era cannot help but look for scientific justifications for old-fashioned horrors. That habit of mind has, of course, also produced a vast audience for science fiction tales that give ingenious explanations, based on real science, for phenomenal events.

It is not to be wondered at, then, that since the 1950s and the dawn of the atomic age, science writers should have been tempted to offer up explanations for the existence of vampires. While previously explained as creatures of Satan eager to kill and to damn humankind, vampires are now described as the products of bacteria, mutation, and evolution, and even as extraterrestrials.

Two of the best scientific vampire novels, *I Am Legend* by Richard Matheson (1954) and *The Vampire Tapestry* by Suzy McKee Charnas (1980), are excerpted in this volume. Other memorable books include *Darker Than You Think* by Jack Williamson (1940), which imaginatively employs quantum mechanics to rationalize werewolves, witchcraft, and vampires; and *Sabella, or The Bloodstone*, by Tanith Lee (1980), which transplants an enigmatic female vampire to the scarlet hills of Mars. Like Charnas' *The Vampire Tapestry*, both *The Hunger*, by Whitley Strieber (1981, excerpted here), and *Fever Dream*, by George R. R. Martin (1982), present vampires as an entirely different species who appear to have evolved alongside humans.

Of the following stories, the most explanatory is the selection from *I Am Legend*. "Unicorn Tapestry" moves the dialogue of explanation into the psychotherapist's office, while Susan Casper's "A Child of Darkness" leaves the reader hovering between explanation and wonder. "Shambleau," written by a science fiction author and set on another planet, deals with the classical male fear of woman.

C. L. MOORE
(1911–1987)

Catherine Lucille Moore was born in Indianapolis, Indiana where, because she was a sickly child, she became an early and avid reader.

Moore gained instant fame and recognition for her first published story, "Shambleau," which appeared in Weird Tales *in 1933. She then went on to use its main character, Northwest Smith, in later novels. In 1949, Moore married Henry Kuttner, himself a famous science fiction writer. Thus began a prolific partnership; they published dozens of novels both separately and together. Kuttner's wit and powerful ideas complemented Moore's talents of fluency and precision. They often worked together under pseudonyms, the most famous being Lewis Padgett and Laurence O'Donnell. The popular* Clash By Night *(1943) was written by Moore alone (under the O'Donnell pseudonym); the sequel,* Fury, *a collaboration between the two writers, was set after holocaust in cities under the sea of Venus.*

Moore was the more prestigious writer in their partnership, though her husband received much of the credit. Her contribution can be accurately judged from the collection The Best of C. L. Moore *(1975). Other collections in which her work appears include* A Gnome There Was *(1950),* Robots Have No Tails *(1952),* Line To Tomorrow *(1954),* No Boundaries *(1955), and* Clash By Night and Other Stories *(1980). After Kuttner's death in 1958, Moore began writing for television, including scripts for such series as* Maverick *and* 77 Sunset Strip, *until she remarried in 1963 and abandoned her writing career.*

In "Shambleau," the tale that follows, we see what canny use Moore makes of classical mythology. Her otherworldly creature is clearly modeled on the Greek story of Medusa, one of the three Gorgons whose hair had been transformed into a nest of serpents. Upon seeing her face, any creature would be turned into stone. Perseus was able to slay the monstrous Medusa by keeping his eyes on her reflection in his shield, never looking at her directly. In "Shambleau," Northwest Smith's friend also makes use of a mirror to help in his battle against the repulsively sweet title character.

"Shambleau" was considered at the time a strange story to be written by a woman because of its grotesque imagery and sexual innuendoes. Its daring and fresh subject matter greatly affected later science fiction writers, who were inspired by this odd tale of the first alien vampire ever to be given a voice in science fiction.

SHAMBLEAU

Man has conquered space before. You may be sure of that. *Somewhere beyond the Egyptians, in that dimness out of which come echoes of half-mythical name—Atlantis, Mu—somewhere back of history's first beginnings there must have been an age when mankind, like us today, built cities of steel to house its star-roving ships and knew the names of the planets in their own native tongues—heard Venus' people call their wet world "Sha-ardol" in that soft, sweet, slurring speech and mimicked Mars' guttural "Lakkdiz" from the harsh tongues of Mars' dryland dwellers. You may be sure of it. Man has conquered Space before, and out of that conquest faint, faint echoes run still through a world that has forgotten the very fact of a civilization which must have been as mighty as our own. There have been too many myths and legends for us to doubt it. The myth of the Medusa, for instance, can never have had its roots in the soil of Earth. That tale of the snake-haired Gorgon whose gaze turned the gazer to stone never originated about any creature that Earth nourished. And those ancient Greeks who told the story must have remembered, dimly and half believing, a tale of antiquity about some strange being from one of the outlying planets their remotest ancestors once trod.*

"Shambleau! Ha . . . Shambleau!" The wild hysteria of the mob rocketed from wall to wall of Lakkdarol's narrow streets and the storming of heavy boots over the slag-red pavement made an ominous undernote to that swelling bay, "Shambleau! Shambleau!"

Northwest Smith heard it coming and stepped into the nearest doorway, laying a wary hand on his heat-gun's grip, and his colorless eyes narrowed. Strange sounds were common enough in the streets of Earth's latest colony on Mars—a raw, red little town where anything might happen, and very often did. But Northwest Smith, whose name is known and respected in every dive and wild outpost on a dozen wild planets, was a cautious man, despite his reputation. He set his back against the wall and gripped his pistol, and heard the rising shout come nearer and nearer.

Then into his range of vision flashed a red running figure, dodging like a hunted hare from shelter to shelter in the narrow street. It was a girl—a berry-brown girl in a single tattered garment whose scarlet burnt the eyes with its brilliance. She ran wearily, and he could hear her gasping breath from where he stood. As she came into view he saw her hesitate and lean one hand against the wall for support, and glance wildly around for shelter. She must not have seen him in the depths of the doorway, for as the bay of he mob grew louder and the pounding feet sounded almost at the corner she gave a despairing little moan and dodged into the recess at his very side.

When she saw him standing there, tall and leather-brown, hand on his heat-gun, she sobbed once, inarticulately, and collapsed at his feet, a huddle of burning scarlet and bare, brown limbs.

Smith had not seen her face, but she was a girl, and sweetly made and in danger; and though he had not the reputation of a chivalrous man, something in her hopeless huddle at his feet touched that chord of sympathy for the underdog that stirs in every Earthman, and he pushed her gently into the corner behind him and jerked out his gun, just as the first of the running mob rounded the corner.

It was a motley crowd, Earthmen and Martians and a sprinkling of Venusian swampmen and strange, nameless denizens of unnamed planets—a typical Lakkdarol mob. When the first of them turned the corner and saw the empty street before them there was a faltering in the rush and the foremost spread out and began to search the doorways on both sides of the street.

"Looking for something?" Smith's sardonic call sounded clear above the clamor of the mob.

They turned. The shouting died for a moment as they took in the scene before them—tall Earthman in the space-explorer's leathern garb, all one color from the burning of savage suns save for the sinister pallor of his no-colored eyes in a scarred and resolute face, gun in his steady hand and the scarlet girl crouched behind him, panting.

The foremost of the crowd—a burly Earthman in tattered leather from which the Patrol insignia had been ripped away—stared for a moment with a strange expression of incredulity on his face over-spreading the savage exultation of the chase. Then he let loose a deep-throated bellow, "Shambleau!" and lunged forward. Behind him the mob took up the cry again, "Shambleau! Shambleau! Shambleau!" and surged after.

Smith, lounging negligently against the wall, arms folded and gun-hand draped over his left forearm, looked incapable of swift motion, but at the leader's first forward step the pistol swept in a practiced half-circle and the dazzle of blue-white heat leaping from its muzzle seared an arc in the slag pavement at his feet. It was an old gesture, and not a man in the crowd but understood it. The foremost recoiled swiftly against the surge of those in the rear, and for a moment there was confusion as the two tides met and struggled. Smith's mouth curled into a grim curve as he watched. The man in the mutilated Patrol uniform lifted a threatening fist and stepped to the very edge of the deadline, while the crowd rocked to and fro behind him.

"Are you crossing that line?" queried Smith in an ominously gentle voice.

'We want the girl!"

"Come and get her!" Recklessly Smith grinned into his face. He saw danger there, but his defiance was not the foolhardy gesture it seemed. An expert psychologist of mobs from long experience, he sensed no murder here. Not a gun had appeared in any hand in the crowd. They desired the girl with an inexplicable bloodthirstiness he was at a loss to understand, but toward himself he sensed no such fury. A mauling he might expect, but his life was in no danger. Guns would have appeared before now if they were coming out at all. So he grinned in the man's angry face and leaned lazily against the wall.

Behind their self-appointed leader the crowd milled impatiently, and threatening voices began to rise again. Smith heard the girl moan at his feet.

"What do you want with her?" he demanded.

"She's Shambleau! Shambleau, you fool! Kick her out of there—we'll take care of her!"

"I'm taking care of her," drawled Smith.

"She's Shambleau, I tell you! Damn your hide, man, we never let those things live! Kick her out here!"

The repeated name had no meaning to him, but Smith's innate stubbornness rose defiantly as the crowd surged forward to the very edge of the arc, their clamor growing louder. "Shambleau! Kick her out here! Give us Shambleau! Shambleau!"

Smith dropped his indolent pose like a cloak and planted both feet wide, swinging up his gun threateningly. "Keep back!" he yelled. "She's mine! Keep back!"

He had no intention of using that heat-beam. He knew by now that they would not kill him unless he started the gunplay himself, and he did not mean to give up his life for any girl alive. But a severe mauling he expected, and he braced himself instinctively as the mob heaved within itself.

To his astonishment a thing happened then that he had never known to happen before. At his shouted defiance the foremost of the mob—those who had heard him clearly—drew back a little, not in alarm but evidently surprised. The ex-Patrolman said, "Yours! She's *yours?*" in a voice from which puzzlement crowded out the anger.

Smith spread his booted legs wide before the crouching figure and flourished his gun.

"Yes," he said. "And I'm keeping her! Stand back there!"

The man stared at him wordlessly, and horror, disgust, and incredulity mingled on his weather-beaten face. The incredulity triumphed for a moment and he said again,

"*Yours!*"

Smith nodded defiance.

The man stepped back suddenly, unutterable contempt in his very pose. He waved an arm to the crowd and said loudly, "It's—his!" and the press melted away, gone silent, too, and the look of contempt spread from face to face.

The ex-Patrolman spat on the slag-paved street and turned his back indifferently. "Keep her, then," he advised briefly over one shoulder. "But don't let her out again in this town!"

Smith stared in perplexity almost open-mouthed as the suddenly scornful mob began to break up. His mind was in a whirl. That such bloodthirsty animosity should vanish in a breath he could not believe. And the curious mingling of contempt and disgust on the faces he saw baffled him even more. Lakkdarol was anything but a puritan town—it did not enter his head for a moment that his claiming the brown girl as his own had caused that strangely shocked revulsion to spread through the crowd. No, it was something more deeply-rooted than that. Instinctive, instant disgust had been in the faces he saw—they would have looked less so if he had admitted cannibalism or *Pharol*-worship.

And they were leaving his vicinity as swiftly as if whatever unknowing sin he had committed were contagious. The street was emptying as rapidly as it had filled. He saw a sleek Venusian glance back over his shoulder as he turned the corner and sneer, "Shambleau!" and the word awoke a new line of speculation in Smith's mind. Shambleau! Vaguely of French origin, it must be. And strange enough to hear it from the lips of Venusians and Martian drylanders, but it was their use of it that puzzled him more. "We never let those things live," the ex-Patrolman had said. It reminded him dimly of something . . . an ancient line from some writing in his own tongue . . . "Thou shalt not suffer a witch to live." He smiled to himself at the similarity, and simultaneously was aware of the girl at his elbow.

She had risen soundlessly. He turned to face her, sheathing his gun, and stared at first with curiosity and then in the entirely frank openness with which men regard that which is not wholly human. For she was not. He knew it at a glance, though the brown, sweet body was shaped like a woman's and she wore the garment of scarlet—he saw it was leather— with an ease that few unhuman beings achieve toward clothing. He knew it from the moment he looked into her eyes, and a shiver of unrest went over him as he met them. They were frankly green as young grass, with slit-like, feline pupils that pulsed unceasingly, and there was a look of dark, animal wisdom in their depths—that look of the beast which sees more than man.

There was no hair upon her face—neither brows nor lashes, and he would have sworn that the tight scarlet turban bound around her head covered baldness. She had three fingers and a thumb, and her feet had four digits apiece too, and all sixteen of them were tipped with round claws that sheathed back into the flesh like a cat's. She ran her tongue over her lips—a thin, pink, flat tongue as feline as her eyes—and spoke

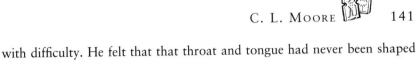

with difficulty. He felt that that throat and tongue had never been shaped for human speech.

"Not—afraid now," she said softly, and her little teeth were white and pointed as a kitten's.

"What did they want you for?" he asked her curiously. "What had you done? Shambleau . . . is that your name?"

"I—not talk your—speech," she demurred hesitantly.

"Well, try to—I want to know. Why were they chasing you? Will you be safe on the street now, or hadn't you better get indoors somewhere? They looked dangerous."

"I—go with you." She brought it out with difficulty.

"Say you!" Smith grinned. "What are you, anyhow? You look like a kitten to me."

"Shambleau." She said it somberly.

"Where d'you live? Are you a Martian?"

"I come from—from far—from long ago—far country——"

"Wait!" laughed Smith. "You're getting your wires crossed. You're not a Martian?"

She drew herself up very straight beside him, lifting the turbaned head, and there was something queenly in the pose of her.

"Martian?" she said scornfully. "My people—are—are—you have no word. Your speech—hard for me."

"What's yours? I might know it—try me."

She lifted her head and met his eyes squarely, and there was in hers a subtle amusement—he could have sworn it.

"Some day I—speak to you in—my own language," she promised, and the pink tongue flicked out over her lips, swiftly, hungrily.

Approaching footsteps on the red pavement interrupted Smith's reply. A dryland Martian came past, reeling a little and exuding an aroma of *segir*-whisky, the Venusian brand. When he caught the red flash of the girl's tatters he turned his head sharply, and as his *segir*-steeped brain took in the fact of her presence he lurched toward the recess unsteadily, bawling, "Shambleau, by *Pharol!* Shambleau!" and reached out a clutching hand.

Smith struck it aside contemptuously.

"On your way, drylander," he advised.

The man drew back and stared, blear-eyed.

"Yours, eh?" he croaked. "*Zut!* You're welcome to it!" And like the ex-Patrolman before him he spat on the pavement and turned away, muttering harshly in the blasphemous tongue of the drylands.

Smith watched him shuffle off, and there was a crease between his colorless eyes, a nameless unease rising within him.

"Come on," he said abruptly to the girl. "If this sort of thing is going to happen we'd better get indoors. Where shall I take you?"

"With—you," she murmured.

He stared down into the flat green eyes. Those ceaselessly pulsing pupils disturbed him, but it seemed to him, vaguely, that behind the animal shallows of her gaze was a shutter—a closed barrier that might at any moment open to reveal the very deeps of that dark knowledge he sensed there.

Roughly he said again, "Come on, then," and stepped down into the street.

She pattered along a pace or two behind him, making no effort to keep up with his long strides, and though Smith—as men know from Venus to Jupiter's moons—walks as softly as a cat, even in spacemen's boots, the girl at his heels slid like a shadow over the rough pavement, making so little sound that even the lightness of his footsteps was loud in the empty street.

Smith chose the less frequented ways of Lakkdarol, and somewhat shamefacedly thanked his nameless gods that his lodgings were not far away, for the few pedestrians he met turned and stared after the two with that by now familiar mingling of horror and contempt which he was as far as ever from understanding.

The room he had engaged was a single cubicle in a lodging-house on the edge of the city. Lakkdarol, raw camp-town that it was in those days, could have furnished little better anywhere within its limits, and Smith's errand there was not one he wished to advertise. He had slept in worse places than this before, and knew that he would do so again.

There was no one in sight when he entered, and the girl slipped up the stairs at his heels and vanished through the door, shadowy, unseen by anyone in the house. Smith closed the door and leaned his broad shoulders against the panels, regarding her speculatively.

She took in what little the room had to offer in a glance—frowsy bed, rickety table, mirror hanging unevenly and cracked against the wall, unpainted chairs—a typical camp-town room in an Earth settlement abroad. She accepted its poverty in that single glance, dismissed it, then crossed to the window and leaned out for a moment, gazing across the low roof-tops toward the barren countryside beyond, red slag under the late afternoon sun.

"You can stay here," said Smith abruptly, "until I leave town. I'm waiting here for a friend to come in from Venus. Have you eaten?"

"Yes," said the girl quickly. "I shall—need no—food for—a while."

"Well—" Smith glanced around the room. "I'll be in sometime tonight. You can go or stay just as you please. Better lock the door behind me."

With no more formality than that he left her. The door closed and he heard the key turn, and smiled to himself. He did not expect, then, ever to see her again.

He went down the steps and out into the late-slanting sunlight with a mind so full of other matters that the brown girl receded very quickly into the background. Smith's errand in Lakkdarol, like most of his errands, is better not spoken of. Man lives as he must, and Smith's living was a perilous affair outside the law and ruled by the ray-gun only. It is enough to say that the shipping-port and its cargoes outbound interested him deeply just now, and that the friend he awaited was Yarol the Venusian, in that swift little Edsel ship the *Maid* that can flash from world to world with a derisive speed that laughs at Patrol boats and leaves pursuers floundering in the ether far behind. Smith and Yarol and the *Maid* were a trinity that had caused the Patrol leaders much worry and many gray hairs in the past, and the future looked very bright to Smith himself that evening as he left his lodging-house.

Lakkdoral roars by night, as Earthmen's camp-towns have a way of doing on every planet where Earth's outposts are, and it was beginning lustily as Smith went down among the awakening lights toward the center of town. His business there does not concern us. He mingled with the crowds where the lights were brightest, and there was the click of ivory counters and the jingle of silver, and red *segir* gurgled invitingly from black Venusian bottles, and much later Smith strolled homeward under the moving moons of Mars, and if the street wavered a little under his feet now and then—why, that is only understandable. Not even Smith could drink red *segir* at every bar from the *Martian Lamb* to the *New Chicago* and remain entirely steady on his feet. But he found his way back with very little difficulty—considering—and spent a good five minutes hunting for his key before he remembered he had left it in the inner lock for the girl.

He knocked then, and there was no sound of footsteps from within, but in a few moments the latch clicked and the door swung open. She retreated soundlessly before him as he entered, and took up her favorite place against the window, leaning back on the sill and outlined against the starry sky beyond. The room was in darkness.

Smith flipped the switch by the door and then leaned back against the panels, steadying himself. The cool night air had sobered him a little, and his head was clear enough—liquor went to Smith's feet, not his head, or he would never have come this far along the lawless way he had chosen. He lounged against the door now and regarded the girl in the sudden glare of the bulbs, blinded a little as much at the scarlet of her clothing as at the light.

"So you stayed," he said.

"I—waited," she answered softly, leaning farther back against the sill and clasping the rough wood with slim, three-fingered hands, pale brown against the darkness.

"Why?"

She did not answer that, but her mouth curved into a slow smile. On a woman it would have been reply enough—provocative, daring. On Shambleau there was something pitiful and horrible in it—so human on the face of one half-animal. And yet . . . that sweet brown body curving so softly from the tatters of scarlet leather—the velvety texture of that brownness—the white-flashing smile. . . . Smith was aware of a stirring excitement within him. After all—time would be hanging heavy now until Yarol came. . . . Speculatively he allowed the steel-pale eyes to wander over her, with a slow regard that missed nothing. And when he spoke he was aware that his voice had deepened a little. . . .

"Come here," he said.

She came forward slowly, on bare clawed feet that made no sound on the floor, and stood before him with downcast eyes and mouth trembling in that pitifully human smile. He took her by the shoulders—velvety soft shoulders, of a creamy smoothness that was not the texture of human flesh. A little tremor went over her, perceptibly, at the contact of his hands. Northwest Smith caught his breath suddenly and dragged her to him . . . sweet yielding brownness in the circle of his arms . . . heard her own breath catch and quicken as her velvety arms closed about his neck And then he was looking down into her face, very near, and the green animal eyes met his with the pulsing pupils and the flicker of—something—deep behind their shallows—and through the rising clamor of his blood, even as he stooped his lips to hers, Smith felt something deep within him shudder away—inexplicable, instinctive, revolted. What it might be he had no words to tell, but the very touch of her was suddenly loathsome—so soft and velvet and unhuman—and it might have been an animal's face that lifted itself to his mouth—the dark knowledge looked hungrily from the darkness of those slit pupils—and for a mad instant he knew that same wild, feverish revulsion he had seen in the faces of the mob. . . .

"God!" he gasped, a far more ancient invocation against evil than he realized, then or ever, and he ripped her arms from his neck, swung her away with such a force that she reeled half across the room. Smith fell back against the door, breathing heavily, and stared at her while the wild revolt died slowly within him.

She had fallen to the floor beneath the window, and as she lay there against the wall with bent head he saw, curiously, that her turban had slipped—the turban that he had been so sure covered baldness—and a lock of scarlet hair fell below the binding leather, hair as scarlet as her garment, as unhumanly red as her eyes were unhumanly green. He stared, and shook his head dizzily and stared again, for it seemed to him that the thick lock of crimson had moved, *squirmed* of itself against her cheek.

At the contact of it her hands flew up and she tucked it away with a very human gesture and then dropped her head again into her hands. And from the deep shadow of her fingers he thought she was staring up at him covertly.

Smith drew a deep breath and passed a hand across his forehead. The inexplicable moment had gone as quickly as it came—too swiftly for him

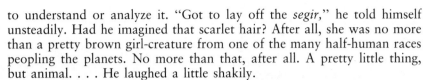

to understand or analyze it. "Got to lay off the *segir*," he told himself unsteadily. Had he imagined that scarlet hair? After all, she was no more than a pretty brown girl-creature from one of the many half-human races peopling the planets. No more than that, after all. A pretty little thing, but animal. . . . He laughed a little shakily.

"No more of that," he said. "God knows I'm no angel, but there's got to be a limit somewhere. Here." He crossed to the bed and sorted out a pair of blankets from the untidy heap, tossing them to the far corner of the room. "You can sleep there."

Wordlessly she rose from the floor and began to rearrange the blankets, the uncomprehending resignation of the animal eloquent in every line of her.

Smith had a strange dream that night. He thought he had awakened to a room full of darkness and moonlight and moving shadows, for the nearer moon of Mars was racing through the sky and everything on the planet below her was endued with a restless life in the dark. And something . . . some nameless, unthinkable *thing* . . . was coiled about his throat . . . something like a soft snake, wet and warm. It lay loose and light about his neck . . . and it was moving gently, very gently, with a soft, caressive pressure that sent little thrills of delight through every nerve and fiber of him, a perilous delight—beyond physical pleasure, deeper than joy of the mind. That warm softness was caressing the very roots of his soul with a terrible intimacy. The ecstasy of it left him weak, and yet he knew—in a flash of knowledge born of this impossible dream—that the soul should not be handled. . . . And with that knowledge a horror broke upon him, turning the pleasure into a rapture of revulsion, hateful, horrible—but still most foully sweet. He tried to lift his hands and tear the dream-monstrosity from his throat—tried but half-heartedly; for though his soul was revolted to its very deeps, yet the delight of his body was so great that his hands all but refused the attempt. But when at last he tried to lift his arms a cold shock went over him and he found that he could not stir . . . his body lay stony as marble beneath the blankets, a living marble that shuddered with a dreadful delight through every rigid vein.

The revulsion grew strong upon him as he struggled against the paralyzing dream—a struggle of soul against sluggish body—titanically, until the moving dark was streaked with blankness that clouded and closed about him at last and he sank back into the oblivion from which he had awakened.

Next morning, when the bright sunlight shining through Mars' clear thin air awakened him, Smith lay for a while trying to remember. The dream had been more vivid than reality, but he could not now quite recall . . . only that it had been more sweet and horrible than anything else in life. He lay puzzling for a while, until a soft sound from the corner aroused him from his thoughts and he sat up to see the girl lying in a catlike coil on her blankets, watching him with round, grave eyes. He regarded her somewhat ruefully.

"Morning," he said. "I've just had the devil of a dream. . . . Well, hungry?"

She shook her head silently, and he could have sworn there was a covert gleam of strange amusement in her eyes.

He stretched and yawned, dismissing the nightmare temporarily from his mind.

"What am I going to do with you?" he inquired, turning to more immediate matters. "I'm leaving here in a day or two and I can't take you along, you know. Where'd you come from in the first place?"

Again she shook her head.

"Not telling? Well, it's your own business. You can stay here until I give up the room. From then on you'll have to do your own worrying."

He swung his feet to the floor and reached for his clothes.

Ten minutes later, slipping the heat-gun into its holster at his thigh, Smith turned to the girl. "There's food-concentrate in that box on the table. It ought to hold you until I get back. And you'd better lock the door again after I've gone."

Her wide, unwavering stare was his only answer, and he was not sure she had understood, but at any rate the lock clicked after him as before, and he went down the steps with a faint grin on his lips.

The memory of last night's extraordinary dream was slipping from him, as such memories do, and by the time he had reached the street, the girl and the dream and all of yesterday's happenings were blotted out by the sharp necessities of the present.

Again the intricate business that had brought him here claimed his attention. He went about it to the exclusion of all else, and there was a good reason behind everything he did from the moment he stepped out into the street until the time when he turned back again at evening; though had one chosen to follow him during the day his apparently aimless rambling through Lakkdarol would have seemed very pointless.

He must have spent two hours at the least idling by the space-port, watching with sleepy, colorless eyes the ships that came and went, the passengers, the vessels lying at wait, the cargoes—particularly the cargoes. He made the rounds of the town's saloons once more, consuming many glasses of varied liquors in the course of the day and engaging in idle conversation with men of all races and worlds, usually in their own languages, for Smith was a linguist of repute among his contemporaries. He heard the gossip of the spaceways, news from a dozen planets of a thousand different events. He heard the latest joke about the Venusian Emperor and the latest report on the Chino-Aryan war and the latest song hot from the lips of Rose Robertson, whom every man on the civilized planets adored as "the Georgia Rose." He passed the day quite profitably, for his own purposes, which do not concern us now, and it was not until

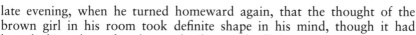

late evening, when he turned homeward again, that the thought of the brown girl in his room took definite shape in his mind, though it had been lurking there, formless and submerged, all day.

He had no idea what comprised her usual diet, but he bought a can of New York roast beef and one of Venusian frog-broth and a dozen fresh canal-apples and two pounds of that Earth lettuce that grows so vigorously in the fertile canal-soil of Mars. He felt that she must surely find something to her liking in this broad variety of edibles, and—for his day had been very satisfactory—he hummed *The Green Hills of Earth* to himself in a surprisingly good baritone as he climbed the stairs.

The door was locked, as before, and he was reduced to kicking the lower panels gently with his boot, for his arms were full. She opened the door with that softness that was characteristic of her and stood regarding him in the semi-darkness as he stumbled to the table with his load. The room was unlit again.

"Why don't you turn on the lights?" he demanded irritably after he had barked his shin on the chair by the table in an effort to deposit his burden there.

"Light and—dark—they are alike—to me," she murmured.

"Cat eyes, eh? Well, you look the part. Here, I've brought you some dinner. Take your choice. Fond of roast beef? Or how abut a little frog-broth?"

She shook her head and backed away a step.

"No," she said. "I can not—eat your food."

Smith's brows wrinkled. "Didn't you have any of the food tablets?"

Again the red turban shook negatively.

"Then you haven't had anything for—why, more than twenty-four hours! You must be starved."

"Not hungry," she denied.

"What can I find for you to eat, then? There's time yet if I hurry. You've got to eat, child."

"I shall—eat," she said softly. "Before long—I shall—feed. Have no—worry."

She turned away then and stood at the window, looking out over the moonlit landscape as if to end the conversation. Smith cast her a puzzled glance as he opened the can of roast beef. There had been an odd undernote in that assurance that, undefinably, he did not like. And the girl had teeth and tongue and presumably a fairly human digestive system, to judge from her human form. It was nonsense for her to pretend that he could find nothing that she could eat. She must have had some of the food concentrate after all, he decided, prying up the thermos lid of the inner container to release the long-sealed savor of the hot meal inside.

"Well, if you won't eat you won't," he observed philosophically as he poured hot broth and diced beef into the dishlike lid of the thermos can and extracted the spoon from its hiding-place between the inner and outer receptacles. She turned a little to watch him as he pulled up a rickety chair and sat down to the food, and after a while the realization that her green gaze was fixed so unwinkingly upon him made the man nervous, and he said between bites of creamy canal-apple, "Why don't you try a little of this? It's good."

"The food—I eat is—better," her soft voice told him in its hesitant murmur, and again he felt rather than heard a faint undernote of unpleasantness in the words. A sudden suspicion struck him as he pondered on that last remark—some vague memory of horror-tales told about campfires in the past—and he swung round in the chair to look at her, a tiny, creeping fear unaccountably arising. There had been that in her words—in her unspoken words, that menaced. . . .

She stood up beneath his gaze demurely, wide green eyes with their pulsing pupils meeting his without a falter But her mouth was scarlet, and her teeth were sharp. . . .

"What food do you eat?" he demanded. And then, after a pause, very softly, "Blood?"

She stared at him for a moment, uncomprehending; then something like amusement curled her lips and she said scornfully, "You think me—vampire, eh? No—I am Shambleau!"

Unmistakably there were scorn and amusement in her voice at the suggestion, but as unmistakably she knew what he meant—accepted it as a logical suspicion—vampires! Fairy tales—but fairy tales this unhuman, outland creature was most familiar with. Smith was not a credulous man, nor a superstitious one, but he had seen too many strange things himself to doubt that the wildest legend might have a basis of fact And there was something namelessly strange about her. . . .

He puzzled over it for a while between deep bites of the canal-apple. And though he wanted to question her about a great many things, he did not, for he knew how futile it would be.

He said nothing more until the meat was finished and another canal-apple had followed the first, and he had cleared away the meal by the simple expedient of tossing the empty can out of the window. Then he lay back in the chair and surveyed her from half-closed eyes, colorless in a face tanned like saddle-leather. And again he was conscious of the brown, soft curves of her, velvety—subtle arcs and planes of smooth flesh under the tatters of scarlet leather. Vampire she might be, unhuman she certainly was, but desirable beyond words as she sat submissive beneath his low regard, her red-turbaned head bent, her clawed fingers lying in her lap. They sat very still for a while, and the silence throbbed between them.

She was so like a woman—an Earth woman—sweet and submissive and demure, and softer than soft fur, if he could forget the three-fingered claws and the pulsing eyes—and that deeper strangeness beyond words. . . . (Had he dreamed that red lock of hair that moved? Had it been *segir* that woke the wild revulsion he knew when he held her in his

arms? Why had the mob so thirsted for her?) He sat and stared, and despite the mystery of her and the half-suspicions that thronged his mind—for she was so beautifully soft and curved under those revealing tatters—he slowly realized that his pulses were mounting, became aware of a kindling within . . . brown girl-creature with downcast eyes . . . and then the lids lifted and the green flatness of a cat's gaze met his, and last night's revulsion woke swiftly again, like a warning bell that clanged as their eyes met—animal, after all, too sleek and soft for humanity, and that inner strangeness. . . .

Smith shrugged and sat up. His failings were legion, but the weakness of the flesh was not among the major ones. He motioned the girl to her pallet of blankets in the corner and turned to his own bed.

From deeps of sound sleep he awoke much later. He awoke suddenly and completely, and with that inner excitement that presages something momentous. He awoke to brilliant moonlight, turning the room so bright that he could see the scarlet of the girl's rags as she sat up on her pallet. She was awake, she was sitting with her shoulder half turned to him and her head bent, and some warning instinct crawled coldly up his spine as he watched what she was doing. And yet it was a very ordinary thing for a girl to do—any girl, anywhere. She was unbinding her turban. . . .

He watched, not breathing, a presentiment of something horrible stirring in his brain, inexplicably. . . . The red folds loosened, and—he knew then that he had not dreamed—again a scarlet lock swung down against her cheek . . . a hair, was it? a lock of hair? . . . . thick as a thick worm it fell, plumply, against that smooth cheek . . . more scarlet than blood and thick as a crawling worm . . . and like a worm it crawled.

Smith rose on an elbow, not realizing the motion, and fixed an unwinking stare, with a sort of sick, fascinated incredulity, on that—that lock of hair. He had not dreamed. Until now he had taken it for granted that it was the *segir* which had made it seem to move on that evening before. But now . . . it was lengthening, stretching, moving of itself. It must be hair, but it *crawled*; with a sickening life of its own it squirmed down against her cheek, caressingly, revoltingly, impossibly.

Wet, it was, and round and thick and shining. . . .

She unfastened the last fold and whipped the turban off. From what he saw then Smith would have turned his eyes away—and he had looked on dreadful things before, without flinching—but he could not stir. He could only lie there on his elbow staring at the mass of scarlet, squirming—worms, hair, what?—that writhed over her head in a dreadful mockery of ringlets. And it was lengthening, falling, somehow growing before his eyes, down over her shoulders in a spilling cascade, a mass that even at the beginning could never have been hidden under the skull-tight turban she had worn. He was beyond wondering, but he realized that. And still it squirmed and lengthened and fell, and she shook it out in a horrible

travesty of a woman shaking out her unbound hair—until the unspeakable tangle of it—twisting, writhing, obscenely scarlet—hung to her waist and beyond, and still lengthened, an endless mass of crawling horror that until now, somehow, impossibly, had been hidden under the tight-bound turban. It was like a nest of blind, restless red worms . . . it was—it was like naked entrails endowed with an unnatural aliveness, terrible beyond words.

Smith lay in the shadows, frozen without and within in a sick numbness that came of utter shock and revulsion.

She shook out the obscene, unspeakable tangle over her shoulders, and somehow he knew that she was going to turn in a moment and that he must meet her eyes. The thought of that meeting stopped his heart with dread, more awfully than anything else in this nightmare horror; for nightmare it must be, surely. But he knew without trying that he could not wrench his eyes away—the sickened fascination of that sight held him motionless, and somehow there was a certain beauty. . . .

Her head was turning. The crawling awfulness rippled and squirmed at the motion, writhing thick and wet and shining over the soft brown shoulders about which they fell now in obscene cascades that all but hid her body. Her head was turning. Smith lay numb. And very slowly he saw the round of her cheek foreshorten and her profile come into view, all the scarlet horrors twisting ominously, and the profile shortened in turn and her full face came slowly round toward the bed—moonlight shining brilliantly as day on the pretty girl-face, demure and sweet, framed in tangled obscenity that crawled. . . .

The green eyes met his. He felt a perceptible shock, and a shudder rippled down his paralyzed spine, leaving an icy numbness in its wake. He felt the goose-flesh rising. But that numbness and cold horror he scarcely realized, for the green eyes were locked with his in a long, long look that somehow presaged nameless things—not altogether unpleasant things—the voiceless voice of her mind assailing him with little murmurous promises. . . .

For a moment he went down into a blind abyss of submission; and then somehow the very sight of that obscenity in eyes that did not then realize they saw it, was dreadful enough to draw him out of the seductive darkness . . . the sight of her crawling and alive with unnamable horror.

She rose, and down about her in a cascade fell the squirming scarlet of—of what grew upon her head. It fell in a long, alive cloak to her bare feet on the floor, hiding her in a wave of dreadful, wet, writhing life. She put up her hands and like a swimmer she parted the waterfall of it, tossing the masses back over her shoulders to reveal her own brown body, sweetly curved. She smiled exquisitely, and in starting waves back from her forehead and down about her in a hideous background writhed the snaky wetness of her living tresses. And Smith knew that he looked upon Medusa.

The knowledge of that—the realization of vast backgrounds reaching into misted history—shook him out of his frozen horror for a moment, and in that moment he met her eyes again, smiling, green as glass in the moonlight, half hooded under drooping lids. Through the twisting scarlet she held out her arms. And there was something soul-shakingly desirable about her, so that all the blood surged to his head suddenly and he stumbled to his feet like a sleeper in a dream as she swayed toward him, infinitely graceful, infinitely sweet in her cloak of living horror.

And somehow there was beauty in it, the wet scarlet writhings with moonlight sliding and shining along the thick, worm-round tresses and losing itself in the masses only to glint again and move silvery along writhing tendrils—an awful, shuddering beauty more dreadful than any ugliness could be.

But all this, again, he but half realized, for the insidious murmur was coiling again through his brain, promising, caressing, alluring, sweeter than honey; and the green eyes that held his were clear and burning like the depths of a jewel, and behind the pulsing slits of darkness he was staring into a greater dark that held all things. . . . He had known—dimly he had known when he first gazed into those flat animal shallows that behind them lay this—all beauty and terror, all horror and delight, in the infinite darkness upon which her eyes opened like windows, paned with emerald glass.

Her lips moved, and in a murmur that blended indistinguishably with the silence and the sway of her body and the dreadful sway of her—her hair—she whispered—very softly, very passionately, "I shall speak to you now—in my own tongue—oh, beloved!"

And in her living cloak she swayed to him, the murmur swelling, seductive and caressing in his innermost brain—promising, compelling, sweeter than sweet. His flesh crawled to the horror of her, but it was a perverted revulsion that clasped what it loathed. His arms slid round her under the sliding cloak, wet, wet and warm and hideously alive—and the sweet velvet body was clinging to his, her arms locked about his neck—and with a whisper and a rush the unspeakable horror closed about them both.

In nightmares until he died he remembered that moment when the living tresses of Shambleau first folded him in their embrace. A nauseous, smothering odor as the wetness shut around him—thick, pulsing worms clasping every inch of his body, sliding, writhing, their wetness and warmth striking through his garments as if he stood naked to their embrace.

All this in a grave instant—and after that a tangled flash of conflicting sensation before oblivion closed over him. For he remembered the dream—and knew it for nightmare reality now, and the sliding, gently moving caresses of those wet, warm worms upon his flesh was an ecstasy above words—that deeper ecstasy that strikes beyond the body and beyond the mind and tickles the very roots of the soul with unnatural delight. So he stood, rigid as marble, as helplessly stony as any of Medusa's victims in ancient legends were, while the terrible pleasure of Shambleau thrilled and shuddered through every fiber of him; through every atom of his body and the intangible atoms of what men call the soul, through all that was Smith the dreadful pleasure ran. And it was truly dreadful. Dimly he knew it, even as his body answered to the root-deep ecstasy, a foul and dreadful wooing from which his very soul shuddered away—and yet in the innermost depths of that soul some grinning traitor shivered with delight. But deeply, behind all this, he knew horror and revulsion and despair beyond telling, while the intimate caresses crawled obscenely in the secret places of his soul—knew that the soul should not be handled— and shook with the perilous pleasure through it all.

And this conflict and knowledge, this mingling of rapture and revulsion all took place in the flashing of a moment while the scarlet worms coiled and crawled upon him, sending deep, obscene tremors of that infinite pleasure into every atom that made up Smith. And he could not stir in that slimy, ecstatic embrace—and a weakness was flooding that grew deeper after each succeeding wave of intense delight, and the traitor in his soul strengthened and drowned out the revulsion—and something within him ceased to struggle as he sank wholly into a blazing darkness that was oblivion to all else but that devouring rapture. . . .

The young Veunsian climbing the stairs to his friend's lodging-room pulled out his key absent-mindedly, a pucker forming between his fine brows. He was slim, as all Venusians are, as fair and sleek as any of them, and as with most of his countrymen the look of cherubic innocence on his face was wholly deceptive. He had the face of a fallen angel, without Lucifer's majesty to redeem it; for a black devil grinned in his eyes and there were faint lines of ruthlessness and dissipation about his mouth to tell of the long years behind him that had run the gamut of experiences and made his name, next to Smith's, the most hated and the most respected in the records of the Patrol.

He mounted the stairs now with a puzzled frown between his eyes. He had come into Lakkdarol on the noon liner—the *Maid* in her hold very skillfully disguised with paint and otherwise—to find in lamentable disorder the affairs he had expected to be settled. And cautious inquiry elicited the information that Smith had not been seen for three days. That was not like his friend—he had never failed before, and the two stood to lose not only a large sum of money but also their personal safety by the inexplicable lapse on the part of Smith. Yarol could think of one solution only: fate had at last caught up with his friend. Nothing but physical disability could explain it.

Still puzzling, he fitted his key in the lock and swung the door open.

In that first moment, as the door opened, he sensed something very wrong. . . . The room was darkened, and for a while he could see nothing, but at the first breath he scented a strange, unnamable odor, half sick-

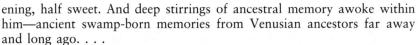

ening, half sweet. And deep stirrings of ancestral memory awoke within him—ancient swamp-born memories from Venusian ancestors far away and long ago. . . .

Yarol laid his hand on his gun, lightly, and opened the door wider. In the dimness all he could see at first was a curious mound in the far corner. . . . Then his eyes grew accustomed to the dark, and he saw it more clearly, a mound that somehow heaved and stirred within itself.

A mound of—he caught his breath sharply—a mound like a mass of entrails, living, moving, writhing with an unspeakable aliveness. Then a hot Venusian oath broke from his lips and he cleared the doorsill in a swift stride, slammed the door and set his back against it, gun ready in his hand, although his flesh crawled—for he *knew*. . . .

"Smith!" he said softly, in a voice thick with horror. "Northwest!"

The moving mass stirred—shuddered—sank back into crawling quiescence again.

"Smith! Smith!" The Venusian's voice was gentle and insistent, and it quivered a little with terror.

An impatient ripple went over the whole mass of aliveness in the corner. It stirred again, reluctantly, and then tendril by writhing tendril, it began to part itself and fall aside, and very slowly the brown of a spaceman's leather appeared beneath it, all slimed and shining.

"Smith! Northwest!" Yarol's persistent whisper came again, urgently, and with a dreamlike slowness the leather garments moved . . . a man sat up in the midst of the writhing worms, a man who once, long ago, might have been Northwest Smith. From head to foot he was slimy, from the embrace of the crawling horror about him. His face was that of some creature beyond humanity—dead-alive, fixed in a gray stare, and the look of terrible ecstasy that overspread it seemed to come from somewhere far within, a faint reflection from immeasurable distances beyond the flesh. And as there is mystery and magic in the moonlight which is after all but a reflection of the everyday sun, so in that gray face turned to the door was a terror unnamable and sweet, a reflection of ecstasy beyond the understanding of any who have known only earthly ecstasy themselves. And as he sat there turning a blank, eyeless face to Yarol the red worms writhed ceaselessly about him, very gently, with a soft, caressive motion that never slacked.

"Smith . . . come here! Smith . . . get up . . . Smith, Smith!" Yarol's whisper hissed in the silence, commanding, urgent—but he made no move to leave the door.

And with a dreadful slowness, like a man rising, Smith stood up in the nest of slimy scarlet. He swayed drunkenly on his feet, and two or three crimson tendrils came writhing up his legs to the knees and wound themselves there, supportingly, moving with a ceaseless caress that seemed to give him some hidden strength, for he said then, without inflection,

"Go away. Go away. Leave me alone." And the dead ecstatic face never changed.

"Smith!" Yarol's voice was desperate. "Smith, listen! Smith, can't you hear me?"

"Go away," the monotonous voice said. "Go away. Go away. Go—"

"Not unless you come too. Can't you hear? Smith! Smith! I'll—"

He hushed in mid-phrase, and once more the ancestral prickle of race-memory shivered down his back, for the scarlet mass was moving again, violently, rising. . . .

Yarol pressed back against the door and gripped his gun, and the name of a god he had forgotten years ago rose to his lips unbidden. For he knew what was coming next, and the knowledge was more dreadful than any ignorance could have been.

The red, writhing mass rose higher, and the tendrils parted and a human face looked out—no, half human, with green cat-eyes that shone in the dimness like lighted jewels, compellingly. . . .

Yarol breathed "Shar!" again, and flung up an arm across his face, and the tingle of meeting that green gaze for even an instant went thrilling through him perilously.

"Smith!" he called in despair. "Smith, can't you hear me?"

"Go away," said that voice that was not Smith's. "Go away."

And somehow, although he dared not look, Yarol knew that the—the other—had parted those worm-thick tresses and stood there in all the human sweetness of the brown, curved woman's body, cloaked in living horror. And he felt the eyes upon him, and something was crying insistently in his brain to lower that shielding arm. . . . He was lost—he knew it, and the knowledge gave him that courage which comes from despair. The voice in his brain was growing, swelling, deafening him with a roaring command that all but swept him before it—command to lower that arm—to meet the eyes that opened upon darkness—to submit—and a promise, murmurous and sweet and evil beyond words, of pleasure to come. . . .

But somehow he kept his head—somehow, dizzily, he was gripping his gun in his upflung hand—somehow, incredibly, crossing the narrow room with averted face, groping for Smith's shoulder. There was a moment of blind fumbling in emptiness, and then he found it, and ripped the leather that was slimy and dreadful and wet—and simultaneously he felt something loop gently about his ankle and a shock of repulsive pleasure went through him, and then another coil, and another, wound about his feet. . . .

Yarol set his teeth and gripped the shoulder hard, and his hand shuddered of itself, for the feel of that leather was slimy as the worms about his ankles, and a faint tingle of obscene delight went through him from the contact.

That caressive pressure on his legs was all he could feel, and the voice in his brain drowned out all other sounds, and his body obeyed him reluctantly—but somehow he gave one heave of tremendous effort and swung Smith, stumbling, out of that nest of horror. The twining tendrils ripped loose with a little sucking sound, and the whole mass quivered and reached after, and then Yarol forgot his friend utterly and turned his whole being to the hopeless task of freeing himself. For only a part of him was fighting now—only a part of him struggled against the twining obscenities, and in his innermost brain the sweet, seductive murmur sounded, and his body clamored to surrender. . . .

"Shar! Shar y'danis . . . Shar mor'la-rol—" prayed Yarol, gasping and half unconscious that he spoke, boy's prayers that he had forgotten years ago, and with his back half turned to the central mass he kicked desperately with his heavy boots at the red, writhing worms about him. They gave back before him, quivering and curling themselves out of reach, and though he knew that more were reaching for his throat from behind, at least he could go on struggling until he was forced to meet those eyes. . . .

He stamped and kicked and stamped again, and for one instant he was free of the slimy grip as the bruised worms curled back from his heavy feet, and he lurched away dizzily, sick with revulsion and despair as he fought off the coils, and then he lifted his eyes and saw the cracked mirror on the wall. Dimly in its reflection he could see the writhing scarlet horror behind him, cat face peering out with its demure girl-smile, dreadfully human, and all the red tendrils reaching after him. And remembrance of something he had read long ago swept incongruously over him, and the gasp of relief and hope that he gave shook for a moment the grip of the command in his brain.

Without pausing for a breath he swung the gun over his shoulder, the reflected barrel in line with the reflected horror in the mirror, and flicked the catch.

In the mirror he saw its blue flame leap in a dazzling spate across the dimness, full into the midst of that squirming, reaching mass behind him. There was a hiss and a blaze and a high, thin scream of inhuman malice and despair—the flame cut a wide arc and went out as the gun fell from his hand, and Yarol pitched forward to the floor.

Northwest Smith opened his eyes to Martian sunlight steaming thinly through the dingy window. Something wet and cold was slapping his face, and the familiar fiery sting of *segir*-whisky burnt his throat.

"Smith!" Yarol's voice was saying from far away. "N. W.! Wake up, damn you! Wake up!"

"I'm—awake," Smith managed to articulate thickly. "Wha's matter?"

Then a cup-rim was thrust against his teeth and Yarol said irritably, "Drink it, you fool!"

Smith swallowed obediently and more of the fire-hot *segir* flowed down his grateful throat. It spread a warmth through his body that awakened him from the numbness that had gripped him until now, and helped a little toward driving out the all-devouring weakness he was becoming aware of slowly. He lay still for a few minutes while the warmth of the whisky went through him, and memory sluggishly began to permeate his brain with the spread of the *segir*. Nightmare memories . . . sweet and terrible . . . memories of—

"God!" gasped Smith suddenly, and tried to sit up. Weakness smote him like a blow, and for an instant the room wheeled as he fell back against something firm and warm—Yarol's shoulder. The Venusian's arm supported him while the room steadied, and after a while he twisted a little and stared into the other's black gaze.

Yarol was holding him with one arm and finishing the mug of *segir* himself, and the black eyes met his over the rim and crinkled into sudden laughter, half hysterical after that terror that was passed.

"By *Pharol!*" gasped Yarol, choking into his mug. "By *Pharol*, N. W.! I'm never gonna let you forget this! Next time you have to drag me out of a mess I'll say—"

"Let it go," said Smith. "What's been going on? How—"

"Shambleau." Yarol's laughter died. "Shambleau! What were you doing with a thing like that?"

"What was it?" Smith asked soberly.

"Mean to say you didn't know? But where'd you find it? How—"

"Suppose you tell me first what you know," said Smith firmly. "And another swig of that *segir*, too, please. I need it."

"Can you hold the mug now? Feel better?"

"Yeah—some. I can hold it—thanks. Now go on."

"Well—I don't know just where to start. They call them Shambleau—"

"Good God, is there more than one?"

"It's a—a sort of race, I think, one of the very oldest. Where they come from nobody knows. The name sounds a little French, doesn't it? But it goes back beyond the start of history. There have always been Shambleau."

"I never heard of 'em."

"Not many people have. And those who know don't care to talk about it much."

"Well, half this town knows. I hadn't any idea what they were talking about, then. And I still don't understand, but—"

"Yes, it happens like this, sometimes. They'll appear, and the news will spread and the town will get together and hunt them down, and after that—well, the story doesn't get around very far. It's too—too unbelievable."

"But—my God, Yarol!—what was it? Where'd it come from? How—"

"Nobody knows just where they come from. Another planet—maybe some undiscovered one. Some day Venus—I know there are some rather awful legends of them handed down in our family—that's how I've heard

about it. And the minute I opened that door, awhile back—I—I think I knew that smell. . . ."

"But—what *are* they?"

"God knows. Not human, though they have the human form. Or that may be only an illusion . . . or maybe I'm crazy. I don't know. They're a species of the vampire—or maybe the vampire is a species of—of them. Their normal form must be that—that mass, and in that form they draw nourishment from the—I suppose the life-forces of men. And they take some form—usually a woman form, I think, and key you up to the highest pitch of emotion before they—begin. That's to work the life-force up to intensity so it'll be easier. . . . And they give, always, that horrible, foul pleasure as they—feed. There are some men who, if they survive the first experience, take to it like a drug—can't give it up—keep the thing with them all their lives—which isn't long—feeding it for that ghastly satisfaction. Worse than smoking *ming* or—or 'praying to *Pharol*.' "

"Yes," said Smith. "I'm beginning to understand why that crowd was so surprised and—and disgusted when I said—well, never mind. Go on."

"Did you get to talk to—to it?" asked Yarol.

"I tried to. It couldn't speak very well. I asked it where it came from and it said—'from far away and long ago'—something like that."

"I wonder. Possibly some unknown planet—but I think not. You know there are so many wild stories with some basis of fact to start from, that I've sometimes wondered—mightn't there be a lot more of even worse and wilder superstitions we've never even heard of? Things like this, blasphemous and foul, that those who know have to keep still about? Awful, fantastic things running around loose that we never hear rumors of at all!

"These things—they've been in existence for countless ages. No one knows when or where they first appeared. Those who've seen them, as we saw this one, don't talk about it. It's just one of those vague, misty rumors you find half hinted at in old books sometimes. . . . I believe they are an older race than man, spawned from ancient seed in times before ours, perhaps on planets that have gone to dust, and so horrible to man that when they are discovered the discoverers keep still about it—forget them again as quickly as they can.

"And they go back to time immemorial. I suppose you recognized the legend of Medusa? There isn't any question that the ancient Greeks knew of them. Does it mean that there have been civilizations before yours that set out from Earth and explored other planets? Or did one of the Shambleau somehow make its way into Greece three thousand years ago? If you think about it long enough you'll go off your head! I wonder how many other legends are based on things like this—things we don't suspect, things we'll never know.

"The Gorgon, Medusa, a beautiful woman with—with snakes for hair, and a gaze that turned men to stone, and Perseus finally killed her—I

remember this just by accident, N. W., and it saved your life and mine—Perseus killed her by using a mirror as he fought to reflect what he dared not look at directly. I wonder what the old Greek who first started that legend would have thought if he'd known that three thousand years later his story would save the lives of two men on another planet. I wonder what that Greek's own story was, and how he met the thing, and what happened. . . .

"Well, there's a lot we'll never know. Wouldn't the records of that race of—of *things,* whatever they are, be worth reading! Records of other planets and other ages and all the beginnings of mankind! But I don't suppose they've kept any records. I don't suppose they've even any place to keep them—from what little I know, or anyone knows about it, they're like the Wandering Jew, just bobbing up here and there at long intervals, and where they stay in the meantime I'd give my eyes to know! But I don't believe that terribly hypnotic power they have indicates any superhuman intelligence. It's their means of getting food—just like a frog's long tongue or a carnivorous flower's odor. Those are physical because the frog and the flower eat physical food. The Shambleau uses a—a mental reach to get mental food. I don't quite know how to put it. And just as a beast that eats the bodies of other animals acquires with each meal greater power over the bodies of the rest, so the Shambleau, stoking itself up with the life-forces of men, increases its power over the minds and the souls of other men. But I'm talking about things I can't define—things I'm not sure exist.

"I only know that when I felt—when those tentacles closed around my legs—I didn't want to pull loose, I felt sensations that—that—oh, I'm fouled and filthy to the very deepest part of me by that—pleasure—and yet—"

"I know," said Smith slowly. The effect of the *segir* was beginning to wear off, and weakness was washing back over him in waves, and when he spoke he was half meditating in a low voice, scarcely realizing that Yarol listened. "I know it—much better than you do—and there's something so indescribably awful that the thing emanates, something so utterly at odds with everything human—there aren't any words to say it. For a while I was a part of it, literally, sharing its thoughts and memories and emotions and hungers, and—well, it's over now and I don't remember very clearly, but the only part left free was that part of me that was but insane from the—the obscenity of the thing. And yet it was a pleasure so sweet—I think there must be some nucleus of utter evil in me—in everyone—that needs only the proper stimulus to get complete control; because even while I was sick all through from the touch of those—things—there was something in me that was—was simply gibbering with delight. . . . Because of that I saw things—and knew things—horrible, wild things I can't quite remember—visited unbelievable places, looked backward

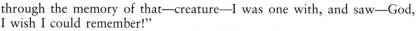

through the memory of that—creature—I was one with, and saw—God, I wish I could remember!"

"You ought to thank your God you can't," said Yarol soberly.

His voice roused Smith from the half-trance he had fallen into, and he rose on his elbow, swaying a little from weakness. The room was wavering before him, and he closed his eyes, not to see it, but he asked, "You say they—they don't turn up again? No way of finding—another?"

Yarol did not answer for a moment. He laid his hands on the other man's shoulders and pressed him back, and then sat staring down into the dark, ravaged face with a new, strange, undefinable look upon it that he had never seen there before—whose meaning he knew, too well.

"Smith," he said finally, and his black eyes for once were steady and serious, and the little grinning devil had vanished from behind them, "Smith, I've never asked your word on anything before, but I've—I've earned the right to do it now, and I'm asking you to promise me one thing."

Smith's colorless eyes met the black gaze unsteadily. Irresolution was in them, and a little fear of what that promise might be. And for just a moment Yarol was looking, not into his friend's familiar eyes, but into a wide gray blankness that held all horror and delight—a pale sea with unspeakable pleasures sunk beneath it. Then the wide stare focused again and Smith's eyes met his squarely and Smith's voice said, "Go ahead. I'll promise."

"That if you ever should meet a Shambleau again—ever, anywhere—you'll draw your gun and burn it to hell the instant you realize what it is. Will you promise me that?"

There was a long silence. Yarol's somber eyes bored relentlessly into the colorless ones of Smith, not wavering. And the veins stood out on Smith's tanned forehead. He never broke his word—he had given it perhaps half a dozen times in his life, but once he had given it, he was incapable of breaking it. And once more the gray seas flooded in a dim tide of memories, sweet and horrible beyond dreams. Once more Yarol was staring into blankness that hid nameless things. The room was very still.

The gray tide ebbed. Smith's eyes, pale and resolute as steel, met Yarol's levelly.

"I'll—try," he said. And his voice wavered.

WHITLEY STRIEBER
(b. 1945)

A native Texan, Whitley Strieber was born in Texas and attended the University of Texas. He spent a decade in the advertising business before turning his attention to writing.

Strieber wrote The Wolfen (1980) and The Hunger (1981)—both of which were made into movies—in which the protagonists encounter a highly evolved form of wolf culling the weak inhabitants of Manhattan. His other works include Black Magic (1982), Catmagic (1986), The Wild (1991), and The Forbidden Zone (1993). He is perhaps most known for Communion: A True Story (1987) and Transformation: The Breakthrough (1988), in which he detailed the supposedly true account of his abduction by aliens.

The Hunger is written in a comparatively restrained style. Strieber, whose temptation as a writer is to be facile, shows here that he can be a sensitively acute observer of human behavior.

The story is set in contemporary New York City, where a couple named Blaylock live in a large East Side house. Miriam Blaylock is the authentic vampire (although the word "vampire" does not appear in Strieber's novel), doomed to immortality. Her lovers all lead extended but not eternal lives; they live for two hundred years and then rapidly age and die within a few days, like her last companion, John.

Miriam has since made love to Dr. Sarah Roberts and introduced her to blood drinking. Soon, Sarah will be transformed into this new species of being with a two-hundred-year life span. What is notable about this particular chapter in the book is that Strieber is as explicit as Joyce Carol Oates in the excerpt from Bellefleur; both elaborate the erotic power of the vampiric embrace. In Strieber's narrative, human lovemaking is juxtaposed with the satiation of vampiric hunger. The temptation of the blood drinker is described with the same agonizing terms used by drug addicts desperate for a fix.

Excerpt from
THE HUNGER

"Open up!" Tom pounded on the front door. He hadn't expected to be ignored. All the more it confirmed to him that Sarah was in there and his presence was not appreciated. "I'll kick this damn door in!" His voice echoed up and down the street but he didn't care. Let somebody call the police. He would welcome the help. He stepped back and gave the door a hard kick—and almost fell into the hallway. The door had opened on its own.

The entrance gaped black. A whispering sound abruptly stopped. Tom could see somebody back in the shadows, crouching low. "I want to see Sarah Roberts," he said as he strode across the threshold. He had intended to leave the door open to get some light from the street, but it closed as soon as he was inside. The smoothness of its motion and the decisive *chunk* of the lock made him suspect that it was being controlled from elsewhere in the house. "All right, Miriam, enough is enough!" He flailed, seeking the wall, then began to slide his hands along its smooth surface trying to find a light. He pressed an old-fashioned button switch but no lights came on. "Oh, for God's sake!"

The whispering began again, closer this time. He recoiled. There was something awful about it, something avid. He pressed back against the front door. The handle would not turn. "Get away from me!" He kicked, met air. The whispering grew louder and louder, becoming a frenetic chatter. It was not a voice at all but rather the sound of movements, as if a swarm of insects were crawling down the hallway.

Tom twisted the handle of the door, threw his weight against it, hammered on it. It might look like wood but it felt like steel.

To his left was an archway leading into a living room.

Windows.

He stepped forward. Something came around his right ankle. He yanked his leg free but now it attached itself to the other ankle. He stamped his feet but it was no use. Both ankles were grasped. *Sarah!* The pressure became pain, searing, excruciating, forcing him to his knees. He clawed the darkness before him, grabbed toward his agonized ankles, and fell forward into a tangled, ropy mass. His legs kicked, his arms flailed. Every movement seemed to entangle him further with whatever it was. Thin fingers groped in his hair, slipped around his neck. He screamed and screamed, pulling at the ropy substance as best he could. A fingernail popped into his cheek and cut through all the way down to his chin. The pain made him bellow, but he managed to move so that it missed the critical blood vessels behind the jaw. "Sarah!"

Tom's hands connected with something solid—a head. He pushed back with all his might. There was a crackling sound and the fingers released his hair. Again and again he smashed at the thing, feeling it break like glass beneath his blows.

He pulled himself to his feet and lunged past it into the living room, rolling across the floor, brushing the stinking dust it had left on him to the floor.

His cheek, his ankles and his hands screamed in pain. He stared into the darkness. Had he killed it?

What the hell was it?

"Sarah, it's me! Come back! You've got to get out of here!"

He saw the shadow of somebody standing at the far end of the room, a tall, thin individual with a bobbing head. It did not look any more human than the thing that attacked him had felt. Its outline was dim in the light from the street.

He didn't understand at all what was happening in this place. Only Sarah was here—somewhere. Every fiber of his body screamed at him to jump out a widow, to escape, to get away from whatever monstrous evil had infected this house—

But Sarah was here.

"You! Where is she?" He took a step toward it. Another. Its head stopped moving. Abruptly it dropped to the floor.

Another one appeared in a doorway that led into the rear part of the house. He could see it marching like a man whose knee joints had been fused. Then it too dropped to the floor.

The scrabbling sound began again.

"Sarah Roberts!"

The sound rose as the things crossed the floor. Tom's hand went to his cheek, touching the open wound. In that instant he knew that he had to leave this place. If they reached him again he was going to die.

To his left was a sun porch with French doors leading to a garden. He stumbled toward the doors, grabbed the handle and jerked at it. Locked.

He didn't try to unlock the door, but took a chair and hurled it through.

He ran wildly across the garden, flailing in the shrubs, seeking some kind of a fence. At last he came to the edge of the property and climbed the brick wall he found there, cutting his fingers deeply on the shards of glass embedded in the top.

Atop the wall he paused, looked back at the house. There were no lights. Not far behind him the shrubbery was waving madly as something struggled through it.

He jumped six feet to the sidewalk.

Back in the world again. A woman walked toward him leading a dachshund. He brushed past her to the corner and hailed a cab.

"Riverside emergency," he gasped out.

"You bet."

They stitched him in the brightly lit emergency room and bandaged his hands. He told them a window had fallen out at his apartment.

What had actually happened he did not know. Perhaps it had been real, perhaps some kind of complex illusion designed to frighten him away.

He had them call over some detectives from the Twenty-third Precinct. Half an hour later he met them in his office.

"So you want us to go to this house and get out your girl friend?"

"That's right, officer. I have every reason to believe she's there against her will."

"Kidnapped?"

"Psychically kidnapped. Influenced."

"It doesn't sound like a crime. She's not under age—"

"Of course not! You're telling me I can't get help."

"Doctor Haver, you haven't reported a crime."

He let them leave. When the door closed he could contain himself no longer. In his defeat and loss he wept, muffling his face in his hands to deaden the sound.

Sarah had been at peace until she heard somebody call her name.

Tom?

She was drifting on the softest of waters, in the moonlit sea . . .

He screamed.

She opened her eyes. In her mind was a vivid image of Tom. "I love you." The screams pealed again and again, so frantic that Sarah had clapped her hands over her ears.

Abruptly it was over. After a moment Miriam's voice drifted through the door. "It's all right," the voice said, "sleep now."

"Thank you," she replied. But she thought, 'please don't let him be dead.' She had to go to him. For that she somehow had to get out of this bed. She swayed when she sat up, shook when she put her feet on the floor, had to grab the bedpost for support when she tried to move.

Helpless, almost overcome with sleep, she sank to the floor.

She laid her head down, wishing she had never left the bed. It was so cold! Her eyes opened, she tried to gather enough energy to pull herself back up.

It was some time before she realized that she was staring into a face. Somebody was lying under the bed, still and silent. Sarah sighed, all that escaped of a scream.

It was not a peaceful face, but a sad one.

So this was Miriam's "food." Sarah gagged with the memory of it. And yet it sang in her veins. Slowly she extended her hand. Her own eyes closing as if she were under the influence of some opiate, she stroked the forehead of the person whose life she had taken.

She Slept.

*   *   *

Miriam moved about the house struggling with her failures. The body of Tom Haver was nowhere to be found. She was not really surprised at his escape. His attackers were fierce but they had little real strength. Poor man. All his survival had gained him was a harder death. He could not be allowed to survive, not with what he now knew. If she was clever, his death could be arranged in such a way that it served a purpose.

She followed a trail of broken plants to the garden wall. There was Eumenes, arms outstretched, mouth lolling open, lusting toward food he could never swallow. Astonishingly repulsive.

She remembered lying with her head in his lap on the slopes of Hymettus.

She returned them all to their resting places, forcing their remains into the chests. At last there was John, slumped against the wall of the attic. She picked him up, holding the wrists together with one hand, carrying him with the other. "I know you can hear me, my love," she said as she placed him in his container. "I'll make you the same promise I made the others. Listen well, because you must hold this in your memory forever. John, I will keep you beside me until time itself comes to an end. I will neither abandon nor forget you. I will never stop loving you."

She pressed him down into his steel tomb until his knees were against his chest and slid the cover closed. Weeping, she spun the bolts one by one.

Tom lay in their bed alone. Each time he had dropped off, shouting terrors had jolted him back awake. His face was a dull haze of throbbing pain, his left eye was swollen closed.

He kept trying to understand what had happened to him. No matter how he worked it out, however, there just wasn't a satisfactory explanation.

He thought of Sarah and cried aloud. She was in the hands of a monster. It was as simple as that. Perhaps science would never explain such things, perhaps it couldn't.

And yet Miriam was real, living in the real world, right now. Her life mocked the laws of nature, at least as Tom understood them.

Slowly, the first shaft of sunlight spread across the wall. Tom imagined the earth, a little green mote of dust sailing around the sun, lost in the enormous darkness. The universe seemed a cold place indeed, malignant and secret.

Was that the truth of it?

Something tickled his unwounded cheek. Tears again. He threw back the covers and got out of bed. All at once he froze. This room was the only one with any sunlight in it. The rest of the apartment was still dark.

He was frozen with terror. He could not move from the place where he stood.

It came at him shrieking, tearing with its long knives of fingernails, its jaws snapping—

And was gone.

He shook his head, went to the bathroom, splashed his chest and neck with cold water. He must not let the image of that thing creep into his mind again. It was not outside the realm of possibility to be driven catatonic by fear. That had to be guarded against if there was to be any hope left at all.

He looked like hell. One eye was an angry purple mass of flesh. The other was black. He badly needed a shave but the bandages were going to get in the way.

Suddenly, the sound of the intercom broke into his thoughts. How long had it been buzzing? Turning on lights as he went, he moved to the foyer and answered it.

Three minutes later Geoff and Phyllis stood at the door. They had food and coffee and the didn't buy any stories about broken windows. They wanted to know what Miriam had done with Sarah.

Miriam stood beside the bed watching Sarah, waiting for her to wake up. The transformation was working well. Miriam touched Sarah's cheek, feeling the cool dryness of the skin. That was another good sign.

It was a happy moment.

The only barrier left to complete transformation was the emotional one. Loyalty was, as always, the issue. Sarah must be made to realize the truth of her situation. She now belonged to a new species and must leave the values of the old behind.

Miriam turned her thoughts to Tom Haver. She could see a good way to use him to further Sarah's change of allegiance. He would be the medium.

A slight variation in Sarah's breathing pattern alerted Miriam to the fact that the Sleep was about to end. Very well. When Sarah awoke, she would find love waiting for her.

An ugly dream receded. Sarah opened her eyes. The thing looming over the bed startled her for an instant. Miriam, of course. Her eyes were glaring, the stare avid. Sarah's impulse was to run.

She thought of the body under the bed, the dead skin dull and dry.

"Don't," Miriam said. "You can't change the past."

"You're a murderer!"

Miriam sat on the edge of the bed. It made Sarah shudder when Miriam stroked her face, but she was afraid to turn away. As a child in Savannah she had captured a baby rabbit. She remembered how it had huddled so quietly in her hand, and she had thought, 'I've tamed it with my touch.' But it wasn't tame at all, it was in a rapture of fear. She had cuddled it to her face and, giving it a friendly snuffle, found that it was dead.

Sarah almost wished something similar would happen to her. But it did not. Instead she remembered last night. "Tom—"

"He's quite well."

"I've got to call him!" Some of her old self was returning, it seemed, as she recalled Tom's screams. "Where's the phone?"

Miriam's expression was hard to read. She seemed at once angry and curiously at peace. "I don't think you should phone him. Go to him instead."

Sarah hid her amazement. She had assumed herself a prisoner. "Can I go now?"

"Certainly. You're no prisoner."

At once Sarah got out of bed. She could stand up easily. The hunger, the grogginess, were gone. Her body seemed unusually light and healthy. The sense of physical well-being was remarkable.

Then the image of the dead girl swam into memory again. Her own experiences crowded out all happiness. She remembered the blood hot in her throat, the delicate sadness of her victim's face. She moved away from the bed.

"The room is clean," Miriam said. "We remove evidence very quickly, you'll find."

Sarah couldn't stand to hear it. She clapped her hands over her ears.

"You took a life. That's what you feel in you now. Her life. She was a healthy young woman of about twenty-five, about your size and build. She was wearing jeans and a brown sweat shirt when I captured her."

"Shut up!"

Sarah's heart had started pounding, her temples throbbing. She longed somehow to expel what was in her. All she could do was escape. She ran from the room, down the hallway toward the stairs.

Miriam's strong hand grabbed her shoulder, spun her around. "Get dressed," she snapped. "You can't go out like that."

"I'm sorry."

"Your clothes are in the bedroom closet."

Sarah hesitated. She didn't want to go back in that bedroom. Miriam pushed her. "Face it, Sarah. You killed. *You.*" She pushed again. "And you'll kill others. You'll keep killing." Another hard shove and Sarah stumbled through the door. Miriam rushed past her, strode to the windows and swept back the heavy drapes.

Dawn was spreading up from the east, the red sun gleaming on the East River, sending a spear of light across Miriam's garden. Such beauty hurt.

"You haven't got any reason to cry," Miriam said. "You should be rejoicing."

"You said I could go." How small her voice sounded.

In answer Miriam swept her clothes out of the closet. Sarah threw them on, thinking only of Tom and the salvation she would find in his arms.

In a few more minutes she was setting out into a magnificent spring morning. The door of the house swung shut behind her. As Sarah walked down the street she was conscious of Miriam's face at the window of the library. Only when she was able to turn a corner and get out of that line of sight did she begin to feel free.

Never, as long as she lived, would she return to that house.

She was actually going back home. She felt all the delight of one who escapes from an unjust imprisonment. She was going back to her place as part of humanity. She was resurrected.

Tom shared as much of his tragedy as he dared with Charlie and Phyllis. He could not tell them of the things he had seen. They might have thought he was hallucinating, which would only confuse matters. Phyllis wept a little when Tom told her that he did not know what had happened to Sarah. She was Sarah's closest associate and a good friend, and she shared some of Tom's anguish.

Tom didn't know if he would ever see Sarah again. He suspected she might be dead. This black thought was in his mind when the lock clicked and Sarah came in.

She burst in. Tom was astonished and glad, and yet somehow assaulted. There was something about the total surprise of the arrival and the quickness of her movements that made him want to retreat.

He refused to accept such a feeling. Her poor, small frame was shaking with tearful joy and he was afraid of her. Or was it joy that moved her? What was that look in her eyes?

"Sarah!" Phyllis' voice rang through the silence.

Sarah glared. Tom had never seen such an expression on her face before. For a moment he was afraid she might strike Phyllis.

"Tom, please hold me!" She came toward him, then paused. He did not understand her hesitation. Her expression became almost desperate.

"You're home now," was all he could think to say. "You made it home." His emotions were beginning to overwhelm him. He wanted to sob. Never again would he let her go. They circled one another, a slow dance.

He recalled their past: lying on a beach in Florida, Sarah holding forth on age vectors in the baking sun. He had laughed aloud at her intensity. Sarah in her lab, her voice strident, the atmosphere charged with her energy. Sarah in bed, loving.

As the shock of her arrival wore off she became more real to Tom. He kissed her. Her mouth was sour and he drew back. Tears appeared in her eyes. "I have a confession—"

"Not yet."

Her eyes widened. Her fingers came up to his bandages. "She hurt me," he said.

"Don't call her 'she.' Miriam isn't a 'she.' That's a human word."

"What, then? Woman?"

"A female of another species. A woman is a human being. Miriam is a mockery of humanity. Women stand for life. Miriam stands for death."

"You're pale," he said. He didn't want to pursue any conversations about Miriam right now. Not until they both felt a lot better.

Phyllis and Charlie had drawn close, instinct making them seek the comfort of the group. Tom could not blame them. He felt it too: something black and cold was in this room.

"I may look pale but I feel good," Sarah said. "I wish I didn't feel like this." Tom detected more than a little desperation in her voice. He began to wish Phyllis and Charlie would leave. He wanted Sarah alone.

"We didn't understand how dangerous she was," Phyllis said.

Sarah turned to her. "I failed, Phyl. You believed in me, but I failed." She was starting to back away, as if their closeness disturbed her.

"We got a lot of data, Sarah."

"Not enough. You don't know the half of it. She didn't let you have anything of real value."

Sarah kept backing away. Tom made a gesture to Phyllis and Charlie, nodded toward the door. "Yes," Sarah said, "it's best if they leave."

"Sarah," Phyllis said, "I don't want you to think you failed."

"Please, Phyl."

"I'll go, but just don't think you've failed. It isn't over yet. Remember that. We haven't even begun to work on that data."

"Yes, Phyl."

"I think you'd better cut it short," Tom said at last. Sarah looked as if she were about to explode. When the door closed behind them at last, Sarah took a ragged breath. She was now on the far side of the room, poised like a cornered animal.

Sarah had known from the moment she entered the apartment what Miriam had done to her. Another trick.

They smelled so good.

She wanted to handle them, to caress their warm, moist skin, to draw them close to her.

How accommodating Miriam had been. And why not, when she knew what this was going to do to Sarah. She wanted to run . . . and then again she didn't. There was something very pleasing about them, about Tom especially, the slow way he moved and the trust in his eyes. This odd feeling isolated her from them, forced her into a kind of loneliness she had never known before.

When the door closed behind Charlie and Phyllis, Sarah knew that Tom was endangered. He should not be alone with her. Not when she was like this.

She strove for control. "Stay on that side of the room," she said.

He looked across at her, a question in his eyes. The wall was directly behind her. She could not get farther away from that wonderful scent. If she opened her arms, called to him, he would come. She must not allow herself to do that.

"Darling?"

"Tom, don't come any closer!"

"You're joking."

"I am not."

"Didn't you come here to be with me?"

There was such hurt in his tone. She wanted to go to him, but she did not dare. He took a step closer. Her flesh crawled, but her arms came up. Another Sarah, mean and evil, smiled, another voice welcomed him. She could hear his pulse as he approached, hear the whisper of his breath, the faint liquid sound as his lips parted.

"We had good times. Don't you remember?" She did remember, as he had no doubt intended she should. Sweaty hours banging away at one another. Such innocence and pleasure.

"Tom, *stop!*"

Thank God it had finally come out. The shout stunned him. He stood still, his smile fading. "Why?"

"Just do it. Don't come a step nearer. Not one step!"

He bowed his head, remained motionless.

"Go into the bedroom and close the door. I made a major error coming here. I've got to get out and I can't possibly make myself do it unless you leave the room."

"What are you talking about?"

"Tom, I can't stand it much longer! Please just do as I say, even if you don't understand."

"I think we ought to talk about it."

"No! Go away!"

He was moving closer again. In a moment she was going to open her arms once more and this time she would not be able to stop.

Miriam called it hunger. A mild word.

"Please!" She cast her eyes down, felt her muscles tensing for the kill. Her body was preparing to spring at him. Hot, anguished tears poured out of her eyes. Very softly, she made a last plea. "Don't touch me."

"You're serious. You're absolutely serious!"

She looked up at him. He was four feet away. She could not warn him again.

"OK, I get the point. But why, Sarah?"

"Just do as I say. Do it now."

At last he began to move toward the bedroom. For a horrible moment she thought she was following him, but she managed to go out the front door instead. Her movements were sinuous and quick. She reminded herself of a rat questing through a maze. There was another person in her, powerful and evil, and she was losing control.

The hallway was empty. That was a small miracle, and Sarah was grateful. She could smell them all around her, behind the doors of their apartments. The moan of need that came out of her mouth was hardly human.

Sarah knew where she had to go, where it was intended she go. There was only one place that did not smell human, only one being who did not tempt the hunger. Miriam had made her point. For Sarah the only thing that now mattered was getting back to that house. Doing it through the crowded Manhattan street was going to be hell. She clung to the notion that she would not kill another human being.

As the elevator descended, she tried to prepare herself for her ordeal. She had moved in the streets before, after all, and hadn't eaten at all the last time. She remembered the man on the sidewalk whom she had nearly killed, the apartment balcony she had climbed.

That was with the streets empty. Now they were going to be jampacked. 'I am a human being,' she thought. 'I will not harm my fellow man.' With all the willpower left to her, she resolved to remain a human being. The hunger she felt, after all, was not her own.

It belonged to the creature's blood. The need to kill was not her need, it was Miriam's. She resolved to keep telling herself that. Then the elevator doors opened and she saw Alex at his post. 'Miriam's hunger,' she repeated, 'not mine.'

She managed to slip past him, get through the front door and out onto the sidewalk.

Madness. People everywhere, more even than she had imagined. She made an involuntary lunge at a passing businessman, managed to dash past him into the middle of the street. Brakes squealed, horns blared. A cab swerved, slurred to a stop. The driver was cursing, the passenger staring terrified from the backseat.

There was no time to waste, no opportunity to miss. She got in. "Whassamatter with you? I got a goddamn fare in here!"

"Emergency!"

"Call a cop, lady. You nearly got yourself run over. Now get outa here."

"Somebody's about to die. I'm a doctor."

The driver rolled his eyes. "OK," he said, "where to?"

Sarah told him Miriam's address and opened the window. The fumes from the street would perhaps mask some of the smells within the cab. She listened as the driver reassured his passenger that all was well, the detour wouldn't take long. Many drivers would have refused to budge, she knew that. But she had gotten lucky. This guy had a heart.

As soon as the house appeared Sarah leaped from the cab, raced up the steps and began hammering the knocker, pressing the buzzer, trying the door.

She could feel Miriam standing just the other side of the door. "Please," she said softly, "please open it." She did not want to shout. Attracting the attention of the neighbors was dangerous.

After the longest thirty seconds of Sarah's life the door clicked and swung open. She staggered in and slammed it shut behind her, on all the bustle and beauty, and the hideous temptation, of the world of man.

Miriam knew at once that Sarah's will had proved stronger than her need. She sighed with displeasure, let the poor thing into the house, waited for the inevitable recriminations.

Sarah's hunger would eventually break her will, but until it did Miriam would have to endure this annoying independence. She hardly heard Sarah's wails of anguish, her roaring anger, hardly felt the clawing and the pummeling as she pulled the girl up the stairs and back into their bedroom.

"I'll return when you're feeling more reasonable," she said. "Try to calm yourself." There was little point in saying more. Sarah was stronger than the others, a lot stronger. Too bad. It was going to make things that much more difficult for her. She had a romantic vision of herself as the great healer. A fool's vision. The world has forgotten that romance has two aspects, that of love and that of death. Sarah didn't know it, but she had moved to the side of death.

The walls of the apartment were closing in on Tom. He stood in the foyer, his mind racked with indecision. He should follow Sarah, go back to that house again.

But he could not. That pretty little house held nothing for him but terror. Pink brickwork, window boxes, romantic white shutters, all seemed evil and grotesque, like makeup smeared on some sneering face. The screaming terrors of last night seemed to come close to him. His hand touched the bandages on his face. Had they been demons? Were such things real? His belief in science had evaporated. All the grand procession of knowledge now seemed nothing more than smugness and ignorance.

In the face of something such as Miriam had a man any power at all? There was no place to turn. Prayer meant nothing to him. His childhood prayers had gotten only silence in reply.

If that silence was sacred, he had not known it until now, and he felt it was too late to challenge the rock of his disbelief. He could not turn to God for strength.

There seemed nowhere to turn. He just didn't have the courage to break the spell of Miriam. Or did he? He imagined taking Sarah in his arms and shouting out his love so loud it would penetrate to the depth of her soul.

That love, that was truth.

That was his weapon.

He took a step toward the door. One step, no more. He remembered the look in Sarah's face as she had pleaded with him not to come near her. "I love you, Sarah! I love you!" His voice echoed. Sunlight spread across the living room. He saw little clouds beyond the window, white and fluffy. He screamed the scream of nightmare.

Miriam decided to wait a bit before telephoning the victim. It would be best if he could get up the courage to come on his own. That way she could let him force his way to Sarah, to succeed where he had failed last night. It was doubtful, however. Human courage had its limits.

She went to the garden to pick flowers. It was a soothing pastime and it would be best if the house appeared as cheerful and sweet as possible. The windows must be opened, the curtains drawn back. There should be music on the stereo, something soothing, perhaps Delius' *Florida Suite,* or the overture from *The Land of Smiles.* Perhaps there should be some fruit and wine set out. No, just wine. Fruit was too much trouble. She didn't even know if they still sold natural fruit, it had been so long since she had noticed.

Carefully avoiding even a glance at her destroyed rose arbor, Miriam clipped until her basket was heavy with marigolds, snapdragons, iris, all the wealth of her garden. She loved the exuberant life of the flowers. Nature demanded nothing more of them than that they open each morning to the sun. Miriam's race was not so lucky. From her and her kind much more was demanded. Not all that nature wants from its children is innocent.

She carried the cut flowers onto the sun porch, laid them on the table which contained the portrait of Lamia. She looked into her mother's eyes, rendered by the artist as pale blue. Before the invention of contact lenses and shaded glasses Miriam's species was marked as having the evil eye. The artist had not wanted to offend his client by giving her eyes their true color.

The portrait was a source of peace and reassurance to Miriam. The eyes said to her, 'Go on, never stop. For me, be immortal.'

Tom had managed to get as far as Miriam's front door. The house stood before him, the vortex of a deadly whirlpool. He was reminded of the flowers that eat flies, using their nectar and their beauty as bait. Tom hated most the beauty of the place. It should have foreboded somehow of the danger within. Must Miriam always smile?

It was a sunny morning, the sky now clear blue. Before him the house glowed in sunlight dappled through budding trees. The green shutters were open. Behind them silk curtains billowed in the fresh breeze. He heard music and saw shadowy movement in the living room.

For an instant he was ready to run, but the music seemed at odds with danger. It was happy, rich music, the kind of thing he might have heard drifting up from the bandshell on a summer night of his boyhood. He supposed that he had been seen, and the music was meant to make him feel just as he did.

He had imagined how life was going to be without Sarah, and had wound up here, telling himself how he loved her. Still, it was going to be hard to get to that front door to ring the bell. If anything the obvious musical attempt to soothe him made him more uneasy than ever.

Either he go in that house now or face the fact that he would never see Sarah again.

How desperately she needed him. When somebody you loved has nowhere left to turn, you help. If there was such a thing as a human compact, that was part of it.

Sarah had to be gotten out of there and taken by force to Riverside. And as for Miriam—she belonged in a specimen container.

A face appeared at a downstairs window. Miriam smiled at him.

In a moment she opened the front door. He mounted the steps and went in. It was as simple as that. She stood before him, blond and beautiful, smelling of flowery old-fashioned perfume, her expression welcoming. As the door closed she regarded him with concern. "I'm so glad you came. I was just going to call you. Sarah needs help."

"I'm aware of that. I came to get her."

"I had hoped she would stay with you this morning. When she came back I just didn't know what to do."

"I want to take her to Riverside."

"That would be best. Tom, I'm afraid I'm at my wit's end. Sarah's reactions have been all wrong. I—I never intended to harm her." The gleam of a tear appeared in one eye. "Now she's up in that bedroom and she won't unlock the door!"

"Upstairs? What room?"

"First door on the right at the head of the stairs."

"You lead the way." Tom had absolutely no intention of wandering around this house on his own. Miriam walked ahead of him, down the very hall where he had been attacked the night before. It was nothing but beautiful now, with flowers on the tables and a cheerful coaching print on one wall. The room's innocent appearance only intensified his caution.

Miriam seemed aware of his feeling, as if the act downstairs had been little more than a formality. "Sarah," she said, "please let me in. I have a surprise for you." She turned to Tom. "I've got a key, but I hate to open a door somebody else has locked."

"Why don't I just bust it down," he said caustically.

She used her key.

It was the most beautiful room Tom had ever seen. The windows opened across a magnificent garden. He could see thousands of flowers, and there were more arrangements of cut flowers on the desk and nightstands. There was something a little obscene about the profusion of flowers. They were a kind of overstatement for an innocence that did not exist, and Tom was beginning to see them as the exact opposite of what they were obviously intended to suggest. They seemed to confirm Miriam's guilt.

The breeze blew past gossamer pink curtains and sunlight poured in the windows. Tom found himself estimating the distance to the ground, and then saw in the garden something that chilled him. There was a path of broken shrubs and upturned earth right across to the brick wall at the garden's far edge. He could see from here the brown scuff marks his shoes had left on the wall.

Sarah lay in a magnificent rosewood bed. She was not asleep, but in a sort of trance-state. Her eyes followed him from beneath half-closed lids. She looked languid, but he had the impression that she was far from it. The eyes hardly blinked.

A fly came in the window, buzzing energetically. Tom watched it spiral up to the ceiling. For a moment he was stunned. He had not noticed that the ceiling was magnificently painted to resemble a blue, cloud-flecked sky. Clouds billowed and larks soared in that magical, ineffably romantic air. The fly, crawling across the painted birds and clouds, was the only thing that disturbed the perfection of the illusion.

Sarah moaned. Tom went beside the bed. Gone were the protests he had heard in the apartment. Her face, beaded with perspiration, became almost sensual. Her eyes were dreamy, softened by desire. Her arms opened wide. He bent close to her, kissed the tears that stained her cheeks.

The next thing he knew her arms had come around him and he was lying beside her on the bed, drawing the delicate silk sheets away from her body. She was more beautiful now than he had ever remembered her.

He was vaguely aware that Miriam had retreated to the hall and pulled the door closed behind her. He feasted his eyes on Sarah's body. It was smoother, softer. He touched her cool breast, felt the heart beating there beneath the firm flesh. Only her eyes told him that she was conscious of his touch. What turmoil was in those eyes. They looked at once delighted, avid with need, and as deeply troubled as any eyes he had ever seen. He tried to comfort her with soft sounds, soothing caresses. This was what he had longed to do at home. This was the truth of love. Surely this would reach her.

Sarah was anguished. She could not even speak, much less cry out. Her body screamed with silent need, her mind hummed with excuses and justifications.

She had determined to lie here until she died. Then Tom had appeared. She hoped at first that it was a hallucination. Then their eyes met and she knew that he was real.

How could anyone be so foolish.

She hadn't the strength for both of them, not anymore. Every cell of

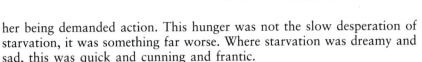

her being demanded action. This hunger was not the slow desperation of starvation, it was something far worse. Where starvation was dreamy and sad, this was quick and cunning and frantic.

"'Sarah, we can conquer this thing together."

He lay close to her, unendurably close. She let her arms twine around him. It felt so good to give in. So very good. "Yes," she said, "we'll do it together."

His body was growing tense with passion. She noticed his eyes flick to the door.

"Miriam won't bother us," she said. "This is exactly what she wants."

She ran her hands under his shirt. She knew just what Tom liked. Deep within, a voice shrieked at her to warn him, to drive him away once again. She purred and arched her back, offering herself to him.

She knew just how to excite him and he found himself responding to her more passionately than ever before. The beauty of the surroundings, the quiet, the warm sunlight combined to encourage him to forget the horrible problems that were besetting them, to forget for just a few minutes. He caressed her breasts, her thighs, sought her lips with his own. 'It'll help,' he told himself, 'it's healthy and normal and positive.'

She unbuttoned his shirt, touched his nipples with her deft little hands. Their delicacy had always delighted him, and he kissed them now. He felt himself growing erect and guided the hands to his zipper.

"Yes, Tom," she said. She was smiling now. He burst out of his un-zippered pants.

He hugged her. "We'll be free again," he said, "you'll see."

"Oh, Tom, I hope so!"

He entered her. Every tiniest move brought intense pleasure. This was what they had needed. They should have trusted love more.

Tom closed his eyes, heard her whispering his name to the rhythm of their movements. Her voice merged with the hypnotic buzzing of the fly on the ceiling. He nuzzled close behind her ear and buried his face in her hair, where it was as soft as the fur of a rabbit.

A new feeling entered him, one that hurt like the contemplation of great beauty. He held her to him, riding her.

With every bit of concentration remaining to her, Sarah tried to resist her need. He lay atop her in his disheveled clothes, sweating out his passion. Beads of perspiration glittered on his forehead. His cheeks were red, as if he had been running.

She was emptied of hope.

Tom's passion rose. She loved him, she realized, as she might love a child. His sexual significance, in the past few days, had dwindled to nothing.

Bang-slap, his body went as it plunged against her. She felt his heat, smelled his breath, tasted the salt of his hot flesh as she waited.

She knew perfectly well what Miriam wanted. And that she wasn't going to do. She couldn't, even if she wanted to. Miriam had forgotten one simple thing. There was no weapon in the room, and without one she could not make Tom's blood flow.

She had almost called out to Miriam for one. But now she was sure she wouldn't do that. Her suffering became a kind of hypnotism. She was lost in it when a flash of light on her face made her open her eyes.

Miriam stood at the foot of the bed, holding up an object so bright it dazzled Sarah.

Tom went on making love, his human senses oblivious to the silent drama being enacted around him.

Miriam was closer now. The object in her hand was a gleaming knife. A scalpel.

Miriam placed it on the bedside table and departed at once.

Sarah touched the sharpness of it with her fingers.

"Oh, Tom, Tom!"

"*Sarah!* I love you, love you! Oh, *God!*"

His pumping shook her. The scalpel dazzled in her hand. So light, so strong.

His face, melting with love, gazed down into hers. She closed her eyes, held her breath. 'No, I will not,' she thought, a chant within her. 'No no, nono, no no.'

It came rolling up from the depths, the *thing* within her.

The scalpel belonged to it. Had always belonged to it.

No no no no.

This was her truth. She pushed it into him.

"SARAAAAAH!"

She took it out, shoved it in again. It whispered through his flesh and all at once the purple miracle of his life was pouring into her.

Alive again. She heard a song that hurt like a memory. Somebody was sobbing. She was sobbing.

Why? She was happy.

His head bobbed, his jaw went slack. To escape his collapsing weight she wriggled out from under him, slipped from the bed. He shook horribly, huddling in the sheets. Blood spread. Then she touched him, bent to him, made believe she was kissing him. She took his life out of him.

She twirled slowly around and around, her whole body rapturing with a fine pleasure. She spread her arms in the warm air. The world had become dream-golden, touched with every beauty she had ever known. She could feel everything—the gentle movement of air past her body, the slow warmth of the sun, the secret pumping of her own blood.

She could feel Tom.

Feel him!

Her eyes went to his dead body. Something extraordinary was happening. Emotions almost seemed to pour from him like some healing water: sorrow, pity, peace.

Such peace.

She heard his voice in the air around her, saying her name in the rhythm of their lovemaking. It got fainter and fainter. More than anything she had ever wanted, she wanted the sound of that voice.

She was desolated.

RICHARD MATHESON
(b. 1926)

Richard Matheson was born in Allendale, New Jersey, and received his degree in journalism from the University of Missouri School of Journalism in 1949. Matheson began his career primarily as a science fiction writer; his first story, "Born of Man and Woman," was published in The Magazine of Fantasy and Science Fiction *in 1950. Since then, his work has included horror stories, science fiction stories, novels, and screenplays.*

Matheson was one of the first writers whose work was adapted for film, marking him as one of the "liberators" of magazine-published science fiction in the early 1950s. He adapted his second science fiction novel, The Shrinking Man *(1956), and sold it to Universal as a screenplay under the title* The Incredible Shrinking Man *(1957). Matheson's next major venture was to write fourteen scripts for the TV series* The Twilight Zone *in 1959. He went on to have a very fruitful career in the film industry, adapting scripts to the big screen for directors such as Roger Corman, including* The Fall of The House of Usher *in 1953.*

The excerpt from I Am Legend *included here is a nearly perfect model of the science fiction vampire story. Matheson imagines that the plague of vampirism decimating the earth is the result of a bacterial infection which creates blood lust in its victims. Even the vampire's traditional antipathy to garlic and to daylight are attributed to the infection. Robert Neville, the narrator of the novel, is immune to the bacteria and becomes the last non-vampire on Earth.*

I Am Legend *is widely regarded as one of the most original and influential vampire novels of the this century. Filmed twice as both* The Last Man on Earth *(1964) and* The Omega Man *(1971), it was the acknowledged but unofficial inspiration for George Romero's groundbreaking horror film,* The Night of the Living Dead *(1968).*

Over the course of his career, Matheson has won numerous awards, including the Bram Stoker Award, the Edgar, the Spur, and the Writer's Guild Award. He was the first author to be named a grand master by the World Horror Convention.

Excerpt from
I AM LEGEND

 "The strength of the vampire is that no one will believe in him."

Thank *you,* Dr. Van Helsing, he thought, putting down his copy of "Dracula." He sat staring moodily at the bookcase, listening to Brahms' second piano concerto, a whisky sour in his right hand, a cigarette between his lips.

It was true. The book was a hodgepodge of superstitions and soap-opera clichés, but that line was true; no one had believed in them, and how could they fight something they didn't even believe in?

That was what the situation had been. Something black and of the night had come crawling out of the Middle Ages. Something with no framework or credulity, something that had been consigned, fact and figure, to the pages of imaginative literature. Vampires were passé, Summers' idylls or Stoker's melodramatics or a brief inclusion in the Britannica or grist for the pulp writer's mill or raw material for the B-film factories. A tenuous legend passed from century to century.

Well, it was true.

He took a sip from his drink and closed his eyes as the cold liquid trickled down his throat and warmed his stomach. True, he thought, but no one ever got the chance to know it. Oh, they knew it was something, but it couldn't be that—not *that. That* was imagination, *that* was superstition, there was no such thing as *that.*

And, before science had caught up with the legend, the legend had swallowed science and everything.

He hadn't found any doweling that day. He hadn't checked the generator. He hadn't cleaned up the pieces of mirror. He hadn't eaten supper; he'd lost his appetite. That wasn't hard. He lost it most of the time. He couldn't do the things he'd done all afternoon and then come home to a hearty meal. Not even after five months.

He thought of the eleven—no, the twelve children that afternoon, and he finished his drink in two swallows.

He blinked and the room wavered a little before him. You're getting blotto, Father, he told himself. So what? he returned. Has anyone more right?

He tossed the book across the room. Begone, Van Helsing and Mina and Jonathan and blood-eyed Count and all! All figments, all driveling extrapolations on a somber theme.

A coughing chuckle emptied itself from his throat. Outside, Ben Cortman called for him to come out. Be right out, Benny, he thought. Soon as I get my tuxedo on.

He shuddered and gritted his teeth edges together. Be right out. Well, why not? Why *not* go out? It was a sure way to be free of them.

Be one of them.

He chuckled at the simplicity of it, then shoved himself up and walked crookedly to the bar. Why not? His mind plodded on. Why go through all this complexity when a flung-open door and a few steps would end at all?

For the life of him, he didn't know. There was, of course, the faint possibility that others like him existed somewhere, trying to go on, hoping that someday they would be among their own kind again. But how could he ever find them if they weren't within a day's drive of his house?

He shrugged and poured more whisky in the glass; he'd given up the use of jiggers months ago. Garlic on the windows and nets over the hothouse and burn the bodies and cart the rocks away and, fraction of an inch by fraction of an inch, reduce their unholy numbers. Why kid himself? He'd never find anyone else.

His body dropped down heavily on the chair. Here we are, kiddies, sitting like a bug in a rug, snugly, surrounded by a battalion of bloodsuckers who wish no more than to sip freely of my bonded, 100-proof hemoglobin. Have a drink, men, this one's really on me.

His face twisted into an expression of raw, unqualified hatred. *Bastards!* I'll kill every mother's son of you before I'll give in! His right hand closed like a clamp and the glass shattered in his grip.

He looked down, dull-eyed, at the fragments on the floor, at the jagged piece of glass still in his hand, at the whisky-diluted blood dripping off his palm.

Wouldn't they like to get some of it, though? he thought. He started up with a furious lurch and almost opened the door so he could wave the hand in their faces and hear them howl.

Then he closed his eyes and a shudder ran through his body. Wise up, buddy, he thought. Go bandage your goddamn hand.

He stumbled into the bathroom and washed his hand carefully, gasping as he daubed iodine into the sliced-open flesh. Then he bandaged it clumsily, his broad chest rising and falling with jerky movements, sweat dripping from his forehead. I need a cigarette, he thought.

In the living room again, he changed Brahms for Bernstein and lit a cigarette. What will I do if I ever run out of coffin nails? he wondered, looking at the cigarette's blue trailing smoke. Well, there wasn't much chance of that. He had about a thousand cartons in the closet of Kathy's—

He clenched his teeth together. In the closet of the *larder,* the *larder,* the *larder.*

Kathy's room.

He sat staring with dead eyes at the mural while "The Age of Anxiety" pulsed in his ears. Age of anxiety, he mused. You thought you had anxiety, Lenny boy. Lenny and Benny; you two should meet. Composer, meet corpse. Mamma, when I grow up I wanna be a wampir like Dada. Why, bless you, hon, of course you shall.

The whisky gurgled into the glass. He grimaced a little at the pain in his hand and shifted the bottle to his left hand.

He sat down and sipped. Let the jagged edge of sobriety be now dulled, he thought. Let the crumby balance of clear vision be expunged, but post haste. I hate 'em.

Gradually the room shifted on its gyroscopic center and wove and undulated about his chair. A pleasant haze, fuzzy at the edges, took over sight. He looked at the glass, at the record player. He let his head flop from side to side. Outside, they prowled and muttered and waited.

Pore vampires, he thought, pore little cusses, pussy-footin' round my house, so thirsty, so all forlorn.

A thought. He raised a forefinger that wavered before his eyes.

Friends, I come before you to discuss the vampire; a minority element if there ever was one, and there was one.

But to concision: I will sketch out the basis for my thesis, which thesis is this: Vampires are prejudiced against.

The keynote of minority prejudice is this: They are loathed because they are feared. Thus . . .

He made himself a drink. A long one.

At one time, the Dark and Middle Ages, to be succinct, the vampire's power was great, the fear of him tremendous. He was anathema and still remains anathema. Society hates him without ration.

But are his needs any more shocking than the needs of other animals and men? Are his deeds more outrageous than the deeds of the parent who drained the spirit from his child? The vampire may foster quickened heartbeats and levitated hair. But is he worse than the parent who gave to society a neurotic child who became a politician? Is he worse than the manufacturer who set up belated foundations with the money he made by handing bombs and guns to suicidal nationalists? Is he worse than the distiller who gave bastardized grain juice to stultify further the brains of those who, sober, were incapable of a progressive thought? (Nay, I apologize for this calumny; I nip the brew that feeds me.) Is he worse, then, than the publisher who filled ubiquitous racks with lust and death wishes? Really, now, search your soul, lovie—is the vampire so bad?

All he does is drink blood.

Why, then, this unkind prejudice, this thoughtless bias? Why cannot the vampire live where he chooses? Why must he seek out hiding places where none can find him out? Why do you wish him destroyed? Ah, see, you have turned the poor guileless innocent into a haunted animal. He has no means of support, no measures for proper education, he has not the voting franchise. No wonder he is compelled to seek out a predatory nocturnal existence.

Robert Neville grunted a surly grunt. Sure, sure, he thought, but would you let your sister marry one?

He shrugged. You got me there, buddy, you got me there.

The music ended. The needle scratched back and forth in the black grooves. He sat there, feeling a chill creeping up his legs. That's what was wrong with drinking too much. You became immune to drunken delights. There was no solace in liquor. Before you got happy, you collapsed. Already the room was straightening out, the sounds outside were starting to nibble at his eardrums.

"Come out, Neville!"

His throat moved and a shaking breath passed his lips. Come out. The women were out there, their dresses open or taken off, their flesh waiting for his touch, their lips waiting for—

My blood, my *blood*!

As if it were someone else's hand, he watched his whitened fist rise up slowly, shuddering, to drive down on his leg. The pain made him suck in a breath of the house's stale air. Garlic. Everywhere the smell of garlic. In his clothes and in the furniture and in his food and even in his drink. Have a garlic and soda; his mind rattled out the attempted joke.

He lurched up and started pacing. What am I going to do now? Go through the routine again? I'll save you the trouble. Reading-drinking-soundproof-the-house—the women. The women, the lustful, bloodthirsty, naked women flaunting their hot bodies at him. No, not hot.

A shuddering whine wrenched up through his chest and throat. God-damn them, what were they waiting for? Did they think he was going to come out and hand himself over?

Maybe I am, maybe I am. He actually found himself jerking off the crossbar from the door. Coming, girls, I'm coming. Wet your lips, now.

Outside, they heard the bar being lifted, and a howl of anticipation sounded in the night.

Spinning, he drove his fists one after the other into the wall until he'd cracked the plaster and broken his skin. Then he stood there trembling helplessly, his teeth chattering.

After a while it passed. He put the bar back across the door and went into the bedroom. He sank down on the bed and fell back on the pillow with a groan. His left hand beat once, feebly, on the bedspread.

Oh, *God*, he thought, how long, how long?

The alarm never went off because he'd forgotten to set it. He slept soundly and motionlessly, his body like cast iron. When he finally opened his eyes, it was ten o'clock.

With a disgusted muttering, he struggled up and dropped his legs over the side of the bed. Instantly his head began throbbing as if his brains were trying to force their way through his skull. Fine, he thought, a hangover. That's all I need.

He pushed himself up with a groan and stumbled into the bathroom, threw water in his face and splashed some over his head. No good, his mind complained, no good. I still feel like hell. In the mirror his face was gaunt, bearded, and very much like the face of a man in his forties. Love, your magic spell is everywhere; inanely, the words flapped across his brain like wet sheets in a wind.

He walked slowly into the living room and opened the front door. A curse fell thickly from his lips at the sight of the woman crumpled across the sidewalk. He started to tighten angrily, but it made his head throb too much and he had to let it go. I'm sick, he thought.

The sky was gray and dead. Great! he thought. Another day stuck in this boarded-up rat hole! He slammed the door viciously, then winced, groaning, at the brain-stabbing noise. Outside, he heard the rest of the mirror fall out and shatter on the porch cement. Oh, *great!* His lips contorted back into a white twist of flesh.

Two cups of burning black coffee only made his stomach feel worse. He put down the cup and went into the living room. To hell with it, he thought, I'll get drunk again.

But the liquor tasted like turpentine, and with a rasping snarl he flung the glass against the wall and stood watching the liquor run down onto the rug. Hell, I'm runnin' out of glasses. The thought irritated him while breath struggled in through his nostrils and out again in faltering bursts.

He sank down on the couch and sat there, shaking his head slowly. It was no use; they'd beaten him, the black bastards had beaten him.

That restless feeling again; the feeling as if he were expanding and the house were contracting and any second now he'd go bursting through its frame in an explosion of wood, plaster, and brick. He got up and moved quickly to the door, his hands shaking.

On the lawn, he stood sucking in great lungfuls of the wet morning air, his face turned away from the house he hated. But he hated the other houses around there too, and he hated the pavement and the sidewalks and the lawns and everything that was on Cimarron Street.

It kept building up. And suddenly he knew he had to get out of there. Cloudy day or not, he had to get out of there.

He locked the front door, unlocked the garage, and dragged up the thick door on its overhead hinges. He didn't bother putting down the door. I'll be back soon, he thought. I'll just go away for a while.

He backed the station wagon quickly down the driveway, jerked it around, and pressed down hard on the accelerator, heading for Compton Boulevard. He didn't know where he was going.

He went around the corner doing forty and jumped that to sixty-five before he'd gone another block. The car leaped forward under his foot and he kept the accelerator on the floor, forced down by a rigid leg. His hands were like carved ice on the wheel and his face was the face of a statue. At eighty-nine miles an hour, he shot down the lifeless, empty boulevard, one roaring sound in the great stillness.

Things rank and gross in nature possess it merely, he thought as he walked slowly across the cemetery lawn.

The grass was so high that the weight of it had bent it over and it crunched under his heavy shoes as he walked. There was no sound but that of his shoes and the now senseless singing of birds. Once I thought they sang because everything was right with the world, Robert Neville thought. I know now I was wrong. They sing because they're feeble-minded.

He had raced six miles, the gas pedal pressed to the floor, before he'd realized where he was going. It was strange the way his mind and body had kept it secret from his consciousness. Consciously, he'd known only that he was sick and depressed and had to get away from the house. He didn't know he was going to visit Virginia.

But he'd driven there directly and as fast as he could. He'd parked at the curb and entered through the rusted gate, and now his shoes were pressing and crackling through the thick grass.

How long had it been since he'd come here? It must have been at least a month. He wished he'd brought flowers, but then, he hadn't realized he was coming here until he was almost at the gate.

His lips pressed together as an old sorrow held him again. Why couldn't he have Kathy there too? Why had he followed so blindly, listening to those fools who set up their stupid regulations during the plague? If only she could be there, lying across from her mother.

Don't start that again, he ordered himself.

Drawing closer to the crypt, he stiffened as he noticed that the iron door was slightly ajar. Oh, *no,* he thought. He broke into a run across the wet grass. If they've been at her, I'll burn down the city, he vowed. I swear to God, I'll burn it to the ground if they've touched her.

He flung open the door and it clanged against the marble wall with a hollow, echoing sound. His eyes moved quickly to the marble base on which the sealed casket rested.

The tension sank; he drew in breath again. It was still there, untouched.

Then, as he started in, he saw the man lying in one corner of the crypt, body curled up on the cold floor.

With a grunt of rage, Robert Neville rushed at the body, and, grabbing the man's coat in taut fingers, he dragged him across the floor and flung him violently out onto the grass. The body rolled onto its back, the white face pointing at the sky.

Robert Neville went back into the crypt, chest rising and falling with harsh movements. Then he closed his eyes and stood with his palms resting on the cover of the casket.

I'm here, he thought. I'm back. Remember me.

He threw out the flowers he'd brought the time before and cleared away the few leaves that had blown in because the door had been opened.

Then he sat down beside the casket and rested his forehead against its cold metal side.

Silence held him in its cold and gentle hands.

If I could die now, he thought; peacefully, gently, without a tremor or a crying out. If I could be with her. If I could believe I would be with her.

His fingers tightened slowly and his head sank forward on his chest.

Virginia. Take me where you are.

A tear, crystal, fell across his motionless hand. . . .

He had no idea how long he'd been there. After a while, though, even the deepest sorrow faltered, even the most penetrating despair lost its scalpel edge. The flagellant's curse, he thought, to grow inured even to the whip.

He straightened up and stood. Still alive, he thought, heart beating senselessly, veins running without point, bones and muscles and tissue all alive and functioning, with no purpose at all.

A moment longer he stood looking down at the casket, then he turned away with a sigh and left, closing the door behind him quietly so as not to disturb her sleep.

He'd forgotten about the man. He almost tipped over him now, stepping aside with a muttered curse and starting past the body.

Then, abruptly, he turned back.

What's this? He looked down incredulously at the man. The man was dead; really dead. But how could that be? The change had occurred so quickly, yet already the man looked and smelled as though he'd been dead for days.

His mind began churning with a sudden excitement. Something had killed the vampire; something brutally effective. The heart had not been touched, no garlic had been present, and yet . . .

It came, seemingly, without effort. Of course—the daylight!

A bolt of self-accusation struck him. To know for five months that they remained indoors by day and never *once* to make the connection! He closed his eyes, appalled by his own stupidity.

The rays of the sun; the infrared and ultraviolet. It had to be them. But why? Damn it, why didn't he know anything about the effects of sunlight on the human system?

Another thought: That man had been one of the true vampires; the living dead. Would sunlight have the same effect on those who were still alive?

The first excitement he'd felt in months made him break into a run for the station wagon.

As the door slammed shut beside him, he wondered if he should have taken away the dead man. Would the body attract others, would they invade the crypt? No, they wouldn't go near the casket, anyway; it was sealed with garlic. Besides, the man's blood was dead now, it—

Again his thoughts broke off as he leaped to another conclusion. The sun's rays must have done something to their blood!

Was it possible, then, that all things bore relations to the blood? The garlic, the cross, the mirror, the stake, daylight, the earth some of them slept in? He didn't see how, and yet . . .

He had to do a lot of reading, a lot of research. It might be just the thing he needed. He'd been planning for a long time to do it, but lately it seemed as if he'd forgotten it altogether. Now this new idea started the desire again.

He started the car and raced up the street, turning off into a residential section and pulling up before the first house he came to.

He ran up the pathway to the front door, but it was locked and he couldn't force it in. With an impatient growl, he ran to the next house. The door was open and he ran to the stairs through the darkened living room and jumped up the carpeted steps two at a time.

He found the woman in the bedroom. Without hesitation, he jerked back the covers and grabbed her by the wrists. She grunted as her body hit the floor, and he heard her making tiny sounds in her throat as he dragged her into the hall and started down the stairs.

As he pulled her across the living room, she started to move.

Her hands closed over his wrists and her body began to twist and flop on the rug. Her eyes were still closed, but she gasped and muttered and her body kept trying to writhe out of his grip. Her dark nails dug into his flesh. He tore out of her grasp with a snarl and dragged her the rest of the way by her hair. Usually he felt a twinge when he realized that, but for some affliction he didn't understand, these people were the same as he. But now an experimental fervor had seized him and he could think of nothing else.

Even so, he shuddered at the strangled sound of horror she made when he threw her on the sidewalk outside.

She lay twisting helplessly on the sidewalk, hands opening and closing, lips drawn back from red-spotted lips. Robert Neville watched her tensely.

His throat moved. It wouldn't last, the feeling of callous brutality. He bit his lips as he watched her. All right, she's suffering, he argued with himself, but she's one of them and she'd kill me gladly if she got the chance. You've got to look at it that way, it's the only way. Teeth clenched, he stood there and watched her die.

In a few minutes she stopped moving, stopped muttering, and her hands uncurled slowly like white blossoms on the cement. Robert Neville crouched down and felt for her heartbeat. There was none. Already her flesh was growing cold.

He straightened up with a thin smile. It was true, then. He didn't need the stakes. After all this time, he'd finally found a better method.

Then his breath caught. But how did he know the woman was really dead? How could he know until sunset?

The thought filled him with a new, more restless anger. Why did each question blight the answers before it?

He thought about it as he sat drinking a can of tomato juice taken from the supermarket behind which he was parked.

How was he going to know? He couldn't very well stay with the woman until sunset came.

Take her home with you, fool.

Again his eyes closed and he felt a shudder of irritation go through him. He was missing all the obvious answers today. Now he'd have to go all the way back and find her, and he wasn't even sure where the house was.

He started the motor and pulled away from the parking lot, glancing down at his watch. Three o'clock. Plenty of time to get back before they came. He eased the gas pedal down and the station wagon pulled ahead faster.

It took him about a half hour to relocate the house. The woman was still in the same position on the sidewalk. Putting on his gloves, Neville lowered the back gate of the station wagon and walked over to the woman. As he walked, he noticed her figure. No, don't start that again, for God's sake.

He dragged the woman back to the station wagon and tossed her in. Then he closed the gate and took off his gloves. He held up the watch and looked at it. Three o'clock. Plenty of time to—

He jerked up the watch and held it against his ear, his heart suddenly jumping.

The watch had stopped.

LESLIE ROY CARTER
(b. 1946)

Leslie Roy Carter was born in 1946 in Washington, D.C. He followed in his father's footsteps and became a naval officer in 1971 after graduating from The College of William and Mary in Virginia. With his family, he lives in Annapolis, Maryland, while on active duty with the U.S. Navy.

Carter's published stories include "Carmen's Flight" in the Towers of Darkover *anthology (1993) and "Final Class," a vampire tale, in the magazine* Vampire's Crypt *(1994).*

In the fanciful tale that follows, we learn about two sorts of vampires. There are the classical supernatural vampires who are a race apart from humankind. The others are mutants who have been absorbed into the larger culture, who "don't go around wearing capes and acting strangely." These "adapting" vampires live anonymously among ordinary mortals, feeding moderately so as to avoid detection. The problem for these vampires is only too human: integration or segregation. The matter is finally resolved, but the solution is awkward.

VANISHING BREED

Carl Rhyner was reading when his window vibrated with a soft thud. He ignored it, knowing what it meant, because at this moment he did not want to be disturbed. *With a plunge he seizes her neck in his fang-like teeth*—the window shuddered again, this time with such violence that Carl was afraid the glass would crack. He disgustedly put the book down and walked across his apartment to the window. The lights of the city, shining through the glass, distinctly outlined the dark object hovering outside. Carl stared at it, dislike pouring from his eyes onto the giant bat. "Go around!"

The bat skittered up and down the glass, its eyes burning red. Its mouth opened and closed, and a faint screech came through the window. "No, damn it, go around." The bat fluttered out into the lights of the city, disappearing among the neon stars. As Carl turned away, his eye caught a movement, and he hurled himself against the "raise" button. The window snapped open just as the bat flashed through into the room. It settled on the living room floor and folded its wings across its body. The wavering mist flowed up from the ground, and Dr. Valpa stepped out.

Carl slammed his hand against the "lower" button and turned to his guest. "Hell, I told you to go around. I'm tired of this stupid rigmarole. If you keep coming in here like that, you'll give me away."

The good doctor scowled at Carl, displeasure written in the lines of his thin lips. "My dear boy—for you are one, you know, lad—all vampires come through windows."

"I don't," asserted Carl. "And furthermore, I don't come dressed in those ridiculous clothes."

Dr. Valpa looked down at his long, flowing black cape, opening his arms outward as if to present himself to an audience. "Enough—I knew you would start on that theme again." Valpa lowered himself into the easy chair, folding his cape behind him. He picked up the novel, turning to the cover. *"Varney the Vampyre!* and you question my methods— really, Carl, how hypocritical." Carl's face flamed. Valpa cut short a laugh and pointed. "There, there is the reason. What true vampire can blush like that? You young mutants are all alike—dress modern, scorn the old ways, run wild. Ah, in my youth—"

"Stop, Doctor. Your youth was a couple of thousand years ago. We, the new vampires, must live in this world, in this time. We can't go around wearing capes and acting strangely. We'd be picked up by the proctors in minutes if we did."

"Sad, but true, lad." Dr. Valpa nodded his head at this point. "Even I

at the university must dress in the current fad in order to keep my job."
He looked up sharply at Carl. "But I still hold to the old ways when I
go on my rounds. At least you could do that."

Carl sat down opposite the old man and stared into his red eyes. "Dr.
Valpa, you don't understand, do you? You still don't grasp what's happening. You wouldn't last a second in the city. If I followed the old ways
of feeding, I'd be caught all too quickly. Here in the city, in this apartment
complex, I have over five hundred people on which I feed. I take a sip
here, a sip there—no one misses it, and if I overindulge a little, they
chalk it up to iron-poor blood. No one guesses, or even can believe that
I'm around."

Dr. Valpa sat back, his arms outstretched along the steep sides of the
chair. "Another point, dear boy. But how can you say you are a vampire?"
Valpa stood up and began pacing up and down. "A vampire involves
himself with his prey; he lures it to him, seducing it with hypnotic trances
that wrap them both in a world of their own. He—"

"Nonsense." Carl propped his leg across his other knee.

Dr. Valpa stopped before the easy chair, stricken to the heart. He turned
slowly, his face paler than death. "Nonsense," he stuttered out. "Nonsense!" he roared.

"Nonsense," Carl repeated quietly. Valpa's mouth stood open, his eyes
wide and staring. "We don't need it. After all, being human, we can enjoy
the, ah—" Carl coughed into his hand, "say, better things of life."

Valpa stood rooted to the floor. His mouth slowly closed, and he
seemed to melt down into the chair. "Is this what we have become, bastards upon the human race, losing our own identity and becoming more
alien every day?" He lowered his head, his eyes riveted to the floral pattern
on the tiles.

Carl stirred uneasily. "Doctor, what do you mean alien? I know you
and the other forefathers are dead come to life, but that makes you
human still."

"No, Carl. You just don't really understand yourself. The true history
of our race has never been written." Dr. Valpa's eyes became blank, and
he seemed to sink into himself. His voice sounded as if he were speaking
in an empty auditorium. Hollow, deep, and quiet. "Didn't they teach you
anything when you were born?"

Carl shook his head. He stared uncomfortably at the old man. "You
know, the usual—speed calculation, speed reading, computer technology—"

"No!" groaned Valpa. "Anything about being a vampire!"

"Well, no. Dr. Jamison, the psychologist attached to our coven, did try
to stress the fact that although we were vampires, we had our place in
society, that we were not truly deviants, misfits—"

"Curses upon him!" cried Dr. Valpa. "The old lure is lost. I told them
to beware of Jamison, he would ruin us!" Valpa was raging now. Carl

was afraid and tried to quiet him. Valpa struck down Carl's hands and grabbed his shoulders. "Didn't they teach you anything about history, boy? Anything?"

Carl pried the clawlike hands away. "Yes, they did. The general atomic wars feared in the '50s and '60s were averted, and the world turned instead to peace. All races were declared equal, and thereby all men. Now, in the twenty-second century, all people live their own lives as long as they bother no one. Each of us has his place—"

"Unholy Powers," Dr. Valpa sighed. "Carl, tomorrow night a warden will come to pick you up." His cape folded over his eyes as he sank down into the floor. The monstrous bat cried shrilly and fluttered up from the floor, striking the wall. The window opened, and the bat flitted out.

"Valpa, wait. Tell me—" Carl cried as the bat disappeared into the night. The cool night air breathed across Carl's face, chilling the sweat that streamed from his pores. He closed the window, and his reflection stared back at him—stark, hard features. Eyes bleak and cold. His flesh was firm upon his face. His teeth were even and white—no trace of fangs—no need, since the use of hyper-fine needles left no marks. "Damn, what did he mean?" Carl asked the still room.

The next night, around two, Carl was leaving on his evening rounds when he again heard the sounds at the windowpane. He hurried over and opened the window, through which a bat of large proportions flew. It settled in the living room and transformed into a middle-aged man, dressed in much the same attire as Dr. Valpa had worn. Only this man was a warden. Carl knew him from his days in the school where he had been instructed, along with the other young vampires, in the ways of men. The wardens were to the human vampires what the proctors were to society as a whole.

The tall vampire walked forward, his cape billowing out behind him. He touched Carl's arm. "You are to come."

Carl leaped as if he had been struck.

The warden eyed him for several moments, then quietly spoke to him. "You are summoned by the council. You must come."

Carl's ashen face convulsed into horror. "Valpa said so, but the council—the council has not been called for fifty years."

"I know." The warden turned and beckoned Carl to the window.

"I can't go that way, sir."

The warden grimaced. "I am not ignorant of your lacks. Come here and observe the dark aircar on the taxi strip. You are to walk down and board it immediately." As he spoke, he slowly vanished, and the bat flew out the window, crying shrilly into the night.

Stepping into the car, Carl saw Steven and Maria Collins. Their faces, like his own, were lined with worry. Maria cried out when she saw him, "Carl, a council—a full council has been called. We are summoned."

Carl sat down beside Maria and put his hand in hers. "He just came for me. I thought I had done something, maybe something I said to Dr. Valpa—"

"Dr. Valpa—the prime leader!"

Carl looked sharply. "Prime leader—since when? He was just an adviser when I heard last."

Steve shook his head. "He was levied into prime position last May. A power play among the old ones put him in. There has been a shake-up in the organization, and it looks like we are the cause of it."

"What do you mean, Steve—we? Do you mean us in particular—unlikely, since I have done little to cause trouble—or," here Carl hesitated, afraid to say it, "or is it the human vamps as a whole?"

Maria's eyes, looking into his, were red, but from crying. "All of us, Carl. We, the first group, and the last three groups they have created."

Carl sat gloomily in the car as it sped away from the city and into the hills. Steve and Maria were also quiet, each locked in his own thoughts, the idea that perhaps the experiment had failed.

The car turned into a deep valley and followed a steep, winding road up the hillside until it came to the house. One should say "castle," but none existed in North America. The house was dark and foreboding, just as Carl, Steve, and Maria remembered it as young vampires playing in the surrounding hills. They always laughed at the antiquity of their elders and the place they chose to live.

Inside they were numbered by the sheer size of the gathering of vampires from all over the world. Great men and women they had only heard of in tales were present. Each one indefinably old, but still outwardly young. Bats whirled through the shadows under the vaulted ceiling. A dim flickering light was shed by a few antique candelabra, whose flames burned blue.

Carl and his friends stood in the rear of the great hall, for they were the last to arrive. No one really noticed them, because all eyes were fixed on Lord Ruthven, who stood before them on the raised dais.

He stretched out his arms, and the murmur of voices stopped. Silence filled the room as the earl's dead gray eyes searched over the gathering. His lips moved slowly, as if talking were an impossibility for him. In a dry voice, cracked and broken with ageless time, he whispered out over the gathering. As the words fell upon their ranks, a shock of silence hit the room. "The experiment has failed."

For a moment, an age, no one moved, talked, existed. For the true vampires, a dream of the centuries had been destroyed. The dream that had been fanned into being, nurtured, given hope and encouragement— gone. And for the human vamps, disbelief and anger. Shame filled their faces, and hatred filled the room. With the apathy and depression of their elders, theirs passion increased, and a tumult broke loose in the rear. The newer human vampires were pushing to the front. Shouts of, "Liar!

Fabricator!" flooded the aisles. Carl stood up on a chair and shouted to be heard.

"Vamps, hear me. These old fools want the experiment to fail. They want us to believe that we cannot be human and still be vampires. They are filled with the ages of mankind and are beginning to believe their own legends."

Steve yelled affirmation, and the air vibrated with the noise of the human vamps crying in the night. Then the screech of a great bat split the air, and the vampires cowered to the floor. The earl stood tall on the platform, his great wings overshadowing the stage. His mouth, sharp-fanged and evil, gaped in anger.

"Fools—listen to me again. What is decided here will rule your lives from now to eternity." Ruthven gestured to a figure standing in the crowd near the stage. Meek it stood, beside Ruthven, a mere shadow of the image of him, but Carl recognized the prime leader.

"Thank you, my good Earl, but I think after I explain to these young hotheads why the experiment has failed, then they will cease this needless disorder." An atmosphere of a classroom seemed to pervade over all as the professor stood behind the podium and straightened his notes. He spoke.

"It seems a certain amount of history was deleted from our younger friends' education, and lacking this, a grave misunderstanding has arisen. I have found in many cases, such as Carl Rhyner's—" heads turned and looked at Carl's flushed face—"a seeking of understanding and self-explanation. The human vamps have been raised in *our* society, and they truly do not know who they are."

Dr. Valpa shuffled his notes and allowed the murmuring to die down. He glanced over his glasses at the rear of the room and noticed the look of acknowledgment in Carl's eyes.

"Yes, they read the old human classics and find only the legends they accuse us of portraying—though in reality the legends are true, and what they read is really us. But they cannot identify with these legends, because they are human and do not believe in what are called 'fantasies' in the world. They are, however, truly vampires, in that they exist by feeding on blood, but human, in that they can't fly, have no problem with mirrors, eat garlic, etc., etc." Dr. Valpa waved his hands as if dismissing the traditional symptoms of vampirism. "Instead of questioning why vampires are affected this way, they took their human 'souls' into hand and began to live their lives in society as an integral part of it. They blended into the background, became respected commoners, upheld the UN and hated the perverts, all the time carrying on a heritage which they accepted as being a norm for their particular subculture. Human vampires. Now this we wanted, expected, ahem, prayed for. But—" His hand shot up, and the index finger quivered over the crowd. Carl knew he would ball up his hand and slam it down on the podium. Crash! "But, we did not expect them to become so human as to not realize their true heritage—that they are, and we are, all of us are aliens to this world."

"Never!" shouted Carl. "I'm as human as anyone on this planet. I'm, I'm—" Oh, my God, he's right. If the legends are true, he must be.

"Carl, all of you, we are aliens. We came over ten thousand years ago. We were forced from our last home by the same thing which is facing us now. We are parasites, Carl, pure and simple. We draw our existence from human life. If we are discovered, openly and under the full light of human understanding, we will be wiped out as cancer and heart disease were in the twenty-first century. No human being can abide the thought of a creature feeding on him. We would be hunted down and destroyed."

Valpa paced the stage, his eyes now not seeing the crowd. His hands fluttered in the direction of Gilles de Rais and his group—the true vampires. "We would be the first to go. They have documented us pretty well. They know all about our peculiarities, and once mankind *really* believed in vampires, then we would quickly go. You," pointing to Carl, Valpa's red eyes glimmered, "would be safe—for a while. But not long enough. Medical checks would be made, impure blood diagnosed as vampire feeding, guards posted in sleeping areas, traps set. Oh, vampires of old, can we ever forget the persecutions of our forefathers on the twilight world of Antares Four!"

"That still doesn't explain, Doctor, why the experiment has failed." All eyes turned to Carl.

Dr. Valpa watched Carl for a moment, then turned to the crowd. The great hall waited for his reply. "They know we are here now. The experiment failed because one of the human vamps was analyzed by a psychproctor. The vamp talked freely about his entire life. He complained of his feelings of non-belonging, his desire for acceptance. And he told the proctor every detail, not knowing what reaction he would get from the human. The vamp had been so humanized that he thought being a vampire was like being a homosexual, deviant but accepted and permitted. We didn't expect the proctor to believe him, but he did, and he forced the young man to reveal his adviser, Sir Romuald." Valpa's face turned paler than ever. "Sir Romuald was terminated, while sleeping, with a stake through his heart, and a real-time record of the execution stored in permanent cybernetic memory."

A cry of agony poured from the true vampires. "It is come, then."

The starship, though ultramodern and wondrous to the humans, was tired and old. It had been old long before its last trip, and it was even older now. But its gleaming hull stood beckoning to the vampires as they filed up from the valley and into the airlock. At the entry ramp Dr. Valpa stood, checking the boarding list against the men and women and whirling bats that thronged inside. Although busy, his eyes noted Carl's hesitant approach up the ramp. He felt a twinge of expectancy of what the young man was going to say. As the last of the humans were coming aboard, Valpa saw how Steven and Maria were gazing back at Carl, and he knew for certain now.

Carl stood beside him, and together they watched Steve and Maria walk into the vast cargo hold of the ship. Maria turned and waved, her small face bright with tears, then disappeared. Dr. Valpa pulled his cape around him, trying to ward off the chill wind blowing up from the valley. His blood-red eyes gazed back down the winding road, out across the valley, to the plasti-domed metropolis on the horizon.

"It was a good world, Carl. Good for our people. We watched it grow from distant Greece to powerful UN. Our people have aided the Terrans in many ways, most of which they will never know. Someday they may feel indebtedness to us. Perhaps, Carl, you may have a hand in that."

"Doctor, I—" Carl stopped. Valpa's arm was around his shoulder, and he felt, for the first time, a humanness, a warmth, coming from the old vampire.

"I know, Carl. You can't go. You can't leave this world for another— however near we can come to it in the universe. I know, because I too wanted to stay on our last journey. I could almost do so now." The old man shook his head sadly, the white curls floating in the chill night air. "Funny as it seems, Carl, I liked being a professor. Always have. However, I suppose I'll be a general or a medicine man or some other type on the next world." Carl couldn't help smiling at the picture of Valpa striding across the fields leading great hulking barbarians into battle.

"Then you will speak comfort to Maria for me, sir?"

Valpa nodded his head and turned to walk up the ramp. He still held Carl close around the shoulders, hugging him to his side. Carl could smell dank earth, a musty odor heavy in his nostrils, and he breathed deeply. Valpa let him go with a shake of the head, as if he were flinging tears from his eyes.

The door slid silently down before Carl, and he turned and raced down the ramp. The ship lifted on its anti-gravs, turning ever so slightly, searching with its starnavs for the correct hole in space. As it winked out of existence, Carl heard again the last words that Valpa had spoken to him.

"We will all think of you, Carl, for you will be something special. For us, for Earth, you will be all that remains of a legend."

SUZY MCKEE CHARNAS
(b. 1939)

Suzy McKee Charnas, born in New York City, was educated at Barnard College and New York University. She was trained as a teacher and worked as a Peace Corps volunteer in Nigeria. She is the author of several novels, among them The Vampire Tapestry (1980) which is composed of five linked stories of varying lengths. One of these stories, "Unicorn Tapestry" (reprinted here), won a 1980 Nebula Award. She recently published another vampire novel, The Ruby Tear (1997), under the pseudonym Rebecca Brand, and has written additional vampire stories for such anthologies as A Whisper of Blood (1991) and Under the Fang (1991). A werewolf story, "Boobs," won a Hugo Award in 1989.

Charnas's very modern vampire tale is certainly one of the finest written in this century. In addition to providing a convincing scientific treatment of vampirism, the novel, because of its prose rhythms, is delicate, rich, complex, and emotionally satisfying.

Charnas's use of the unicorn invites speculation about her tale. In medieval folklore, unicorns were said to be attracted to young virgins. A hunter would use a virgin as bait to attract a unicorn, which, when it had put its head in the young woman's lap, was easily captured.

The medieval mind saw in the story of the unicorn a Christian allegory, with the Virgin Mary as the maiden and the wounded unicorn as Christ. In a story as richly and densely imagined as "Unicorn Tapestry," it is, perhaps, not reading too much into Charnas's story to assume that we are reading an allegory of Christ.

UNICORN TAPESTRY

"Hold on," Floria said. "I know what you're going to say: I agreed not to take any new clients for a while. But wait till I tell you—you're not going to believe this—first phone call, setting up an initial appointment, he comes out with what his problem is: 'I seem to have fallen victim to a delusion of being a vampire.' "

"Christ H. God!" cried Lucille delightedly. "Just like that, over the telephone?"

"When I recovered my aplomb, so to speak, I told him that I prefer to wait with the details until our first meeting, which is tomorrow."

They were sitting on the tiny terrace outside the staff room of the clinic, a converted town house on the upper West Side. Floria spent three days a week here and the remaining two in her office on Central Park South where she saw private clients like this new one. Lucille, always gratifyingly responsive, was Floria's most valued professional friend. Clearly enchanted with Floria's news, she sat eagerly forward in her chair, eyes wide behind Coke-bottle lenses.

She said, "Do you suppose he thinks he's a revivified corpse?"

Below, down at the end of the street, Floria could see two kids skidding their skateboards near a man who wore a woolen cap and a heavy coat despite the May warmth. He was leaning against a wall. He had been there when Floria had arrived at the clinic this morning. If corpses walked, some, not nearly revivified enough, stood in plain view in New York.

"I'll have to think of a delicate way to ask," she said.

"How did he come to you, this 'vampire'?"

"He was working in an upstate college, teaching and doing research, and all of a sudden he just disappeared—vanished, literally, without a trace. A month later he turned up here in the city. The faculty dean at the school knows me and sent him to see me."

Lucille gave her a sly look. "So you thought, ahah, do a little favor for a friend, this looks classic and easy to transfer if need be: repressed intellectual blows stack and runs off with spacey chick, something like that."

"You know me too well," Floria said with a rueful smile.

"Huh," grunted Lucille. She sipped ginger ale from a chipped white mug. "I don't take panicky middle-aged men anymore, they're too depressing. And you shouldn't be taking this one, intriguing as he sounds."

Here comes the lecture, Floria told herself.

Lucille got up. She was short, heavy, prone to wearing loose garments that swung about her like ceremonial robes. As she paced, her hem brushed at the flowers starting up in the planting boxes that rimmed the little terrace. "You know damn well this is just more overwork you're loading on. Don't take this guy; refer him."

Floria sighed. "I know, I know. I promised everybody I'd slow down. But you said it yourself just a minute ago—it looked like a simple favor. So what do I get? Count Dracula, for God's sake! Would you give that up?"

Fishing around in one capacious pocket, Lucille brought out a dented package of cigarettes and lit up, scowling. "You know, when you give me advice I try to take it seriously. Joking aside, Floria, what am I supposed to say? I've listened to you moaning for months now, and I thought we'd figured out that what you need is to shed some pressure, to start saying no—and here you are insisting on a new case. You know what I think: you're hiding in other people's problems from a lot of your own stuff that you should be working on.

"Okay, okay, don't glare at me. Be pigheaded. Have you gotten rid of Chubs, at least?" This was Floria's code name for a troublesome client named Kenny whom she'd been trying to unload for some time.

Floria shook her head.

"What gives with you? It's weeks since you swore you'd dump him! Trying to do everything for everybody is wearing you out. I bet you're still dropping weight. Judging by the very unbecoming circles under your eyes, sleeping isn't going too well, either. Still no dreams you can remember?"

"Lucille, don't nag, I don't want to talk about my health."

"Well, what about his health—Dracula's? Did you suggest that he have a physical before seeing you? There might be some physiological—"

"You're not going to be able to whisk him off to an M.D. and out of my hands," Floria said wryly. "He told me on the phone that he wouldn't consider either medication or hospitalization."

Involuntarily she glanced down at the end of the street. The woolen-capped man had curled up on the sidewalk at the foot of the building, sleeping or passed out or dead. The city was tottering with sickness. Compared with that wreck down there and others like him, how sick could this "vampire" be, with his cultured baritone voice, his self-possessed approach?

"And you won't consider handing him off to somebody else," Lucille said.

"Well, not until I know a little more. Come on, Luce—wouldn't you want at least to know what he looks like?"

Lucille stubbed out her cigarette against the low parapet. Down below a policeman strolled along the street ticketing the parked cars. He didn't even look at the man lying at the corner of the building. They watched his progress without comment. Finally Lucille said, "Well, if you won't drop Dracula, keep me posted on him, will you?"

*   *   *

He entered the office on the dot of the hour, a gaunt but graceful figure. He was impressive. Wiry gray hair, worn short, emphasized the massiveness of his face with its long jaw, high cheekbones, and granite cheeks grooved as if by winters of hard weather. His name, typed in caps on the initial information sheet that Floria proceeded to fill out with him, was Edward Lewis Weyland.

Crisply he told her about the background of the vampire incident, describing in caustic terms his life at Cayslin College: the pressures of collegial competition, interdepartmental squabbles, student indifference, administrative bungling. History has limited use, she knew, since memory distorts; still, if he felt most comfortable establishing the setting for his illness, that was as good a way to start off as any.

At length his energy faltered. His angular body sank into a slump, his voice became flat and tired as he haltingly worked up to the crucial event: night work at the sleep lab, fantasies of blood-drinking as he watched the youthful subjects of his dream research slumbering, finally an attempt to act out the fantasy with a staff member at the college. He had been repulsed; then panic had assailed him. Word would get out, he'd be fired, blacklisted forever. He'd bolted. A nightmare period had followed—he offered no details. When he had come to his senses he'd seen that just what he feared, the ruin of his career, would come from his running away. So he'd phoned the dean, and now here he was.

Throughout this recital she watched him diminish from the dignified academic who had entered her office to a shamed and frightened man hunched in his chair, his hands pulling fitfully at each other.

"What are your hands doing?" she said gently. He looked blank. She repeated the question.

He looked down at his hands. "Struggling," he said.

"With what?"

"The worst," he muttered. "I haven't told you the worst." She had never grown hardened to this sort of transformation. His long fingers busied themselves fiddling with a button on his jacket while he explained painfully that the object of his "attack" at Cayslin had been a woman. Not young but handsome and vital, she had first caught his attention earlier in the year during a *festschrift*—an honorary seminar—for a retiring professor.

A picture emerged of an awkward Weyland, lifelong bachelor, seeking this woman's warmth and suffering her refusal. Floria knew she should bring him out of his past and into his here-and-now, but he was doing so beautifully on his own that she was loath to interrupt.

"Did I tell you there was a rapist active on the campus at this time?" he said bitterly. "I borrowed a leaf from his book: I tried to take from this woman, since she wouldn't give. I tried to take some of her blood." He stared at the floor. "What does that mean—to take someone's blood?"

"What do you think it means?"

The button, pulled and twisted by his fretful fingers, came off. He put it into his pocket, the impulse, she guessed, of a fastidious nature. "Her energy," he murmured, "stolen to warm the aging scholar, the walking corpse, the vampire—myself."

His silence, his downcast eyes, his bent shoulders, all signaled a man brought to bay by a life crisis. Perhaps he was going to be the kind of client therapists dream of and she needed so badly these days: a client intelligent and sensitive enough, given the companionship of a professional listener, to swiftly unravel his own mental tangles. Exhilarated by his promising start, Floria restrained herself from trying to build on it too soon. She made herself tolerate the silence, which lasted until he said suddenly, "I notice that you make no notes as we speak. Do you record these sessions on tape?"

A hint of paranoia, she thought; not unusual. "Not without your knowledge and consent, just as I won't send for your personnel file from Cayslin without your knowledge and consent. I do, however, write notes after each session as a guide to myself and in order to have a record in case of any confusion about anything we do or say here. I can promise you that I won't show my notes or speak of you by name to anyone— except Dean Sharpe at Cayslin, of course, and even then only as much as is strictly necessary—without your written permission. Does that satisfy you?"

"I apologize for my question," he said. "The . . . incident has left me . . . very nervous; a condition that I hope to get over with your help."

The time was up. When he had gone, she stepped outside to check with Hilda, the receptionist she shared with four other therapists here at the Central Park South office. Hilda always sized up new clients in the waiting room.

Of this one she said, "Are you sure there's anything wrong with that guy? I think I'm in love."

Waiting at the office for a group of clients to assemble Wednesday evening, Floria dashed off some notes on the "vampire."

> Client described incident, background. No history of mental illness, no previous experience of therapy. Personal history so ordinary you almost don't notice how bare it is: only child of German immigrants, schooling normal, field work in anthropology, academic posts leading to Cayslin College professorship. Health good, finances adequate, occupation satisfactory, housing pleasant (though presently installed in a N.Y. hotel); never married, no kids, no family, no religion, social life strictly job-related; leisure—says he likes to drive. Reaction to question about drinking, but no signs of alcohol problems. Physically very smooth-moving for his age (over fifty) and height; catlike, alert. Some apparent stiffness in the midsection—slight protective stoop—tightening up of

middle age? Paranoic defensiveness? Voice pleasant, faint accent (German-speaking childhood at home). Entering therapy condition of consideration for return to job.

What a relief: his situation looked workable with a minimum of strain on herself. Now she could defend to Lucille her decision to do therapy with the "vampire."

After all, Lucille was right. Floria did have problems of her own that needed attention, primarily her anxiety and exhaustion since her mother's death more than a year before. The breakup of Floria's marriage had caused misery, but not this sort of endless depression. Intellectually the problem was clear: with both her parents dead she was left exposed. No one stood any longer between herself and the inevitability of her own death. Knowing the source of her feelings didn't help: she couldn't seem to mobilize the nerve to work on them.

The Wednesday group went badly again. Lisa lived once more her experiences in the European death camps and everyone cried. Floria wanted to stop Lisa, turn her, extinguish the droning horror of her voice in illumination and release, but she couldn't see how to do it. She found nothing in herself to offer except some clever ploy out of the professional bag of tricks—dance your anger, have a dialog with yourself of those days—useful techniques when they flowed organically as part of a living process in which the therapist participated. But thinking out responses that should have been intuitive wouldn't work. The group and its collective pain paralyzed her. She was a dancer without a choreographer, knowing all the moves but unable to match them to the music these people made.

Rather than act with mechanical clumsiness she held back, did nothing, and suffered guilt. Oh God, the smart, experienced people in the group must know how useless she was here.

Going home on the bus she thought about calling up one of the therapists who shared the downtown office. He had expressed an interest in doing co-therapy with her under student observation. The Wednesday group might respond well to that. Suggest it to them next time? Having a partner might take pressure off Floria and revitalize the group, and if she felt she must withdraw he would be available to take over. Of course he might take over anyway and walk off with some of her clients.

Oh boy, terrific, who's paranoid now? Wonderful way to think about a good colleague. God, she hadn't even known she was considering chucking the group.

Had the new client, running from his "vampirism," exposed her own impulse to retreat? This wouldn't be the first time that Floria had obtained help from a client while attempting to give help. Her old supervisor, Rigby, said that such mutual aid was the only true therapy—the rest was fraud. What a perfectionist, old Rigby, and what a bunch of young idealists he'd turned out, all eager to save the world.

Eager, but not necessarily able. Jane Fennerman had once lived in the world, and Floria had been incompetent to save her. Jane, an absent member of tonight's group, was back in the safety of a locked ward, hazily gliding on whatever tranquilizers they used there.

Why still mull over Jane? she asked herself severely, bracing against the bus's lurching halt. Any client was entitled to drop out of therapy and commit herself. Nor was this the first time that sort of thing had happened in the course of Floria's career. Only this time she couldn't seem to shake free of the resulting depression and guilt.

But how could she have helped Jane more? How could you offer reassurance that life was not as dreadful as Jane felt it to be, that her fears were insubstantial, that each day was not a pit of pain and danger?

She was taking time during a client's canceled hour to work on notes for the new book. The writing, an analysis of the vicissitudes of salaried versus private practice, balked her at every turn. She longed for an interruption to distract her circling mind.

Hilda put through a call from Cayslin College. It was Doug Sharpe, who had sent Dr. Weyland to her.

"Now that he's in your capable hands, I can tell people plainly that he's on what we call 'compassionate leave' and make them swallow it." Doug's voice seemed thinned by the long-distance connection. "Can you give me a preliminary opinion?"

"I need time to get a feel for the situation."

He said, "Try not to take too long. At the moment I'm holding off pressure to appoint someone in his place. His enemies up here—and a sharp-tongued bastard like him acquires plenty of those—are trying to get a search committee authorized to find someone else for the directorship of the Cayslin Center for the Study of Man."

"Of People," she corrected automatically, as she always did. "What do you mean, 'bastard'? I thought you liked him, Doug. 'Do you want me to have to throw a smart, courtly, old-school gent to Finney or MaGill?' Those were your very words." Finney was a Freudian with a mouth like a pursed-up little asshole and a mind to match, and MaGill was a primal yowler in a padded gym of an office.

She heard Doug tapping at his teeth with a pen or pencil. "Well," he said, "I have a lot of respect for him, and sometimes I could cheer him for mowing down some pompous moron up here. I can't deny, though, that he's earned a reputation for being an accomplished son-of-a-bitch and tough to work with. Too damn cold and self-sufficient, you know?"

"Mmm," she said. "I haven't seen that yet."

He said, "You will. How about yourself? How's the rest of your life?"

"Well, offhand, what would you say if I told you I was thinking of going back to art school?"

"What would I say? I'd say bullshit, that's what I'd say. You've had fifteen years of doing something you're good at, and now you want to throw all that out and start over in an area you haven't touched since Studio 101 in college? If God had meant you to be a painter, She'd have sent you to art school in the first place."

"I did think about art school at the time."

"The point is that you're good at what you do. I've been at the receiving end of your work and I know what I'm talking about. By the way, did you see that piece in the paper about Annie Barnes, from the group I was in? That's an important appointment. I always knew she'd wind up in Washington. What I'm trying to make clear to you is that your 'graduates' do too well for you to be talking about quitting. What's Morton say about that idea, by the way?"

Mort, a pathologist, was Floria's lover. She hadn't discussed this with him, and she told Doug so.

"You're not on the outs with Morton, are you?"

"Come on, Douglas, cut it out. There's nothing wrong with my sex life, believe me. It's everyplace else that's giving me trouble."

"Just sticking my nose into your business," he replied. "What are friends for?"

They turned to lighter matters, but when she hung up Floria felt glum. If her friends were moved to this sort of probing and kindly advice-giving, she must be inviting help more openly and more urgently than she'd realized.

The work on the book went no better. It was as if, afraid to expose her thoughts, she must disarm criticism by meeting all possible objections beforehand. The book was well and truly stalled—like everything else. She sat sweating over it, wondering what the devil was wrong with her that she was writing mush. She had two good books to her name already. What was this bottleneck with the third?

"But what do you think?" Kenny insisted anxiously. "Does it sound like my kind of job?"

"How do you feel about it?"

"I'm all confused, I told you."

"Try speaking for me. Give me the advice I would give you."

He glowered. "That's a real cop-out, you know? One part of me talks like you, and then I have a dialog with myself like a TV show about a split personality. It's all me that way; you just sit there while I do all the work. I want something from *you*."

She looked for the twentieth time at the clock on the file cabinet. This time it freed her. "Kenny, the hour's over."

Kenny heaved his plump, sulky body up out of his chair. "You don't care. Oh, you pretend to, but you don't really—"

"Next time, Kenny."

He stumped out of the office. She imagined him towing in his wake the raft of decisions he was trying to inveigle her into making for him. Sighing, she went to the window and looked out over the park, filling her eyes and her mind with the full, fresh green of late spring. She felt dismal. In two years of treatment the situation with Kenny had remained a stalemate. He wouldn't go to someone else who might be able to help him, and she couldn't bring herself to kick him out, though she knew she must eventually. His puny tyranny couldn't conceal how soft and vulnerable he was . . .

Dr. Weyland had the next appointment. Floria found herself pleased to see him. She could hardly have asked for a greater contrast to Kenny: tall, lean, that august head that made her want to draw him, good clothes, nice big hands—altogether, a distinguished-looking man. Though he was informally dressed in slacks, light jacket, and tieless shirt, the impression he conveyed was one of impeccable leisure and reserve. He took not the padded chair preferred by most clients but the wooden one with the cane seat.

"Good afternoon, Dr. Landauer," he said gravely. "May I ask your judgment of my case?"

"I don't regard myself as a judge," she said. She decided to try to shift their discussion onto a first-name basis if possible. Calling this old-fashioned man by his first name so soon might seem artificial, but how could they get familiar enough to do therapy while addressing each other as "Dr. Landauer" and "Dr. Weyland" like two characters out of a vaudeville sketch?

"This is what I think, Edward," she continued. "We need to find out about this vampire incident—how it tied into your feelings about yourself, good and bad, at the time; what it did for you that led you to try to 'be' a vampire even though that was bound to complicate your life terrifically. The more we know, the closer we can come to figuring out how to insure that this vampire construct won't be necessary to you again."

"Does this mean that you accept me formally as a client?" he said.

Comes right out and says what's on his mind, she noted; no problem there. "Yes."

"Good. I too have a treatment goal in mind. I will need at some point a testimonial from you that my mental health is sound enough for me to resume work at Cayslin."

Floria shook her head. "I can't guarantee that. I can commit myself to work toward it, of course, since your improved mental health is the aim of what we do here together."

"I suppose that answers the purpose for the time being," he said. "We can discuss it again later on. Frankly, I find myself eager to continue our work today. I've been feeling very much better since I spoke with you, and I thought last night about what I might tell you today."

She had the distinct feeling of being steered by him; how important was it to him, she wondered, to feel in control? She said, "Edward, my own feeling is that we started out with a good deal of very useful verbal work, and that now is a time to try something a little different."

He said nothing. He watched her. When she asked whether he remembered his dreams he shook his head, no.

She said, "I'd like you to try to do a dream for me now, a waking dream. Can you close your eyes and daydream, and tell me about it?"

He closed his eyes. Strangely, he now struck her as less vulnerable rather than more, as if strengthened by increased vigilance.

"How do you feel now?" she said.

"Uneasy." His eyelids fluttered. "I dislike closing my eyes. What I don't see can hurt me."

"Who wants to hurt you?"

"A vampire's enemies, of course—mobs of screaming peasants with torches."

Translating into what, she wondered—young Ph.D.s pouring out of the graduate schools panting for the jobs of older men like Weyland? "Peasants, these days?"

"Whatever their daily work, there is still a majority of the stupid, the violent, and the credulous, putting their feather-brained faith in astrology, in this cult or that, in various branches of psychology."

His sneer at her was unmistakable. Considering her refusal to let him fill the hour his own way, this desire to take a swipe at her was healthy. But it required immediate and straightforward handling.

"Edward, open your eyes and tell me what you see."

He obeyed. "I see a woman in her early forties," he said, "clever-looking face, dark hair showing gray; flesh too thin for her bones, indicating either vanity or illness; wearing slacks and a rather creased batik blouse—describable, I think, by the term 'peasant style'—with a food stain on the left side."

Damn! Don't blush. "Does anything besides my blouse suggest a peasant to you?"

"Nothing concrete, but with regard to me, my vampire self, a peasant with a torch is what you could easily become."

"I hear you saying that my task is to help you get rid of your delusion, though this process may be painful and frightening for you."

Something flashed in his expression—surprise, perhaps alarm, something she wanted to get in touch with before it could sink away out of reach again. Quickly she said, "How do you experience your face at this moment?"

He frowned. "As being on the front of my head. Why?"

With a rush of anger at herself she saw that she had chosen the wrong technique for reaching that hidden feeling: she had provoked hostility instead. She said, "Your face looked to me just now like a mask for concealing what you feel rather than an instrument of expression."

He moved restlessly in the chair, his whole physical attitude tense and guarded. "I don't know what you mean."

"Will you let me touch you?" she said, rising.

His hands tightened on the arms of his chair, which protested in a sharp creak. He snapped, "I thought this was a talking cure."

Strong resistance to body work—ease up. "If you won't let me massage some of the tension out of your facial muscles, will you try to do it yourself?"

"I don't enjoy being made ridiculous," he said, standing and heading for the door, which clapped smartly to behind him.

She sagged back in her seat; she had mishandled him. Clearly her initial estimation of this as a relatively easy job had been wrong and had led her to move far too quickly with him. Certainly it was much too early to try body work. She should have developed a firmer level of trust first by letting him do more of what he did so easily and so well—talk.

The door opened. Weyland came back in and shut it quietly. He did not sit again but paced about the room, coming to rest at the window.

"Please excuse my rather childish behavior just now," he said. "Playing these games of yours brought it on."

"It's frustrating, playing games that are unfamiliar and that you can't control," she said. As he made no reply, she went on in a conciliatory tone, "I'm not trying to belittle you, Edward. I just need to get us off whatever track you were taking us down so briskly. My feeling is that you're trying hard to regain your old stability.

"But that's the goal, not the starting point. The only way to reach your goal is through the process, and you don't drive the therapy process like a train. You can only help the process happen, as though you were helping a tree grow."

"These games are part of the process?"

"Yes."

"And neither you nor I control the games?"

"That's right."

He considered. "Suppose I agree to try this process of yours; what would you want of me?"

Observing him carefully, she no longer saw the anxious scholar bravely struggling back from madness. Here was a different sort of man—armored, calculating. She didn't know just what the change signaled, but she felt her own excitement stirring, and that meant she was on the track of—something.

"I have a hunch," she said slowly, "that this vampirism extends further back into your past than you've told me and possibly right up into the present as well. I think it's still with you. My style of therapy stresses dealing with the now at least as much as the then; if the vampirism is part of the present, dealing with it on that basis is crucial."

Silence.

"Can you talk about being a vampire: being one now?"

"You won't like knowing," he said.

"Edward, try."

He said, "I hunt."

"Where? How? What sort of—of victims?"

He folded his arms and leaned his back against the window frame. "Very well, since you insist. There are a number of possibilities here in the city in summer. Those too poor to own air-conditioners sleep out on rooftops and fire escapes. But often, I've found, their blood is sour with drugs or liquor. The same is true of prostitutes. Bars are full of accessible people but also full of smoke and noise, and there too the blood is fouled. I must choose my hunting grounds carefully. Often I go to openings of galleries or evening museum shows or department shores on their late nights—places where women may be approached."

And take pleasure in it, she thought, if they're out hunting also—for acceptable male companionship. Yet he said he's never married. Explore where this is going. "Only women?"

He gave her a sardonic glance, as if she were a slightly brighter student than he had at first assumed.

"Hunting women is liable to be time-consuming and expensive. The best hunting is in the part of Central Park they call the Ramble, where homosexual men seek encounters with others of their kind. I walk there too at night."

Floria caught a faint sound of conversation and laughter from the waiting room; her next client had probably arrived, she realized, looking reluctantly at the clock. "I'm sorry, Edward, but our time seems to be—"

"Only a moment more," he said coldly. "You asked; permit me to finish my answer. In the Ramble I find someone who doesn't reek of alcohol or drugs, who seems healthy, and who is not insistent on 'hooking up' right there among the bushes. I invite such a man to my hotel. He judges me safe, at least: older, weaker than he is, unlikely to turn out to be a dangerous maniac. So he comes to my room. I feed on his blood.

"Now, I think, our time is up."

He walked out.

She sat torn between rejoicing at his admission of the delusion's persistence and dismay that his condition was so much worse than she had first thought. Her hope of having an easy time with him vanished. His initial presentation had been just that—a performance, an act. Forced to abandon it, he had dumped on her this lump of material, too much—and too strange—to take in all at once.

Her next client liked the padded chair, not the wooden one that Weyland had sat in during the first part of the hour. Floria started to move the wooden one back. The armrests came away in her hands.

She remembered him starting up in protest against her proposal of touching him. The grip of his fingers had fractured the joints, and the shafts now lay in splinters on the floor.

Floria wandered into Lucille's room at the clinic after the staff meeting. Lucille was lying on the couch with a wet cloth over her eyes.

"I thought you looked green around the gills today," Floria said. "What's wrong?"

"Big bash last night," said Lucille in sepulchral tones. "I think I feel about the way you do after a session with Chubs. You haven't gotten rid of him yet, have you?"

"No. I had him lined up to see Marty instead of me last week, but damned if he didn't show up at my door at his usual time. It's a lost cause. What I wanted to talk to you about was Dracula."

"What about him?"

"He's smarter, tougher, and sicker than I thought, and maybe I'm even less competent than I thought, too. He's already walked out on me once—I almost lost him. I never took a course in treating monsters."

Lucille groaned. "Some days they're all monsters." This from Lucille, who worked longer hours than anyone else at the clinic, to the despair of her husband. She lifted the cloth, refolded it, and placed it carefully across her forehead. "And if I had ten dollars for every client who's walked out on me . . . Tell you what: I'll trade you Madame X for him, how's that? Remember Madame X, with the jangling bracelets and the parakeet eye makeup and the phobia about dogs? Now she's phobic about things dropping on her out of the sky. Just wait—it'll turn out that one day when she was three a dog trotted by and pissed on her leg just as an over-passing pigeon shat on her head. What are we doing in this business?"

"God knows," Floria laughed. "But am I in this business these days— I mean, in the sense of practicing my so-called skills? Blocked with my group work, beating my brains out on a book that won't go, and doing something—I'm not sure it's therapy—with a vampire . . . You know, once I had this sort of natural choreographer inside myself that hardly let me put a foot wrong and always knew how to correct a mistake if I did. Now that's gone. I feel as if I'm just going through a lot of mechanical motions. Whatever I had once that made me useful as a therapist, I've lost it."

Ugh, she thought, hearing the descent of her voice into a tone of gloomy self-pity.

"Well, don't complain about Dracula," Lucille said. "You were the one who insisted on taking him on. At least he's got you concentrating on his problem instead of just wringing your hands. As long as you've started, stay with it—illumination may come. And now I'd better change the ribbon in my typewriter and get back to reviewing Silverman's latest best-seller on self-shrinking while I'm feeling mean enough to do it justice." She got up gingerly. "Stick around in case I faint and fall into the wastebasket."

"Luce, this case is what I'd like to try to write about."

"Dracula?" Lucille pawed through a desk drawer full of paper clips, pens, rubber bands and old lipsticks.

"Dracula. A monograph . . ."

"Oh, I know that game: you scribble down everything you can and then read what you wrote to find out what's going on with the client, and with luck you end up publishing. Great! But if you are going to publish, don't piddle this away on a dinky paper. Do a book. Here's your subject, instead of those depressing statistics you've been killing yourself over. This one is really exciting—a case study to put on the shelf next to Freud's own wolf-man, have you thought of that?"

Floria liked it. "What a book that could be—fame if not fortune. Notoriety, most likely. How in the world could I convince our colleagues that it's legit? There's a lot of vampire stuff around right now—plays on Broadway and TV, books all over the place, movies. They'll say I'm just trying to ride the coattails of a fad."

"No, no, what you do is show how this guy's delusion is related to the fad. Fascinating." Lucille, having found a ribbon, prodded doubtfully at the exposed innards of her typewriter.

"Suppose I fictionalize it," Floria said, "under a pseudonym. Why not ride the popular wave and be free in what I can say?"

"Listen, you've never written a word of fiction in your life, have you?" Lucille fixed her with a bloodshot gaze. "There's no evidence that you could turn out a best-selling novel. On the other hand, by this time you have a trained memory for accurately reporting therapeutic transactions. That's a strength you'd be foolish to waste. A solid professional book would be terrific—and a feather in the cap of every woman in the field. Just make sure you get good legal advice on disguising your Dracula's identity well enough to avoid libel."

The cane-seated chair wasn't worth repairing, so she got its twin out of the bedroom to put in the office in its place. Puzzling: by his history Weyland was fifty-two, and by his appearance no muscle man. She should have asked Doug—but how, exactly? "By the way, Doug, was Weyland ever a circus strong man or a blacksmith? Does he secretly pump iron?" Ask the client himself—but not yet.

She invited some of the younger staff from the clinic over for a small party with a few of her outside friends. It was a good evening; they were not a heavy-drinking crowd, which meant the conversation stayed intelligent. The guests drifted about the long living room or stood in twos and threes at the windows looking down on West End Avenue as they talked.

Mort came, warming the room. Fresh from a session with some amateur chamber-music friends, he still glowed with the pleasure of making his cello sing. His own voice was unexpectedly light for so large a man. Sometimes Floria thought that the deep throb of the cello was his true voice.

He stood beside her talking with some others. There was no need to lean against his comfortable bulk or to have him put his arm around her waist. Their intimacy was long-standing, an effortless pleasure in each other that required neither demonstration nor concealment.

He was easily diverted from music to his next favorite topic, the strengths and skills of athletes.

"Here's a question for a paper I'm thinking of writing," Floria said. "Could a tall, lean man be exceptionally strong?"

Mort rambled on in his thoughtful way. His answer seemed to be no.

"But what about chimpanzees?" put in a young clinician. "I went with a guy once who was an animal handler for TV, and he said a three-month-old chimp could demolish a strong man."

"It's all physical conditioning," somebody else said. "Modern people are soft."

Mort nodded. "Human beings in general are weakly made compared to other animals. It's a question of muscle insertions—the angles of how the muscles are attached to the bones. Some angles give better leverage than others. That's how a leopard can bring down a much bigger animal than itself. It has a muscular structure that gives it tremendous strength for its streamlined build."

Floria said, "If a man were built with muscle insertions like a leopard's, he'd look pretty odd, wouldn't he?"

"Not to an untrained eye," Mort said, sounding bemused by an inner vision. "And my God, what an athlete he'd make—can you imagine a guy in the decathlon who's as strong as a leopard?"

When everyone else had gone Mort stayed, as he often did. Jokes about insertions, muscular and otherwise, soon led to sounds more expressive and more animal, but afterward Floria didn't feel like resting snuggled together with Mort and talking. When her body stopped racing, her mind turned to her new client. She didn't want to discuss him with Mort, so she ushered Mort out as gently as she could and sat down by herself at the kitchen table with a glass of orange juice.

How to approach the reintegration of Weyland the eminent, gray-haired academic with the rebellious vampire-self that had smashed his life out of shape?

She thought of the broken chair, of Weyland's big hands crushing the wood. Old wood and dried-out glue, of course, or he never could have done that. He was a man, after all, not a leopard.

The day before the third session Weyland phoned and left a message with Hilda: he would not be coming to the office tomorrow for his appoint-

ment, but if Dr. Landauer were agreeable she would find him at their usual hour at the Central Park Zoo.

Am I going to let him move me around from here to there? she thought. I shouldn't—but why fight it? Give him some leeway, see what opens up in a different setting. Besides, it was a beautiful day, probably the last of the sweet May weather before the summer stickiness descended. She gladly cut Kenny short so that she would have time to walk over to the zoo.

There was a fair crowd there for a weekday. Well-groomed young matrons pushed clean, floppy babies in strollers. Weyland she spotted at once.

He was leaning against the railing that enclosed the seals' shelter and their murky green pool. His jacket, slung over his shoulder, draped elegantly down his long back. Floria thought him rather dashing and faintly foreign-looking. Women who passed him, she noticed, tended to glance back.

He looked at everyone. She had the impression that he knew quite well that she was walking up behind him.

"Outdoors makes a nice change from the office, Edward," she said, coming to the rail beside him. "But there must be more to this than a longing for fresh air." A fat seal lay in sculptural grace on the concrete, eyes blissfully shut, fur drying in the sun to a translucent water-color umber.

Weyland straightened from the rail. They walked. He did not look at the animals; his eyes moved continually over the crowd. He said, "Someone has been watching for me at your office building."

"Who?"

"There are several possibilities. Pah, what a stench—though humans caged in similar circumstances smell as bad." He sidestepped a couple of shrieking children who were fighting over a balloon and headed out of the zoo under the musical clock.

They walked the uphill path northward through the park. By extending her own stride a little Floria found that she could comfortably keep pace with him.

"Is it peasants with torches?" she said. "Following you?"

He said, "What a childish idea."

All right, try another tack, then: "You were telling me last time about hunting in the Ramble. Can we return to that?"

"If you wish." He sounded bored—a defense? Surely—she was certain this must be the right reading—surely his problem was a transmutation into "vampire" fantasy of an unacceptable aspect of himself. For men of his generation the confrontation with homosexual drives could be devastating.

"When you pick up someone in the Ramble, is it a paid encounter?"

"Usually."

"How do you feel about having to pay?" She expected resentment.

He gave a faint shrug. "Why not? Others work to earn their bread. I work, too, very hard, in fact. Why shouldn't I use my earnings to pay for my sustenance?"

Why did he never play the expected card? Baffled, she paused to drink from a fountain. They walked on.

"Once you've got your quarry, how do you . . ." She fumbled for a word.

"Attack?" he supplied, unperturbed. "There's a place on the neck, here, where pressure can interrupt the blood flow to the brain and cause unconsciousness. Getting close enough to apply that pressure isn't difficult."

"You do this before or after any sexual activity?"

"Before, if possible," he said aridly, "and instead of." He turned aside to stalk up a slope to a granite outcrop that overlooked the path they had been following. There he settled on his haunches, looking back the way they had come. Floria, glad she'd worn slacks today, sat down near him.

He didn't seem devastated—anything but. Press him, don't let him get by on cool. "Do you often prey on men in preference to women?"

"Certainly. I take what is easiest. Men have always been more accessible because women have been walled away like prizes or so physically impoverished by repeated childbearing as to be unhealthy prey for me. All this has begun to change recently, but gay men are still the simplest quarry." While she was recovering from her surprise at his unforeseen and weirdly skewed awareness of female history, he added suavely, "How carefully you control your expression, Dr. Landauer—no trace of disapproval."

She did disapprove, she realized. She would prefer him not to be committed sexually to men. Oh, hell.

He went on, "Yet no doubt you see me as one who victimizes the already victimized. This is the world's way. A wolf brings down the stragglers at the edges of the herd. Gay men are denied the full protection of the human herd and are at the same time emboldened to make themselves known and available.

"On the other hand, unlike the wolf I can feed without killing, and these particular victims pose no threat to me that would cause me to kill. Outcasts themselves, even if they comprehend my true purpose among them they cannot effectively accuse me."

God, how neatly, completely, and ruthlessly he distanced the homosexual community from himself! "And how do you feel, Edward, about their purposes—their sexual expectations of you?"

"The same way I feel about the sexual expectations of women whom I choose to pursue: they don't interest me. Besides, once my hunger is active, sexual arousal is impossible. My physical unresponsiveness seems to surprise no one. Apparently impotence is expected in a gray-haired man, which suits my intention."

Some kids carrying radios swung past below, trailing a jumble of amplified thump, wail, and jabber. Floria gazed after them unseeingly, thinking, astonished again, that she had never heard a man speak of his own impotence with such cool indifference. She had induced him to talk about his problem all right. He was speaking as freely as he had in the first session, only this time it was no act. He was drowning her in more than she had ever expected or for that matter wanted to know about vampirism. What the hell: she was listening, she thought she understood—what was it all good for? Time for some cold reality, she thought; see how far he can carry all this incredible detail. Give the whole structure a shove.

She said, "You realize, I'm sure, that people of either sex who make themselves so easily available are also liable to be carriers of disease. When was your last medical checkup?"

"My dear Dr. Landauer, my first medical checkup will be my last. Fortunately, I have no great need of one. Most serious illnesses—hepatitis, for example—reveal themselves to me by a quality in the odor of the victim's skin. Warned, I abstain. When I do fall ill, as occasionally happens, I withdraw to some place where I can heal undisturbed. A doctor's attention would be more dangerous to me than any disease."

Eyes on the path below, he continued calmly, "You can see by looking at me that there are no obvious clues to my unique nature. But believe me, an examination of any depth by even a half-sleeping medical practitioner would reveal some alarming deviations from the norm. I take pains to stay healthy, and I seem to be gifted with an exceptionally hardy constitution."

Fantasies of being unique and physically superior; take him to the other pole. "I'd like you to try something now. Will you put yourself into the mind of a man you contact in the Ramble and describe your encounter with him from his point of view?"

He turned toward her and for some moments regarded her without expression. Then he resumed his surveillance of the path. "I will not. Though I do have enough empathy with my quarry to enable me to hunt efficiently. I must draw the line at erasing the necessary distance that keeps prey and predator distinct.

"And now I think our ways part for today." He stood up, descended the hillside, and walked beneath some low-canopied trees, his tall back stooped, toward the Seventy-second Street entrance of the park.

Floria arose more slowly, aware suddenly of her shallow breathing and the sweat on her face. Back to reality or what remained of it. She looked at her watch. She was late for her next client.

Floria couldn't sleep that night. Barefoot in her bathrobe she paced the living room by lamplight. They had sat together on that hill as isolated as in her office—more so, because there was no Hilda and no phone. He was, she knew, very strong, and he had sat close enough to her to reach out for that paralyzing touch to the neck—

Just suppose for a minute that Weyland had been brazenly telling the truth all along, counting on her to treat it as a delusion because on the face of it the truth was inconceivable.

Jesus, she thought, if I'm thinking that way about him, this therapy is more out of control than I thought. What kind of therapist becomes an accomplice to the client's fantasy? A crazy therapist, that's what kind.

Frustrated and confused by the turmoil in her mind, she wandered into the workroom. By morning the floor was covered with sheets of newsprint, each broadly marked by her felt-tipped pen. Floria sat in the midst of them, gritty-eyed and hungry.

She often approached problems this way, harking back to art training: turn off the thinking, put hand to paper and see what the deeper, less verbally sophisticated parts of the mind have to offer. Now that her dreams had deserted her, this was her only access to those levels.

The newsprint sheets were covered with rough representations of Weyland's face and form. Across several of them were scrawled words: *"Dear Doug, your vampire is fine, it's your ex-therapist who's off the rails. Warning: Therapy can be dangerous to your health. Especially if you are the therapist. Beautiful vampire, awaken to me. Am I really ready to take on a legendary monster? Give up—refer this one out. Do your job—work is a good doctor."*

That last one sounded pretty good, except that doing her job was precisely what she was feeling so shaky about these days.

Here was another message: *"How come this attraction to someone so scary?"* Oh, ho, she thought, is that a real feeling or an aimless reaction out of the body's early-morning hormone peak? You don't want to confuse honest libido with mere biological clockwork.

Deborah called. Babies cried in the background over the Scotch Symphony. Nick, Deb's husband, was a musicologist with fervent opinions on music and nothing else.

"We'll be in town a little later in the summer," Deborah said, "just for a few days at the end of July. Nicky has this seminar-convention thing. Of course, it won't be easy with the babies . . . I wondered if you might sort of coordinate your vacation so you could spend a little time with them?"

Baby-sit, that meant. Damn. Cute as they were and all that, damn! Floria gritted her teeth. Visits from Deb were difficult. Floria had been so proud of her bright, hard-driving daughter, and then suddenly Deborah had dropped her studies and rushed to embrace all the dangers that Floria had warned her against: a romantic, too-young marriage, instant breeding, no preparation for self-support, the works. Well, to each her own, but it was so wearing to have Deb around playing the empty-headed hausfrau.

"Let me think, Deb. I'd love to see all of you, but I've been considering spending a couple of weeks in Maine with your Aunt Nonnie." God knows I need a real vacation, she thought, though the peace and quiet up there is hard for a city kid like me to take for long. Still, Nonnie,

Floria's younger sister, was good company. "Maybe you could bring the kids up there for a couple of days. There's room in that great barn of a place, and of course Nonnie'd be happy to have you."

"Oh, no, Mom, it's so dead up there, it drives Nick crazy—don't tell Nonnie I said that. Maybe Nonnie could come down to the city instead. You could cancel a date or two and we could all go to Coney Island together, things like that."

Kid things, which would drive Nonnie crazy and Floria too before long. "I doubt she could manage," Floria said, "but I'll ask. Look, hon, if I do go up there, you and Nick and the kids could stay here at the apartment and save some money."

"We have to be at the hotel for the seminar," Deb said shortly. No doubt she was feeling just as impatient as Floria was by now. "And the kids haven't seen you for a long time—it would be really nice if you could stay in the city just for a few days."

"We'll try to work something out." Always working something out. Concord never comes naturally—first we have to butt heads and get pissed off. Each time you call I hope it'll be different, Floria thought.

Somebody shrieked for "oly," jelly that would be, in the background— Floria felt a sudden rush of warmth for them, her grandkids for God's sake. Having been a young mother herself, she was still young enough to really enjoy them (and to fight with Deb about how to bring them up).

Deb was starting an awkward goodbye. Floria replied, put the phone down, and sat with her head back against the flowered kitchen wallpaper, thinking, Why do I feel so rotten now? Deb and I aren't close, no comfort, seldom friends, though we were once. Have I said everything wrong, made her think I don't want to see her and don't care about her family? What does she want from me that I can't seem to give her? Approval? Maybe she thinks I still hold her marriage against her. Well, I do, sort of. What right have I to be critical, me with my divorce? What terrible things would she say to me, would I say to her, that we take such care not to say anything important at all?

"I think today we might go into sex," she said.

Weyland responded dryly, "Might we indeed. Does it titillate you to wring confessions of solitary vice from men of mature years?"

Oh no you don't, she thought. You can't sidestep so easily. "Under what circumstances do you find yourself sexually aroused?"

"Most usually upon waking from sleep," he said indifferently.

"What do you do about it?"

"The same as others do. I am not a cripple, I have hands."

"Do you have fantasies at these times?"

"No. Women, and men for that matter, appeal to me very little, either in fantasy or reality."

"Ah—what about female vampires?" she said, trying not to sound arch.

"I know of none."

Of course: the neatest out in the book. "They're not needed for reproduction, I suppose, because people who die of vampire bites become vampires themselves."

He said testily, "Nonsense. I am not a communicable disease."

So he had left an enormous hole in his construct. She headed straight for it: "Then how does your kind reproduce?"

"I have no kind, so far as I am aware," he said, "and I do not reproduce. Why should I, when I may live for centuries still, perhaps indefinitely? My sexual equipment is clearly only detailed biological mimicry, a form of protective coloration." How beautiful, how simple a solution, she thought, full of admiration in spite of herself. "Do I occasionally detect a note of prurient interest in your questions, Dr. Landauer? Something akin to stopping at the cage to watch the tigers mate at the zoo?"

"Probably," she said, feeling her face heat. He had a great backhand return shot there. "How do you feel about that?"

He shrugged.

"To return to the point," she said. "Do I hear you saying that you have no urge whatever to engage in sexual intercourse with anyone?"

"Would you mate with your livestock?"

His matter-of-fact arrogance took her breath away. She said weakly, "Men have reportedly done so."

"Driven men. I am not driven in that way. My sex urge is of low frequency and is easily dealt with unaided—although I occasionally engage in copulation out of the necessity to keep up appearances. I am capable, but not—like humans—obsessed."

Was he sinking into lunacy before her eyes? "I think I hear you saying," she said, striving to keep her voice neutral, "that you're not just a man with a unique way of life. I think I hear you saying that you're not human at all."

"I thought that this was already clear."

"And that there are no others like you."

"None that I know of."

"Then—you see yourself as what? Some sort of mutation?"

"Perhaps. Or perhaps your kind are the mutation."

She saw disdain in the curl of his lip. "How does your mouth feel now?"

"The corners are drawn down. The feeling is contempt."

"Can you let the contempt speak?"

He got up and went to stand at the window, positioning himself slightly to one side as if to stay hidden from the street below.

"Edward," she said.

He looked back at her. "Humans are my food. I draw the life out of their veins. Sometimes I kill them. I am greater than they are. Yet I must spend my time thinking about their habits and their drives, scheming to avoid the dangers they pose—I hate them."

She felt the hatred like a dry heat radiating from him. God, he really lived all this! She had tapped into a furnace of feeling. And now? The sensation of triumph wavered, and she grabbed at a next move: hit him with reality now, while he's burning.

"What about blood banks?" she said. "Your food is commercially available, so why all the complication and danger of the hunt?"

"You mean I might turn my efforts to piling up a fortune and buying blood by the case? That would certainly make for an easier, less risky life in the short run. I could fit quite comfortably into modern society if I became just another consumer.

"However, I prefer to keep the mechanics of my survival firmly in my own hands. After all, I can't afford to lose my hunting skills. In two hundred years there may be no blood banks, but I will still need my food."

Jesus, you set him a hurdle and he just flies over it. Are there no weaknesses in all this, has he no blind spots? Look at his tension—go back to that. Floria said, "What do you feel now in your body?"

"Tightness." He pressed his spread fingers to his abdomen.

"What are you doing with your hands?"

"I put my hands to my stomach."

"Can you speak for your stomach?"

" 'Feed me or die,' " he snarled.

Elated again, she closed in: "And for yourself, in answer?"

" 'Will you never be satisfied?' " He glared at her. "You shouldn't seduce me into quarreling with the terms of my own existence!"

"Your stomach is your existence," she paraphrased.

"The gut determines," he said harshly. "That first, everything else after."

"Say, 'I resent . . .' "

He held to a tense silence.

" 'I resent the power of my gut over my life,' " she said for him.

He stood with an abrupt motion and glanced at his watch, an elegant flash of slim silver on his wrist. "Enough," he said.

That night at home she began a set of notes that would never enter his file at the office, notes toward the proposed book.

Couldn't do it, couldn't get properly into the sex thing with him. Everything shoots off in all directions. His vampire concept so thoroughly worked out, find myself half believing sometimes—my own childish fantasy-response to his powerful death-avoidance, contact-avoidance fantasy. Lose professional distance every time—is that what scares me about him? Don't really want to shatter his delusion (my life a mess, what right to tear down others' patterns?)—so see it as real? Wonder how much of "vampirism" he acts out, how far, how often. Something

attractive in his purely selfish, predatory stance—the lure of the great outlaw.

Told me today quite coolly about a man he killed recently—inadvertently—by drinking too much from him. *Is* it fantasy? Of course—the victim, he thinks, was a college student. Breathes there a professor who hasn't dreamed of murdering some representative youth, retaliation for years of classroom frustration? Speaks of teaching with acerbic humor—amuses him to work at cultivating the minds of those he regards strictly as bodies, containers of his sustenance. He shows the alienness of full-blown psychopathology, poor bastard, plus clean-cut logic. Suggested he find another job (assuming his delusion at least in part related to pressures at Cayslin); his fantasy-persona, the vampire, more realistic than I about job-switching:

"For a man of my apparent age it's not so easy to make such a change in these tight times. I might have to take a position lower on the ladder of 'success' as you people assess it." Status is important to him? "Certainly. An eccentric professor is one thing; an eccentric pipefitter, another. And I like good cars, which are expensive to own and run." Then, thoughtful addition. "Although there are advantages to a simpler, less visible life." He refuses to discuss other "jobs" from former "lives." We are deep into the fantasy—where the hell going? Damn right I don't control the "games"—preplanned therapeutic strategies get whirled away as soon as we begin. Nerve-wracking.

Tried again to have him take the part of his enemy-victim, peasant with torch. Asked if he felt himself rejecting that point of view? Frosty reply: "Naturally. The peasant's point of view is in no way my own. I've been reading in your field, Dr. Landauer. You work from the Gestalt orientation—" Originally yes, I corrected; eclectic now. "But you do proceed from the theory that I am projecting some aspect of my own feelings outward onto others, whom I then treat as my victims. Your purpose then must be to maneuver me into accepting as my own the projected 'victim' aspect of myself. This integration is supposed to effect the freeing of energy previously locked into maintaining the projection. All this is an interesting insight into the nature of ordinary human confusion, but I am not an ordinary human, and I am not confused. I cannot afford confusion." Felt sympathy for him—telling me he's afraid of having own internal confusions exposed in therapy, too threatening. Keep chipping away at delusion, though with what prospect? It's so complex, deep-seated.

Returned to his phrase "my apparent age." He asserts he has lived many human lifetimes, all details forgotten, however, during periods of suspended animation between lives. Perhaps sensing my skepticism at such handy amnesia, grew cool and distant, claimed to know little about the hibernation process itself: "The essence of this state is that I sleep through it—hardly an ideal condition for making scientific observations."

Edward thinks his body synthesizes vitamins, minerals (as all our bodies synthesize vitamin D), even proteins. Describes unique design he deduces in himself: special intestinal microfauna plus superefficient body chemistry extracts enough energy to live on from blood. Damn good mileage per calorie, too. (Recall observable tension, first interview, at question about drinking—my note on possible alcohol problem!)

Speak for blood: " 'Lacking me, you have no life. I flow to the heart's soft drumbeat through lightless prisons of flesh. I am rich, I am nourishing, I am difficult to attain.' " Stunned to find him positively lyrical on subject of his "food." Drew attention to whispering voice of blood. " 'Yes. I am secret, hidden beneath the surface, patient, silent, steady. I work unnoticed, an unseen thread of vitality running from age to age—beautiful, efficient, self-renewing, self-cleansing, warm, filling—' " Could *see* him getting worked up. Finally he stood: "My appetite is pressing. I must leave you." And he did.

Sat and trembled for five minutes after.

New development (or new perception?): he sometimes comes across very unsophisticated about own feelings—lets me pursue subjects of extreme intensity and delicacy to him.

Asked him to daydream—a hunt. (Hands—mine—shaking now as I write. God. What a session.) He told of picking up a woman at poetry reading, 92nd Street Y—has N.Y.C. all worked out, circulates to avoid too much notice any one spot. Spoke easily, eyes shut without observable strain: chooses from audience a redhead in glasses, dress with drooping neckline (ease of access), no perfume (strong smells bother him). Approaches during the intermission, encouraged to see her fanning away smoke of others' cigarettes—meaning she doesn't smoke, health sign. Agreed in not enjoying the reading, they adjourn together to coffee shop.

"She asks whether I'm a teacher," he says, eyes shut, mouth amused. "My clothes, glasses, manner all suggest this, and I emphasize the impression—it reassures. She's a copy editor for a publishing house. We talk about books. The waiter brings her a gummy-looking pastry. As a non-eater, I pay little attention to the quality of restaurants, so I must apologize to her. She waves this away—is engrossed, or pretending to be engrossed, in talk." A longish dialog between interested woman and Edward doing shy-lonesome-scholar act—dead wife, competitive young colleagues who don't understand him, quarrels in professional journals with big shots in his field—a version of what he first told me. She's attracted (of course—lanky, rough-cut elegance plus hints of vulnerability all very alluring, as intended). He offers to take her home.

Tension in his body at this point in narrative—spine clear of chair back, hands braced on thighs. "She settles beside me in the back of the cab, talking about problems of her own career—illegible manuscripts of Biblical length, mulish editors, suicidal authors—and I make comforting comments, I lean nearer and put my arm along the back of the seat, behind her shoulders. Traffic is heavy, we move slowly. There is time to make my meal here in the taxi and avoid a tedious extension of the situation into her apartment—if I move soon."

How do you feel?

"Eager," he says, voice husky. "My hunger is so roused I can scarcely restrain myself. A powerful hunger, not like yours—mine compels. I embrace her shoulders lightly, make kindly-uncle remarks, treading that fine line between the game of seduction she perceives and the game of friendly interest I pretend to affect. My real purpose underlies all: what I say, how I look, every gesture is part of the stalk. There is an added excitement, and fear, because I'm doing my hunting in the presence of a third person—behind the cabbie's head."

Could scarcely breathe. Studied him—intent face, masklike with closed eyes, nostrils slightly flared; legs tensed, hands clenched on knees. Whispering: "I press the place on her neck. She starts, sighs faintly, silently drops against me. In the stale stench of the cab's interior, with the ticking of the meter in my ears and the mutter of the radio—I take hold here, at the tenderest part of her throat. Sound subsides into the background—I feel the sweet blood beating under her skin, I taste salt at the moment before I—strike. My saliva thins her blood so that it flows out, I draw the blood into my mouth swiftly, swiftly, before she can wake, before we can arrive . . ."

Trailed off, sat back loosely in chair—saw him swallow. "Ah. I feed." Heard him sigh. Managed to ask about physical sensation. His low murmur, "Warm. Heavy, here—" touches his belly—"in a pleasant way. The good taste of blood, tart and rich, in my mouth . . ."

And then? A flicker of movement beneath his closed eyelids: "In time I am aware that the cabbie has glanced back once and has taken our—embrace for just that. I can feel the cab slowing, hear him move to turn off the meter. I withdraw, I quickly wipe my mouth on my handkerchief. I take her by the shoulders and shake her gently; does she often have these attacks, I inquire, the soul of concern. She comes around, bewildered, weak, thinks she has fainted. I give the driver extra money and ask him to wait. He looks intrigued—'What was that all about,' I can see the question in his face—but as a true New Yorker he won't expose his own ignorance by asking.

"I escort the woman to her front door, supporting her as she staggers. Any suspicion of me that she may entertain, however formless and hazy, is allayed by my stern charging of the doorman to see that she reaches her apartment safely. She grows embarrassed, thinks perhaps that if not put off by her 'illness' I would spend the night with her, which moves her to press upon me, unasked, her telephone number. I bid her a solicitous good night and take the cab back to my hotel, where I sleep."

No sex? No sex.

How did he feel about the victim as a person? "She was food."

This was his "hunting" of last night, he admits afterward, not a made-up dream. No boasting in it, just telling. Telling me! Think: I can go talk to Lucille, Mort, Doug, others about most of what matters to me. Edward has only me to talk to and that for a fee—what isolation! No wonder the stone, monumental face—only those long, strong lips (his point of contact, verbal and physical-in-fantasy, with the world and with "food") are truly expressive. An exciting narration; uncomfortable to find I felt not only empathy but enjoyment. Suppose he picked up and victimized—even in fantasy—Deb or Hilda, how would I feel then?

Later: truth—I also found this recital sexually stirring. Keep visualizing how he looked finishing this "dream"—he sat very still, head up, look of thoughtful pleasure on his face. Like handsome intellectual listening to music.

Kenny showed up unexpectedly at Floria's office on Monday, bursting with malevolent energy. She happened to be free, so she took him—something was definitely up. He sat on the edge of his chair.

"I know why you're trying to unload me," he accused. "It's that new one, the tall guy with the snooty look—what is he, an old actor or something? Anybody could see he's got you itching for him."

"Kenny, when was it that I first spoke to you about terminating our work together?" she said patiently.

"Don't change the subject. Let me tell you, in case you don't know it: that guy isn't really interested, Doctor, because he's a fruit. A faggot. You want to know how I know?"

Oh Lord, she thought wearily, he's regressed to age ten. She could see that she was going to hear the rest whether she wanted to or not. What in God's name was the world like for Kenny, if he clung so fanatically to her despite her failure to help him?

"Listen, I knew right away there was something flaky about him, so I followed him from here to that hotel where he lives. I followed him the other afternoon too. He walked around like he does a lot, and then he went into one of those ritzy movie houses on Third that open early and show risqué foreign movies—you know, Japs cutting each other's things off and glop like that. This one was French, though.

"Well, there was a guy came in, a Madison Avenue type carrying his attaché case, taking a work break or something. Your man moved over and sat down behind him and reached out and sort of stroked the guy's neck, and the guy leaned back, and your man leaned forward and started nuzzling at him, you know—kissing him.

"I saw it. They had their heads together and they stayed like that a while. It was disgusting: complete strangers, without even 'hello.' The Madison Avenue guy just sat there with his head back looking zonked, you know, just swept away, and what he was doing with his hands under his raincoat in his lap I couldn't see, but I bet you can guess.

"And then your fruity friend got up and walked out. I did, too, and I hung around a little outside. After a while the Madison Avenue guy came out looking all sleepy and loose, like after you-know-what, and he wandered off on his own someplace.

"What do you think now?" he ended, on a high, triumphant note.

Her impulse was to slap his face the way she would have slapped Deb-as-a-child for tattling. But this was a client, not a kid. God give me strength, she thought.

"Kenny, you're fired."

"You can't!" he squealed. "You can't! What will I—who can I—"

She stood up, feeling weak but hardening her voice. "I'm sorry. I absolutely cannot have a client who makes it his business to spy on other clients. You already have a list of replacement therapists from me."

He gaped at her in slack-jawed dismay, his eyes swimmy with tears.

"I'm sorry, Kenny. Call this a dose of reality therapy and try to learn from it. There are some things you simply will not be allowed to do." She felt better: it was done at last.

"I hate you!" He surged out of his chair, knocking it back against the wall. Threateningly he glared at the fish tank, but, contenting himself with a couple of kicks at the nearest table leg, he stamped out.

Floria buzzed Hilda: "No more appointments for Kenny, Hilda. You can close his file."

"Whoopee," Hilda said.

Poor, horrid Kenny. Impossible to tell what would happen to him, better not to speculate or she might relent, call him back. She had encouraged him, really, by listening instead of shutting him up and throwing him out before any damage was done.

Was it damaging, to know the truth? In her mind's eye she saw a cream-faced young man out of a Black Thumb Vodka ad wander from a movie theater into daylight, yawning and rubbing absently at an irritation on his neck . . .

She didn't even look at the telephone on the table or think about whom to call, now that she believed. No; she was going to keep quiet about Dr. Edward Lewis Weyland, her vampire.

Hardly alive at staff meeting, clinic, yesterday—people asking what's the matter, fobbed them off. Settled down today. Had to, to face him.

Asked him what he felt were his strengths. He said speed, cunning, ruthlessness. Animal strengths, I said. What about imagination, or is that strictly human? He defended at once: not human only. Lion, waiting at water hole where no zebra yet drinks, thinks "Zebra—eat," therefore performs feat of imagining event yet-to-come. Self experienced as animal? Yes—reminded me that humans are also animals. Pushed for his early memories; he objected: "Gestalt is here-and-now, not history-taking." I insist, citing anomalous nature of his situation, my own refusal to be bound by any one theoretical framework. He defends tensely: "Suppose I became lost there in memory, distracted from dangers of the present, left unguarded from those dangers."

Speak for memory. He resists, but at length attempts it: " 'I am heavy with the multitudes of the past.' " Fingertips to forehead propping up all that weight of lives. " 'So heavy, filling worlds of time laid down eon by eon, I accumulate, I persist, I demand recognition, I am as real as the life around you—more real, weightier, richer.' " His voice sinking, shoulders bowed, head in hands—I begin to feel pressure at the back of my own skull. " 'Let me in.' " Only a rough whisper now. " 'I offer beauty as well as terror. Let me in.' " Whispering also, I suggest he reply to his memory.

"Memory, you want to crush me," he groans. "You would overwhelm me with the cries of animals, the odor and jostle of bodies, old betrayals, dead joys, filth and anger from other times—I must concentrate on the danger now. Let me be." All I can take of this crazy conflict, I gabble us off onto something else. He looks up—relief?—follows my lead—where? Rest of session a blank.

No wonder sometimes no empathy at all—a species boundary! He has to be utterly self-centered just to keep balance—self-centeredness of an animal. Thought just now of our beginning, me trying to push him to produce material, trying to control him, manipulate—no way, no way; so here we are, someplace else—I feel dazed, in shock, but stick with it—it's real.

Therapy with a dinosaur, a Martian.

"You call me 'Weyland' now, not 'Edward.' " I said first name couldn't mean much to one with no memory of being called by that name as a child, silly to pretend it signifies intimacy where it can't. I think he knows now that I believe him. Without prompting, told me truth of disappearance from Cayslin. No romance; he tried to drink from a woman who worked there, she shot him, stomach and chest. Luckily for him, small-caliber pistol, and he was wearing a lined coat over three-piece suit. Even so, badly hurt. (Midsection stiffness I noted when he first came—he was still in some pain at that time.) He didn't "vanish"—fled, hid, was bound by questionable types who caught on to what he was, sold him "like a chattel" to someone here in the city. He was imprisoned, fed, put on exhibition—very privately—for gain. Got away. "Do you believe any of this?" Never asked anything like that before, seems of concern to him now. I said my belief or lack of same was immaterial; remarked on hearing a lot of bitterness.

He steepled his fingers, looked brooding at me over tips: "I nearly died there. No doubt my purchaser and his diabolist friend still search for me. Mind you, I had some reason at first to be glad of the attentions of the people who kept me prisoner. I was in no condition to fend for myself. They brought me food and kept me hidden and sheltered, whatever their motives. There are always advantages . . ."

Silence today started a short session. Hunting poor last night, Weyland still hungry. Much restless movement, watching goldfish darting in tank, scanning bookshelves. Asked him to be books. " 'I am old and full of knowledge, well made to last long. You see only the title, the substance is hidden. I am a book that stays closed.' " Malicious twist of the mouth, not quite a smile: "This is a good game." Is he feeling threatened, too—already "opened" too much to me? Too strung out with him to dig when he's skimming surfaces that should be probed. Don't know how to *do* therapy with Weyland—just have to let things happen, hope it's good. But what's "good"? Aristotle? Rousseau? Ask Weyland what's good, he'll say "Blood."

Everything in a spin—these notes too confused, too fragmentary—worthless for a book, just a mess, like me, my life. Tried to call Deb last night, cancel visit. Nobody home, thank God. Can't tell her to stay away—but damn it—do not need complications now!

Floria went down to Broadway with Lucille to get more juice, cheese and crackers for the clinic fridge. This week it was their turn to do the provisions, a chore that rotated among the staff. Their talk about grant proposals for the support of the clinic trailed off.

"Let's sit a minute," Floria said. They crossed to a traffic island in the middle of the avenue. It was a sunny afternoon, close enough to lunchtime so that the brigade of old people who normally occupied the benches had thinned out. Floria sat down and kicked a crumpled beer can and some greasy fast-food wrappings back under the bench.

"You look like hell but wide awake at least," Lucille commented.

"Things are still rough," Floria said. "I keep hoping to get my life under control so I'll have some energy left for Deb and Nick and the kids when they arrive, but I can't seem to do it. Group was awful last night—a member accused me afterward of having abandoned them all. I think I have, too. The professional messes and the personal are all related somehow, they run into each other. I should be keeping them apart so I can deal with them separately, but I can't. I can't concentrate, my mind is all over the place. Except with Dracula, who keeps me riveted with astonishment when he's in the office and bemused the rest of the time."

A bus roared by, shaking the pavement and the benches. Lucille waited until the noise faded. "Relax about the group. The others would have defended you if you'd been attacked during the session. They all understand, even if you don't seem to: it's the summer doldrums, people don't want to work, they expect you to do it all for them. But don't push so hard. You're not a shaman who can magic your clients back into health."

Floria tore two cans of juice out of a six-pack and handed one to her. On a street corner opposite, a violent argument broke out in typewriter-fast Spanish between two women. Floria sipped tinny juice and watched. She'd seen a guy last winter straddle another on that same corner and try to smash his brains out on the icy sidewalk. The old question again: What's crazy, what's health?

"It's a good thing you dumped Chubs, anyhow," Lucille said. "I don't know what finally brought that on, but it's definitely a move in the right direction. What about Count Dracula? You don't talk about him much anymore. I thought I diagnosed a yen for his venerable body."

Floria shifted uncomfortably on the bench and didn't answer. If only she could deflect Lucille's sharp-eyed curiosity.

"Oh," Lucille said. "I see. You really are hot—or at least warm. Has he noticed?"

"I don't think so. He's not on the lookout for that kind of response from me. He says sex with other people doesn't interest him, and I think he's telling the truth."

"Weird," Lucille said. "What about *Vampire on My Couch?* Shaping up all right?"

"It's shaky, like everything else. I'm worried that I don't know how things are going to come out. I mean, Freud's wolf-man case was a success, as therapy goes. Will my vampire case turn out successfully?"

She glanced at Lucille's puzzled face, made up her mind, and plunged ahead. "Luce, think of it this way: suppose, just suppose, that my Dracula is for real, an honest-to-God vampire—"

"Oh *shit!*" Lucille erupted in anguished exasperation. "Damn it, Floria, enough is enough—will you stop futzing around and get some help? Coming to pieces yourself and trying to treat this poor nut with a vampire fixation—how can you do him any good? No wonder you're worried about his therapy!"

"Please, just listen, help me think this out. My purpose can't be to cure him of what he is. Suppose vampirism isn't a defense he has to learn to drop? Suppose it's the core of his identity? Then what do I do?"

Lucille rose abruptly and marched away from her through a gap between the rolling waves of cabs and trucks. Floria caught up with her on the next block.

"Listen, will you? Luce, you see the problem? I don't need to help him see who and what he is, he knows that perfectly well, and he's not crazy, far from it—"

"Maybe not," Lucille said grimly, "but you are. Don't dump this junk on me outside of office hours, Floria. I don't spend my time listening to nut-talk unless I'm getting paid."

"Just tell me if this makes psychological sense to you: he's healthier than most of us because he's always true to his identity, even when he's engaged in deceiving others. A fairly narrow, rigorous set of requirements necessary to his survival—that *is* his identity, and it commands him completely. Anything extraneous could destroy him. To go on living, he has to act solely out of his own undistorted necessity, and if that isn't authenticity, what is? So he's healthy, isn't he?" She paused, feeling a sudden lightness in herself. "And that's the best sense I've been able to make of this whole business so far."

They were in the middle of the block. Lucille, who could not on her short legs outwalk Floria, turned on her suddenly. "What the hell do you think you're doing, calling yourself a therapist? For God's sake, Floria, don't try to rope me into this kind of professional irresponsibility. You're just dipping into your client's fantasies instead of helping him to handle them. That's not therapy, it's collusion. Have some sense! Admit you're over your head in troubles of your own, retreat to firmer ground—go get treatment for yourself!"

Floria angrily shook her head. When Lucille turned away and hurried on up the block toward the clinic, Floria let her go without trying to detain her.

Thought about Lucille's advice. After my divorce going back into therapy for a while did help, but now? Retreat again to being a client, like old days in training—so young, inadequate, defenseless then. Awful prospect. And I'd have to hand over W. to somebody else—who? I'm not up to handling him, can't cope, too anxious, yet with all that we do good therapy together somehow. I can't control, can only offer; he's free to take, refuse, use as suits, as far as he's willing to go. I serve as resource while he does own therapy—isn't that therapeutic ideal, free of "shoulds," "shouldn'ts"?

Saw ballet with Mort, lovely evening—time out from W.—talking, singing, pirouetting all the way home, feeling safe as anything in the shadow of Mort-mountain; rolled later with that humming (off-key), sun-warm body. Today W. says he saw me at Lincoln Center last night, avoided me because of Mort. W. is ballet fan! Started attending to pick up victims, now also because dance puzzles and pleases.

"When a group dances well, the meaning is easy—the dancers make a visual complement to the music, all their moves necessary, coherent, flowing. When a gifted soloist performs, the pleasure of making the moves is echoed in my own body. The soloist's absorption is total, much like my own in the actions of the hunt. But when a man and a woman dance together, something else happens. Sometimes one is hunter, one is prey, or they shift these roles between them. Yet some other level of significance exists—I suppose to do with sex—and I feel it—a tugging sensation, here"—touched his solar plexus—"but I do not understand it."

Worked with his reactions to ballet. The response he feels to pas de deux is a kind of pull, "Like hunger but not hunger." Of course he's baffled—Balanchine writes that the pas de deux is always a love story between man and woman. W. isn't man, isn't woman, yet the drama connects. His hands hovering as he spoke, fingers spread toward each other. Pointed this out. Body work comes easier to him now: joined his hands, interlaced fingers, spoke for hands without prompting: " 'We are similar, we want the comfort of like closing to like.' " How would that be for him, to find—likeness, another of his kind? "Female?" Starts impatiently explaining how unlikely this is— No, forget sex and pas de deux for now; just to find your like, another vampire.

He springs up, agitated now. There are none, he insists; adds at once, "But what would it be like? What would happen? I fear it!" Sits again, hands clenched. "I long for it."

Silence. He watches goldfish, I watch him. I withhold fatuous attempt to pin down this insight, if that's what it is—what can I know about his insight? Suddenly he turns, studies me intently till I lose my nerve, react, cravenly suggest that if I make him uncomfortable he might wish to switch to another therapist—

"Certainly not." More follows, all gold: "There is value to me in what we do here, Dr. Landauer, much against my earlier expectations. Although people talk appreciatively of honest speech they generally avoid it, and I myself have found scarcely any use for it at all. Your straightforwardness with me—and the straightforwardness you require in return—this is healthy in a life so dependent on deception as mine."

Sat there, wordless, much moved, thinking of what I don't show him—my upset life, seat-of-pants course with him and attendant strain, attraction to him—I'm holding out on him while he appreciates my honesty.

Hesitation, then lower-voiced, "Also, there are limits on my methods of self-discovery, short of turning myself over to a laboratory for vivisection. I have no others like myself to look at and learn from. Any tools that may help are worth much to me, and these games of yours are—potent." Other stuff besides, not important. Important: he moves me and he draws me and he keeps on coming back. Hang in if he does.

Bad night— Kenny's aunt called: no bill from me this month, so if he's not seeing me who's keeping an eye on him, where's he hanging out?

Much implied blame for what *might* happen. Absurd, but shook me up: I did fail Kenny. Called off group this week also; too much.

No, it was a *good* night—first dream in months I can recall, contact again with own depths—but disturbing. Dreamed myself in cab with W. in place of the woman from the Y. He put his hand not on my neck but breast—I felt intense sensual response in the dream, also anger and fear so strong they woke me.

Thinking about this: anyone leans toward him sexually, to him a sign his hunting technique has maneuvered prospective victim into range, maybe arouses his appetite for blood. *I don't want that.* "She was food." I am not food, I am a person. No thrill at languishing away in his arms in a taxi while he drinks my blood—that's disfigured sex, masochism. My sex response in dream signaled to me I would be his victim—I rejected that, woke up.

Mention of *Dracula* (novel). W. dislikes: meandering, inaccurate, those absurd fangs. Says he himself has a sort of needle under his tongue, used to pierce skin. No offer to demonstrate, and no request from me. I brightly brought up historical Vlad Dracul—celebrated instance of Turkish envoys who, upon refusing to uncover to Vlad to show respect, were killed by spiking their hats to their skulls. "Nonsense," snorts W. "A clever ruler would use very small thumbtacks and dismiss the envoys to moan about the streets of Varna holding their tacked heads." First spontaneous play he's shown—took head in hands and uttered plaintive groans, "Ow, oh, ooh." I cracked up. W. reverted at once to usual dignified manner. "You can see that this would serve the ruler much more effectively as an object lesson against rash pride."

Later, same light vein: "I know why I'm a vampire; why are you a therapist?" Off balance as usual, said things about helping, mental health, etc. He shook his head: "And people think of a vampire as arrogant! You want to perform cures in a world which exhibits very little health of any kind—and it's the same arrogance with all of you. This one wants to be President or Class Monitor or Department Chairman or Union Boss, another must be first to fly to the stars or to transplant the human brain, and on and on. As for me, I wish only to satisfy my appetite in peace."

And those of us whose appetite is for competence, for effectiveness? Thought of Green, treated eight years ago, went on to be indicted for running a hellish "home" for aged. I had helped him stay functional so he could destroy the helpless for profit.

W. not my first predator, only most honest and direct. Scared; not of attack by W., but of process we're going through. I'm beginning to be up to it (?), but still—utterly unpredictable, impossible to handle or manage. Occasional stirrings of inward choreographer that used to shape my work so surely. Have I been afraid of that, holding it down in myself, choosing mechanical manipulation instead? Not a choice with W.—thinking no good, strategy no good, nothing left but instinct, clear and uncluttered responses if I can find them. Have to be my own authority with him, as he is always his own authority with a world in which he's unique. So work with W. not just exhausting—exhilarating too, along with strain, fear.

Am I growing braver? Not much choice.

Park again today (air-conditioning out at office). Avoiding Lucille's phone calls from clinic (very reassuring that she calls despite quarrel, but don't want to take all this up with her again). Also meeting W. in open feels saner somehow—wild creatures belong outdoors? Sailboat pond N. of 72nd, lots of kids, garbage, one beautiful tall boat drifting. We walked.

W. maintains he remembers no childhood, no parents. I told him my astonishment, confronted by someone who never had a life of the previous generation (even adopted parent) shielding him from death—how naked we stand when the last shield falls. Got caught in remembering a death dream of mine, dream it now and then—couldn't concentrate, got scared, spoke of it—a dog tumbled under a passing truck, ejected to side of the road where it lay unable to move except to lift head and shriek; couldn't help. Shaking nearly to tears—remembered Mother got into dream somehow—had blocked that at first. Didn't say it now. Tried to rescue situation, show W. how to work with a dream (sitting in vine arbor near band shell, some privacy).

He focused on my obvious shakiness: "The air vibrates constantly with the death cries of countless animals large and small. What is the death of one dog?" Leaned close, speaking quietly, instructing. "Many creatures are dying in ways too dreadful to imagine. I am part of the world; I listen to the pain. You people claim to be above all that. You deafen yourselves with your own noise and pretend there's nothing else to hear. Then these screams enter your dreams, and you have to seek therapy because you have lost the nerve to listen."

Remembered myself, said, Be a dying animal. He refused: "You are the one who dreams this." I had a horrible flash, felt I was the dog—helpless, doomed, hurting—burst into tears. The great therapist, bringing her own hangups into session with client! Enraged with self, which did not help stop bawling.

W. disconcerted, I think; didn't speak. People walked past, glanced over, ignored us. W. said finally, "What is this?" Nothing, just the fear of death. "Oh, the fear of death. That's with me all the time. One must simply get used to it." Tears into laughter. Goddamn wisdom of the ages. He got up to go, paused: "And tell that stupid little man who used to precede me at your office to stop following me around. He puts himself in danger that way."

Kenny, damn it! Aunt doesn't know where he is, no answer on his phone. Idiot!

Sketching all night—useless. W. beautiful beyond the scope of line—the beauty of singularity, cohesion, rooted in absolute devotion to demands of his specialized body. In feeding (woman in taxi) utter absorption one wants from a man in sex—no score-keeping, no fantasies, just hot urgency of appetite, of senses, the moment by itself.

His sleeves worn rolled back today to the elbows—strong, sculptural forearms, the long bones curved in slightly, suggest torque, leverage. How old?

Endurance: huge, rich cloak of time flows back from his shoulders like wings of a dark angel. All springs from, elaborates, the single, stark, primary condition: he is a predator who subsists on human blood. Harmony, strength, clarity, magnificence—all from that basic animal integrity. Of course I long for all that, here in the higgledy-piggledy hodgepodge of my life! Of course he draws me!

Wore no perfume today, deference to his keen, easily insulted sense of smell. He noticed at once, said curt thanks. Saw something bothering him, opened my mouth seeking desperately for right thing to say—up rose my inward choreographer, wide awake, and spoke plain from my heart: thinking on my floundering in some of our sessions—I am aware that you see this confusion of mine. I know you see by your occasional impatient look, sudden disengagement—yet you continue to reveal yourself to me (even shift our course yourself if it needs shifting and I don't do it). I think I know why. Because there's no place for you in world as you truly are. Because beneath your various façades your true self suffers; like all true selves, it wants, needs to be honored as real and valuable through acceptance by another. I try to be that other, but often you are beyond me.

He rose, paced to window, looked back, burning at me. "If I seem sometimes restless or impatient, Dr. Landauer, it's not because of any professional shortcomings of yours. On the contrary—you are all too effective. The seductiveness, the distraction of our—human contact worries me. I fear for the ruthlessness that keeps me alive."

Speak for ruthlessness. He shook his head. Saw tightness in shoulders, feet braced hard against floor. Felt reflected tension in my own muscles.

Prompted him: " 'I resent . . .' "

"I resent your pretension to teach me about myself! What will this work that you do here make of me? A predator paralyzed by an unwanted empathy with his prey? A creature fit only for a cage and keeper?" He was breathing hard, jaw set. I saw suddenly the truth of his fear: his integrity is not human, but my work is specifically human,

designed to make humans more human—what if it does that to him? Should have seen it before, should have seen it. No place left to go: had to ask him, in small voice, Speak for my pretension.

"No!" Eyes shut, head turned away.

Had to do it: Speak for me.

W. whispered, "As to the unicorn, out of your own legends—'Unicorn, come lay your head in my lap while the hunters close in. You are a wonder, and for love of wonder I will tame you. You are pursued, but forget your pursuers, rest under my hand till they come and destroy you.' " Looked at me like steel: "Do you see? The more you involve yourself in what I am, the more you become the peasant with the torch!"

Two days later Doug came into town and had lunch with Floria.

He was a man of no outstanding beauty who was nevertheless attractive: he didn't have much chin and his ears were too big, but you didn't notice because of his air of confidence. His stability had been earned the hard way—as a gay man facing the straight world. Some of his strength had been attained with effort and pain in a group that Floria had run years earlier. A lasting affection had grown between herself and Doug. She was intensely glad to see him.

They ate near the clinic. "You look a little frayed around the edges," Doug said. "I heard about Jane Fennerman's relapse—too bad."

"I've only been able to bring myself to visit her once since."

"Feeling guilty?"

She hesitated, gnawing on a stale breadstick. The truth was, she hadn't thought of Jane Fennerman in weeks. Finally she said, "I guess I must be."

Sitting back with his hands in his pockets, Doug chided her gently. "It's got to be Jane's fourth or fifth time into the nuthatch, and the others happened when she was in the care of other therapists. Who are you to imagine—to demand—that her cure lay in your hands? God may be a woman, Floria, but She is not you. I thought the whole point was some recognition of individual responsibility—you for yourself, the client for himself or herself."

"That's what we're always saying," Floria agreed. She felt curiously divorced from this conversation. It had an old-fashioned flavor. Before Weyland. She smiled a little.

The waiter ambled over. She ordered bluefish. The serving would be too big for her depressed appetite, but Doug wouldn't be satisfied with his customary order of salad (he never was) and could be persuaded to help out.

He worked his way around to Topic A. "When I called to set up this lunch, Hilda told me she's got a crush on Weyland. How are you and he getting along?"

"My God, Doug, now you're going to tell me this whole thing was to fix me up with an eligible suitor!" She winced at her own rather strained laughter. "How soon are you planning to ask Weyland to work at Cayslin again?"

"I don't know, but probably sooner than I thought a couple of months ago. We hear that he's been exploring an attachment to an anthropology department at a Western school, some niche where I guess he feels he can have less responsibility, less visability, and a chance to collect himself. Naturally, this news is making people at Cayslin suddenly eager to nail him down for us. Have you a recommendation?"

"Yes," she said. "Wait."

He gave her an inquiring look. "What for?"

"Until he works more fully through certain stresses in the situation at Cayslin. Then I'll be ready to commit myself about him." The bluefish came. She pretended distraction: "Good God, that's too much fish for me. Doug, come on and help me out here."

Hilda was crouched over Floria's file drawer. She straightened up, looking grim. "Somebody's been in the office!"

What was this, had someone attacked her? The world took on a cock-eyed, dangerous tilt. "Are you okay?"

"Yes, sure, I mean there are records that have been gone through. I can tell. I've started checking and so far it looks as if none of the files themselves are missing. But if any papers were taken out of them, that would be pretty hard to spot without reading every folder in the place. Your files, Floria. I don't think anybody else's were touched."

Mere burglary; weak with relief, Floria sat down on one of the waiting-room chairs. But only her files? "Just my stuff, you're sure?"

Hilda nodded. "The clinic got hit, too. I called. They see some new-looking scratches on the lock of your file drawer over there. Listen, you want me to call the cops?"

"First check as much as you can, see if anything obvious is missing."

There was no sign of upset in her office. She found a phone message on her table: Weyland had canceled his next appointment. She knew who had broken into her files.

She buzzed Hilda's desk. "Hilda, let's leave the police out of it for the moment. Keep checking." She stood in the middle of the office, looking at the chair replacing the one he had broken, looking at the window where he had so often watched.

Relax, she told herself. There was nothing for him to find here or at the clinic.

She signaled that she was ready for the first client of the afternoon.

That evening she came back to the office after having dinner with friends. She was supposed to be helping set up a workshop for next month, and she'd been putting off even thinking about it, let alone doing any real work. She set herself to compiling a suggested bibliography for her section. The phone light blinked.

It was Kenny, sounding muffled and teary. "I'm sorry," he moaned. "The medicine just started to wear off. I've been trying to call you everyplace. God, I'm so scared—he was waiting in the alley."

"Who was?" she said, dry-mouthed. She knew.

"Him. The tall one, the faggot—only he goes with women too, I've seen him. He grabbed me. He hurt me. I was lying there a long time. I couldn't do anything. I felt so funny—like floating away. Some kids found me. Their mother called the cops. I was so cold, so scared—"

"Kenny, where are you?"

He told her which hospital. "Listen, I think he's really crazy, you know? And I'm scared he might . . . you live alone . . . I don't know—I didn't mean to make trouble for you. I'm so scared."

God damn you, you meant exactly to make trouble for me, and now you've bloody well made it. She got him to ring for a nurse. By calling Kenny her patient and using "Dr." in front of her own name without qualifying the title she got some information: two broken ribs, multiple contusions, a badly wrenched shoulder, and a deep cut on the scalp which Dr. Wells thought accounted for the blood loss the patient had sustained. Picked up early today, the patient wouldn't say who had attacked him. You can check with Dr. Wells tomorrow, Dr.—?

Can Weyland think I've somehow sicked Kenny on him? No, he surely knows me better than that. Kenny must have brought this on himself.

She tried Weyland's number and then the desk at his hotel. He had closed his account and gone, providing no forwarding information other than the address of a university in New Mexico.

Then she remembered: this was the night Deb and Nick and the kids were arriving. Oh, God. Next phone call. The Americana was the hotel Deb had mentioned. Yes, Mr. and Mrs. Nicholas Redpath were registered in room whatnot. Ring, please.

Deb's voice came shakily on the line. "I've been trying to call you." Like Kenny.

"You sound upset," Floria said, steadying herself for whatever calamity had descended: illness, accident, assault in the streets of the dark, degenerate city.

Silence, then a raggedy sob. "Nick's not here. I didn't phone you earlier because I thought he still might come, but I don't think he's coming, Mom." Bitter weeping.

"Oh, Debbie. Debbie, listen, you just sit tight, I'll be right down there."

The cab ride took only a few minutes. Debbie was still crying when Floria stepped into the room.

"I don't know, I don't know," Deb wailed, shaking her head. "What did I do wrong? He went away a week ago, to do some research, he said, and I didn't hear from him, and half the bank money is gone—just half, he left me half. I kept hoping . . . they say most runaways come back in a few days or call up, they get lonely . . . I haven't told anybody—I thought since we were supposed to be here at this convention thing together, I'd better come, maybe he'd show up. But nobody's seen him, and there are no messages, not a word, nothing."

"All right, all right, poor Deb," Floria said, hugging her.

"Oh God, I'm going to wake the kids with all this howling." Deb pulled away, making a frantic gesture toward the door of the adjoining room. "It was so hard to get them to sleep—they were expecting Daddy to be here, I kept telling them he'd be here." She rushed out into the hotel hallway. Floria followed, propping the door open with one of her shoes since she didn't know whether Deb had a key with her or not. They stood out there together, ignoring passersby, huddling over Deb's weeping.

"What's been going on between you and Nick?" Floria said. "Have you two been sleeping together lately?"

Deb let out a squawk of agonized embarrassment, "Mo-*ther!*" and pulled away from her. Oh, hell, wrong approach.

"Come on, I'll help you pack. We'll leave word you're at my place. Let Nick come looking for you." Floria firmly squashed down the miserable inner cry, How am I going to stand this?

"Oh, no, I can't move till morning now that I've got the kids settled down. Besides, there's one night's deposit on the rooms. Oh, Mom, what did I do?"

"You didn't do anything, hon," Floria said, patting her shoulder and thinking in some part of her mind, Oh boy, that's great, is that the best you can come up with in a crisis with all your training and experience? Your touted professional skills are not so hot lately, but this bad? Another part answered. Shut up, stupid, only an idiot does therapy on her own family. Deb's come to her mother, not to a shrink, so go ahead and be Mommy. If only Mommy had less pressure on her right now—but that was always the way: everything at once or nothing at all.

"Look, Deb, suppose I stay the night here with you."

Deb shook the pale, damp-streaked hair out of her eyes with a determined, grown-up gesture. "No, thanks, Mom. I'm so tired I'm just going to fall out now. You'll be getting a bellyful of all this when we move in on you tomorrow anyway. I can manage tonight, and besides—"

And besides, just in case Nick showed up, Deb didn't want Floria around complicating things; of course. Or in case the tooth fairy dropped by.

Floria restrained an impulse to insist on staying; an impulse, she recognized, that came from her own need not to be alone tonight. That was not something to load on Deb's already burdened shoulders.

"Okay," Floria said. "But look, Deb, I'll expect you to call me up first thing in the morning, whatever happens." *And if I'm still alive, I'll answer the phone.*

All the way home in the cab she knew with growing certainty that Weyland would be waiting for her there. *He can't just walk away,* she thought; *he has to finish things with me. So let's get it over.*

In the tiled hallway she hesitated, keys in hand. What about calling the cops to go inside with her? Absurd. You don't set the cops on a unicorn.

She unlocked and opened the door to the apartment and called inside, "Weyland! Where are you?"

Nothing. Of course not—the door was still open, and he would want to be sure she was by herself. She stepped inside, shut the door and snapped on a lamp as she walked into the living room.

He was sitting quietly on a radiator cover by the street window, his hands on his thighs. His appearance here in a new setting, her setting, this faintly lit room in her home place, was startlingly intimate. She was sharply aware of the whisper of movement—his clothing, his shoe soles against the carpet underfoot—as he shifted his posture.

"What would you have done if I'd brought somebody with me?" she said unsteadily. "Changed yourself into a bat and flown away?"

"Two things I must have from you," he said. "One is the bill of health that we spoke of when we began, though not, after all, for Cayslin College. I've made other plans. The story of my disappearance has of course filtered out along the academic grapevine so that even two thousand miles from here people will want evidence of my mental soundness. Your evidence. I would type it myself and forge your signature, but I want your authentic tone and language. Please prepare a letter to the desired effect, addressed to these people."

He drew something white from an inside pocket and held it out. She advanced and took the envelope from his extended hand. It was from the Western anthropology department that Doug had mentioned at lunch.

"Why not Cayslin?" she said. "They want you there."

"Have you forgotten your own suggestion that I find another job? That was a good idea after all. Your reference will serve me best out there—with a copy for my personnel file at Cayslin, naturally."

She put her purse down on the seat of a chair and crossed her arms. She felt reckless—the effect of stress and weariness, she thought, but it was an exciting feeling.

"The receptionist at the office does this sort of thing for me," she said.

He pointed. "I've been in your study. You have a typewriter there, you have stationery with your letterhead, you have carbon paper."

"What was the second thing you wanted?"

"Your notes on my case."

"Also at the—"

"You know that I've already searched both your work places, and the very circumspect jottings in your file on me are not what I mean. Others must exist: more detailed."

"What makes you think that?"

"How could you resist?" He mocked her. "You have encountered nothing like me in your entire professional life, and never shall again. Perhaps you hope to produce an article someday, even a book—a memoir of something impossible that happened to you one summer. You're an ambitious woman, Dr. Landauer."

Floria squeezed her crossed arms tighter against herself to quell her shivering. "This is all just supposition," she said.

He took folded papers from his pocket, some of her thrown-aside notes on him, salvaged from the wastebasket. "I found these. I think there must be more. Whatever there is, give it to me, please."

"And if I refuse, what will you do? Beat me up the way you beat up Kenny?"

Weyland said calmly, "I told you he should stop following me. This is serious now. There are pursuers who intend me ill—my former captors, of whom I told you. Whom do you think I keep watch for? No records concerning me must fall into their hands. Don't bother protesting to me your devotion to confidentiality. There is a man named Alan Reese who would take what he wants and be damned to your professional ethics. So I must destroy all evidence you have about me before I leave the city."

Floria turned away and sat down by the coffee table, trying to think beyond her fear. She breathed deeply against the fright trembling in her chest.

"I see," he said dryly, "that you won't give me the notes; you don't trust me to take them and go. You see some danger."

"All right, a bargain," she said. "I'll give you whatever I have on your case if in return you promise to go straight out to your new job and keep away from Kenny and my offices and anybody connected with me—"

He was smiling slightly as he rose from the seat and stepped soft-footed toward her over the rug. "Bargains, promises, negotiations—all foolish, Dr. Landauer. I want what I came for."

She looked up at him. "But then how can I trust you at all? As soon as I give you what you want—"

"What is it that makes you afraid—that you can't render me harmless to you? What a curious concern you show suddenly for your own life and the lives of those around you! You are the one who led me to take chances in our work together—to explore the frightful risks of self-revelation. Didn't you see in the air between us the brilliant shimmer of those hazards? I thought your business was not smoothing the world over but adventuring into it, discovering its true nature, and closing valiantly with everything jagged, cruel, and deadly."

In the midst of her terror the inner choreographer awoke and stretched. Floria rose to face the vampire.

"All right, Weyland, no bargains. I'll give you freely what you want."
Of course she couldn't make herself safe from him—or make Kenny or
Lucille or Deb or Doug safe—any more than she could protect Jane Fennerman from the common dangers of life. Like Weyland, some dangers
were too strong to bind or banish. "My notes are in the workroom—
come on, I'll show you. As for the letter you need, I'll type it right now
and you can take it away with you."

She sat at the typewriter arranging paper, carbon sheets, and white-out,
and feeling the force of his presence. Only a few feet away, just at the
margin of the light from the gooseneck lamp by which she worked, he
leaned against the edge of the long table that was twin to the table in her
office. Open in his large hands was the notebook she had given him from
the table drawer. When he moved his head over the notebook's pages,
his glasses glinted.

She typed the heading and the date. How surprising, she thought, to
find that she had regained her nerve here, and now. When you dance as
the inner choreographer directs, you act without thinking, not in command of events but in harmony with them. You yield control, accepting
the chance that a mistake might be part of the design. The inner choreographer is always right but often dangerous: giving up control means accepting the possibility of death. What I feared I have pursued right here
to this moment in this room.

A sheet of paper fell out of the notebook. Weyland stooped and caught
it up, glanced at it. "You had training in art?" Must be a sketch.

"I thought once I might be an artist," she said.

"What you chose to do instead is better," he said. "This making of
pictures, plays, all art, is pathetic. The world teems with creation, most
of it unnoticed by your kind just as most of the deaths are unnoticed.
What can be the point of adding yet another tiny gesture? Even you, these
notes—for what, a moment's celebrity?"

"You tried it yourself," Floria said. "The book you edited, *Notes on a
Vanished People.*" She typed: ". . . temporary dislocation resulting from
a severe personal shock . . ."

"That was professional necessity, not creation," he said in the tone of
a lecturer irritated by a question from the audience. With disdain he tossed
the drawing on the table. "Remember, I don't share your impulse toward
artistic gesture—your absurd frills—"

She looked up sharply. "The ballet, Weyland. Don't lie." She typed:
". . . exhibits a powerful drive toward inner balance and wholeness in a
difficult life situation. The steadying influence of an extraordinary basic
integrity . . ."

He set the notebook aside. "My feeling for ballet is clearly some sort
of aberration. Do you sigh to hear a cow calling in a pasture?"

"There are those who have wept to hear whales singing in the ocean."

He was silent, his eyes averted.

"This is finished," she said. "Do you want to read it?"

He took the letter. "Good," he said at length. "Sign it, please. And type an envelope for it." He stood closer, but out of arm's reach, while she complied. "You seem less frightened."

"I'm terrified but not paralyzed," she said and laughed, but the laugh came out a gasp.

"Fear is useful. It has kept you at your best throughout our association. Have you a stamp?"

Then there was nothing to do but take a deep breath, turn off the gooseneck lamp, and follow him back into the living room. "What now, Weyland?" she said softly. "A carefully arranged suicide so that I have no chance to retract what's in that letter or to reconstruct my notes?"

At the window again, always on watch at the window, he said, "Your doorman was sleeping in the lobby. He didn't see me enter the building. Once inside, I used the stairs, of course. The suicide rate among therapists is notoriously high. I looked it up."

"You have everything all planned?"

The window was open. He reached out and touched the metal grille that guarded it. One end of the grille swung creaking outward into the night air, like a gate opening. She visualized him sitting there waiting for her to come home, his powerful fingers patiently working the bolts at that side of the grille loose from the brick-and-mortar window frame. The hair lifted on the back of her neck.

He turned toward her again. She could see the end of the letter she had given him sticking palely out of his jacket pocket.

"Floria," he said meditatively. "An unusual name—is it after the heroine of Sardou's *Tosca*? At the end, doesn't she throw herself to her death from a high castle wall? People are careless about the names they give their children. I will not drink from you—I hunted today, and I fed. Still, to leave you living . . . is too dangerous."

A fire engine tore past below, siren screaming. When it had gone Floria said, "Listen, Weyland, you said it yourself: I can't make myself safe from you—I'm not strong enough to shove you out the window instead of being shoved out myself. Must you make yourself safe from me? Let me say this to you, without promises, demands, or pleadings: I will not go back on what I wrote in that letter. I will not try to re-create my notes. I mean it. Be content with that."

"You tempt me to it," he murmured after a moment, "to go from here with you still alive behind me for the remainder of your little life—to leave woven into Dr. Landauer's quick mind those threads of my own life that I pulled for her . . . I want to be able sometimes to think of you thinking of me. But the risk is very great."

"Sometimes it's right to let the dangers live, to give them their place," she urged. "Didn't you tell me yourself a little while ago how risk makes us more heroic?"

He looked amused. "Are you instructing me in the virtues of danger? You are brave enough to know something, perhaps, about that, but I have studied danger all my life."

"A long, long life with more to come," she said, desperate to make him understand and believe her. "Not mine to jeopardize. There's no torch-brandishing peasant here; we left that behind long ago. Remember when you spoke for me? You said, 'For love of wonder.' That was true."

He leaned to turn off the lamp near the window. She thought that he had made up his mind, and that when he straightened it would be to spring.

But instead of terror locking her limbs, from the inward choreographer came a rush of warmth and energy into her muscles and an impulse to turn toward him. Out of a harmony of desires she said swiftly, "Weyland, come to bed with me."

She saw his shoulders stiffen against the dim square of the window, his head lift in scorn. "You know I can't be bribed that way," he said contemptuously. "What are you up to? Are you one of those who come into heat at the sight of an upraised fist?"

"My life hasn't twisted me that badly, thank God," she retorted. "And if you've known all along how scared I've been, you must have sensed my attraction to you too, so you know it goes back to—very early in our work. But we're not at work now, and I've given up being 'up to' anything. My feeling is real—not a bribe, or a ploy, or a kink. No 'love me now, kill me later,' nothing like that. Understand me, Weyland: if death is your answer, than let's get right to it—come ahead and try."

Her mouth was dry as paper. He said nothing and made no move; she pressed on. "But if you can let me go, if we can simply part company here, then this is how I would like to mark the ending of our time together. This is the completion I want. Surely you feel something, too—curiosity at least?"

"Granted, your emphasis on the expressiveness of the body has instructed me," he admitted, and then he added lightly, "Isn't it extremely unprofessional to proposition a client?"

"Extremely, and I never do; but this, now, feels right. For you to indulge in courtship that doesn't end in a meal would be unprofessional, too, but how would it feel to indulge anyway—this once? Since we started, you've pushed me light-years beyond my profession. Now I want to travel all the way with you, Weyland. Let's be unprofessional together."

She turned and went into the bedroom, leaving the lights off. There was a reflected light, cool and diffuse, from the glowing night air of the great city. She sat down on the bed and kicked off her shoes. When she looked up, he was in the doorway.

Hesitantly, he halted a few feet from her in the dimness, then came and sat beside her. He would have lain down in his clothes, but she said quietly, "You can undress. The front door's locked and there isn't anyone here but us. You won't have to leap up and flee for your life."

He stood again and began to take off his clothes, which he draped neatly over a chair. He said, "Suppose I am fertile with you; could you conceive?"

By her own choice any such possibility had been closed off after Deb. She said, "No," and that seemed to satisfy him.

She tossed her own clothes onto the dresser.

He sat down next to her again, his body silvery in the reflected light and smooth, lean as a whippet and as roped with muscle. His cool thigh pressed against her own fuller, warmer one as he leaned across her and carefully deposited his glasses on the bedtable. Then he turned toward her, and she could just make out two puckerings of tissue on his skin: bullet scars, she thought, shivering.

He said, "But why do I wish to do this?"

"Do you?" She had to hold herself back from touching him.

"Yes." He stared at her. "How did you grow so real? The more I spoke to you of myself, the more real you became."

"No more speaking, Weyland," she said gently. "This is body work."

He lay back on the bed.

She wasn't afraid to take the lead. At the very least she could do for him as well as he did for himself, and at the most, much better. Her own skin was darker than his, a shadowy contrast where she browsed over his body with her hands. Along the contours of his ribs she felt knotted places, hollows—old healings, the tracks of time. The tension of his muscles under her touch and the sharp sound of his breathing stirred her. She lived the fantasy of sex with an utter stranger; there was no one in the world so much a stranger as he. Yet there was no one who knew him as well as she did, either. If he was unique, so was she, and so was their confluence here.

The vividness of the moment inflamed her. His body responded. His penis stirred, warmed, and thickened in her hand. He turned on his hip so that they lay facing each other, he on his right side, she on her left. When she moved to kiss him he swiftly averted his face: of course—to him, the mouth was for feeding. She touched her fingers to his lips, signifying her comprehension.

He offered no caresses but closed his arms around her, his hands cradling the back of her head and neck. His shadowed face, deep-hollowed under brow and cheekbone, was very close to hers. From between the parted lips that she must not kiss his quick breath came, roughened by groans of pleasure. At length he pressed his head against hers, inhaling deeply; taking her scent, she thought, from her hair and skin.

He entered her, hesitant at first, probing slowly and tentatively. She found this searching motion intensely sensuous, and clinging to him all along his sinewy length she rocked with him through two long swelling waves of sweetness. Still half submerged, she felt him strain tight against her, she heard him gasp through his clenched teeth. Panting, they subsided and lay loosely interlocked. His head was tilted back; his eyes were closed. She had no desire to stroke him or to speak with him, only to rest spent against his body and absorb the sounds of his breathing, her breathing.

He did not lie long to hold or be held. Without a word he disengaged his body from hers and got up. He moved quietly about the bedroom, gathering his clothing, his shoes, the drawings, the notes from the workroom. He dressed without lights. She listened in silence from the center of a deep repose.

There was no leavetaking. His tall figure passed and repassed the dark rectangle of the doorway, and then he was gone. The latch on the front door clicked shut.

Floria thought of getting up to secure the deadbolt. Instead she turned on her stomach and slept.

She woke as she remembered coming out of sleep as a youngster—peppy and clearheaded.

"Hilda, let's give the police a call about that break-in. If anything ever does come of it, I want to be on record as having reported it. You can tell them we don't have any idea who did it or why. And please make a photocopy of this letter carbon to send to Doug Sharpe up at Cayslin. Then you can put the carbon into Weyland's file and close it."

Hilda sighed. "Well, he was too old anyway."

He wasn't, my dear, but never mind.

In her office Floria picked up the morning's mail from her table. Her glance strayed to the window where Weyland had so often stood. God, she was going to miss him; and God, how good it was to be restored to plain working days.

Only not yet. Don't let the phone ring, don't let the world push in here now. She needed to sit alone for a little and let her mind sort through the images left from . . . from the pas de deux with Weyland. It's the notorious morning after, old dear, she told herself; just where have I been dancing, anyway?

In a clearing in the enchanted forest with the unicorn, of course, but not the way the old legends have it. According to them, hunters set a virgin to attract the unicorn by her chastity so they can catch and kill him. My unicorn was the chaste one, come to think of it, and this lady meant no treachery. No, Weyland and I met hidden from the hunt, to celebrate a private mystery of our own. . . .

Your mind grappled with my mind, my dark leg over your silver one, unlike closing with unlike across whatever likeness may be found: your memory pressing on my thoughts, my words drawing out your words in which you may recognize your life, my smooth palm gliding down your smooth flank . . .

Why, this will make me cry, she thought, blinking. And for what? Does an afternoon with the unicorn have any meaning for the ordinary days that come later? What has this passage with Weyland left me? Have I anything in my hands now besides the morning's mail?

What I have in my hands is my own strength, because I had to reach deep to find the strength to match him.

She put down the letters, noticing how on the backs of her hands the veins stood, blue shadows, under the thin skin. How can these hands be strong? Time was beginning to wear them thin and bring up the fragile inner structure in clear relief. That was the meaning of the last parent's death: that the child's remaining time has a limit of its own.

But not for Weyland. No graveyards of family dead lay behind him, no obvious and implacable ending of his own span threatened him. Time has to be different for a creature of an enchanted forest, as morality has to be different. He was a predator and a killer formed for a life of centuries, not decades; of secret singularity, not the busy hum of the herd. Yet his strength, suited to that nonhuman life, had revived her own strength. Her hands were slim, no longer youthful, but she saw now that they were strong enough.

For what? She flexed her fingers, watching the tendons slide under the skin. Strong hands don't have to clutch. They can simply open and let go.

She dialed Lucille's extension at the clinic.

"Luce? Sorry to have missed your calls lately. Listen, I want to start making arrangements to transfer my practice for a while. You were right, I do need a break, just as all my friends have been telling me. Will you pass the word for me to the staff over there today? Good, thanks. Also, there's the workshop coming up next month. . . . Yes. Are you kidding? They'd love to have you in my place. You're not the only one who's noticed that I've been falling apart, you know. It's awfully soon—can you manage, do you think? Luce, you are a brick and a lifesaver and all that stuff that means I'm very, very grateful."

Not so terrible, she thought, but only a start. Everything else remained to be dealt with. The glow of euphoria couldn't carry her for long. Already, looking down, she noticed jelly on her blouse, just like old times, and she didn't even remember having breakfast. If you want to keep the strength you've found in all this, you're going to have to get plenty of practice being strong. Try a tough one now.

She phoned Deb. "Of course you slept late, so what? I did, too, so I'm glad you didn't call and wake me up. Whenever you're ready—if you need help moving uptown from the hotel, I can cancel here and come down. . . . Well, call if you change your mind. I've left a house key for you with my doorman.

"And listen, hon, I've been thinking—how about all of us going up together to Nonnie's over the weekend? Then when you feel like it maybe you'd like to talk about what you'll do next. Yes, I've already started setting up some free time for myself. Think about it, love. Talk to you later."

Kenny's turn. "Kenny, I'll come by during visiting hours this afternoon."

"Are you okay?" he squeaked.

"I'm okay. But I'm not your mommy, Ken, and I'm not going to start trying to hold the big bad world off you again. I'll expect you to be ready to settle down seriously and choose a new therapist for yourself. We're going to get that done today once and for all. Have you got that?"

After a short silence he answered in a desolate voice, "All right."

"Kenny, nobody grown up has a mommy around to take care of things for them and keep them safe—not even me. You just have to be tough enough and brave enough yourself. See you this afternoon."

How about Jane Fennerman? No, leave it for now, we are not Wonder Woman, we can't handle that stress today as well.

Too restless to settle down to paperwork before the day's round of appointments began, she got up and fed the goldfish, then drifted to the window and looked out over the city. Same jammed-up traffic down there, same dusty summer park stretching away uptown—yet not the same city, because Weyland no longer hunted there. Nothing like him moved now in those deep, grumbling streets. She would never come upon anyone there as alien as he—and just as well. Let last night stand as the end, unique and inimitable, of their affair. She was glutted with strangeness and looked forward frankly to sharing again in Mort's ordinary human appetite.

And Weyland—how would he do in that new and distant hunting ground he had found for himself? Her own balance had been changed. Suppose his once perfect, solitary equilibrium had been altered too? Perhaps he had spoiled it by involving himself too intimately with another being— herself. And then he had left her alive—a terrible risk. Was this a sign of his corruption at her hands?

"Oh, no," she whispered fiercely, focusing her vision on her reflection in the smudged window glass. Oh, no, I am not the temptress. I am not the deadly female out of legends whose touch defiles the hitherto unblemished being, her victim. If Weyland found some human likeness in himself, that had to be in him to begin with. Who said he was defiled anyway? Newly discovered capacities can be either strengths or weaknesses, depending on how you use them.

Very pretty and reassuring, she thought grimly; but it's pure cant. Am I going to retreat now into mechanical analysis to make myself feel better?

She heaved open the window and admitted the sticky summer breath of the city into the office. There's your enchanted forest, my dear, all nitty-gritty and not one flake of fairy dust. You've survived here, which means you can see straight when you have to. Well, you have to now.

Has he been damaged? No telling yet, and you can't stop living while you wait for the answers to come in. I don't know all that was done between us, but I do know who did it: I did it, and he did it, and neither of us withdrew until it was done. We were joined in a rich complicity—he in the wakening of some flicker of humanity in himself, I in keeping and, yes, enjoying the secret of his implacable blood hunger. What that complicity means for each of us can only be discovered by getting on with living and watching for clues from moment to moment. His business is to continue from here, and mine is to do the same, without guilt and without resentment. Doug was right: the aim is individual responsibility. From that effort, not even the lady and the unicorn are exempt.

Shaken by a fresh upwelling of tears, she thought bitterly, Moving on is easy enough for Weyland; he's used to it, he's had more practice. What about me? Yes, be selfish, woman—if you haven't learned that, you've learned damn little.

The Japanese say that in middle age you should leave the claims of family, friends, and work, and go ponder the meaning of the universe while you still have the chance. Maybe I'll try just existing for a while, and letting grow in its own time my understanding of a universe that includes Weyland—and myself—among its possibilities.

Is that looking out for myself? Or am I simply no longer fit for living with family, friends, and work? Have *I* been damaged by *him*—by my marvelous, murderous monster?

Damn, she thought, I wish he were here, I wish we could talk about it. The light on her phone caught her eye; it was blinking the quick flashes that meant Hilda was signaling the imminent arrival of—not Weyland—the day's first client.

We're each on our own now, she thought, shutting the window and turning on the air-conditioner.

But think of me sometimes, Weyland, thinking of you.

SUSAN CASPER
(b. 1947)

Born in Philadelphia, Susan Casper graduated from Temple University. She published her first story, "Spring-Fingered Jack," in the anthology Fears *(1983), and has published several others in collaboration with her husband, Gardner Dozois (editor of* Asimov's Science Fiction *magazine and the annual* Year's Best Science Fiction *anthology). These stories have been collected in* Slow Dancing Through Time *(1990). Casper and Dozois also edited the anthology* Ripper! *in 1988.*

Though much different in tone, prose style, and characterization, "A Child of Darkness" bears comparison both with Richard Matheson's I Am Legend *and with Suzy McKee Charnas's "Unicorn Tapestry."* I Am Legend *theorizes that vampirism is the result of illness, while "Unicorn Tapestry" wrestles with whether or not the protagonist is truly a vampire.*

In "A Child of Darkness," Casper tells her story in the present tense interspersed with flashbacks. The protagonist, Daria, is told that she is suffering from a blood disease known as porphyria, a type of anemia that shares many symptoms with vampirism. Or is Daria suffering from a psychological disorder? Casper, a wise fiction writer, reserves the answer to that question to the very last possible moment.

A CHILD OF DARKNESS

The air is damp and tainted with the odors of tobacco, sweat, and urine. What light there is comes from a small bulb in the ceiling, its plastic cover green with ancient grime. Voices echo, reecho along the concrete walls of the corridor until they sound like an old recording. It is Daria's only contact with the world outside of her little cell and she is torn between a nervous desire to shut it all out, and a need to listen greedily.

Far away a woman begins to sing an old gospel song. Her voice is thin and slightly off-key; it gives Daria a shiver. *It makes my blood run cold,* she thinks, then laughs bitterly at the idea. Hers is not the only laughter. From somewhere in the depths comes the cackle of a mad woman—and then another voice joins in, slurred, unsteady, taunting. "That singin' won't help you none, bitch. God knows what you are. Whore of Babylon, that's what *you* are."

The singing stops. "What the hell do you know?" a Spanish accent replies.

"Ain't what I know that counts, bitch. It's what God knows. God knows you're a sinner. He's gonna get you, girl."

The accent protests. She prays, sobs, moans, repents, accuses, but her anguished voice is softer, and weaker, and somehow more frightening then the others.

Suddenly, a shrill, soprano, scream cuts across all the other noises. "Oh, the pain. Oh my God, the pain. I'm dying. Somebody please . . . help me."

"Hey, you, knock it off down there," a cold male voice replies.

Daria can see nothing from her cell but the stained gray wall across the corridor which seems to go on forever, but she finds that if she presses herself into the corner, she can just make out the place where the hallway ends on one side. A guard is sitting there. He is eating a sandwich that he peels from a wax-paper bag as if it were a banana. A Styrofoam cup is perched on the floor by his side. Another cop comes by. She can see him briefly as he passes through her narrow channel of vision, but he must have stopped to talk, because the first man's face splits into a grin and then she can see his lips move. His thumb points down her corridor and he begins to laugh.

Lousy bastard, she thinks.

The Kool-Aid looked a lot like wine in her mother's good stemware. Especially when the light shone through it, making the liquid glow like rubies, or maybe the glorious seeds of an autumn pomegranate. She lifted the glass, pinky raised in a grotesque child's parody, and delicately sipped the liquid. *Wine must taste a lot like this,* she thought, swirling the sugary drink in her mouth. This was what it would be like when she was a lady. She would pile her hair high atop her head in curls and wear deliciously tight dresses, her shoulders draped in mink. Just like Marilyn Monroe.

"Ha, ha, Dary's drinking wi-ine. Dary's drinking wi-ine," Kevin sang as he raced back and forth across the kitchen floor.

"It's not either wine," she said, more embarrassed then frightened at being caught by her little brother.

"If it's not wine then prove it," he said, snatching the glass from her hand. He held it tightly in his fist, one pinky shooting straight out into the air, mocking her already exaggerated grip. He sipped it, then made a face, eyes bugged and whirling. "Ugh, it is wine," he said, looking at her impishly. "I must be drunk." He began to stagger about, flinging himself around the room. Daria saw it coming. She wanted to cry out and stop him, or at least to cover her eyes so that she couldn't see the disaster, but it happened before she could do any of those things. Kevin tripped over the leg of a chair and went down in a crash of shattered crystal.

Her first thought was for the glass. That was one of the things that she hated herself for later. All she could think about was how it was Kevin's fault that the glass was broken, but she would be the one who got the spanking for it. Especially the way he was howling. Then she saw the blood all over her brother's arm. Already there was a small puddle on the floor. She knew that she should get a bandage, or call the emergency number that her mother always kept near the phone, or at the very least, run and get a neighbor, but she couldn't move. She couldn't take her eyes off of the bright-red stain. It was not as if she had never seen blood before, but suddenly she was drawn to it as she had never been drawn to anything before. Without knowing what she was doing, she found herself walking toward her brother, taking his arm in her hands and pulling it slowly toward her face. And then she could taste the salt and copper taste as she sucked at her brother's wound, filling a need that she hadn't even known existed. It was a hunger so all-consuming that she could not be distracted even by Kevin's fists flailing away at her back, or the sound of her mother's scream when she entered the room.

Daria realizes that she has wedged her face too tightly between the bars and the cold metal is bruising her cheeks. She withdraws into the dimness. There is a metal shelf bolted to the wall. It has a raised edge running around its sides and was obviously designed to hold a mattress that is long since gone. There are cookie-sized holes in the metal, placed with no discernible pattern along its length. Words have been scratched into this cot frame with nail files, hair pins, paper clips—mostly names like Barbara and Mike, and Gloria S. There are many expletives and an occasional statement about the "pigs," but no poems or limericks to occupy her attention for even a brief time. The metal itself is studded with rock-hard lumps of used chewing gum, wadded bits of paper and who knows what else. It is uncomfortable to sit on even without these things—too wide. Her skirt is too tight for her to sit cross-legged, and so if she sits back far enough to lean against the wall, the metal lip cuts sharply into the back of her calves. Already, there are bright red welts on her legs, and so she lies on her side with her knees drawn up and her head pedestaled on her arm, the holes in the metal leaving rings along the length of her body. She pulls a crumpled package of cigarettes out of her pocket and stares at them longingly. Only three left. With a sigh, she puts them back. It is going to be a long night.

The doctor's name was printed in thick black letters on the frosted glass. Who knew what horrors waited for her on the other side. She knew that she had promised her mother that she would behave, but it was all too much for her. With tears streaming down her cheeks, she tried to pull free from her mother's grasp.

"No! Please. No, Mommy! I'll be a good girl, I promise."

Her mother grabbed her by both shoulders and stooped down until she could look into her daughter's eyes. With trembling fingers she brushed the child's hair. "Dary, honey, the doctor won't hurt you. All he wants to do is have a little talk with you. That's all. You can talk with the nice doctor, can't you?"

Daria sniffed and wiped her eyes with the backs of her hands. She knew what kind of people went to see psychiatrists. Crazy people. And crazy people got "put away" in the nuthouse. She allowed her mother to lead her into the doctor's office, a queen walking bravely to the gallows.

The waiting room was supposed to look inviting. One whole side was set up as a playroom, with a child-sized table and two little chairs, an open toybox with dolls and blocks spilling out of the top. A lady in starched white greeted them at the door and pointed Daria toward the corner, but she was not the least interested in playing. Instead, she hoisted herself onto a large wooden chair and sat there in perfect stillness, her hands folded across her lap. There she could hear some of the words that passed between her mother and the nurse. Their voices were hushed and they were quite far away, but she could hear enough to tell that her mother was ashamed to tell the white lady what Daria had done. She could hear the word "crazy" pass back and forth between them just as she had heard it pass between her father and mother all the last week. And she could tell, even though she could only see the back of her head, that her mother was crying.

Suddenly, the door opened up behind the nurse's desk and Daria's mother disappeared through it. The nurse tried to talk to the sullen little girl, but Daria remained motionless, knowing that she would wait there forever, if necessary, but she would not move from that spot until her mother returned.

Then, like a miracle, her mother was back. Daria forgot all about her resolve to stay in the seat. She rushed to her mother's side. She would go anywhere, even inside the doctor's room if only her mother wouldn't leave her again. When her mother opened the door to the doctor's office and waved Daria through, the child went without hesitation, but then, her mother shut the door without following, and Daria was more frightened than ever.

"You must be Daria," Doctor Wells said without moving from his desk. He reminded Daria of the stuffed walrus in the museum, and he smelled of tobacco and Sen-Sen and mustache wax. He smiled, and it was a pleasant smile. "Your mother tells me that you're very smart and that you like to do puzzles. I have a puzzle here that's very hard. Would you like to try and do my puzzle?"

Daria nodded, but she did not move from her place near the door. Dr. Wells got up and walked over to a shelf and removed a large wooden puzzle. It was a cow. A three-dimensional puzzle. Daria had never seen anything like it before. He placed the puzzle on a little table that was a twin to the one in the waiting room and went back behind his desk.

"Well, you don't have to do it if you don't want to," he said after a minute, and then began to look through some papers on his desk, ignoring her. Soon, Daria's curiosity got the better of her and she found herself standing at the table looking at the puzzle, taking it apart.

Daria had expected the doctor would talk to her, but he didn't really seem interested in talking. He seemed content to watch her play with the puzzles and toys and he asked her very few questions. By the time she left his office, Daria had decided that she liked Dr. Wells very much.

She wakes slowly, unsure whether minutes or hours have passed. Her eyes are weeping from the cold of the metal where her head has been resting, and her muscles ache with stiffness. Her neck and chest, still covered with crusted blood that the arresting officers had refused to let her wash away, have begun to itch unmercifully. She sits up and realizes that her bladder is full. There is a toilet in the cell. It is a filthy affair with no seat, no paper, no sink, and no privacy from the eyes of the policemen who occasionally stroll up and down the corridor. She will live with the pain a while longer.

Suddenly, she realizes what it is that has woken her up. Silence. It is a silence as profound as the noise had been earlier. No singing, no taunting voices, nobody howling in pain. It is so quiet that she can hear the rustling newspaper of the guard at the end of the hall. She feels that she ought to be grateful not to have to listen to the racket, but instead, she finds the silence frightening.

Once again, she pulls the crumpled pack of cigarettes from her pocket. This time she cannot resist. She pulls one from the pack and straightens its bent form, then holds it between her lips for a long time before she begins the finalizing act of lighting it. She lets out the smoke in a long plume, pleased by the hominess of its smell. A familiar scent in this alien world.

"Can you spare one . . . please?" a soft voice calls from the next cell. "Please?" it asks again. The noise acts like a trigger as the tiny gospel singer starts in once more. A hand pokes through the bars in the corner of the cell. It is black and scarred and shaking with the strain of the reach. It is easily the largest hand she has ever seen. Large even for a man. Daria stares at the two cigarettes remaining in her pack. What the hell, she figures, they'll be gone soon anyway. She removes one and places it in the hand. It squeezes her own gently and withdraws.

"So, it has happened again, Daria?" Dr. Wells asked. The child nodded, looking down at her feet. "After three years we had great hope that it wouldn't happen again. But now that you are a little older, perhaps you can tell me what went on in your mind. What were you thinking when it happened? Do you have any idea why you did it?"

"I don't remember thinking anything. I don't even remember doing it. It was like a dream. They had us all lined up outside for gym. We were going to play field hockey. Tanya and Melinda were playing and Tanya hit her with her stick. I only wanted to help, but there was blood all over everything. I remember being afraid. I remember doing it, but it was almost more like watching television, when the camera's supposed to be you. The next thing I knew, Mrs. Rollie was holding me down and there were people everywhere." There was a long pause. "None of the other girls will talk to me now. They call me . . ." The child burst into tears. "They call me a vampire," she said.

"And how do you feel about that?" Dr. Wells goaded her.

"I don't know. Maybe it's true. It must be true, else why would I do what I do?" Tears streamed down her cheeks and she blotted them with a tissue.

"What do you know about vampires, Daria?"

"That they sleep in coffins and hate the sun . . . I know, but maybe it's only partly true. I do hate the sunlight. It hurts my eyes. And garlic, too. It makes me sick. Even the smell of it. Maybe the legends aren't quite right. Maybe I'm just a different kind of vampire. Why else would I do what I do?"

"Do you want to be a vampire, Daria?" Dr. Wells asked softly.

"No!" she shouted, the tears streaming down her face unimpeded, then again more softly, "No. Do you think I'm a vampire?" she asked.

"No, Daria. I don't believe in vampires. I think you're a young lady with a problem. And . . . I think if we work together, we can find out why you have this problem and what we can do about it."

There is the jingle of keys and the crisp sound of heavy feet. The dying

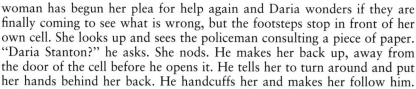

woman has begun her plea for help again and Daria wonders if they are finally coming to see what is wrong, but the footsteps stop in front of her own cell. She looks up and sees the policeman consulting a piece of paper. "Daria Stanton?" he asks. She nods. He makes her back up, away from the door of the cell before he opens it. He tells her to turn around and put her hands behind her back. He handcuffs her and makes her follow him.

She is surprised to see there is only one cell between hers and the main corridor, something that she hadn't noticed on the way in. The cop she saw earlier is still sitting there, still eating, or perhaps eating again. She wants to ask him why he doesn't at least check on the woman who is screaming, but he doesn't look up at her as she passes. She is taken down an endless maze of corridors, all covered with the same green tile, except where they branch out into hallways full of cells. Eventually, she is taken to a room where her cuffs are removed and she is told to wait. He is careless shutting the door behind him and she can see that it isn't locked, but she makes no move to go through it. What difference can it make. Her fate was decided long ago.

"Daria Stanton? Please sit down, I have some questions to ask you."

Even after six months it still felt strange, coming to this new building, walking down a new corridor. She still missed Dr. Wells and hated him for dying that way, without any warning, as though it had been an act against her, personally. This new doctor didn't feel like a doctor at all; letting her call him Mark. And there should be a law against anyone's shrink being so cute, with all those new-fangled ideas. She paused outside the door, pulled off her mirrored sunglasses, and adjusted her hair and makeup in the lenses.

"Morning, Mark," she said as she seated herself in his green padded chair by the window. She couldn't bring herself to lie down on the couch, because all she could think of was how much she wanted him lying there with her. Seated where she was, she could watch the street outside while they talked. Two boys were standing around the old slide-bolt gum machine that had stood outside Wexler's Drug Store for as long as she could remember. It was easy to tell by their attitude that they were up to something. The dark-haired boy looked around furtively several times, then started sliding the bolt back and forth.

"I have some news for you this morning," Dr. Bremner told her. "Good news, I hope." The blond child kicked the machine and tried the bolt again. "The reports of your blood workup are back and I've gone over them with Dr. Walinski. Your blood showed a marked anemia of a type known as iron-deficiency porphyria. Now, ordinarily, I wouldn't be telling a patient that it was good news that she was sick, but in your case, it could mean that your symptoms are purely physical." A woman walked down the street. The two boys stopped tampering with the machine, turned and stared into the drugstore window until she had passed ". . . a very rare disease. It is even more unusual for it to evince the symptoms that you have, but . . . it has been known to happen. Your body craves the iron porphyrins that it can't produce, and somehow, it knows what *you* don't . . . that whole blood is a source." The boys went back to the machine. One of them pulled a wire from his pocket and inserted it into the coin slot. "I've also talked with Dr. Ruth Tracey at the Eilman Clinic for Blood Disorders. She says your sensitivity to light and to garlic are all tied up in this too. For one thing, garlic breaks down old red blood cells. Just what a person with your condition can't afford to have happen." Once again the boys were interrupted and once again they removed themselves to the drugstore window. "Do you understand what all this means?"

Daria nodded morosely.

"How does it feel to know that there is a physiological cause for your problem?"

"I don't see what difference it makes," she said, brushing a wisp of straight black hair from her forehead in irritation. "Insanity, vampirism, porphyria? What difference does it make what name you put on it? Even my family barely speaks to me any more. Besides, it's getting worse. I can't even stand to go out during the day anymore, and look at this." She pulled the sunglasses from her face to show him the dark circles under her eyes.

"Yes, I know, but Dr. Tracey can help you. With the right medications your symptoms should disappear. Imagine a time when you can see someone cut themselves without being afraid of what you'll do. You'll be able to go to the beach and get a suntan for Chrissake."

Daria looked back out the window, but the boys were gone. She wasn't sure whether the half-empty globe had been full of gumballs a moment ago.

Hours—weeks—years later they bring her back to her cell. Though she has only been there since early evening, already it is like coming home. The chorus has changed. Two drunken, giggling voices have been added and someone is drumming on the bars with ringed fingers. The taunter still goads the gospel singer even though she has stopped singing and the dying woman is still dying, with a tough new voice telling her to do it already and shut up. Daria slumps back on her slab of metal, her back against the wall with her straight skirt hiked up so that her legs can be folded in front of her. She no longer cares what anybody sees. She has been questioned, photographed, and given one phone call. Mark will be there for the arraignment. He will see about getting her a lawyer. She has been told not to worry, that everything will be all right—but she is not worried . . . she knows that nothing will ever be all right for her again.

She stares at the dim and dirty green light that is always on and wonders if prison will be worse. From what she has read about penal institutions, she will not last very long once they send her away. A vampire in prison. She laughs at the thought and wonders what Dracula would do.

The fire was warmth seeping into her body, making her feel alive for the first time in years. She inched herself a little closer to the hearth. Mark came into the room holding a pair of cocktail glasses. He placed one by her elbow and joined her on the rug.

"Daria, there are things I wanted to tell you. So many things that I just couldn't say while you were my patient. You do understand why I couldn't go on treating you? Not the way I felt."

She reached out and squeezed his hand, reluctant to turn her face away from the fire for even the time it would have taken to look at him. He stroked her hair. Why did it make her feel like purring? She wanted him to take her in his arms, but she was afraid. Unlike most twenty-year-old women, she had no idea what to do; how to react. The boys that she met had often told her that she was beautiful, flirted, made passes or asked her out, but the moment they found out anything about her, they always became frightened and backed off. Mark was different. He already knew everything, even though he didn't choose to believe it all.

He took her face in his hands and kissed her. At first she wanted to pull away, but soon a burning started inside of her that made the fireplace unnecessary.

Daria can no longer stand the boredom. She climbs on the bars of her cell just for something to do. It is morning. She can tell by the shuffling of feet and slamming of doors that come from the main corridor. She can tell by the food trays being brought down the hall, though none comes to her, and by the fact that the man in the chair has been replaced by a sloppy matron. She wonders if Mark is in the building yet. Probably. He has been in love with her since the first day she walked into his office, though she is convinced it is her condition and not herself that he loves. She would like to love him back, but though she needs him and wants him, truly enjoys his intimacy, she is sure that love is just another emotion that she cannot feel.

A different policeman stops outside her cell. He is carrying handcuffs, but he does not take them from his belt as he opens her cell door. "Time for your arraignment," he says cheerfully. Docile, she follows him down the same, and then a different, set of corridors. They take a long ride in a rickety elevator and when the doors open they are standing in a paneled hall. Spears of morning light stab through the windows making Daria cover her eyes. In the distance she can see a courtroom packed with people. Mark is there. He is standing by the double doors that lead inside. Someone is with him. Even on such short notice, he has found a lawyer— a friend of a friend. Mark takes her hand and they go through the double doors together. There are several cases to wait through before her name is called and he whispers reassurances to her while they sit there.

Finally, it is her turn, but the lawyer and Mark have taken that burden from her and she has no need to speak. Instead, she watches the judge. His face is puffy from sleep as he reads down the list of charges, aggravated assault, assault and battery . . . the list is long and Daria is surprised that they haven't thrown in witchcraft. The judge has probably slept through many such arraignments, but Daria knows that he will not sleep through this one. Indeed, she sees his eyes grow wide as the details of her crime are discussed. Interfering at the scene of an accident, obstructing the paramedics . . . there is no mercy in that face for her.

Then Mark begins to talk. Lovingly, he tells of her condition, of the work that Dr. Tracey is doing, of the hope for an imminent cure. He is so eloquent that for the very first time *she* is almost willing to believe that she is merely "sick." The judge's face softens. Illness is another matter. Daria has been so resigned to her fate that she is surprised to find that she has been freed. Released on her own recognizance until her trial. No bail. Mark throws his arms around her, but she is too stunned to hug him back.

"I love you," Mark tells her as he leads her out of the courtroom. He has brought glasses to shield her eyes from the sun.

A vein in his neck is throbbing.

"I love you too," she answers automatically. She tries not to stare at the throbbing vein. *This is a compulsion caused by illness,* she tells herself, *a chemical imbalance in the blood. It can be cured.*

"Daria, we're going to fight this. First we'll get you off on those ridiculous charges, and then Dr. Tracey is going to make you well. You'll see. Everything's going to be all right." He puts his arm around her shoulders, but something inside make her stiffen and pull away.

Once again she looks at the throbbing vein and wonders what it will be like not to feel this hunger. All it will take is just the right compound stabbed into her arm with a little glass needle. A second of pain.

No, she thinks to herself in the crowded aloneness of the jailhouse steps. She finds herself a well of resolve, of acceptance that she has never tapped before. She will no longer be put off by bottles of drugs, by diets that don't work, by hours of laborious talk. She will be what she is, the thing that makes her different, the thing that makes her herself. She is not just a young woman with a rare blood disease; she is a vampire, child of darkness, and she had been fighting it for way too long.

Allowing her expression to soften to a smile, she turns to Mark and places her hand gently on his neck, feeling the pulse of the vein under her thumb. "Yes, Mark, you're right," she says softly. "You *will* have to get me off on these charges." So many little blue veins in so many necks. She will have to stay free if she is to feed.

THE
NON-HUMAN
VAMPIRE

E ven if we limit our definition of the vampire to creatures who drink
blood, there are numerous non-human vampires in the natural
world—among them mosquitoes, fleas, bedbugs, ticks, gnats, and lice.
Then there are leeches and spiders. And, finally, there are the vampire bats.

The vast majority of non-human vampires in fiction appear in children's
humorous literature, where cute animal vampires have proliferated in recent years. There is "Bunnicula," a vampire rabbit who sucks the juices
out of helpless fruits and vegetables. Created by James and Deborah Howe
in 1980, Bunnicula has appeared in numerous pictures books, young adult
novels, and even an animated television special. Bunnicula's competitors
include the Vampire Cat series by Louise Munro Foley (1996 to present).

But the creatures explored in the following pages are *not* natural, in
the usual understanding of the word. And that is what makes them especially interesting.

The vampire you will meet in Tanith Lee's "Bite-Me-Not or, Fleur de
Feu," though not human, rouses great sympathy. Roger Zelazny's "The
Stainless Steel Leech" has a strong comic dimension. All of the stories in this
section, which include "The Spider" and "Negotium Perambulans," extend
the fictional possibilities of vampires beyond those that simply mimic human
form and behavior.

HANNS HEINZ EWERS
(1871–1943)

Hanns Heinz Ewers was a German writer (born in Düsseldorf); much of his fiction remains untranslated. He is noted mainly for a series of novels featuring anthropologist Frank Braun, a character who wields his influence over supposedly "inferior" people. Ewers is the author of Der Sanberlehrling *(1907, reprinted in the United States as* The Sorcerer's Apprentice *in 1927),* Vampir *(1921), and* Alraune *(also known as* The Mandrakes, *1911). His short fiction was collected in* Das Graven *(1908) and* Nachtmahr *(1922).*

Ewers led a complex and disturbing life; he was a spy in Mexico and the United States during World War I and an early member of the Nazi Party. He wrote the official biography of Horst Wessel, a Nazi officer killed by Communists in a street fight, as well as a biography of Edgar Allan Poe. Ewers's views about the link between German and Jewish destiny, as they are expressed in Vampir, *are macabre. There, the character Braun must drink the blood of his Jewish mistress—voluntarily offered by her—if he is to be an eloquent fund-raiser for the cause of Germany in World War I.*

The plot of Ewers's "The Spider" is not uncommon: There is a haunted house, castle, room, or cave. Someone is challenged to spend an hour, or a night in the dangerous place. He or she accepts the challenge and is found either dead or raving mad after the ordeal; or survives by being brave or clever.

What makes "The Spider" a superlative story, despite its well-worn plot, is the mimetic dialogue that Clairimonda, the vampire, and Richard Bracquemont, her victim, carry on together from windows on opposite sides of the street. Bracquemont calls it a game, but it seems more nearly a kind of simultaneous dance whose meaning becomes clear only at the story's end. The gesturing is surreal, unimaginable, and at the same time so apt for an encounter between a victim who yearns to be victimized and the creature who wants to victimize him. It is a fair, if disastrous, exchange.

THE SPIDER

When the student of medicine, Richard Bracquemont, decided to move into room #7 of the small Hotel Stevens, Rue Alfred Stevens (Paris 6), three persons had already hanged themselves from the cross-bar of the window in that room on three successive Fridays.

The first was a Swiss traveling salesman. They found his corpse on Saturday evening. The doctor determined that the death must have occurred between five and six o'clock on Friday afternoon. The corpse hung on a strong hook that had been driven into the window's cross-bar to serve as a hanger for articles of clothing. The window was closed, and the dead man had used the curtain cord as a noose. Since the window was very low, he hung with his knees practically touching the floor—a sign of the great discipline the suicide must have exercised in carrying out his design. Later, it was learned that he was a married man, a father. He had been a man of a continually happy disposition; a man who had achieved a secure place in life. There was not one written word to be found that would have shed light on his suicide . . . not even a will. Furthermore, none of his acquaintances could recall hearing anything at all from him that would have permitted anyone to predict his end.

The second case was not much different. The artist, Karl Krause, a high wire cyclist in the nearby Medrano Circus, moved into room #7 two days later. When he did not show up at Friday's performance, the director sent an employee to the hotel. There, he found Krause in the unlocked room hanging from the window cross-bar in circumstances exactly like those of the previous suicide. This death was as perplexing as the first. Krause was popular. He earned a very high salary, and had appeared to enjoy life at its fullest. Once again, there was no suicide note; no sinister hints. Krause's sole survivor was his mother to whom the son had regularly sent 300 marks on the first of the month.

For Madame Dubonnet, the owner of the small, cheap guesthouse whose clientele was composed almost completely of employees in a nearby Montmartre vaudeville theater, this second curious death in the same room had very unpleasant consequences. Already several of her guests had moved out, and other regular clients had not come back. She appealed for help to her personal friend, the inspector of police of the ninth precinct, who assured her that he would do everything in his power to help her. He pushed zealously ahead not only with the investigation into the grounds for the suicides of the two guests, but he also placed an officer in the mysterious room.

This man, Charles-Maria Chaumié, actually volunteered for the task.

Chaumié was an old "Marsouin," a marine sergeant with eleven years of service, who had lain so many nights at posts in Tonkin and Annam, and had greeted so many stealthily creeping river pirates with a shot from his rifle that he seemed ideally suited to encounter the "ghost" that everyone on Rue Alfred Stevens was talking about.

From then on, each morning and each evening, Chaumié paid a brief visit to the police station to make his report, which, for the first few days, consisted only of his statement that he had not noticed anything unusual. On Wednesday evening, however, he hinted that he had found a clue. Pressed to say more, he asked to be allowed more time before making any comment, since he was not sure that what he had discovered had any relationship to the two deaths, and he was afraid he might say something that would make him look foolish.

On Thursday, his behavior seemed a bit uncertain, but his mood was noticeably more serious. Still, he had nothing to report. On Friday morning, he came in very excited and spoke, half humorously, half seriously, of the strangely attractive power that his window had. He would not elaborate this notion and said that, in any case, it had nothing to do with the suicides; and that it would be ridiculous of him to say any more. When, on that same Friday, he failed to make his regular evening report, someone went to his room and found him hanging from the cross-bar of the window.

All the circumstances, down to the minutest detail, were the same here as in the previous cases. Chaumié's legs dragged along the ground. The curtain cord had been used for a noose. The window was closed, the door to the room had not been locked and death had occurred at six o'clock. The dead man's mouth was wide open, and his tongue protruded from it.

Chaumié's death, the third in as many weeks in room #7, had the following consequences: all the guests, with the exception of a German high-school teacher in room #16, moved out. The teacher took advantage of the occasion to have his rent reduced by a third. The next day, Mary Garden, the famous Opéra Comique singer, drove up to the Hotel Stevens and paid two hundred francs for the red curtain cord, saying it would bring her luck. The story, small consolation for Madame Dubonnet, got into the papers.

If these events had occurred in summer, in July or August, Madame Dubonnet would have secured three times that price for her cord, but as it was in the middle of a troubled year, with elections, disorders in the Balkans, bank crashes in New York, the visit of the King and Queen of England, the result was that the *affaire Rue Alfred Stevens* was talked of less than it deserved to be. As for the newspaper accounts, they were brief, being essentially the police reports word for word.

These reports were all that Richard Bracquemont, the medical student, knew of the matter. There was one detail about which he knew nothing because neither the police inspector nor any of the eyewitnesses had mentioned it to the press. It was only later, after what happened to the medical student, that anyone remembered that when the police removed Sergeant Charles-Maria Chaumié's body from the window cross-bar a large black spider crawled from the dead man's open mouth. A hotel porter flicked it away, exclaiming. "Ugh, another of those damned creatures." When in later investigations which concerned themselves mostly with Bracquemont the servant was interrogated, he said that he had seen a similar spider crawling on the Swiss traveling salesman's shoulder when his body was removed from the window cross-bar. But Richard Bracquemont knew nothing of all this.

It was more than two weeks after the last suicide that Bracquemont moved into the room. It was a Sunday. Bracquemont conscientiously recorded everything that happened to him in his journal. That journal now follows.

Monday, February 28

I moved in yesterday evening. I unpacked my two wicker suitcases and straightened the room a little. Then I went to bed. I slept so soundly that it was nine o'clock the next morning before a knock at my door woke me. It was my hostess, bringing me breakfast herself. One could read her concern for me in the eggs, the bacon and the superb *café au lait* she brought me. I washed and dressed, then smoked a pipe as I watched the servant make up the room.

So, here I am. I know well that the situation may prove dangerous, but I think I may just be the one to solve the problem. If, once upon a time, Paris was worth a mass (conquest comes at a dearer rate these days), it is well worth risking my life *pour un si bel enjeu*. I have at least one chance to win, and I mean to risk it.

As it is, I'm not the only one who has had this notion. Twenty-seven people have tried for access to the room. Some went to the police, some went directly to the hotel owner. There were even three women among the candidates. There was plenty of competition. No doubt the others are poor devils like me.

And yet, it was I who was chosen. Why? Because I was the only one who hinted that I had some plan—or the semblance of a plan. Naturally, I was bluffing.

These journal entries are intended for the police. I must say that it amuses me to tell those gentlemen how neatly I fooled them. If the Inspector has any sense, he'll say, "Hm. This Bracquemont is just the man we need." In any case, it doesn't matter what he'll say. The point is I'm here now, and I take it as a good sign that I've begun my task by bamboozling the police.

I had gone first to Madame Dubonnet, and it was she who sent me to the police. They put me off for a whole week—as they put off my rivals as well. Most of them gave up in disgust, having something better to do than hang around the musty squad room. The Inspector was beginning to get irritated at my tenacity. At last, he told me I was wasting my time. That the police had no use for bungling amateurs. "Ah, if only you had a plan. Then . . ."

On the spot, I announced that I had such a plan, though naturally I had no such thing. Still, I hinted that my plan was brilliant, but dangerous, that it might lead to the same end as that which had overtaken the police officer, Chaumié. Still, I promised to describe it to him if he would give me his word that he would personally put it into effect. He made excuses, claiming he was too busy but when he asked me to give him at least a hint of my plan, I saw that I had picqued his interest.

I rattled off some nonsense made up of whole cloth. God alone knows where it all came from. I told him that six o'clock of a Friday is an occult hour. It is the last hour of the Jewish week; the hour when Christ disappeared from his tomb and descended into hell. That he would do well to remember that the three suicides had taken place at approximately that hour. That was all I could tell him just then, I said, but I pointed him to *The Revelations of St. John*.

The Inspector assumed the look of a man who understood all that I had been saying, then he asked me to come back that evening.

I returned, precisely on time, and noted a copy of the *New Testament* on the Inspector's desk. I had, in the meantime, been at the *Revelations* myself, without however having understood a syllable. Perhaps the Inspector was cleverer than I. Very politely—nay—deferentially, he let me know that, despite my extremely vague intimations, he believed he grasped my line of thought and was ready to expedite my plan in every way.

And here, I must acknowledge that he has indeed been tremendously helpful. It was he who made the arrangement with the owner that I was to have anything I needed so long as I stayed in the room. The Inspector gave me a pistol and a police whistle, and he ordered the officers on the beat to pass through the Rue Alfred Stevens as often as possible, and to watch my window for any signal. Most important of all, he had a desk telephone installed which connects directly with the police station. Since the station is only four minutes away, I see no reason to be afraid.

Wednesday, March 1
Nothing has happened. Not yesterday. Not today.

Madame Dubonnet brought a new curtain cord from another room— the rooms are mostly empty, of course. Madame Dubonnet takes every opportunity to visit me, and each time she brings something with her. I have asked her to tell me again everything that happened here, but I have learned nothing new. She has her own opinion of the suicides. Her view is that the music hall artist, Krause, killed himself because of an unhappy love affair. During the last year that Krause lived in the hotel, a young woman had made frequent visits to him. These visits had stopped, just before his death. As for the Swiss gentleman, Madame Dubonnet confessed herself baffled. On the other hand, the death of the policeman was easy to explain. He had killed himself just to annoy her.

These are sad enough explanations, to be sure, but I let her babble on to take the edge off my boredom.

Thursday, March 3
Still nothing. The Inspector calls twice a day. Each time, I tell him that all is well. Apparently, these words do not reassure him.

I have taken out my medical books and I study, so that my self-imposed confinement will have some purpose.

Friday, March 4
I ate uncommonly well at noon. The landlady brought me half a bottle of champagne. It seemed a meal for a condemned man. Madame Dubonnet looked at me as if I were already three-quarters dead. As she was leaving, she begged me tearfully to come with her, fearing no doubt that I would hang myself "just to annoy her."

I studied the curtain cord once again. Would I hang myself with it? Certainly, I felt little desire to do so. The cord is stiff and rough—not the sort of cord one makes a noose of. One would need to be truly determined before one could imitate the others.

I am seated now at my table. At my left, the telephone. At my right, the revolver. I'm not frightened; but I am curious.

Six o'clock, the same evening
Nothing has happened. I was about to add, "Unfortunately." The fatal hour has come—and has gone, like any six o'clock on any evening. I won't hide the fact that I occasionally felt a certain impulse to go to the window, but for a quite different reason than one might imagine.

The Inspector called me at least ten times between five and six o'clock. He was as impatient as I was. Madame Dubonnet, on the other hand, is happy. A week has passed without someone in #7 hanging himself. Marvelous.

Monday, March 7
I have a growing conviction that I will learn nothing; that the previous suicides are related to the circumstances surrounding the lives of the three men. I have asked the Inspector to investigate the cases further, convinced that someone will find their motivations. As for me, I hope to stay here as long as possible. I may not conquer Paris here, but I live very well and I'm fattening up nicely. I'm also studying hard, and I am making real progress. There is another reason, too, that keeps me here.

Wednesday, March 9
So! I have taken one step more. Clarimonda.

I haven't yet said anything about Clarimonda. It is she who is my "third" reason for staying here. She is also the reason I was tempted to go to the window during the "fateful" hour last Friday. But of course, not to hang myself.

Clarimonda. Why do I call her that? I have no idea what her name is, but it ought to be Clarimonda. When finally I ask her name, I'm sure it will turn out to be Clarimonda.

I noticed her almost at once . . . in the very first days. She lives across the narrow street; and her window looks right into mine. She sits there, behind her curtains.

I ought to say that she noticed me before I saw her; and that she was obviously interested in me. And no wonder. The whole neighborhood knows I am here, and why. Madame Dubonnet has seen to that.

I am not of a particularly amorous disposition. In fact, my relations with women have been rather meager. When one comes from Verdun to Paris to study medicine, and has hardly money enough for three meals a day, one has something else to think about besides love. I am then not very experienced with women, and I may have begun my adventure with her stupidly. Never mind. It's exciting just the same.

At first, the idea of establishing some relationship with her simply did not occur to me. It was only that, since I was here to make observations, and, since there was nothing in the room to observe, I thought I might as well observe my neighbor—openly, professionally. Anyhow, one can't sit all day long just reading.

Clarimonda, I have concluded, lives alone in the small flat across the way. The flat has three windows, but she sits only before the window that looks into mine. She sits there, spinning on an old-fashioned spindle, such as my grandmother inherited from a great aunt. I had no idea anyone still used such spindles. Clarimonda's spindle is a lovely object. It appears to be made of ivory; and the thread she spins is of an exceptional fineness. She works all day behind her curtains, and stops spinning only as the sun goes down. Since darkness comes abruptly here in this narrow street and in this season of fogs, Clarimonda disappears from her place at five o'clock each evening.

I have never seen a light in her flat.

What does Clarimonda look like? I'm not quite sure. Her hair is black and wavy; her face pale. Her nose is short and finely shaped with delicate nostrils that seem to quiver. Her lips, too, are pale; and when she smiles, it seems that her small teeth are as keen as those of some beast of prey. Her eyelashes are long and dark; and her huge dark eyes have an intense glow. I guess all these details more than I know them. It is hard to see clearly through the curtains.

Something else: she always wears a black dress embroidered with a lilac motif; and black gloves, no doubt to protect her hands from the effects of her work. It is a curious sight: her delicate hands moving perpetually, swiftly grasping the thread, pulling it, releasing it, taking it up again; as if one were watching the indefatigable motions of an insect.

Our relationship? For the moment, still very superficial, though it *feels* deeper. It began with a sudden exchange of glances in which each of us noted the other. I must have pleased her, because one day she studied me a while longer, then smiled tentatively. Naturally, I smiled back. In this fashion, two days went by, each of us smiling more frequently with the passage of time. Yet something kept me from greeting her directly.

Until today. This afternoon, I did it. And Clarimonda returned my greeting. It was done subtly enough, to be sure, but I saw her nod.

Thursday, March 10

Yesterday, I sat for a long time over my books, though I can't truthfully say that I studied much. I built castles in the air and dreamed of Clarimonda.

I slept fitfully.

This morning, when I approached my window, Clarimonda was already in her place. I waved, and she nodded back. She laughed and studied me for a long time.

I tried to read, but I felt much too uneasy. Instead, I sat down at my window and gazed at Clarimonda. She too had laid her work aside. Her hands were folded in her lap. I drew my curtain wider with the window cord, so that I might see better. At the same moment, Clarimonda did the same with the curtains at her window. We exchanged smiles.

We must have spent a full hour gazing at each other.

Finally, she took up her spinning.

Saturday, March 12

The days pass, I eat and drink. I sit at the desk. I light my pipe; I look down at my book but I don't read a word, though I try again and again. Then I go to the window where I wave to Clarimonda. She nods. We smile. We stare at each other for hours.

Yesterday afternoon, at six o'clock, I grew anxious. The twilight came early, bringing with it something like anguish. I sat at my desk. I waited until I was invaded by an irresistible need to go to the window—not to hang myself; but just to see Clarimonda. I sprang up and stood beside the curtain where it seemed to me I had never been able to see so clearly, though it was already dark. Clarimonda was spinning, but her eyes looked into mine. I felt myself strangely contented even as I experienced a light sensation of fear.

The telephone rang. It was the Inspector tearing me out of my trance with his idiotic questions. I was furious.

This morning, the Inspector and Madame Dubonnet visited me. She is enchanted with how things are going. I have now lived for two weeks in room #7. The Inspector, however, does not feel he is getting results. I hinted mysteriously that I was on the trail of something most unusual. The jackass took me at my word and fulfilled my dearest wish. I've been allowed to stay in the room for another week. God knows it isn't Madame Dubonnet's cooking or wine-cellar that keeps me here. How quickly one can be sated with such things. No. I want to stay because of the window Madame Dubonnet fears and hates. That beloved window that shows me Clarimonda.

I have stared out of my window, trying to discover whether she ever leaves her room, but I've never seen her set foot on the street.

As for me, I have a large, comfortable armchair and a green shade over the lamp whose glow envelops me in warmth. The Inspector has left me with a huge packet of fine tobacco—and yet I cannot work. I read two or three pages only to discover that I haven't understood a word. My eyes see the letters, but my brain refuses to make any sense of them. Absurd. As if my brain were posted: "No Trespassing." It is as if there were no room in my head for any other thought than the one: Clarimonda. I push my book away; I lean back deeply into my chair. I dream.

Sunday, March 13

This morning I watched a tiny drama while the servant was tidying my room. I was strolling in the corridor when I paused before a small window in which a large garden spider had her web. Madame Dubonnet will not have it removed because she believes spiders bring luck, and she's had enough misfortunes in her house lately. Today, I saw a much smaller spider, a male, moving across the strong threads towards the middle of the web, but when his movements alerted the female, he drew back shyly to the edge of the web from which he made a second attempt to cross it. Finally, the female in the middle appeared attentive to his wooing, and stopped moving. The male tugged at a strand gently, then more strongly till the whole web shook. The female stayed motionless. The male moved quickly forward and the female received him quietly, calmly, giving herself over completely to his embraces. For a long minute, they hung together motionless at the center of the huge web.

Then I saw the male slowly extricating himself, one leg over the other. It was as if he wanted tactfully to leave his companion alone in the dream of love, but as he started away, the female, overwhelmed by a wild life, was after him, hunting him ruthlessly. The male let himself drop from a thread, the female followed, and for a while the lovers hung there, imitating a piece of art. Then they fell to the window-sill where the male, summoning all his strength, tried again to escape. Too late. The female already had him in her powerful grip, and was carrying him back to the center of the web. There, the place that had just served as the couch for their lascivious embraces took on quite another aspect. The lover wriggled, trying to escape from the female's wild embrace, but she was too much for him. It was not long before she had wrapped him completely in her thread, and he was helpless. Then she dug her sharp pincers into his body, and sucked full draughts of her young lover's blood. Finally, she detached herself from the pitiful and unrecognizable shell of his body and threw it out of her web.

So that is what love is like among these creatures. Well for me that I am not a spider.

Monday, March 14

I don't look at my books any longer. I spend my days at the window. When it is dark, Clarimonda is no longer there, but if I close my eyes, I continue to see her.

This journal has become something other than I intended. I've spoken about Madame Dubonnet, about the Inspector; about spiders and about Clarimonda. But I've said nothing about the discoveries I undertook to make. It can't be helped.

Tuesday, March 15

We have invented a strange game, Clarimonda and I. We play it all day long. I greet her; then she greets me. Then I tap my fingers on the windowpanes. The moment she sees me doing that, she too begins tapping. I wave to her; she waves back. I move my lips as if speaking to her; she does the same. I run my hand through my sleep-disheveled hair and instantly her hand is at her forehead. It is a child's game, and we both laugh over it. Actually, she doesn't laugh. She only smiles a gently contained smile. And I smile back in the same way.

The game is not as trivial as it seems. It's not as if we were grossly imitating each other—that would weary us both. Rather, we are communicating with each other. Sometimes, telepathically, it would seem, since Clarimonda follows my movements instantaneously almost before she has had time to see them. I find myself inventing new movements, or new combinations of movements, but each time she repeats them with disconcerting speed. Sometimes, I change the order of the movements to surprise her, making whole series of gestures as rapidly as possible; or I leave out some motions and weave in others, the way children play "Simon Says." What is amazing is that Clarimonda never once makes a mistake, no matter how quickly I change gestures.

That's how I spend my days . . . but never for a moment do I feel that I'm killing time. It seems, on the contrary, that never in my life have I been better occupied.

Wednesday, March 16

Isn't it strange that it hasn't occurred to me to put my relationship with Clarimonda on a more serious basis than these endless games. Last night, I thought about this . . . I can, of course, put on my hat and coat, walk down two flights of stairs, take five steps across the street and mount two flights to her door which is marked with a small sign that says "Clarimonda." Clarimonda what? I don't know. Something. Then I can knock and . . .

Up to this point I imagine everything very clearly, but I cannot see what should happen next. I know that the door opens. But then I stand before it, looking into a dark void. Clarimonda doesn't come. Nothing comes. Nothing is there, only the black, impenetrable dark.

Sometimes, it seems to me that there can be no other Clarimonda but the one I see in the window; the one who plays gesture-games with me. I cannot imagine a Clarimonda wearing a hat, or a dress other than her black dress with the lilac motif. Nor can I imagine a Clarimonda without black gloves. The very notion that I might encounter Clarimonda somewhere in the streets or in a restaurant eating, drinking or chatting is so improbable that it makes me laugh.

Sometimes I ask myself whether I love her. It's impossible to say, since I have never loved before. However, if the feeling that I have for Clarimonda is really—love, then love is something entirely different from anything I have seen among my friends or read about in novels.

It is hard for me to be sure of my feelings and harder still to think of anything that doesn't relate to Clarimonda or, what is more important, to our game. Undeniably, it is our game that concerns me. Nothing else— and this is what I understand least of all.

There is no doubt that I am drawn to Clarimonda, but with this attraction there is mingled another feeling, fear. No. That's not it either. Say rather a vague apprehension in the presence of the unknown. And this anxiety has a strangely voluptuous quality so that I am at the same time drawn to her even as I am repelled by her. It is as if I were moving in giant circles around her, sometimes coming close, sometimes retreating . . . back and forth, back and forth.

Once, I am sure of it, it will happen, and I will join her.

Clarimonda sits at her window and spins her slender, eternally fine thread, making a strange cloth whose purpose I do not understand. I am amazed that she is able to keep from tangling her delicate thread. Hers is surely a remarkable design, containing mythical beasts and strange masks.

Thursday, March 17
I am curiously excited. I don't talk to people any more. I barely say "hello" to Madame Dubonnet or to the servant. I hardly give myself time to eat. All I can do is sit at the window and play the game with Clarimonda. It is an enthralling game. Overwhelming.

I have the feeling something will happen tomorrow.

Friday, March 18
Yes. Yes. Something will happen today. I tell myself—as loudly as I can—that that's why I am here. And yet, horribly enough, I am afraid.

And in the fear that the same thing is going to happen to me as happened to my predecessors, there is strangely mingled another fear: a terror of Clarimonda. And I cannot separate the two fears.

I am frightened. I want to scream.

Six o'clock, evening

I have my hat and coat on. Just a couple of words.

At five o'clock, I was at the end of my strength. I'm perfectly aware now that there is a relationship between my despair and the "sixth hour" that was so significant in the previous weeks. I no longer laugh at the trick I played the Inspector.

I was sitting at the window, trying with all my might to stay in my chair but the window kept drawing me. I had to resume the game with Clarimonda. And yet, the window horrified me. I saw the others hanging there: the Swiss traveling salesman, fat, with a thick neck and a grey stubbly beard; the thin artist; and the powerful police sergeant. I saw them, one after the other, hanging from the same hook, their mouths open, their tongues sticking out. And then, I saw myself among them.

Oh, this unspeakable fear. It was clear to me that it was provoked as much by Clarimonda as by the cross-bar and the horrible hook. May she pardon me . . . but it is the truth. In my terror, I keep seeing the three men hanging there, their legs dragging on the floor.

And yet, the fact is I had not felt the slightest desire to hang myself; nor was I afraid that I would want to do so. No, it was the window I feared; and Clarimonda. I was sure that something horrid was going to happen. Then I was overwhelmed by the need to go to the window to stand before it. I had to . . .

The telphone rang. I picked up the receiver and before I could hear a word, I screamed. "Come. Come at once."

It was as if my shrill cry had in that instant dissipated the shadows from my soul. I grew calm. I wiped the sweat from my forehead. I drank a glass of water. Then I considered what I should say to the Inspector when he arrived. Finally, I went to the window. I waved and smiled. And Clarimonda too waved and smiled.

Five minutes later, the Inspector was here. I told him that I was getting to the bottom of the matter, but I begged him not to question me just then. That very soon I would be in a position to make important revelations. Strangely enough, though I was lying to him, I myself had the feeling that I was telling the truth. Even now, against my will. I have that same conviction.

The Inspector could not help noticing my agitated state of mind, especially since I apologized for my anguished cry over the telephone. Naturally, I tried to explain it to him, and yet I could not find a single reason to give for it. He said affectionately that there was no need ever to apologize to him; that he was always at my disposal; that that was his duty. It was better that he should come a dozen times to no effect rather than fail to be here when he was needed. He invited me to go out with him for the evening. It would be a distraction for me. It would do me good not to be alone for a while. I accepted the invitation though I was very reluctant to leave the room.

Saturday, March 19

We went to the *Gaieté Rochechouart, La Cigale,* and *La Lune Rousse.* The Inspector was right: It was good for me to get out and breathe the fresh air. At first, I had an uncomfortable feeling, as if I were doing something wrong; as if I were a deserter who had turned his back on the flag. But that soon went away. We drank a lot, laughed and chatted. This morning, when I went to my window, Clarimonda gave me what I thought was a look of reproach, though I may only have imagined it. How could she have known that I had gone out last night? In any case, the look lasted only for an instant, then she smiled again.

We played the game all day long.

Sunday, March 20

Only one thing to record: we played the game.

Monday, March 21

We played the game all day long.

Tuesday, March 22

Yes, the game. We played it again. And nothing else. Nothing at all.

Sometimes I wonder what is happening to me? What is it I want? Where is all this leading? I know the answer: there is nothing else I want except what is happening. *It* is what I want . . . what I long for. This only.

Clarimonda and I have spoken with each other in the course of the last few days, but very briefly; scarcely a word. Sometimes we moved our lips, but more often we just looked at each other with deep understanding.

I was right about Clarimonda's reproachful look because I went out with the Inspector last Friday. I asked her to forgive me. I said it was stupid of me, and spiteful to have gone. She forgave me, and I promised never to leave the window again. We kissed, pressing our lips against each of our windowpanes.

Wednesday, March 23

I know now that I love Clarimonda. That she has entered into the very fiber of my being. It may be that the loves of other men are different. But does there exist one head, one ear, one hand that is exactly like hundreds of millions of others? There are always differences, and it must be so with love. My love is strange, I know that, but is it any the less lovely because of that? Besides, my love makes me happy.

If only I were not so frightened. Sometimes my terror slumbers and I forget it for a few moments, then it wakes and does not leave me. The fear is like a poor mouse trying to escape the grip of a powerful serpent. Just wait a bit, poor sad terror. Very soon, the serpent love will devour you.

Thursday, March 24

I have made a discovery: I don't play with Clarimonda. She plays with me.

Last night, thinking as always about our game, I wrote down five new and intricate gesture patterns with which I intended to surprise Clarimonda today. I gave each gesture a number. Then I practiced the series, so I could do the motions as quickly as possible, forwards or backwards. Or sometimes only the even numbered ones, sometimes the odd. Or the first and the last of the five patterns. It was tiring work, but it made me happy and seemed to bring Clarimonda closer to me. I practiced for hours until I got all the motions down pat, like clockwork.

This morning, I went to the window. Clarimonda and I greeted each other, then our game began. Back and forth! It was incredible how quickly she understood what was to be done; how she kept pace with me.

There was a knock at the door. It was the servant bringing me my shoes. I took them. On my way back to the window, my eye chanced to fall on the slip of paper on which I had noted my gesture patterns. It was then that I understood: in the game just finished, *I had not made use of a single one of my patterns.*

I reeled back and had to hold on to the chair to keep from falling. It was unbelievable. I read the paper again—and again. It was still true: I had gone through a long series of gestures at the window, and not one of the patterns had been mine.

I had the feeling, once more, that I was standing before Clarimonda's wide open door, through which, though I stared, I could see nothing but a dark void. I knew, too, that if I chose to turn from the door now, I might be saved; and that I still had the power to leave. And yet, I did not leave—because I felt myself at the very edge of the mystery: as if I were holding the secret in my hands. "Paris! You will conquer Paris," I thought. And in that instant, Paris was more powerful than Clarimonda.

I don't think about that any more. Now, I feel only love. Love, and a delicious terror.

Still, the moment itself endowed me with strength. I read my notes again, engraving the gestures on my mind. Then I went back to the window only to become aware that *there was not one of my patterns that I wanted to use.* Standing there, it occurred to me to rub the side of my nose; instead I found myself pressing my lips to the windowpane. I tried to drum with my fingers on the window sill; instead, I brushed my fingers through my hair. And so I understood that it was not that Clarimonda did what I did. Rather, my gestures followed her lead and with such lightning rapidity that we seemed to be moving simultaneously. I, who had been so proud because I thought I had been influencing her, I was in fact being influenced by her. Her influence . . . so gentle . . . so delightful.

I have tried another experiment. I clenched my hands and put them in my pockets firmly intending not to move them one bit. Clarimonda raised her hand and, smiling at me, made a scolding gesture with her finger. I did not budge, and yet I could feel how my right hand *wished* to leave my pocket. I shoved my fingers against the lining, but against my will, my hand left the pocket; my arm rose into the air. In my turn, I made a scolding gesture with my finger and smiled. It seemed to me that it was not I who was doing all this. It was a stranger whom I was watching. But, of course, I was mistaken. It was I making the gesture, and the person watching me was the stranger; that very same stranger who, not long ago, was so sure that he was on the edge of a great discovery. In any case, it was not I.

Of what use to me is this discovery? I am here to do Clarimonda's will. Clarimonda, whom I love with an anguished heart.

Friday, March 25
I have cut the telephone cord. I have no wish to be continually disturbed by the idiotic inspector just as the mysterious hour arrives.

God. Why did I write that? Not a word of it is true. It is as if someone else were directing my pen.

But I want to . . . want to . . . to write the truth here . . . though it is costing me great effort. But I want to . . . once more . . . do what *I* want.

I have cut the telephone cord . . . ah . . .

Because I had to . . . there it is. Had to . . .

We stood at our windows this morning and played the game, which is now different from what it was yesterday. Clarimonda makes a movement and I resist it for as long as I can. Then I give in and do what she wants without further struggle. I can hardly express what a joy it is to be so conquered; to surrender entirely to her will.

We played. All at once, she stood up and walked back into her room, where I could not see her; she was so engulfed by the dark. Then she came back with a desk telephone, like mine, in her hands. She smiled and set the telephone on the window sill, after which she took a knife and cut the cord. Then I carried my telephone to the window where I cut the cord. After that, I returned my phone to its place.

That's how it happened . . .

I sit at my desk where I have been drinking tea the servant brought me. He has come for the empty teapot, and I ask him for the time, since my watch isn't running properly. He says it is five fifteen. Five fifteen . . .

I know that if I look out of my window, Clarimonda will be there making a gesture that I will have to imitate. I will look just the same. Clarimonda is there, smiling. If only I could turn my eyes away from hers.

Now she parts the curtain. She takes the cord. It is red, just like the cord in my window. She ties a noose and hangs the cord on the hook in the window cross-bar.

She sits down and smiles.

No. Fear is no longer what I feel. Rather, it is a sort of oppressive terror which I would not want to avoid for anything in the world. Its grip is irresistible, profoundly cruel, and voluptuous in its attraction.

I could go to the window, and do what she wants me to do, but I wait. I struggle. I resist though I feel a mounting fascination that becomes more intense each minute.

Here I am once more. Rashly, I went to the window where I did what Clarimonda wanted. I took the cord, tied a noose, and hung it on the hook . . .

Now, I want to see nothing else—except to stare at this paper. Because if I look, I know what she will do . . . now . . . at the sixth hour of the last day of the week. If I see her, I will have to do what she wants. Have to . . .

I won't see her . . .

I laugh. Loudly. No. I'm not laughing. Something is laughing in me, and I know why. It is because of my "I won't . . ."

I won't, and yet I know very well that I have to . . . have to look at her. I must . . . must . . . and then . . . all that follows.

If I still wait, it is only to prolong this exquisite torture. Yes, that's it. This breathless anguish is my supreme delight. I write quickly, quickly . . . just so I can continue to sit here; so I can attenuate these seconds of pain.

Again, terror. Again. I know that I will look toward her. That I will stand up. That I will hang myself.

That doesn't frighten me. That is beautiful . . . even precious.

There is something else. *What will happen afterwards?* I don't know, but since my torment is so delicious, I feel . . . feel that something horrible must follow.

Think . . . think . . . Write something. Anything at all . . . to keep from looking toward her . . .

My name . . . Richard Bracquemont. Richard Bracquemont . . . Richard Bracquemont . . . Richard . . .

I can't . . . go on. I must . . . no . . . no . . . must look at her . . . Richard Bracquemont . . . no . . . no more . . . Richard . . . Richard Bracque— . . .

The inspector of the ninth precinct, after repeated and vain efforts to telephone Richard, arrived at the Hotel Stevens at 6:05. He found the body of the student Richard Bracquemont hanging from the cross-bar of the window in room #7, in the same position as each of his three predecessors.

The expression on the student's face, however, was different, reflecting an appalling fear. Bracquemont's eyes were wide open and bulging from their sockets. His lips were drawn into a *rictus,* and his jaws were clamped together. A huge black spider whose body was dotted with purple spots lay crushed and nearly bitten in two between his teeth.

On the table, there lay the student's journal. The inspector read it and went immediately to investigate the house across the street. What he learned was that the second floor of that building had not been lived in for many months.

E. F. BENSON
(1867–1940)

Edward Frederic Benson was born and raised in England and was educated at Cambridge. His brothers A. C. Benson and Robert Hugh Benson were also writers, but he was by far the most successful of the three. The brothers came from what we would now regard as a dysfunctional family; one reference book says that "their history reads like a TV soap opera."* *Benson published his first and most acclaimed novel, Dodo, in 1893. The novel's popularity spawned two later sequels: Dodo's Daughter (1914; republished as Dodo the Second) and Dodo Wonders (1921). His second novel, The Rubicon (1894), fared less well with the critics. Then followed years of popularity with readers leavened by serious criticism from reviewers.*

Like many people of his generation Benson was fascinated by seances, psychic phenomena, and magic, and wrote about them in his fiction, including The Luck of the Vails (1901) and The Angel of Pain (1906). His many other successful novels include Mrs. Ames (1912), Queen Lucia (1920), Miss Mapp (1922), and Lucia in London (1927). His writing expanded to other genres as well, including biographies of Queen Victoria, William Gladstone, and William II of Germany. His reminisces include As We Were (1930), As We Are (1932), and Final Edition (1940). Benson's short stories are well known, many displaying strong science fiction elements. Collections include The Room in the Tower and Other Stories (1912), The Countess of Lowndes Square (1912), Visible and Invisible (1923), Spook Stories (1928), and More Spook Stories (1934).

"Negotium Perambulans" ("the plague that walks," in Latin) recalls M. R. James's "Count Magnus." But here, the victim of the vampiric creature clearly, even dearly, deserves his end. As for the Thing itself, the subject of the story, there is hardly a monster in fiction that is quite as wet and loathsome.

---

*The Penguin Encyclopedia of Horror and the Supernatural (Viking, 1986).

NEGOTIUM PERAMBULANS

The casual tourist in West Cornwall may just possibly have noticed, as he bowled along over the bare high plateau between Penzance and the Land's End, a dilapidated signpost pointing down a steep lane and bearing on its battered finger the faded inscription "Polearn 2 miles," but probably very few have had the curiosity to traverse those two miles in order to see a place to which their guide-books award so cursory a notice. It is described there, in a couple of unattractive lines, as a small fishing village with a church of no particular interest except for certain carved and painted wooden panels (originally belonging to an earlier edifice) which form an altar-rail. But the church at St. Creed (the tourist is reminded) has a similar decoration far superior in point of preservation and interest, and thus even the ecclesiastically disposed are not lured to Polearn. So meager a bait is scarce worth swallowing, and a glance at the very steep lane which in dry weather presents a carpet of sharp-pointed stones, and after rain a muddy watercourse, will almost certainly decide him not to expose his motor or his bicycle to risks like these in so sparsely populated a district. Hardly a house has met his eye since he left Penzance, and the possible trundling of a punctured bicycle for half a dozen weary miles seems a high price to pay for the sight of a few painted panels.

Polearn, therefore, even in the high noon of the tourist season, is little liable to invasion, and for the rest of the year I do not suppose that a couple of folk a day traverse those two miles (long ones at that) of steep and stony gradient. I am not forgetting the postman in this exiguous estimate, for the days are few when, leaving his pony and cart at the top of the hill, he goes as far as the village, since but a few hundred yards down the lane there stands a large white box, like a sea-trunk, by the side of the road, with a slit for letters and a locked door. Should he have in his wallet a registered letter or be the bearer of a parcel too large for insertion in the square lips of the sea-trunk, he must needs trudge down the hill and deliver the troublesome missive, leaving it in person on the owner, and receiving some small reward of coin or refreshment for his kindness. But such occasions are rare, and his general routine is to take out of the box such letters as may have been deposited there, and insert in their place such letters as he has brought. These will be called for, perhaps that day or perhaps the next, by an emissary from the Polearn post-office. As for the fishermen of the place, who, in their export trade, constitute the chief link of movement between Polearn and the outside world, they would not dream of taking their catch up the steep lane and so, with six miles farther of travel, to the market at Penzance. The sea

route is shorter and easier, and they deliver their wares to the pier-head. Thus, though the sole industry of Polearn is sea-fishing, you will get no fish there unless you have bespoken your requirements to one of the fishermen. Back come the trawlers as empty as a haunted house, while their spoils are in the fish-train that is speeding to London.

Such isolation of a little community, continued, as it has been, for centuries, produces isolation in the individual as well, and nowhere will you find greater independence of character than among the people of Polearn. But they are linked together, so it has always seemed to me, by some mysterious comprehension: it is as if they had all been initiated into some ancient rite, inspired and framed by forces visible and invisible. The winter storms that batter the coast, the vernal spell of the spring, the hot, still summers, the season of rains and autumnal decay, have made a spell which, line by line, has been communicated to them, concerning the powers, evil and good, that rule the world, and manifest themselves in ways benignant or terrible . . .

I came to Polearn first at the age of ten, a small boy, weak and sickly, and threatened with pulmonary trouble. My father's business kept him in London, while for me abundance of fresh air and a mild climate were considered essential conditions if I was to grow to manhood. His sister had married the vicar of Polearn, Richard Bolitho, himself native to the place, and so it came about that I spent three years, as a paying guest, with my relations. Richard Bolitho owned a fine house in the place, which he inhabited in preference to the vicarage, which he let to a young artist, John Evans, on whom the spell of Polearn had fallen for from year's beginning to year's end he never let it. There was a solid roofed shelter, open on one side to the air, built for me in the garden, and here I lived and slept, passing scarcely one hour out of the twenty-four behind walls and windows. I was out on the bay with the fisher-folk, or wandering along the gorse-clad cliffs that climbed steeply to right and left of the deep combe where the village lay, or pottering about on the pier-head, or bird's-nesting in the bushes with the boys of the village. Except on Sunday and for the few daily hours of my lessons, I might do what I pleased so long as I remained in the open air. About the lessons there was nothing formidable; my uncle conducted me through flowering bypaths among the thickets of arithmetic, and made pleasant excursions into the elements of Latin grammar, and above all, he made me daily give him an account, in clear and grammatical sentences, of what had been occupying my mind or my movements. Should I select to tell him about a walk along the cliffs, my speech must be orderly, not vague, slip-shod notes of what I had observed. In this way, too, he trained my observation, for he would bid me tell him what flowers were in bloom, and what birds hovered fishing over the sea or were building in the bushes. For that I owe him a perennial gratitude, for to observe and to express my thoughts in the clear spoken word became my life's profession.

But far more formidable than my weekday tasks was the prescribed routine for Sunday. Some dark embers compounded of Calvinism and mysticism smoldered in my uncle's soul, and made it a day of terror. His sermon in the morning scorched us with a foretaste of the eternal fires reserved for unrepentant sinners, and he was hardly less terrifying at the children's service in the afternoon. Well do I remember his exposition of the doctrine of guardian angels. A child, he said, might think himself secure in such angelic care, but let him beware of committing any of those numerous offenses which would cause his guardian to turn his face from him, for as sure as there were angels to protect us, there were also evil and awful presences which were ready to pounce; and on them he dwelt with peculiar gusto. Well, too, do I remember in the morning sermon his commentary on the carved panels of the altar-rails to which I have already alluded. There was the angel of the Annunciation there, and the angel of the Resurrection, but not less was there the witch of Endor, and, on the fourth panel, a scene that concerned me most of all. This fourth panel (he came down from his pulpit to trace its time-worn features) represented the lych-gate of the church-yard at Polearn itself, and indeed the resemblance when thus pointed out was remarkable. In the entry stood the figure of a robed priest holding up a Cross, with which he faced a terrible creature like a gigantic slug, that reared itself up in front of him. That, so ran my uncle's interpretation, was some evil agency, such as he had spoken about to us children, of almost infinite malignity and power, which could alone be combated by firm faith and a pure heart. Below ran the legend "Negotium perambulans in tenebris" from the ninety-first Psalm. We should find it translated there, "the pestilence that walketh in darkness," which but feebly rendered the Latin. It was more deadly to the soul than any pestilence that can only kill the body: it was the Thing, the Creature, the Business that trafficked in the outer Darkness, a minister of God's wrath on the unrighteous . . .

I could see, as he spoke, the looks which the congregation exchanged with each other, and knew that his words were evoking a surmise, a remembrance. Nods and whispers passed between them, they understood to what he alluded, and with the inquisitiveness of boyhood I could not rest till I had wormed the story out of my friends among the fisher-boys, as, next morning, we sat basking and naked in the sun after our bathe. One knew one bit of it, one another, but it pieced together into a truly alarming legend. In bald outline it was as follows:

A church far more ancient than that in which my uncle terrified us every Sunday had once stood not three hundred yards away, on the shelf of level ground below the quarry from which its stones were hewn. The owner of the land had pulled this down, and erected for himself a house on the same site out of these materials, keeping, in a very ecstasy of wickedness, the altar, and on this he dined and played dice afterwards. But as he grew old some black melancholy seized him, and he would have lights burning there all night, for he had deadly fear of the darkness. On one winter evening there sprang up such a gale as was never before known, which broke in the windows of the room where he had supped, and extinguished the lamps. Yells of terror brought in his servants, who found him lying on the floor with the blood streaming from his throat. As they entered some huge black shadow seemed to move away from him, crawled across the floor and up the wall and out of the broken window.

"There he lay a-dying," said the last of my informants, "and him that had been a great burly man was withered to a bag o' skin, for the critter had drained all the blood from him. His last breath was a scream, and he hollered out the same words as passon read off the screen."

"*Negotium perambulans in tenebris,*" I suggested eagerly.

"Thereabouts. Latin anyhow."

"And after that?" I asked.

"Nobody would go near the place, and the old house rotted and fell in ruins till three years ago, when along comes Mr. Dooliss from Penzance, and built the half of it up again. But he don't care much about such critters, nor about Latin neither. He takes his bottle of whisky a day and gets drunk's a lord in the evening. Eh, I'm gwine home to my dinner."

Whatever the authenticity of the legend, I had certainly heard the truth about Mr. Dooliss from Penzance, who from that day became an object of keen curiosity on my part, the more so because the quarry-house adjoined my uncle's garden. The Thing that walked in the dark failed to stir my imagination, and already I was so used to sleeping alone in my shelter that the night had no terrors for me. But it would be intensely exciting to wake at some timeless hour and hear Mr. Dooliss yelling, and conjecture that the Thing had got him.

But by degrees the whole story faded from my mind, overscored by the more vivid interests of the day, and, for the last two years of my outdoor life in the vicarage garden, I seldom thought about Mr. Dooliss and the possible fate that might await him for his temerity in living in the place where that Thing of darkness had done business. Occasionally I saw him over the garden fence, a great yellow lump of a man, with slow and staggering gait, but never did I set eyes on him outside his gate, either in the village street or down on the beach. He interfered with none, and no one interfered with him. If he wanted to run the risk of being the prey of the legendary nocturnal monster, or quietly drink himself to death, it was his affair. My uncle, so I gathered, had made several attempts to see him when first he came to live at Polearn, but Mr. Dooliss appeared to have no use for parsons, but said he was not at home and never returned the call.

After three years of sun, wind, and rain, I had completely outgrown my early symptoms and had become a tough, strapping youngster of thirteen. I was sent to Eton and Cambridge, and in due course ate my dinners and became a barrister. In twenty years from that time I was earning a yearly income of five figures, and had already laid by in sound securities a sum that brought me dividends which would, for one of my simple tastes and frugal habits, supply me with all the material comforts I needed on this side of the grave. The great prizes of my profession were already within my reach, but I had no ambition beckoning me on, nor did I want a wife and children, being, I must suppose, a natural celibate. In fact there was only one ambition which through these busy years had held the lure of blue and far-off hills to me, and that was to get back to Polearn, and live once more isolated from the world with the sea and the gorse-clad hills for play-fellows, and the secrets that lurked there for exploration. The spell of it had been woven about my heart, and I can truly say that there had hardly passed a day in all those years in which the thought of it and the desire for it had been wholly absent from my mind. Though I had been in frequent communication with my uncle there during his lifetime, and, after his death, with his widow who still lived there, I had never been back to it since I embarked on my profession, for I knew that if I went there, it would be a wrench beyond my power to tear myself away again. But I had made up my mind that when once I had provided for my own independence, I would go back there not to leave it again. And yet I did leave it again, and now nothing in the world would induce me to turn down the lane from the road that leads from Penzance to the Land's End, and see the sides of the combe rise steep above the roofs of the village and hear the gulls chiding as they fish in the bay. One of the things invisible, of the dark powers, leaped into light, and I saw it with my eyes.

The house where I had spent those three years of boyhood had been left for life to my aunt, and when I made known to her my intention of coming back to Polearn, she suggested that, till I found a suitable house or found her proposal unsuitable, I should come to live with her.

"The house is too big for a lone old woman," she wrote, "and I have often thought of quitting and taking a little cottage sufficient for me and my requirements. But come and share it, my dear, and if you find me troublesome, you or I can go. You may want solitude—most people in Polearn do—and will leave me. Or else I will leave you: one of the main reasons of my stopping here all these years was a feeling that I must not let the old house starve. Houses starve, you know, if they are not lived in. They die a lingering death; the spirit in them grows weaker and weaker, and at last fades out of them. Isn't this nonsense to your London notions? . . ."

Naturally I accepted with warmth this tentative arrangement, and on an evening in June found myself at the head of the lane leading down to Polearn, and once more I descended into the steep valley between the hills. Time had stood still apparently for the combe, the dilapidated signpost (or its successor) pointed a rickety finger down the lane, and a few hundred yards farther on was the white box for the exchange of letters. Point after

remembered point met my eye, and what I saw was not shrunk, as is often the case with the revisited scenes of childhood, into a smaller scale. There stood the post-office, and there the church and close beside it the vicarage, and beyond, the tall shrubberies which separated the house for which I was bound from the road, and beyond that again the gray roofs of the quarry-house damp and shining with the moist evening wind from the sea. All was exactly as I remembered it, and, above all, that sense of seclusion and isolation. Somewhere above the tree-tops climbed the lane which joined the main road to Penzance, but all that had become immeasurably distant. The years that had passed since last I turned in at the well-known gate faded like a frosty breath, and vanished in this warm, soft air. There were law-courts somewhere in memory's dull book which, if I cared to turn the pages, would tell me that I had made a name and a great income there. But the dull book was closed now, for I was back in Polearn, and the spell was woven around me again.

And if Polearn was unchanged, so too was Aunt Hester, who met me at the door. Dainty and china-white she had always been, and the years had not aged but only refined her. As we sat and talked after dinner she spoke of all that had happened in Polearn in that score of years, and yet somehow the changes of which she spoke seemed but to confirm the immutability of it all. As the recollection of names came back to me, I asked her about the quarry-house and Mr. Dooliss, and her face gloomed a little as with the shadow of a cloud on a spring day.

"Yes, Mr. Dooliss," she said, "poor Mr. Dooliss, how well I remember him, though it must be ten years and more since he died. I never wrote to you about it, for it was all very dreadful, my dear, and I did not want to darken your memories of Polearn. Your uncle always thought that something of the sort might happen if he went on in his wicked, drunken ways, and worse than that, and though nobody knew exactly what took place, it was the sort of thing that might have been anticipated."

"But what more or less happened, Aunt Hester?" I asked.

"Well, of course I can't tell you everything, for no one knew it. But he was a very sinful man, and the scandal about him at Newlyn was shocking. And then he lived, too, in the quarry-house . . . I wonder if by any chance you remember a sermon of your uncle's when he got out of the pulpit and explained that panel in the altar-rails, the one, I mean, with the horrible creature rearing itself up outside the lych-gate?"

"Yes, I remember perfectly," said I.

"Ah. It made an impression on you, I suppose, and so it did on all who heard him, and that impression got stamped and branded on us all when the catastrophe occurred. Somehow Mr. Dooliss got to hear about your uncle's sermon, and in some drunken fit he broke into the church and smashed the panel to atoms. He seems to have thought that there was some magic in it, and that if he destroyed that he would get rid of the terrible fate that was threatening him. For I must tell you that before he committed that dreadful sacrilege he had been a haunted man: he hated and feared darkness, for he thought that the creature on the panel was on his track, but that as long as he kept lights burning it could not touch him. But the panel, to his disordered mind, was the root of his terror, and so, as I said, he broke into the church and attempted—you will see why I said 'attempted'—to destroy it. It certainly was found in splinters next morning, when your uncle went into church for matins, and knowing Mr. Dooliss's fear of the panel, he went across to the quarry-house afterwards and taxed him with its destruction. The man never denied it; he boasted of what he had done. There he sat, though it was early morning, drinking his whisky.

" 'I've settled your Thing for you,' he said, 'and your sermon too. A fig for such superstitions.'

"Your uncle left him without answering his blasphemy, meaning to go straight into Penzance and give information to the police about this outrage to the church, but on his way back from the quarry-house he went into the church again, in order to be able to give details about the damage, and there in the screen was the panel, untouched and uninjured. And yet he had himself seen it smashed, and Mr. Dooliss had confessed that the destruction of it was his work. But there it was, and whether the power of God had mended it or some other power, who knows?"

This was Polearn indeed, and it was the spirit of Polearn that made me accept all Aunt Hester was telling me as attested fact. It had happened like that. She went on in her quiet voice.

"Your uncle recognized that some power beyond police was at work, and he did not go to Penzance or give informations about the outrage, for the evidence of it had vanished."

A sudden spate of skepticism swept over me.

"There must have been some mistake," I said. "It hadn't been broken . . ."

She smiled.

"Yes, my dear, but you have been in London so long," she said. "Let me, anyhow, tell you the rest of my story. That night, for some reason, I could not sleep. It was very hot and airless; I dare say you will think that the sultry conditions accounted for my wakefulness. Once and again, as I went to the window to see if I could not admit more air, I could see from it the quarry-house, and I noticed the first time that I left my bed that it was blazing with lights. But the second time that I saw that it was all in darkness, and as I wondered at that, I heard a terrible scream, and the moment afterwards the steps of someone coming at full speed down the road outside the gate. He yelled as he ran; 'Light, light!' he called out. 'Give me light, or it will catch me!' It was very terrible to hear that, and I went to rouse my husband, who was sleeping in the dressing-room across the passage. He wasted no time, but by now the whole village was aroused by the screams, and when he got down to the pier he found that all was over. The tide was low, and on the rocks at its foot was lying the body of Mr. Dooliss. He must have cut some artery when he fell on those sharp edges of stone, for he had bled to death, they thought, and though he was a big burly man, his corpse was but skin and bones. Yet there was no pool of blood round him, such as you would have expected. Just skin and bones as if every drop of blood in his body had been sucked out of him!"

She leaned forward.

"You and I, my dear, know what happened," she said, "or at least can guess. God has His instruments of vengeance on those who bring wickedness into places that have been holy. Dark and mysterious are His ways."

Now what I should have thought of such a story if it had been told me in London I can easily imagine. There was such an obvious explanation: the man in question had been a drunkard, what wonder if the demons of delirium pursued him? But here in Polearn it was different.

"And who is in the quarry-house now?" I asked. "Years ago the fisherboys told me the story of the man who first built it and of his horrible end. And now again it has happened. Surely no one has ventured to inhabit it once more?"

I saw in her face, even before I asked that question, that somebody had done so.

"Yes, it is lived in again," said she, "for there is no end to the blindness . . . I don't know if you remember him. He was tenant of the vicarage many years ago."

"John Evans," said I.

"Yes. Such a nice fellow he was too. Your uncle was pleased to get so good a tenant. And now—"

She rose.

"Aunt Hester, you shouldn't leave your sentences unfinished," I said.

She shook her head.

"My dear, that sentence will finish itself," she said. "But what a time of night! I must go to bed, and you too, or they will think we have to keep lights burning here through the dark hours."

Before getting into bed I drew my curtains wide and opened all the windows to the warm tide of the sea air that flowed softly in. Looking out into the garden I could see in the moonlight the roof of the shelter, in which for three years I had lived, gleaming with dew. That, as much as anything, brought back the old days to which I had now returned, and they seemed of one piece with the present, as if no gap of more than twenty years sundered them. The two flowed into one like globules of mercury uniting into a softly shining globe, of mysterious lights and reflections. Then, raising my eyes a little, I saw against the black hill-side the windows of the quarry-house still alight.

Morning, as is so often the case, brought no shattering of my illusion. As I began to regain consciousness, I fancied that I was a boy again waking up in the shelter in the garden, and though, as I grew more widely awake, I smiled at the impression, that on which it was based I found to be indeed true. It was sufficient now as then to be here, to wander again on the cliffs, and hear the popping of the ripened seed-pods on the gorse-bushes; to stray along the shore to the bathing-cove, to float and drift and swim in the warm tide, and bask on the sand, and watch the gulls fishing, to lounge on the pier-head with the fisher-folk, to see in their eyes and hear in their quiet speech the evidence of secret things not so much known to them as part of their instincts and their very being. There were powers and presences about me; the white poplars that stood by the stream that babbled down the valley knew of them, and showed a glimpse of their knowledge sometimes, like the gleam of their white underleaves; the very cobbles that paved the street were soaked in it . . . All that I wanted was to lie there and grow soaked in it too; unconsciously, as a boy, I had done that, but now the process must be conscious. I must know what stir of forces, fruitful and mysterious, seethed along the hill-side at noon, and sparkled at night on the sea. They could be known, they could even be controlled by those who were masters of the spell, but never could they be spoken of, for they were dwellers in the innermost, grafted into the eternal life of the world. There were dark secrets as well as these clear, kindly powers, and to these no doubt belonged the *negotium perambulans in tenebris* which, though of deadly malignity, might be regarded not only as evil, but as the avenger of sacrilegious and impious deeds . . . All this was part of the spell of Polearn, of which the seeds had long lain dormant in me. But now they were sprouting, and who knew what strange flower would unfold on their stems?

It was not long before I came across John Evans. One morning, as I lay on the beach, there came shambling across the sand a man stout and middle-aged with the face of Silenus. He paused as he drew near and regarded me from narrow eyes.

"Why, you're the little chap that used to live in the parson's garden," he said. "Don't you recognize me?"

I saw who it was when he spoke: his voice, I think, instructed me, and recognizing it, I could see the features of the strong, alert young man in this gross caricature.

"Yes, you're John Evans," I said. "You used to be very kind to me: you used to draw pictures for me."

"So I did, and I'll draw you some more. Been bathing? That's a risky performance. You never know what lives in the sea, nor what lives on the land for that matter. Not that I heed them. I stick to work and whisky. God! I've learned to paint since I saw you, and drink too for that matter. I live in the quarry-house, you know, and it's a powerful thirsty place. Come and have a look at my things if you're passing. Staying with your aunt, are you? I could do a wonderful portrait of her. Interesting face; she knows a lot. People who live at Polearn get to know a lot, though I don't take much stock in that sort of knowledge myself."

I do not know when I have been at once so repelled and interested. Behind the mere grossness of the face there lurked something which, while it appalled, yet fascinated me. His thick lisping speech had the same quality. And his paintings, what would they be like? . . .

"I was just going home," I said. "I'll gladly come in, if you'll allow me."

He took me through the untended and overgrown garden into the house which I had never yet entered. A great gray cat was sunning itself in the window, and an old woman was laying lunch in a corner of the cool hall into which the door opened. It was built of stone, and the carved moldings let into the walls, the fragments of gargoyles and sculptured images, bore testimony to the truth of its having been built out of the demolished church. In one corner was an oblong and carved wooden table littered with a painter's apparatus and stacks of canvases leaned against the walls.

He jerked his thumb towards a head of an angel that was built into the mantelpiece and giggled.

"Quite a sanctified air," he said, "so we tone it down for the purposes of ordinary life by a different sort of art. Have a drink? No? Well, turn over some of my pictures while I put myself to rights."

He was justified in his own estimate of his skill: he could paint (and apparently he could paint anything), but never have I seen pictures so inexplicably hellish. There were exquisite studies of trees, and you knew that something lurked in the flickering shadows. There was a drawing of his cat sunning itself in the window, even as I had just now seen it, and yet it was no cat but some beast of awful malignity. There was a boy stretched naked on the sands, not human, but some evil thing which had come out of the sea. Above all there were pictures of his garden overgrown and jungle-like, and you knew that in the bushes were presences ready to spring out on you . . .

"Well, do you like my style?" he said as he came up, glass in hand. (The tumbler of spirits that he held had not been diluted.) "I try to paint the essence of what I see, not the mere husk and skin of it, but its nature, where it comes from and what gave it birth. There's much in common between a cat and a fuchsia-bush if you look at them closely enough. Everything came out of the slime of the pit, and it's all going back there. I should like to do a picture of you some day. I'd hold the mirror up to Nature, as that old lunatic said."

After the first meeting I saw him occasionally throughout the months of that wonderful summer. Often he kept to his house and to his painting for days together, and then perhaps some evening I would find him lounging on the pier, always alone, and every time we met thus the repulsion and interest grew, for every time he seemed to have gone farther along a path of secret knowledge towards some evil shrine where complete initiation awaited him . . . And then suddenly the end came.

I had met him thus one evening on the cliffs while the October sunset still burned in the sky, but over it with amazing rapidity there spread from the west a great blackness of cloud such as I have never seen for denseness. The light was sucked from the sky, the dusk fell in ever thicker layers. He suddenly became conscious of this.

"I must get back as quick as I can," he said. "It will be dark in a few minutes, and my servant is out. The lamps will not be lit."

He stepped out with extraordinary briskness for one who shambled and could scarcely lift his feet, and soon broke out into a stumbling run. In the gathering darkness I could see that his face was moist with the dew of some unspoken terror.

"You must come with me," he panted, "for so we shall get the lights burning the sooner. I cannot do without light."

I had to exert myself to the full to keep up with him, for terror winged him, and even so I fell behind, so that when I came to the garden gate, he was already half-way up the path to the house. I saw him enter, leaving the door wide, and found him fumbling with matches. But his hand so trembled that he could not transfer the light to the wick of the lamp.

"But what's the hurry about?" I asked.

Suddenly his eyes focused themselves on the open door behind me, and he jumped from his seat beside the table which had once been the altar of God, with a gasp and a scream.

"No, no!" he cried. "Keep it off! . . ."

I turned and saw what he had seen. The Thing had entered and now was swiftly sliding across the floor towards him, like some gigantic caterpillar. A stale phosphorescent light came from it, for though the dusk had grown to blackness outside, I could see it quite distinctly in the awful light of its own presence. From it too there came an odor of corruption and decay, as from slime that has long lain below water. It seemed to have no head, but on the front of it was an orifice of puckered skin which opened and shut and slavered at the edges. It was hairless, and slug-like in shape and in texture. As it advanced its fore-part reared itself from the ground, like a snake about to strike, and it fastened on him . . .

At that sight, and with the yells of his agony in my ears, the panic which had struck me relaxed into a hopeless courage, and with palsied, impotent hands I tried to lay hold of the Thing. But I could not: though something material was there, it was impossible to grasp it; my hands sunk in it as in thick mud. It was like wrestling with a nightmare.

I think that but a few seconds elapsed before all was over. The screams of the wretched man sank to moans and mutterings as the Thing fell on him: he panted once or twice and was still. For a moment longer there came gurglings and sucking noises, and then it slid out even as it had entered. I lit the lamp which he had fumbled with, and there on the floor he lay, no more than a rind of skin in loose folds over projecting bones.

ROGER ZELAZNY
(1937–1995)

Roger Zelazny, a Hugo and Nebula award-winning writer, grew up in Euclid, Ohio. He earned an undergraduate degree from Case Western Reserve University and a masters degree from Columbia University. He was employed by the Social Security Administration from 1962 to 1969 in Cleveland and Baltimore, after which he wrote full time. He published his first story, "Passion Play," in Amazing Stories magazine in 1962. He eventually took on the pseudonym Harrison Denmark.

In the 1960s, Zelazny became a leading figure of the "new wave" of science fiction writing, together with Samuel R. Delany, Thomas M. Disch, and Ursula K. Le Guin. These authors shifted emphasis from the external world of the sciences to a more internal, sociological, and psychological perspective.

Zelazny's best early work is assembled in Four for Tomorrow (1967) and The Doors of His Face, the Lamps of His Mouth, and Other Stories (1971). Novels include the award-winning Lord of Light (1967), Isle of the Dead (1969), and the immensely popular and critically acclaimed Amber series, starting with Nine Princes in Amber (1970). His later works include Deus Irae (with Phillip K. Dick; 1976), Doorways in the Sand (1976), Roadmarks (1979), The Last Defender of Camelot (1980), Uncommon Variations (1983), and Eye of Cat (1982). Zelazny's last novel, Donnerjack (1997), was co-written with Jane Lindskold, while in one of his last published works, he completed a novel started by the late Alfred Bester, entitled Psychoshop (1998).

"The Stainless Steel Leech" is an ingeniously imagined tragicomedy of a were-robot (as in were-wolf, were-tiger) whose best friend is a sadly dwindling vampire, and how the two play out their destiny together. The story's genial, even comic, tone is a delicate counterpoint to what is essentially a sad account of obsolescence.

THE STAINLESS STEEL LEECH

They're really afraid of this place.

During the day they'll clank around the headstones, if they're ordered to, but even Central can't make them search at night, despite the ultras and the infras—and they'll never enter a mausoleum.

Which makes things nice for me.

They're superstitious; it's a part of the circuitry. They were designed to serve man, and during his brief time on earth, awe and devotion, as well as dread, were automatic things. Even the last man, dead Kennington, commanded every robot in existence while he lived. His person was a thing of veneration, and all his orders were obeyed.

And a man is a man, alive or dead—which is why the graveyards are a combination of hell, heaven, and strange feedback, and will remain apart from the cities so long as the earth endures.

But even as I mock them they are looking behind the stones and peering into the gullies. They are searching for—and afraid they might find—me.

I, the unjunked, am legend. Once out of a million assemblies a defective such as I might appear and go undetected, until too late.

At will, I could cut the circuit that connected me with Central Control, and be a free 'bot, and master of my own movements. I liked to visit the cemeteries, because they were quiet and different from the maddening stamp-stamp of the presses and the clanking of the crowds; I liked to look at the green and red and yellow and blue things that grew about the graves. And I did not fear these places, for that circuit, too, was defective. So when I was discovered they removed my vite-box and threw me on the junk heap.

But the next day I was gone, and their fear was great.

I no longer posses a self-contained power unit, but the freak coils within my chest act as storage batteries. They require frequent recharging, however, and there is only one way to do that.

The werebot is the most frightful legend whispered among the gleaming steel towers, when the night wind sighs with its burden of fears out of the past, from days when non-metal beings walked the earth. The half-lifes; the preyers upon order, still cry darkness within the vite-box of every 'bot.

I, the discontent, the unjunked, live here in Rosewood Park, among the dogwood and myrtle, the headstones and broken angels, with Fritz—another legend—in our deep and peaceful mausoleum

Fritz is a vampire, which is a terrible and tragic thing. He is so undernourished that he can no longer move about, but he cannot die either, so

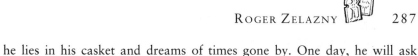

he lies in his casket and dreams of times gone by. One day, he will ask me to carry him outside into the sunlight, and I will watch him shrivel and dim into peace and nothingness and dust. I hope he does not ask me soon.

We talk. At night, when the moon is full and he feel strong enough, he tells me of his better days, in places called Austria and Hungary, where he, too, was feared and hunted.

". . . But only a stainless steel leech can get blood out of a stone—or a robot," he said last night. "It is a proud and lovely thing to be a stainless steel leech—you are possibly the only one of your kind in existence. Live up to your reputation! Hound them! Drain them! Leave your mark on a thousand steel throats!"

And he was right. He is always right. And he knows more about these things than I.

"Kennington!" his thin, bloodless lips smiled. "Oh, what a duel we fought! He was the last man on earth, and I the last vampire. For ten years I tried to drain him. I got at him twice, but he was from the Old Country and knew what precautions to take. Once he learned of my existence, he issued a wooden stake to every robot—but I had forty-two graves in those days and they never found me. They did come close, though. . . .

"But at night, ah, at night!" he chuckled. "Then things were reversed! I was the hunter and he the prey!

"I remember his frantic questing after the last few sprays of garlic and wolfsbane on earth, the crucifix assembly lines he kept in operation around the clock—irreligious soul that he was! I was genuinely sorry when he died, in peace. Not so much because I hadn't gotten to drain him properly, but because he was a worthy opponent and a suitable antagonist. What a game we played!"

His husky voiced weakened.

"He sleeps a scant three hundred paces from here, bleaching and dry. His is the great marble tomb by the gate. . . . Please gather roses tomorrow and place them upon it."

I agreed that I would, for there is a closer kinship between the two of us than between myself and any 'bot, despite the dictates of resemblance. And I must keep my word, before this day passes into evening and although there are searchers above, for such is the law of my nature.

"Damn them! (He taught me that word.) Damn them!" I say. "I'm coming up! Beware, gentle 'bots! I shall walk among you and you shall not know me. I shall join in the search, and you will think I am one of you. I shall gather the red flowers for dead Kennington, rubbing shoulders with you, and Fritz will smile at the joke."

I climb the cracked and hollow steps, the east already spilling twilight, and the sun half-lidded in the west.

I emerge.

The roses live on the wall across the road. From great twisting tubes of vine, with heads brighter than any rust, they burn like danger lights on a control panel, but moistly.

One, two, three roses for Kennington. Four, five . . .

"What are you doing, 'bot?"

"Gathering roses."

"You are supposed to be searching for the werebot. Has something damaged you?"

"No, I'm all right," I say, and I fix him where he stands, by bumping against his shoulder. The circuit completed, I drain his vite-box until I am filled.

"You are the werebot!" he intones weakly.

He falls with a crash.

. . . Six, seven, eight roses for Kennington, dead Kennington, dead as the 'bot at my feet—more dead—for he once lived a full, organic life, nearer to Fritz's or my own than to theirs.

"What happened here, 'bot?"

"He is stopped, and I am picking roses," I tell them.

There are four 'bots and an Over.

"It is time you left this place," I say. "Shortly it will be night and the werebot will walk. Leave, or he will end you."

"You stopped him!" says the Over. "You are the werebot!"

I bunch all the flowers against my chest with one arm and turn to face them. The Over, a large special-order 'bot, moves toward me. Others are approaching from all directions. He had sent out a call.

"You are a strange and terrible thing," he is saying, "and you must be junked, for the sake of the community."

He seizes me and I drop Kennington's flowers.

I cannot drain him. My coils are already loaded near their capacity, and he is specially insulated.

There are dozens around me now, fearing and hating. They will junk me and I will lie beside Kennington.

"Rust in peace," they will say. . . . I am sorry that I cannot keep my promise to Fritz.

"Release him!"

No!

It is shrouded and moldering Fritz in the doorway of the mausoleum, swaying, clutching at the stone. He always knows. . . .

"Release him! I, a human, order it."

He is ashen and gasping, and the sunlight is doing awful things to him.

—The ancient circuits click and suddenly I am free.

"Yes, master," says the Over. "We did not know. . . ."

"Seize that robot!"

He points a shaking emaciated finger at him.

"He is the werebot," he gasps. "Destroy him! The one gathering flowers was obeying my orders. Leave him here with me."

He falls to his knees and the final darts of day pierce his flesh.

"And go! All the rest of you! Quickly! It is my order that no robot ever enter another graveyard again!"

He collapses within and I know that now there are only bones and bits of rotted shroud on the doorstep of our home.

Fritz has had his final joke—a human masquerade.

I take the roses to Kennington, as the silent 'bots file out through the gate forever, bearing the unprotesting Overbot with them. I place the roses at the foot of the monument—Kennington's and Fritz's—the monument of the last, strange, truly living ones.

Now only I remain unjunked.

In the final light of the sun I see them drive a stake through the Over's vite-box and bury him at the crossroads.

Then they hurry back toward their towers of steel, of plastic.

I gather up what remains of Fritz and carry him down to his box. The bones are brittle and silent.

. . . It is a very proud and very lonely thing to be a stainless steel leech.

TANITH LEE
(b. 1947)

Tanith Lee, who has written children's books and sword-and-sorcery novels for adults, is the master of a truly distinguished and sensuous prose style. Her first fantasy novel, The Birthgrave, *was published in 1975; since then she has published more than fifty books and 130 short stories. Her novels include the Scarabae Blood Opera series, which began with* Dark Dance *(1992); her Unicorn seriess for young adults including* Black Unicorn *(1991),* Gold Unicorn *(1993), and* Red Unicorn *(1997); as well as* Lycanthia *(1981),* Anackire *(1983), and* The Gods Are Thirsty *(1996). Lee has also written dozens of short stories collected into many volumes, among them* Dreams of Dark and Light *(1986),* Forests of the Night *(1989), and* Women as Demons: The Male Perception of Women Through Space and Time *(1989).*

The originality and poetic power of "Bite-Me-Not or, Fleur de Feu" is truly astonishing. This is a simple Cinderella tale transformed into an epic romance. Rohise, the little slave in the duke's kitchen, is our Cinderella, living within a castle sealed against the intrusion of a race of vampires. The magnificent black-winged vampire prince, Feroluce, finds a way to break into the castle. There he is set upon by a chained lion that wounds him, allowing him to be captured and caged by the inhabitants of the castle. Though Rohise falls in love with him, he is doomed to be killed at dawn and to have his blood poured over the plant known as fleur de fleu or flower of fire. This plant grows in a secret garden of the castle, and its flower, if it ever blooms, repels vampires.

The rest of the story explores the slow progress toward love of these two, Rohise and Feroluce, who are different species. With such vast differences between them, it takes Lee's truly epic imagination to bring these two together in a believable way.

Lee's prose is baroque, richly metaphoric. At its best, as in this story, her imagery is perfect for the sort of medieval allegorical tapestry she is weaving. The language is grandiose indeed, but so is the conception she has of her story. That her prose should slip perceptibly into near poetry is not surprising.

One last word: the reader should not have qualms about the quasi-French verses that Lee uses from time to time. Invariably, their meaning is made clear within the text itself.

BITE-ME-NOT OR, FLEUR DE FEU

In the tradition of young girls and windows, the young girl looks out of this one. It is difficult to see anything. The panes of the window are heavily leaded, and secured by a lattice of iron. The stained glass of lizard-green and storm-purple is several inches thick. There is no red glass in the window. The color red is forbidden in the castle. Even the sun, behind the glass, is a storm sun, a green-lizard sun.

The young girl wishes she had a gown of palest pastel rose—the nearest affinity to red which is never allowed. Already she has long dark beautiful eyes, a long white neck. Her long hair is however hidden in a dusty scarf and she wears rags. She is a scullery maid. As she scours dishes and mops stone floors, she imagines she is a princess floating through the upper corridors, gliding to the dais in the Duke's hall. The Cursed Duke. She is sorry for him. If he had been her father, she would have sympathized and consoled him. His own daughter is dead, as his wife is dead, but these things, being to do with the cursing, are never spoken of. Except, sometimes, obliquely.

"Rohise!" dim voices cry now, full of dim scolding soon to be actualized.

The scullery maid turns from the window and runs to have her ears boxed and a broom thrust into her hands.

Meanwhile, the Cursed Duke is prowling his chamber, high in the East Turret carved with swans and gargoyles. The room is lined with books, swords, lutes, scrolls, and has two eerie portraits, the larger of which represents his wife, and the smaller his daughter. Both ladies look much the same with their pale, egg-shaped faces, polished eyes, clasped hands. They do not really look like his wife or daughter, nor really remind him of them.

There are no windows at all in the turret, they were long ago bricked up and covered with hangings. Candles burn steadily. It is always night in the turret. Save, of course, by night there are particular *sounds* all about it, to which the Duke is accustomed, but which he does not care for. By night, like most of his court, the Cursed Duke closes his ears with softened tallow. However, if he sleeps, he dreams, and hears in the dream the beating of wings. . . . Often, the court holds loud revel all night long.

The Duke does not know Rohise the scullery maid has been thinking of him. Perhaps he does not even know that a scullery maid is capable of thinking at all.

Soon the Duke descends from the turret and goes down, by various stairs and curving passages, into a large, walled garden on the east side of the castle.

It is a very pretty garden, mannered and manicured, which the gardeners keep in perfect order. Over the tops of the high, high walls, where delicate blooms bell the vines, it is just possible to glimpse the tips of sun-baked mountains. But by day the mountains are blue and spiritual to look at, and seem scarcely real. They might only be inked on the sky.

A portion of the Duke's court is wandering about in the garden, playing games or musical instruments, or admiring painted sculptures, or the flora, none of which is red. But the Cursed Duke's court seems vitiated this noon. Nights of revel take their toll.

As the Duke passes down the garden, his courtiers acknowledge him deferentially. He sees them, old and young alike, all doomed as he is, and the weight of his burden increases.

At the furthest, most eastern end of the garden, there is another garden, sunken and rather curious, beyond a wall with an iron door. Only the Duke possesses the key to this door. Now he unlocks it and goes through. His courtiers laugh and play and pretend not to see. He shuts the door behind him.

The sunken garden, which no gardener ever tends, is maintained by other, spontaneous, means. It is small and square, lacking the hedges and the paths of the other, the sundials and statues and little pools. All the sunken garden contains is a broad paved border, and at its center a small plot of humid earth. Growing in the earth is a slender bush with slender velvet leaves.

The Duke stands and looks at the bush only a short while.

He visits it every day. He has visited it every day for years. He is waiting for the bush to flower. Everyone is waiting for this. Even Rohise, the scullery maid, is waiting, though she does not, being only sixteen, born in the castle and uneducated, properly understand why.

The light in the little garden is dull and strange, for the whole of it is roofed over by a dome of thick smoky glass. It makes the atmosphere somewhat depressing, although the bush itself gives off a pleasant smell, rather resembling vanilla.

Something is cut into the stone rim of the earth-plot where the bush grows. The Duke reads it for perhaps the thousandth time. *O, fleur de feu*—

When the Duke returns from the little garden into the large garden, locking the door behind him, no one seems truly to notice. But their obeisances now are circumspect.

One day, he will perhaps emerge from the sunken garden leaving the door wide, crying out in a great voice. But not yet. Not today.

The ladies bend to the bright fish in the pools, the knights pluck for them blossoms, challenge each other to combat at chess, or wrestling, discuss the menagerie lions; the minstrels sing of unrequited love. The pleasure garden is full of one long and weary sigh.

"Oh flurda fur

"Pourma souffrance—"
Sings Rohise as she scrubs the flags of the pantry floor.
"Ned ormey par,
"May say day mwar—"
"What are you singing, you slut?" someone shouts, and kicks over her bucket.

Rohise does not weep. She tidies her bucket and soaks up the spilled water with her cloths. She does not know what the song, because of which she seems, apparently, to have been chastised, means. She does not understand the words that somehow, somewhere—perhaps from her own dead mother—she learned by rote.

In the hour before sunset, the Duke's hall is lit by flambeaux. In the high windows, the casements of oil-blue and lavender glass and glass like storms and lizards, are fastened tight. The huge window by the dais was long ago obliterated, shut up, and a tapestry hung of gold and silver tissue with all the rubies pulled out and emeralds substituted. It describes the subjugation of a fearsome unicorn by a maiden, and huntsmen.

The court drifts in with its clothes of rainbow from which only the color red is missing.

Music for dancing plays. The lean pale dogs pace about, alert for tidbits as dish on dish comes in. Roast birds in all their plumage glitter and die a second time under the eager knives. Pastry castles fall. Pink and amber fruits, and green fruits and black, glow beside the goblets of fine yellow wine.

The Cursed Duke eats with care and attention, not with enjoyment. Only the very young of the castle still eat in that way, and there are not so many of those.

The murky sun slides through the stained glass. The musicians strike up more wildly. The dances become boisterous. Once the day goes out, the hall will ring to *chanson*, to drum and viol and pipe. The dogs will bark, no language will be uttered except in a bellow. The lions will roar from the menagerie. On some nights the cannons are set off from the battlements, which are now all of them roofed in, fired out through narrow mouths just wide enough to accommodate them, the charge crashing away in thunder down the darkness.

By the time the moon comes up and the castle rocks to its own cacophony, exhausted Rohise has fallen fast asleep in her cupboard bed in the attic. For years, from sunset to rise, nothing has woken her. Once, as a child, when she had been especially badly beaten, the pain woke her and she heard a strange silken scratching, somewhere over her bed. But she thought it a rat, or a bird. Yes, a bird, for later it seemed to her there were also wings. . . . But she forgot all this half a decade ago. Now she sleeps deeply and dreams of being a princess, forgetting, too, how the Duke's daughter died. Such a terrible death, it is better to forget.

"The sun shall not smite thee by day, neither the moon by night," intones the priest, eyes rolling, his voice like a bell behind the Duke's shoulder.

"Ne moi mords pas," whispers Rohise in her deep sleep. "Ne mwar
mor par, ne par mor mwar. . . ."

And under its impenetrable dome, the slender bush has closed its fur
leaves also to sleep. O flower of fire, oh fleur de fur. Its blooms, though
it has not bloomed yet, bear the ancient name *Nona Mordica*. In light
parlance they call it Bite-Me-Not. There is a reason for that.

He is the Prince of a proud and savage people. The pride they acknowledge, perhaps they do not consider themselves to be savages, or at least
believe that savagery is the proper order of things.

Feroluce, that is his name. It is one of the customary names his kind
give their lords. It has connotations with diabolic royalty and, too, with
a royal flower of long petals curved like scimitars. Also the name might
be the partial anagram of another name. The bearer of that name was
also winged.

For Feroluce and his people are winged beings. They are more like a
nest of dark eagles than anything, mounted high among the rocky pilasters
and pinnacles of the mountain. Cruel and magnificent, like eagles, the
somber sentries motionless as statuary on the ledge-edges, their sable
wings folded about them.

They are very alike in appearance (less a race or tribe, more a flock,
an unkindness of ravens). Feroluce also, black-winged, black-haired, aqui-
line of feature, standing on the brink of star-dashed space, his eyes burning
through the night like all the eyes along the rocks, depthless red as claret.

They have their own traditions of art and science. They do not make
or read books, fashion garments, discuss God or metaphysics or men.
Their cries are mostly wordless and always mysterious, flung out like
ribbons over the air as they wheel and swoop and hang in wicked cruci-
form, between the peaks. But they sing, long hours, for whole nights at
a time, music that has a language only they know. All their wisdom and
theosophy, and all their grasp of beauty, truth or love, is in the singing.

They look unloving enough, and so they are. Pitiless fallen angels. A
traveling people, they roam after sustenance. Their sustenance is blood.
Finding a castle, they accepted it, every bastion and wall, as their prey.
They have preyed on it and tried to prey on it for years.

In the beginning, their calls, their songs, could lure victims to the feast.
In this way, the tribe or unkindness of Feroluce took the Duke's wife,
somnambulist, from a midnight balcony. But the Duke's daughter, the
first victim, they found seventeen years ago, benighted on the mountain
side. Her escort and herself they left to the sunrise, marble figures, the
life drunk away.

Now the castle is shut, bolted and barred. They are even more attracted
by its recalcitrance (a woman who says "No"). They do not intend to go
away until the castle falls to them.

By night, they fly like huge black moths round and round the carved turrets, the dull-lit leaded windows, their wings invoking a cloudy tindery wind, pushing thunder against thundery glass.

They sense they are attributed to some sin, reckoned a punishing curse, a penance, and this amuses them at the level whereon they understand it. They also sense something of the flower, the *Nona Mordica*. Vampires have their own legends.

But tonight Feroluce launches himself into the air, speeds down the sky on the black sails of his wings, calling, a call like laughter or derision. This morning, in the tween-time before the light began and the sun-to-be drove him away to his shadowed eyrie in the mountain-guts, he saw a chink in the armor of the beloved refusing-woman-prey. A window, high in an old neglected tower, a window with a small eyelet which was cracked.

Feroluce soon reaches the eyelet and breathes on it, as if he would melt it. (His breath is sweet. Vampires do not eat raw flesh, only blood, which is a perfect food and digests perfectly, while their teeth are sound of necessity.) The way the glass mists at breath intrigues Feroluce. But presently he taps at the cranky pane, taps, then claws. A piece breaks away, and now he sees how it should be done.

Over the rims and upthrusts of the castle, which is only really another mountain with caves to Feroluce, the rumble of the Duke's revel drones on.

Feroluce pays no heed. He does not need to reason, he merely knows, *that* noise masks *this*—as he smashes in the window. Its panes were all faulted and the lattice rusty. It is, of course, more than that. The magic of Purpose has protected the castle, and, as in all balances, there must be, or come to be, some balancing contradiction, some flaw. . . .

The people of Feroluce do not notice what he is at. In a way, the dance with their prey has debased to a ritual. They have lived almost two decades on the blood of local mountain beasts, and bird-creatures like themselves brought down on the wing. Patience is not, with them, a virtue. It is a sort of foreplay, and can go on, in pleasure, a long, long while.

Feroluce intrudes himself through the slender window. Muscularly slender himself, and agile, it is no feat. But the wings catch, are a trouble. They follow him because they must, like two separate entities. They have been cut a little on the glass, and bleed.

He stands in a stony small room, shaking bloody feathers from him, snarling, but without sound.

Then he finds the stairway and goes down.

There are dusty landings and neglected chambers. They have no smell of life. But then there comes to be a smell. It is the scent of a nest, a colony of things, wild creatures, in constant proximity. He recognizes it. The light of his crimson eyes precedes him, deciphering blackness. And then other eyes, amber, green and gold, spring out like stars all across his path.

Somewhere an old torch is burning out. To the human eye, only mounds and glows would be visible, but to Feroluce, the Prince of the vampires, all is suddenly revealed. There is a great stone area, barred with bronze and iron, and things stride and growl behind the bars, or chatter and flee, or only stare. And there, without bars, though bound by ropes of brass to rings of brass, three brazen beasts.

Feroluce, on the steps of the menagerie, looks into the gaze of the Duke's lions. Feroluce smiles, and the lions roar. One is the king, its mane like war-plumes. Feroluce recognizes the king and the king's right to challenge, for this is the lions' domain, their territory.

Feroluce comes down the stair and meets the lion as it leaps the length of its chain. To Feroluce, the chain means nothing, and since he has come close enough, very little either to the lion.

To the vampire Prince the fight is wonderful, exhilarating and meaningful, intellectual even, for it is colored by nuance, yet powerful as sex.

He holds fast with his talons, his strong limbs wrapping the beast which is almost stronger than he, just as its limbs wrap him in turn. He sinks his teeth in the lion's shoulder, and in fierce rage and bliss begins to draw out the nourishment. The lion kicks and claws at him in turn. Feroluce feels the gouges like fire along his shoulders, thighs, and hugs the lion more nearly as he throttles and drinks from it, loving it, jealous of it, killing it. Gradually the mighty feline body relaxes, still clinging to him, its cat teeth embedded in one beautiful swanlike wing, forgotten by both.

In a welter of feathers, stripped skin, spilled blood, the lion and the angel lie in embrace on the menagerie floor. The lion lifts its head, kisses the assassin, shudders, lets go.

Feroluce glides out from under the magnificent deadweight of the cat. He stands. And pain assaults him. His lover has severely wounded him.

Across the menagerie floor, the two lionesses are crouched. Beyond them, a man stands gaping in simple terror, behind the guttering torch. He had come to feed the beasts, and seen another feeding, and now is paralyzed. He is deaf, the menagerie-keeper, previously an advantage saving him the horror of nocturnal vampire noises.

Feroluce starts toward the human animal swifter than a serpent, and checks. Agony envelops Feroluce and the stone room spins. Involuntarily, confused, he spreads his wings for flight, there in the confined chamber. But only one wing will open. The other, damaged and partly broken, hangs like a snapped fan. Feroluce cries out, a beautiful singing note of despair and anger. He drops fainting at the menagerie keeper's feet.

The man does not wait for more. He runs away through the castle, screaming invective and prayer, and reaches the Duke's hall and makes the whole hall listen.

All this while, Feroluce lies in the ocean of almost-death that is sleep or swoon, while the smaller beasts in the cages discuss him, or seem to.

And when he is raised, Feroluce does not wake. Only the great drooping bloody wings quiver and are still. Those who carry him are more than ever revolted and frightened, for they have seldom seen blood. Even the food for the menagerie is cooked almost black. Two years ago, a gardener slashed his palm on a thorn. He was banished from the court for a week. But Feroluce, the center of so much attention, does not rouse. Not until the dregs of the night are stealing out through the walls. Then some nervous instinct invests him. The sun is coming and this is an open place, he struggles through unconsciousness and hurt, through the deepest most bladed waters, to awareness.

And finds himself in a huge bronze cage, the cage of some animal appropriated for the occasion. Bars, bars all about him, and not to be got rid of, for he reaches to tear them away and cannot. Beyond the bars, the Duke's hall, which is only a pointless cold glitter to him in the maze of pain and dying lights. Not an open place, in fact, but too open for his kind. Through the window-spaces of thick glass, muddy sunglare must come in. To Feroluce it will be like swords, acids, and burning fire—

Far off he hears wings beat and voices soaring. His people search for him, call and wheel and find nothing.

Feroluce cries out, a gravel shriek now, and the persons in the hall rush back from him, calling on God. But Feroluce does not see. He has tried to answer his own. Now he sinks down again under the coverlet of his broken wings, and the wine-red stars of his eyes go out.

"And the Angel of Death," the priest intones, "shall surely pass over, but yet like the shadow, not substance—"

The smashed window in the old turret above the menagerie tower has been sealed with mortar and brick. It is a terrible thing that it was for so long overlooked. A miracle that only one of the creatures found and entered by it. God, the Protector, guarded the Cursed Duke and his court. And the magic that surrounds the castle, that too held fast. For from the possibility of a disaster was born a bloom of great value: Now one of the monsters is in their possession. A prize beyond price.

Caged and helpless, the fiend is at their mercy. It is also weak from its battle with the noble lion, which gave its life for the castle's safety (and will be buried with honor in an ornamented grave at the foot of the Ducal family tomb). Just before the dawn came, the Duke's advisers advised him, and the bronze cage was wheeled away into the darkest area of the hall, close by the dais where once the huge window was but is no more. A barricade of great screens was brought, and set around the cage, and the top of it covered. No sunlight now can drip into the prison to harm the specimen. Only the Duke's ladies and gentlemen steal in around the screens and see, by the light of a candlebranch, the demon still lying in its trance of pain and bloodloss. The Duke's alchemist sits on a stool nearby, dictating many notes to a nervous apprentice. The alchemist, and the apothecary for that matter, are convinced the vampire, having drunk the lion almost dry, will recover from its wounds. Even the wings will mend.

The Duke's court painter also came. He was ashamed presently, and went away. The beauty of the demon affected him, making him wish to paint it, not as something wonderfully disgusting, but as a kind of superlative man, vital and innocent, or as Lucifer himself, stricken in the sorrow of his colossal Fall. And all that has caused the painter to pity the fallen one, mere artisan that the painter is, so he slunk away. He knows, since the alchemist and the apothecary told him, what is to be done.

Of course much of the castle knows. Though scarcely anyone has slept or sought sleep, the whole place rings with excitement and vivacity. The Duke has decreed, too, that everyone who wishes shall be a witness. So he is having a progress through the castle, seeking every nook and cranny, while, let it be said, his architect takes the opportunity to check no other windowpane has cracked.

From room to room the Duke and his entourage pass, through corridors, along stairs, through dusty attics and musty storerooms he has never seen, or if seen has forgotten. Here and there some retainer is come on. Some elderly women are discovered spinning like spiders up under the eaves, half-blind and complacent. They curtsy to the Duke from a vague recollection of old habit. The Duke tells them the good news, or rather, his messenger, walking before, announces it. The ancient women sigh and whisper, are left, probably forget. Then again, in a narrow courtyard, a simple boy, who looks after a dovecote, is magnificently told. He has a fit from alarm, grasping nothing; and the doves who love and understand him (by not trying to) fly down and cover him with their soft wings as the Duke goes away. The boy comes to under the doves as if in a heap of warm snow, comforted.

It is on one of the dark staircases above the kitchen that the gleaming entourage sweeps round a bend and comes on Rohise the scullery maid, scrubbing. In these days, when there are so few children and young servants, labor is scarce, and the scullerers are not confined to the scullery.

Rohise stands up, pale with shock, and for a wild instant thinks that, for some heinous crime she has committed in ignorance, the Duke has come in person to behead her.

"Hear then, by the Duke's will," cries the messenger. "One of Satan's night-demons, which do torment us, has been captured and lies penned in the Duke's hall. At sunrise tomorrow, this thing will be taken to that sacred spot where grows the bush of the Flower of the Fire, and here its foul blood shall be shed. Who then can doubt the bush will blossom, and save us all, by the Grace of God."

"And the Angel of Death," intones the priest, on no account to be omitted, "shall surely—"

"Wait," says the Duke. He is as white as Rohise. "Who is this?" he asks. "Is it a ghost?"

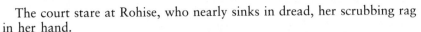

The court stare at Rohise, who nearly sinks in dread, her scrubbing rag in her hand.

Gradually, despite the rag, the rags, the rough hands, the court too begins to see.

"Why, it is a marvel."

The Duke moves forward. He looks down at Rohise and starts to cry. Rohise thinks he weeps in compassion at the awful sentence he is here to visit on her, and drops back on her knees.

"No, no," says the Duke tenderly. "Get up. Rise. You are so like my child, my daughter—"

Then Rohise, who knows few prayers, begins in panic to sing her little song as an orison:

"*Oh fleur de feu*
"*Pour ma souffrance—*"

"Ah!" says the Duke. "Where did you learn that song?"

"From my mother," says Rohise. And, all instinct now, she sings again:

"O flurda fur,
"Pourma souffrance
"Ned orney par
"May say day mwar—"

It is the song of the fire-flower bush, the *Nona Mordica*, called Bite-Me-Not. It begins, and continues: *Oh flower of fire, For my misery's sake, Do not sleep but aid me; wake!* The Duke's daughter sang it very often. In those days the shrub was not needed, being just a rarity of the castle. Invoked as an amulet, on a mountain road, the rhyme itself had besides proved useless.

The Duke takes the dirty scarf from Rohise's hair. She is very, very like his lost daughter, the same pale smooth oval face, the long white neck and long dark polished eyes, and the long dark hair. (Or is it that she is very, very like the painting?)

The Duke gives instructions and Rohise is borne away.

In a beautiful chamber, the door of which has for seventeen years been locked, Rohise is bathed and her hair is washed. Oils and scents are rubbed into her skin. She is dressed in a gown of palest most pastel rose, with a girdle sewn with pearls. Her hair is combed, and on it is set a chaplet of stars and little golden leaves. "Oh, your poor hands," say the maids, as they trim her nails. Rohise has realized she is not to be executed. She has realized the Duke has seen her and wants to love her like his dead daughter. Slowly, an uneasy stir of something, not quite happiness, moves through Rohise. Now she will wear her pink gown, now she will sympathize with and console the Duke. Her daze lifts suddenly.

The dream has come true. She dreamed of it so often it seems quite normal. The scullery was the thing which never seemed real.

She glides down through the castle and the ladies are astonished by her grace. The carriage of her head under the starry coronet is exquisite. Her voice is quiet and clear and musical, and the foreign tone of her mother, long unremembered, is quite gone from it. Only the roughened hands give her away, but smoothed by unguents, soon they will be soft and white.

"Can it be she is truly the princess returned to flesh?"

"Her life was taken so early—yes, as they believe in the Spice-Lands, by some holy dispensation, she might return."

"She would be about the age to have been conceived the very night the Duke's daughter d— That is, the very night the bane began—"

Theosophical discussion ensues. Songs are composed.

Rohise sits for a while with her adoptive father in the East Turret, and he tells her about the books and swords and lutes and scrolls, but not about the two portraits. Then they walk out together, in the lovely garden in the sunlight. They sit under a peach tree, and discuss many things, or the Duke discusses them. That Rohise is ignorant and uneducated does not matter at this point. She can always be trained. She has the basic requirements: docility, sweetness. There are many royal maidens in many places who know as little as she.

The Duke falls asleep under the peach tree. Rohise listens to the love-songs her own (her very own) courtiers bring her.

When the monster in the cage is mentioned, she nods as if she knows what they mean. She supposes it is something hideous, a scaring treat to be shown at dinner time, when the sun has gone down.

When the sun moves towards the western line of mountains just visible over the high walls, the court streams into the castle and all the doors are bolted and barred. There is an eagerness tonight in the concourse.

As the light dies out behind the colored windows that have no red in them, covers and screens are dragged away from a bronze cage. It is wheeled out into the center of the great hall.

Cannons begin almost at once to blast and bang from the roof holes. The cannoneers have had strict instructions to keep up the barrage all night without a second's pause.

Drums pound in the hall. The dogs start to bark. Rohise is not surprised by the noise, for she has often heard it from far up, in her attic, like a sea-wave breaking over and over through the lower house.

She looks at the cage cautiously, wondering what she will see. But she sees only a heap of blackness like ravens, and then a tawny dazzle, torch-light on something like human skin. "You must not go down to look," says the Duke protectively, as his court pours about the cage. Someone pokes between the bars with a gemmed cane, trying to rouse the nightmare which lies quiescent there. But Rohise must be spared this.

So the Duke calls his actors, and a slight, pretty play is put on through-out dinner, before the dais, shutting off from the sight of Rohise the rest of the hall, where the barbaric gloating and goading of the court, unchecked, increases.

The Prince Feroluce becomes aware between one second and the next. It is the sound—heard beyond all others—of the wings of his people beating at the stones of the castle. It is the wings which speak to him, more than their wild orchestral voices. Besides these sensations, the anguish of healing and the sadism of humankind are not much.

Feroluce opens his eyes. His human audience, pleased, but afraid and squeamish, backs away, and asks each other for the two thousandth time if the cage is quite secure. In the torchlight the eyes of Feroluce are more black than red. He stares about. He is, though captive, imperious. If he were a lion or a bull, they would admire this 'nobility.' But the fact is, he is too much like a man, which serves to point up his supernatural differences unbearably.

Obviously, Feroluce understands the gist of his plight. Enemies have him penned. He is a show for now, but ultimately to be killed, for with the intuition of the raptor he divines everything. He had thought the sunlight would kill him, but that is a distant matter, now. And beyond all, the voices and the voices of the wings of his kindred beat the air outside this room-caved mountain of stone.

And so, Feroluce commences to sing, or at least, this is how it seems to the rabid court and all the people gathered in the hall. It seems he sings. It is the great communing call of his kind, the art and science and religion of the winged vampires, his means of telling them, or attempting to tell them, what they must be told before he dies. So the sire of Feroluce sang, and the grandsire, and each of his ancestors. Generally they died in flight, falling angels spun down the gulches and enormous stairs of distant peaks, singing. Feroluce, immured, believes that his cry is somehow audible.

To the crowd in the Duke's hall the song is merely that, a song, but how glorious. The dark silver voice, turning to bronze or gold, whitening in the higher registers. There seem to be words, but in some other tongue. This is how the planets sing, surely, or mysterious creatures of the sea.

Everyone is bemused. They listen, astonished.

No one now remonstrates with Rohise when she rises and steals down from the dais. There is an enchantment which prevents movement and coherent thought. Of all the roomful, only she is drawn forward. So she comes close, unhindered, and between the bars of the cage, she sees the vampire for the first time.

She has no notion what he can be. She imagined it was a monster or a monstrous beast. But it is neither. Rohise, starved for so long of beauty and always dreaming of it, recognizes Feroluce inevitably as part of the

dream-come-true. She loves him instantly. Because she loves him, she is not afraid of him.

She attends while he goes on and on with his glorious song. He does not see her at all, or any of them. They are only things, like mist, or pain. They have no character or personality or worth; abstracts.

Finally, Feroluce stops singing. Beyond the stone and the thick glass of the siege, the wing-beats, too, eddy into silence.

Finding itself mesmerized, silent by night, the court comes to with a terrible joint start, shrilling and shouting, bursting, exploding into a compensation of sound. Music flares again. And the cannons in the roof, which have also fallen quiet, resume with a tremendous roar.

Feroluce shuts his eyes and seems to sleep. It is his preparation for death.

Hands grasp Rohise. "Lady—step back, come away. So close! It may harm you—"

The Duke clasps her in a father's embrace. Rohise, unused to this sort of physical expression, is unmoved. She pats him absently.

"My lord, what will be done?"

"Hush, child. Best you do not know."

Rohise persists.

The Duke persists in not saying.

But she remembers the words of the herald on the stair, and knows they mean to butcher the winged man. She attends thereafter more carefully to snatches of the bizarre talk about the hall, and learns all she needs. At earliest sunrise, as soon as the enemy retreat from the walls, their captive will be taken to the lovely garden with the peach trees. And so to the sunken garden of the magic bush, the fire-flower. And there they will hang him up in the sun through the dome of smoky glass, which will be slow murder to him, but they will cut him, too, so his blood, the stolen blood of the vampire, runs down to water the roots of the fleur de feu. And who can doubt that, from such nourishment, the bush will bloom? The blooms are salvation. Wherever they grow it is a safe place. Whoever wears them is safe from the draining bite of demons. Bite-Me-Not, they call it; vampire-repellent.

Rohise sits the rest of the night on her cushions, with folded hands, resembling the portrait of the princess, which is not like her.

Eventually the sky outside alters. Silence comes down beyond the wall, and so within the wall, and the court lifts its head, a corporate animal scenting day.

At the intimation of sunrise the black plague has lifted and gone away, and might never have been. The Duke, and almost all his castle full of men, women, children, emerge from the doors. The sky is measureless and bluely grey, with one cherry rift in the east that the court refers to as "mauve," since dawns and sunsets are never any sort of red here.

They move through the dimly lightening garden as the last stars melt. The cage is dragged in their midst.

They are too tired, too concentrated now, the Duke's people, to continue baiting their captive. They have had all the long night to do that, and to drink and opine, and now their stamina is sharpened for the final act.

Reaching the sunken garden, the Duke unlocks the iron door. There is no room for everyone within, so mostly they must stand outside, crammed in the gate, or teetering on erections of benches that have been placed around, and peering in over the walls through the glass of the dome. The places in the doorway are the best, of course; no one else will get so good a view. The servants and lower persons must stand back under the trees and only imagine what goes on. But they are used to that.

Into the sunken garden itself there are allowed to go the alchemist and the apothecary, and the priest, and certain sturdy soldiers attendant on the Duke, and the Duke. And Feroluce in the cage.

The east is all 'mauve' now. The alchemist has prepared sorcerous safeguards which are being put into operation, and the priest, never to be left out, intones prayers. The bulge-thewed soldiers open the cage and seize the monster before it can stir. But drugged smoke has already been wafted into the prison, and besides, the monster has prepared itself for hopeless death and makes no demur.

Feroluce hangs in the arms of his loathing guards, dimly aware the sun is near. But death is nearer, and already one may hear the alchemist's apprentice sharpening the knife an ultimate time.

The leaves of the *Nona Mordica* are trembling, too, at the commencement of the light, and beginning to unfurl. Although this happens every dawn, the court points to it with optimistic cries. Rohise, who has claimed a position in the doorway, watches it too, but only for an instant. Though she has sung of the flue de fur since childhood, she had never known what the song was all about. And in just this way, though she has dreamed of being the Duke's daughter most of her life, such an event was never really comprehended either, and so means very little.

As the guards haul the demon forward to the plot of humid earth where the bush is growing, Rohise darts into the sunken garden, and lightning leaps in her hands. Women scream and well they might. Rohise has stolen one of the swords from the East Turret, and now she flourishes it, and now she has swung it and a soldier falls, bleeding red, red, *red,* before them all.

Chaos enters, as in yesterday's play, shaking its tattered sleeves. The men who hold the demon rear back in horror at the dashing blade and the blasphemous gore, and the mad girl in her princess's gown. The Duke makes a pitiful bleating noise, but no one pays him any attention.

The east glows in and like the liquid on the ground.

Meanwhile, the ironically combined sense of impending day and spilled hot blood have penetrated the stunned brain of the vampire. His eyes open and he sees the girl wielding her sword in a spray of crimson as the last guard lets go. Then the girl has run to Feroluce. Though, or because, her face is insane, it communicates her purpose, as she thrusts the sword's hilt into his hands.

No one has dared approach either the demon or the girl. Now they look on in horror and in horror grasp what Feroluce has grasped.

In that moment the vampire springs, and the great swanlike wings are reborn at his back, healed and whole. As the doctors predicted, he has mended perfectly, and prodigiously fast. He takes to the air like an arrow, unhindered, as if gravity does not any more exist. As he does so, the girl grips him about the waist, and slender and light, she is drawn upward too. He does not glance at her. He veers towards the gateway, and tears through it, the sword, his talons, his wings, his very shadow beating men and bricks from his path.

And now he is in the sky above them, a black star which has not been put out. They see the wings flare and beat, and the swirling of a girl's dress and unbound hair, and then the image dives and is gone into the shade under the mountains, as the sun rises.

It is fortunate, the mountain shade in the sunrise. Lion's blood and enforced quiescence have worked wonders, but the sun could undo it all. Luckily the shadow, deep and cold as a pool, envelops the vampire, and in it there is a cave, deeper and colder. Here he alights and sinks down, sloughing the girl, whom he has almost forgotten. Certainly he fears no harm from her. She is like a pet animal, maybe, like the hunting dogs or wolves or lammergeyers that occasionally the unkindness of vampires have kept by them for a while. That she helped him is all he needs to know. She will help again. So when, stumbling in the blackness, she brings him in her cupped hands water from a cascade at the poolcave's back, he is not surprised. He drinks the water, which is the only other substance his kind imbibe. Then he smooths her hair, absently, as he would pat or stroke the pet she seems to have become. He is not grateful, as he is not suspicious. The complexities of his intellect are reserved for other things. Since he is exhausted he falls asleep, and since Rohise is exhausted she falls asleep beside him, pressed to his warmth in the freezing dark. Like those of Feroluce, as it turns out, her thoughts are simple. She is sorry for distressing the Cursed Duke. But she has no regrets, for she could no more have left Feroluce to die than she could have refused to leave the scullery for the court.

The day, which had only just begun, passes swiftly in sleep.

Feroluce wakes as the sun sets, without seeing anything of it. He unfolds himself and goes to the cave's entrance, which now looks out on a whole sky of stars above a landscape of mountains. The castle is far below, and to the eyes of Rohise as she follows him, invisible. She does not even look for it, for there is something else to be seen.

The great dark shapes of angels are wheeling against the peaks, the stars. And their song begins, up in the starlit spaces. It is a lament, their mourning, pitiless and strong, for Feroluce, who has died in the stone heart of the thing they prey upon.

The tribe of Feroluce do not laugh, but, like a bird or wild beast, they have a kind of equivalent to laughter. This Feroluce now utters, and like a flung lance he launches himself into the air.

Rohise at the cave mouth, abandoned, forgotten, unnoted even by the mass of vampires, watches the winged man as he flies towards his people. She supposes for a moment that she may be able to climb down the tortuous ways of the mountain, undetected. Where then should she go? She does not spend much time on these ideas. They do not interest or involve her. She watches Feroluce and, because she learned long ago the uselessness of weeping, she does not shed tears, though her heart begins to break.

As Feroluce glides, body held motionless, wings outspread on a downdraft, into the midst of the storm of black wings, the red stars of eyes ignite all about him. The great lament dies. The air is very still.

Feroluce waits then. He waits, for the aura of his people is not as he has always known it. It is as if he had come among emptiness. From the silence, therefore, and from nothing else, he learns it all. In the stone he lay and he sang of his death, as the Prince must, dying. And the ritual was completed, and now there is the threnody, the grief, and thereafter the choosing of a new Prince. And none of this is alterable. He is dead. Dead. It cannot and will not be changed.

There is a moment of protest, then, from Feroluce. Perhaps his brief sojourn among men has taught him some of their futility. But as the cry leaves him, all about the huge wings are raised like swords. Talons and teeth and eyes burn against the stars. To protest is to be torn in shreds. He is not of their people now. They can attack and slaughter him as they would any other intruding thing. *Go,* the talons and the teeth and the eyes say to him. *Go far off.*

He is dead. There is nothing left him but to die.

Feroluce retreats. He soars. Bewildered, he feels the power and energy of his strength and the joy of flight, and cannot understand how this is, if he is dead. Yet he *is* dead. He knows it now.

So he closes his eyelids, and his wings. Spear swift he falls. And something shrieks, interrupting the reverie of nihilism. Disturbed, he opens his wings, shudders, turns like a swimmer, finds a ledge against his side and two hands outstretched, holding him by one shoulder, and by his hair.

"No," says Rohise. (The vampire cloud, wheeling away, have not heard her; she does not think of them.) His eyes stay shut. Holding him, she kisses these eyelids, his forehead, his lips, gently, as she drives her nails into his skin to hold him. The black wings beat, tearing to be free and fall and die. "No," say Rohise. "I love you," she says. "My life is your life." These are the words of the court and of courtly love songs. No matter, she means them. And though he cannot understand her language or her sentiments, yet her passion, purely that, communicates itself, strong and burning as the passions of his kind, who generally love only one thing, which is scarlet. For a second her intensity fills the void which now contains him. But then he dashes himself away from the ledge, to fall again, to seek death again.

Like a ribbon, clinging to him still, Rohise is drawn from the rock and falls with him.

Afraid, she buries her head against his breast, in the shadow of wings and hair. She no longer asks him to reconsider. This is how it must be. *Love* she thinks again, in the instant before they strike the earth. Then that instant comes, and is gone.

Astonished, she finds herself still alive, still in the air. Touching so close feathers have been left on the rocks, Feroluce has swerved away, and upward. Now, conversely, they are whirling towards the very stars. The world seems miles below. Perhaps they will fly into space itself. Perhaps he means to break their bones instead on the cold face of the moon.

He does not attempt to dislodge her, he does not attempt any more to fall and die. But as he flies, he suddenly cries out, terrible lost lunatic cries.

They do not hit the moon. They do not pass through the stars like static rain.

But when the air grows thin and pure there is a peak like a dagger standing in their path. Here, he alights. As Rohise lets go of him, he turns away. He stations himself, sentry-fashion, in the manner of his tribe, at the edge of the pinnacle. But watching for nothing. He has not been able to choose death. His strength and the strong will of another, these have hampered him. His brain has become formless darkness. His eyes glare, seeing nothing.

Rohise, gasping a little in the thin atmosphere, sits at his back, watching for him, in case any harm may come near him.

At last, harm does come. There is a lightening in the east. The frozen, choppy sea of the mountains below and all about, grows visible. It is a marvelous sight, but holds no marvel for Rohise. She averts her eyes from the exquisitely penciled shapes, looking thin and translucent as paper, the rivers of mist between, the glimmer of nacreous ice. She searches for a blind hole to hide in.

There is a pale yellow wound in the sky when she returns. She grasps Feroluce by the wrist and tugs at him. "Come," she says. He looks at her vaguely, as if seeing her from the shore of another country. "The sun," she says. "Quickly."

The edge of the light runs along his body like a razor. He moves by instinct now, following her down the slippery dagger of the peak, and so

eventually into a shallow cave. It is so small it holds him like a coffin. Rohise closes the entrance with her own body. It is the best she can do. She sits facing the sun as it rises, as if prepared to fight. She hates the sun for his sake. Even as the light warms her chilled body, she curses it. Till light and cold and breathlessness fade together.

When she wakes, she looks up into twilight and endless stars, two of which are red. She is lying on the rock by the cave. Feroluce leans over her, and behind Feroluce his quiescent wings fill the sky.

She has never properly understood his nature: Vampire. Yet her own nature, which tells her so much, tells her some vital part of herself is needful to him, and that he is danger, and death. But she loves him, and is not afraid. She would have fallen to die with him. To help him by her death does not seem wrong to her. Thus, she lies still, and smiles at him to reassure him she will not struggle. From lassitude, not fear, she closes her eyes. Presently she feels the soft weight of hair brush by her cheek, and then his cool mouth rests against her throat. But nothing more happens. For some while, they continue in this fashion, she yielding, he kneeling over her, his lips on her skin. Then he moves a little away. He sits, regarding her. She, knowing the unknown act has not been completed, sits up in turn. She beckons to him mutely, telling him with her gestures and her expression *I consent. Whatever is necessary.* But he does not stir. His eyes blaze, but even of these she has no fear. In the end he looks away from her, out across the spaces of the darkness.

He himself does not understand. It is permissible to drink from the body of a pet, the wolf, the eagle. Even to kill the pet, if need demands. Can it be, outlawed from his people, he has lost their composite soul? Therefore, is he soulless now? It does not seem to him he is. Weakened and famished though he is, the vampire is aware of a wild tingling of life. When he stares at the creature which is his food, he finds he sees her differently. He has borne her through the sky, he has avoided death, by some intuitive process, for her sake, and she has led him to safety, guarded him from the blade of the sun. In the beginning it was she who rescued him from the human things which had taken him. She cannot be human, then. Not pet, and not prey. For no, he could not drain her of blood, as he would not seize upon his own kind, even in combat, to drink and feed. He starts to see her as beautiful, not in the way a man beholds a woman, certainly, but as his kind revere the sheen of water in dusk, or flight, or song. There are no words for this. But the life goes on tingling through him. Though he is dead, life.

In the end, the moon does rise, and across the open face of it something wheels by. Feroluce is less swift than was his wont, yet he starts in pursuit, and catches and brings down, killing on the wing, a great night bird. Turning in the air, Feroluce absorbs its liquors. The heat of life now, as well as its assertion, courses through him. He returns to the rock perch, the glorious flaccid bird dangling from his hand. Carefully, he tears the glory of the bird in pieces, plucks the feathers, splits the bones. He wakes the companion (asleep again from weakness) who is not pet or prey, and feeds her morsels of flesh. At first she is unwilling. But her hunger is so enormous and her nature so untamed that quite soon she accepts the slivers of raw fowl.

Strengthened by blood, Feroluce lifts Rohise and bears her gliding down the moon-slit quill-backed land of the mountains, until there is a rocky cistern full of cold, old rains. Here they drink together. Pale white primroses grow in the fissures where the black moss drips. Rohise makes a garland and throws it about the head of her beloved when he does not expect it. Bewildered but disdainful, he touches at the wreath of primroses to see if it is likely to threaten or hamper him. When it does not, he leaves it in place.

Long before dawn this time, they have found a crevice. Because it is so cold, he folds his wings about her. She speaks of her love to him, but he does not hear, only the murmur of her voice, which is musical and does not displease him. And later, she sings him sleepily the little song of the fleur de fur.

There comes a time then, brief, undated, chartless time, when they are together, these two creatures. Not together in any accepted sense, of course, but together in the strange feeling or emotion, instinct or ritual, that can burst to life in an instant or flow to life gradually across half a century, and which men call *Love*.

They are not alike. No, not at all. Their differences are legion and should be unpalatable. He is a supernatural thing and she a human thing, he was a lord and she a scullery sloven. He can fly, she cannot fly. And he is male, she female. What other items are required to make them enemies? Yet they are bound, not merely by love, they are bound by all they are, the very stumbling blocks. Bound, too, because they are doomed. Because the stumbling blocks have doomed them; everything has. Each has been exiled out of their own kind. Together, they cannot even communicate with each other, save by looks, touches, sometimes by sounds, and by songs neither understands, but which each comes to value since the other appears to value them, and since they give expression to that other. Nevertheless, the binding of the doom, the greatest binding, grows, as it holds them fast to each other, mightier and stronger.

Although they do not know it, or not fully, it is the awareness of doom that keeps them there, among the platforms and steps up and down, and the inner cups, of the mountains.

Here it is possible to pursue the airborne hunt, and Feroluce may now and then bring down a bird to sustain them both. But birds are scarce. The richer lower slopes, pastured with goats, wild sheep and men—they lie far off and far down from this place as a deep of the sea. And Feroluce

does not conduct her there, nor does Rohise ask that he should, or try to
lead the way, or even dream of such a plan.

But yes, birds are scarce, and the pastures far away, and winter is
coming. There are only two seasons in these mountains. High summer,
which dies, and the high cold which already treads over the tips of the
air and the rock, numbing the sky, making all brittle, as though the whole
landscape might snap in pieces, shatter.

How beautiful it is to wake with the dusk, when the silver webs of
night begin to form, frost and ice, on everything. Even the ragged dress—
once that of a princess—is tinseled and shining with this magic substance,
even the mighty wings—once those of a prince—each feather is drawn
glittering with thin rime. And oh, the sky, thick as a daisy-field with the
white stars. Up there, when they have fed and have strength, they fly, or,
Feroluce flies and Rohise flies in his arms, carried by his wings. Up there
in the biting chill like a pane of ghostly vitreous, they have become lovers,
true blind lovers, embraced and linked, their bodies a bow, coupling on
the wing. By the hour that this first happened the girl had forgotten all
she had been, and he had forgotten too that she was anything but the
essential mate. Sometimes, borne in this way, by wings and by fire, she
cries out as she hangs in the ether. These sounds, transmitted through the
flawless silence and amplification of the peaks, scatter over tiny half-buried
villages countless miles away, where they are heard in fright and taken
for the shrieks of malign invisible devils, tiny as bats, and armed with the
barbed stings of scorpions. There are always misunderstandings.

After a while, the icy prologues and the stunning starry fields of winter
nights give way to the main argument of winter.

The liquid of the pool, where the flowers made garlands, has clouded
and closed to stone. Even the volatile waterfalls are stilled, broken cascades of glass. The wind tears through the skin and hair to gnaw the
bones. To weep with cold earns no compassion of the cold.

There is no means to make fire. Besides, the one who was Rohise is an
animal now, or a bird, and beasts and birds do not make fire, save for
the phoenix in the Duke's bestiary. Also, the sun is fire, and the sun is a
foe. Eschew fire.

There begin the calendar months of hibernation. The demon lovers too
must prepare for just such a measureless winter sleep, that gives no hunger, asks no action. There is a deep cave they have lined with feathers
and withered grass. But there are no more flying things to feed them.
Long, long ago, the last warm frugal feast, long, long ago the last flight,
joining, ecstasy and song. So, they turn to their cave, to stasis, to sleep.
Which each understands, wordlessly, thoughtlessly, is death.

What else? He might drain her of blood, he could persist some while
on that, might even escape the mountains, the doom. Or she herself might
leave him, attempt to make her way to the places below, and perhaps she
could reach them, even now. Others, lost here, have done so. But neither

considers these alternatives. The moment for all that is past. Even the death-lament does not need to be voiced again.

Installed, they curl together in their bloodless, icy nest, murmuring a little to each other, but finally still.

Outside, the snow begins to come down. It falls like a curtain. Then the winds take it. Then the night is full of the lashing of whips, and when the sun rises it is white as the snow itself, its flames very distant, giving nothing. The cave mouth is blocked up with snow. In the winter, it seems possible that never again will there be a summer in the world.

Behind the modest door of snow, hidden and secret, sleep is quiet as stars, dense as hardening resin. Feroluce and Rohise turn pure and pale in the amber, in the frigid nest, and the great wings lie like a curious articulated machinery that will not move. And the withered grass and the flowers are crystallized, until the snows shall melt.

At length, the sun deigns to come closer to the earth, and the miracle occurs. The snow shifts, crumbles, crashes off the mountains in rage. The waters hurry after the snow, the air is wrung and racked by splittings and splinterings, by rushes and booms. It is half a year, or it might be a hundred years, later.

Open now, the entry to the cave. Nothing emerges. Then, a flutter, a whisper. Something does emerge. One black feather, and caught in it, the petal of a flower, crumbling like dark charcoal and white, drifting away into the voids below. Gone. Vanished. It might never have been.

But there comes another time (half a year, a hundred years), when an adventurous traveler comes down from the mountains to the pocketed villages the other side of them. He is a swarthy cheerful fellow, you would not take him for herbalist or mystic, but he has in a pot a plant he found high up in the staring crags, which might after all contain anything or nothing. And he shows the plant, which is an unusual one, having slender, dark and velvety leaves, and giving off a pleasant smell like vanilla. "See, the *Nona Mordica*," he says. "The Bite-Me-Not. The flower that repels vampires."

Then the villagers tell him an odd story, about a castle in another country, besieged by a huge flock, a menace of winged vampires, and how the Duke waited in vain for the magic bush that was in his garden, the Bite-Me-Not, to flower and save them all. But it seems there was a curse on this Duke, who on the very night his daughter was lost, had raped a serving woman, as he had raped others before. But this woman conceived. And bearing the fruit, or flower, of this rape, damaged her, so she lived only a year or two after it. The child grew up unknowing, and in the end betrayed her own father by running away to the vampires, leaving the Duke demoralized. And soon after he went mad, and himself stole out one night, and let the winged fiends into his castle, so all there perished.

"Now if only the bush had flowered in time, as your bush flowers, all would have been well," the villagers cry.

The traveler smiles. He in turn does not tell them of the heap of peculiar bones, like parts of eagles mingled with those of a woman and a man. Out of the bones, from the heart of them, the bush was rising, but the traveler untangled the roots of it with care; it looks sound enough now in its sturdy pot, all of it twining together. It seems as if two separate plants are growing from a single stem, one with blooms almost black, and one pink-flowered, like a young sunset.

"Flur de fur," says the traveler, beaming at the marvel, and his luck.

Fleur de feu. Oh flower of fire. That fire is not hate or fear, which makes flowers come, not terror or anger or lust, it is love that is the fire of the Bite-Me-Not, love which cannot abandon, love which cannot harm. Love which never dies.

•••••••V•••••••
THE COMIC
VAMPIRE

Despite the link between horror and humor (they both depend upon distortion and excess), comparatively little vampire comedy has been written. While satirists and stand-up comedians are perfectly comfortable poking fun at every aspect of human existence, blood may be a problem. Blood, as has been pointed out, is a substance singularly laden with meaning—most of it of a very serious sort. And there are only a certain number of clever remarks that can be made about it.

The film industry, though, has had quite a bit of fun with vampires. Abbott and Costello have met Dracula to good effect in *Abbott and Costello Meet Frankenstein* (1948). John Carradine in *Billy the Kid versus Dracula* (1966) enhances the film's campiness so that it becomes sheer comedy. Then there is *Love at First Bite* (1979), in which Susan St. James and George Hamilton play with the big 1970s questions of commitment and recreational sex. And in *The Fearless Vampire Killer* (1967), a chaste chambermaid finds her crucifix powerless against the Jewish vampire that has come to ravish her.

In print, humorous vampires mostly lend themselves to short pieces with funny punch lines and trick endings, as in the stories collected here. Nonetheless, some brave authors have attempted to explore the lighter side of undeath at novel length. *Tabitha fffoulkes* by John Linssen (1978) is a genuine romantic comedy about the rocky relationship between a modern young woman and her vampiric suitor. *The Goldcamp Vampire, or The Sanguinary Sourdough* by Elizabeth Ann Scarborough (1987), is a light-hearted romp set in Jack London's Yukon. *Suckers,* by Anne Billson (1993), is something considerably nastier, a biting black comedy set in Thatcherite London. *Suckers* contains one of the most audacious and perversely amusing end-of-chapter cliffhangers ever conceived: when the heroine goes undercover at a vampires-only pub, her menstrual period suddenly begins.

The definitive vampire comedy has probably yet to be written, but the stories selected here, including the Dracula story by filmmaker Woody Allen, do reveal untapped veins of humor in the conventions of traditional vampire fiction.

FREDERIC BROWN
(1906–1972)

Born in Cincinnati, Ohio, Frederic Brown attended the University of Cincinnati and Hanover College in Indiana. He was a detective story and science fiction writer, and a working journalist for the Milwaukee Journal for many years.

Brown is perhaps most famous for his detective novels, especially The Fabulous Clipjoint (1947), but his science fiction stories are well loved for their humor and elegance. His most well-known science fiction novel, What Mad Universe (1949), is a complex alternate-worlds story. Brown was also attracted to humor writing, making many of his shorter works essentially extended jokes. His collection entitled Nightmares and Geezenstacks (1961) merged with another, Honeymoon in Hell (1958), into an omnibus edition, entitled And the Gods Laughed (1987). Brown's other science fiction works include The Lights in the Sky are Stars (1953) and Martians Go Home (1955).

Many of his previously uncollected stories have recently been published, including "Homicide Sanitarium" (1984), "Before She Kills" (1984), "The Freak Show Murders" (1985), "Thirty Corpses Every Thursday" (1986), "Who Was that Blonde I Saw You Kill Last Night?" (1988), "The Water-Walker" (1990), and "The Pickled Punks" (1991).

The story that follows is typical of Brown's specialty, which is the tiny, explosive joke. So as not to risk spoiling the joke, no annotation or commentary is offered here. Still, readers may want to keep in mind what it is that you can't get from a turnip.

BLOOD

In their time machine, Vron and Dreena, last two survivors of the race of vampires, fled into the future to escape annihilation. They held hands and consoled one another in their terror and their hunger.

In the twenty-second century mankind had found them out, had discovered that the legend of vampires living secretly among humans was not a legend at all, but fact. There had been a pogrom that had found and killed every vampire but these two, who had already been working on a time machine and who had finished in time to escape in it. Into the future, far enough into the future that the very word *vampire* would be forgotten so they could again live unsuspected—and from their loins regenerate their race.

"I'm hungry, Vron. Awfully hungry."

"I too, Dreena dear. We'll stop again soon."

They had stopped four times already and had narrowly escaped dying each time. They had *not* been forgotten. The last stop, half a million years back, had shown them a world gone to the dogs—quite literally: human beings were extinct and dogs had become civilized and man-like. Still they had been recognized for what they were. They'd managed to feed once, on the blood of a tender young bitch, but then they'd been hounded back to their time machine and into flight again.

"Thanks for stopping," Dreena said. She sighed.

"Don't thank me," said Vron grimly. "This is the end of the line. We're out of fuel and we'll find none here—by now all radioactives will have turned to lead. We live here . . . or else."

They went out to scout. "Look," said Dreena excitedly, pointing to something walking toward them. "A new creature! The dogs are gone and something else has taken over. And surely we're forgotten."

The approaching creature was telepathic. "I have heard your thoughts," said a voice inside their brains. "You wonder whether we know 'vampires,' whatever they are. We do not."

Dreena clutched Vron's arm in ecstasy. "Freedom!" she murmured hungrily. "And *food!*"

"You also wonder," said the voice, "about my origin and evolution. All life today is vegetable. I—" He bowed low to them. "I, a member of the dominant race, was once what you called a turnip."

CHARLES BEAUMONT
(1929–1967)

Chicago-born Charles Nutt was self-educated after his second year of high school. He wrote under several pseudonyms, including Charles Beaumont, Keith Grantland, C. B. Lovehill, and S. M. Tenneshaw. It was as Beaumont, under which he wrote "Blood Brother" and most of his science fiction, that he was best known.

Nutt began publishing his brand of horror mixed with science fiction with "The Devil, You Say?" for Amazing Stories *in 1951. He published many short story collections, including* The Hunger *(1957),* Yonder *(1958),* Night Ride and Other Journeys *(1960),* The Magic Man *(1965), and* The Edge *(1966). His work combines humor with horror in a very effective style that downplays the grimness of the subject matter. He also worked as a writer for genre movies, among them* Queen of Outer Space *(1958),* The Premature Burial *(1962),* The Wonderful World of the Brothers Grimm *(1962),* The Haunted Palace *(1963),* The Seven Faces of Dr. Lao *(1964), and* The Masque of the Red Death *(1964). Several of these films were directed by the famous director Roger Corman, well known for his horror and science fiction genre movies. Nutt also wrote numerous scripts for television, including some work for* The Twilight Zone.

"Blood Brother," like satire generally, succeeds because it takes its target seriously. Nutt examines vampire lore with a pragmatic eye, showing us that a twentieth-century urban vampire has almost unsolvable problems. The joke, as the story's ending reveals, is that there are people out there who can solve these problems rather simply.

BLOOD BROTHER

"Now then," said the psychiatrist, looking up from his note pad, "when did you first discover that you were dead?"

"Not dead," said the pale man in the dark suit. "Undead."

"I'm sorry."

"Just try to keep it straight. If I were dead, I'd be in great shape. That's the trouble, though. I can't die."

"Why not?"

"Because I'm not alive."

"I see." The psychiatrist made a rapid notation. "Now, Mr. Smith, I'd like you to start at the beginning, and tell me the whole story."

The pale man shook his head. "At twenty-five dollars an hour," he said, "are you kidding? I can barely afford to have my cape cleaned once a month."

"I've been meaning to ask you about that. Why do you wear it?"

"You ever hear of a vampire without a cape? It's part of the whole schmear, that's all. *I* don't know why!"

"Calm yourself."

"Calm yourself! I wish I could. I tell you, Doctor, I'm going right straight out of my skull. Look at this!" The man who called himself Smith put out his hands. They were a tremblous blur of white. "And look at this!" He pulled down the flaps beneath his eyes, revealing an intricate red lacework of veins. "Believe me," he said, flinging himself upon the couch, "another few days of this and I'll be ready for the funny farm!"

The psychiatrist picked a mahogany letter opener off his desk and tapped his palm. "I would appreciate it," he said, "if you would make an effort to avoid those particular terms."

"All right," said the pale man. "But you try living on blood for a year, and see how polite you are. I mean—"

"The beginning, Mr. Smith."

"Well, I met this girl, Dorcas, and she bit me."

"Yes?"

"That's all. It doesn't take much, you know."

The psychiatrist removed his glasses and rubbed his eyes. "As I understand it," he said, "you think you're a vampire."

"No," said Smith. "I *think* I'm a human being, but I *am* a vampire. That's the hell of it. I can't seem to adjust."

"How do you mean?"

"Well, the hours for instance. I used to have very regular habits. Work from nine to five, home, a little TV, maybe, into bed by ten, up at six-thirty. Now—" He shook his head violently from side to side. "You know how it is with vampires."

"Let's pretend I don't," said the psychiatrist, soothingly. "Tell me. How is it?"

"Like I say, the hours. Everything's upside-down. That's why I made this appointment with you so late. See, you're supposed to sleep during the *day* and work at *night*."

"Why?"

"Boy, you've got me. I asked Dorcas, that's the girl bit me, and she said she'd try and find out, but nobody seems to be real sure about it."

"Dorcas," said the psychiatrist, pursing his lips. "That's an unusual name."

"Dorcas Schultz is an unusual girl, I'll tell you. A real nut. She's on that late-late TV show, you know? The one that runs all those crummy old horror movies?" Smith scraped a stain from his cloak with his fingernail. "Maybe you know her. She recommended you."

"It's possible. But let's get back to you. You were speaking of the hours."

Smith wrung his hands. "They're murdering me," he said. "Eight fly-by-night jobs I've had—eight!—and lost every one!"

"Would you care to explain that?"

"Nothing to explain. I just can't stay awake, that's all. I mean, every night—I mean every *day*—I toss and turn for hours and then when I finally *do* doze off, boom, it's nightfall and I've got to get out of the coffin."

"The coffin?"

"Yeah. That's another sweet wrinkle. The minute you go bat, you're supposed to give up beds and take a casket. Which is not only sick, but expensive as *hell*." Smith shook his head angrily. "First you got to buy the damn thing. Do you know the cost of the average casket?"

"Well—" began the psychiatrist.

"Astronomical! Completely out of proportion. I'm telling you, it's a racket! For anything even halfway decent you're going to drop five bills, easy. But that's just the initial outlay. Then there's the cartage and the cleaning bills."

"I don't—"

"Seventy-five to a hundred every month, month in, month out."

"I'm afraid I—"

"The grave dirt, man. Sacking out in a coffin isn't bad enough, no, you've got to line it with *soil from the family plot*. I ask you, who's got a family plot these days? Have you?"

"No, but—"

"Right. So what do you do? You go out and buy one. Then you bring home a couple pounds of dirt and spread it around in the coffin. Wake up at night and you're *covered* with it." Smith clicked his tongue exasperatedly. "If you could just wear pajamas—but no, the rules say the full bit. Ever *hear* of anything so crazy? You can't even take off your *shoes*, for cry eye!" He began to pace. "Then there's the bloodstains."

The psychiatrist lowered his pad, replaced his glasses, and regarded his patient with a not incurious eye.

"I must go through twenty white shirts a month," continued Smith. "Even at two-fifty a shirt, that's a lot of dough. You're probably thinking, Why isn't he more careful? Well, listen, I try to be. But it isn't like eating a bowl of tomato soup, you know." A shudder, or something like a shudder, passed over the pale man. "That's another thing. The diet. I mean, I always used to like my steaks rare, but this is ridiculous! Blood for breakfast, blood for lunch, blood for dinner. Uch—just the thought of it makes me queasy to the stomach!" Smith flung himself back onto the couch and closed his eyes. "It's the monotony that gets you," he said, "although there's plenty else to complain about. You know what I mean?"

"Well," said the psychiatrist, clearing his throat, "I—"

"Filthy stuff! And the routines I have to go through to get it! What if you had to rob somebody every time you wanted a hamburger—I mean, just supposing. That's the way it is with me. I tried stocking up on plasma, but that's death warmed over. A few nights of it and you've got to go after the real thing, it doesn't matter *how* many promises you've made to yourself."

"The real thing?"

"I don't like to talk about it," said Smith, turning his head to the wall. "I'm actually a very sensitive person, know what I mean? Gentle. Kind. Never could stand violence, not even as a kid. Now . . ." He sobbed wrackingly, leaped to his feet, and resumed pacing. "Do you think I *enjoy* biting people? Do you think I don't *know* how disgusting it is? But, I tell you, I *can't help it!* Every few nights I get this terrible urge . . ."

"Yes?"

"You'll hate me."

"No, Mr. Smith."

"Yes you will. Everybody does. Everybody hates a vampire." The pale man withdrew a large silk handkerchief from his pocket and daubed at sudden tears. "It isn't fair," he choked. "After all, we didn't *ask* to become what we are, did we? Nobody ever thinks of that."

"You feel, then, that you are being persecuted?"

"Damn right," said Smith. "And you know why? I'll tell you why. Because I *am* being persecuted. That's why. Have you ever heard a nice thing said about a vampire? Ever in your whole life? No. Why? Because people hate us. But I'll tell you something even sillier. They *fear* us, too!" The pale man laughed a wild, mirthless laugh. *"Us,"* he said. "The most helpless creatures on the face of the Earth! Why, it doesn't take *anything* to knock us over. If we don't cut our throats trying to shave—you know the mirror bit: no reflection—we stand a chance to land flat on our back because the neighbor downstairs is cooking garlic. Or bring us a little running water, see what happens. We flip our lids. Or silver bullets. *Daylight,* for crying out loud. If I'm not back in that stupid coffin by dawn, zow, I'm out like a light. So I'm out late, and time sort of gets away from me, and I look at my watch and I've got ten minutes. What do I do? Any other vampire in his right mind, he changes into a bat and flies. Not me. You know why?"

The psychiatrist shook his head.

"Because I can't stand the ugly things. They make me sick just to look at, let alone *be*. And then there's all the hassle of taking off your clothes and all. So I grab a cab and just pray there isn't any traffic. Boy. Or take these." He smiled for the first time, revealing two large pointed incisors. "What do you imagine happens to us when our choppers start to go? I've had this one on the left filled it must be half a dozen times. The dentist says if I was smart I'd have 'em all yanked out and a nice denture put in. Sure. Can't you just see me trying to rip out somebody's throat with a pair of false teeth? Or take the routine with the wooden stake. It used to be that was kind of a secret. Now with all these lousy movies, the whole *world* is in on the gag. I ask you, Doctor, how are you supposed to be able to sleep when you know that everybody in the block is just itching to find you so they can drive a piece of wood into your heart? Huh? Man, you talk about *sick!* Those people are in *really* bad shape!" He shuddered again. "I'll tell you about the jazz with crosses, but frankly, even thinking about it makes me jumpy. You know what? I have to walk three blocks out of my way to avoid the church I used to go to every Sunday. But don't get the idea it's just churches. No, it's *anything*. Cross your fingers and I'll start sweating. Lay a fork over a knife and I'll probably jump right out the window. So then what happens? I splatter myself all over the sidewalk, right? But do I die? Oh, hell, no. Doc, listen! You've got to help me! If you don't, I'm going to go off my gourd, I know it!"

The psychiatrist folded his note pad and smiled. "Mr. Smith," he said, "you may be surprised to learn that yours is a relatively simple problem . . . with a relatively simple cure."

"Really?" asked the pale man.

"To be sure," said the psychiatrist. "Just lie down on the couch there. That's it. Close your eyes. Relax. Good." The psychiatrist rose from his chair and walked to his desk. "While it is true that this syndrome is something of a rarity," he said, "I do not foresee any great difficulty." He picked something off the top of the desk and returned. "It is primarily a matter of adjustment and of right thinking. Are you quite relaxed?"

Smith said that he was.

"Good," said the psychiatrist. "Now we begin the cure." With which comment he raised his arm high in the air, held it there for a moment, then plunged it down, burying the mahogany letter opener to its hilt in Mr. Smith's heart.

Seconds later, he was dialing a telephone number.

"Is Dorcas there?" he asked, idly scratching the two circular marks on his neck. "Tell her it's her fiancé."

WOODY ALLEN
(b. 1935)

America's most creative, and often funniest, filmmaker, Woody Allen, was born Allen Stewart Konigsberg in Brooklyn, New York. He was educated at New York University and at the City College of New York.

Allen began his career as a comedy writer and a stand-up comedian, drawing most of his material from events or fantasies in his own life and finding humor in his own insecurities. In his comedy routines and films, Allen often depicts himself as the prototypical modern man, one living in a perpetual state of anxiety, hexed by women, the certainty of death, and the guilt-ridden vestiges of inherited religion. There is a direct line leading from Y. L. Peretz's Yiddish sufferer, "Silent Bontsche," through Charlie Chaplin's Little Tramp to Woody Allen's endlessly beset schlimazel (klutz), an endlessly baffled New York City Jew around whom the contemporary world whirls.

Allen's film triumphs, almost too numerous to list, include such favorites as Annie Hall (1977), Manhattan (1979), Broadway Danny Rose (1984), The Purple Rose of Cairo (1985), and Mighty Aphrodite (1995). His written works include Getting Even (1971), Without Feathers (1975), and The Complete Prose of Woody Allen (1991).

That Allen turned his attention to Count Dracula should not surprise us. Nor should it surprise us that Allen's Count Dracula has an uncanny resemblance to the schlimazel Allen has made famous. In any case, here we have the fruit of that excursion: The answer to the question of what happens to a vampire whose sense of sunrise and sunset is discombobulated by a total eclipse of the sun.

COUNT DRACULA

Somewhere in Transylvania, Dracula the monster lies sleeping in his coffin, waiting for night to fall. As exposure to the sun's rays would surely cause him to perish, he stays protected in the satin-lined chamber bearing his family name in silver. Then the moment of darkness comes, and through some miraculous instinct the fiend emerges from the safety of his hiding place and, assuming the hideous forms of the bat or the wolf, he prowls the countryside, drinking the blood of his victims. Finally, before the first rays of his archenemy, the sun, announce a new day, he hurries back to the safety of his hidden coffin and sleeps, as the cycle begins anew.

Now he starts to stir. The fluttering of his eyelids are a response to some age-old, unexplainable instinct that the sun is nearly down and his time is near. Tonight, he is particularly hungry and as he lies there, fully awake now, in red-lined Inverness cape and tails, waiting to feel with uncanny perception the precise moment of darkness before opening the lid and emerging, he decides who this evening's victims will be. The baker and his wife, he thinks to himself. Succulent, available, and unsuspecting. The thought of the unwary couple whose trust he has carefully cultivated excites his blood lust to a fever pitch, and he can barely hold back these last seconds before climbing out of the coffin to seek his prey.

Suddenly he knows the sun is down. Like an angel of hell, he rises swiftly, and changing into a bat, flies pell-mell to the cottage of his tantalizing victims.

"Why, Count Dracula, what a nice surprise," the baker's wife says, opening the door to admit him. (He has once again assumed human form, as he enters their home, charmingly concealing his rapacious goal.)

"What brings you here so early?" the baker asks.

"Our dinner date," the Count answers. "I hope I haven't made an error. You did invite me for tonight, didn't you?"

"Yes, tonight, but that's not for seven hours."

"Pardon me?" Dracula queries, looking around the room puzzled.

"Or did you come by to watch the eclipse with us?"

"Eclipse?"

"Yes. Today's the total eclipse."

"What?"

"A few moments of darkness from noon until two minutes after. Look out the window."

"Uh-oh—I'm in big trouble."

"Eh?"

"And now if you'll excuse me . . ."

"What, Count Dracula?"

"Must be going—aha—oh, god . . ." Frantically he fumbles for the door knob.

"Going? You just came."

"Yes—but—I think I blew it very badly . . ."

"Count Dracula, you're pale."

"Am I? I need a little fresh air. It was nice seeing you . . ."

"Come. Sit down. We'll have a drink."

"Drink? No, I must run. Er—you're stepping on my cape."

"Sure. Relax. Some wine."

"Wine? Oh no, gave it up—liver and all that, you know. And now I really must buzz off. I just remembered, I left the lights on at my castle—bills'll be enormous . . ."

"Please," the baker says, his arm around the Count in firm friendship. "You're not intruding. Don't be so polite. So you're early."

"Really, I'd like to stay but there's a meeting of old Roumanian Counts across town and I'm responsible for the cold cuts."

"Rush, rush, rush. It's a wonder you don't get a heart attack."

"Yes, right—and now—"

"I'm making Chicken Pilaf tonight," the baker's wife chimes in. "I hope you like it."

"Wonderful, wonderful," the Count says, with a smile, as he pushes her aside into some laundry. Then, opening a closet door by mistake, he walks in. "Christ, where's the goddamn front door?"

"Ach," laughs the baker's wife, "such a funny man, the Count."

"I knew you'd like that," Dracula says, forcing a chuckle, "now get out of my way." At last he opens the front door but time has run out on him.

"Oh, look, Mama," says the baker, "the eclipse must be over. The sun is coming out again."

"Right," says Dracula, slamming the front door. "I've decided to stay. Pull down the window shades quickly—*quickly!* Let's move it!"

"What window shades?" asks the baker.

"There are none, right? Figures. You got a basement in this joint?"

"No," says the wife affably, "I'm always telling Jarslov to build one but he never listens. That's some Jarslov, my husband."

"I'm all choked up. Where's the closet?"

"You did that one already, Count Dracula. Unt Mama and I laughed at it."

"Ach—such a funny man, the Count."

"Look, I'll be in the closet. Knock at seven-thirty." And with that, the Count steps inside the closet and slams the door.

"Hee-hee—he is so funny, Jarslov."

"Oh, Count. Come out of the closet. Stop being a big silly." From inside the closet comes the muffled voice of Dracula.

"Can't—please—take my word for it. Just let me stay here. I'm fine. Really."

"Count Dracula, stop the fooling. We're already helpless with laughter."

"Can I tell you, I love this closet."

"Yes, but . . ."

"I know, I know . . . it seems strange, and yet here I am, having a ball. I was just saying to Mrs. Hess the other day, give me a good closet and I can stand in it for hours. Sweet woman, Mrs. Hess. Fat but sweet . . . Now, why don't you run along and check back with me at sunset. Oh, Ramona, la da da de da da da de, Ramona . . ."

Now the Mayor and his wife, Katia, arrive. They are passing by and have decided to pay a call on their good friends, the baker and his wife.

"Hello, Jarslov. I hope Katia and I are not intruding?"

"Of course not, Mr. Mayor. Come out, Count Dracula! We have company!"

"Is the Count here?" asks the Mayor surprised.

"Yes, and you'll never guess where," says the baker's wife.

"It's so rare to see him around this early. In fact I can't ever remember seeing him around in the daytime."

"Well, he's here. Come out, Count Dracula!"

"Where is he?" Katia asks, not knowing whether to laugh or not.

"Come on out now! Let's go!" The baker's wife is getting impatient.

"He's in the closet," says the baker, apologetically.

"Really?" asks the Mayor.

"Let's go," says the baker with mock good humor as he knocks on the closet door. "Enough is enough. The Mayor's here."

"Come on out, Dracula," His Honor shouts, "let's have a drink."

"No, go ahead. I've got some business in here."

"In the closet?"

"Yes, don't let me spoil your day. I can hear what you're saying. I'll join in if I have anything to add."

Everyone looks at one another and shrugs. Wine is poured and they all drink.

"Some eclipse today," the Mayor says, sipping from his glass.

"Yes," the baker agrees. "Incredible."

"Yeah. Thrilling," says a voice from the closet.

"What, Dracula?"

"Nothing, nothing. Let it go."

And so the time passes, until the Mayor can stand it no longer and forcing open the door to the closet, he shouts, "Come on, Dracula. I always thought you were a mature man. Stop this craziness."

The daylight streams in, causing the evil monster to shriek and slowly dissolve to a skeleton and then to dust before the eyes of the four people present. Leaning down to the pile of white ash on the closet floor, the baker's wife shouts, "Does this mean dinner's off tonight?"

·······VI·······
THE HEROIC
VAMPIRE

Is vampirism an unnatural plague or merely another alternative lifestyle? One hundred years after *Dracula*, readers are finding it easier to identify with vampiric protagonists and even admire them. In a more secular and hostile age, where undeath is not automatically synonymous with damnation, even Dracula can be a hero if seen from the right point of view. Over the last few decades fictional vampires have been transformed from remorseless seducers and killers, to tormented souls wrestling with an affliction beyond their control, to, increasingly, genuinely heroic figures who are morally superior to the petty, short-lived humans who surround them. It is not surprising that more and more young readers identify with the vampire who is exiled from normal experience, a sexual experimenter, a sensualist, and, above all, someone who has found a way to stay young.

There has been a steady drifting of audience or reader sympathy in favor of the vampire, perhaps beginning with the film *Dracula* (1931), in which Bela Lugosi as the title character is fascinating, though perhaps not congenial. Film Draculas following Lugosi have been increasingly attractive figures.

This trend achieved greater visibility in the 1960s, with the creation of Barnabas Collins on television's *Dark Shadows* and the popular comic book heroine Vampirella, and accelerated rapidly from there. Even more admirable and altruistic is Chelsea Quinn Yarbro's popular creation, the Count Saint-Germain. Introduced in *Hôtel Transylvania* in 1977, Saint-Germain is perhaps the purest example of the heroic vampire in modern fiction; he has defended the innocent and battled the corrupt in nearly a dozen books and has a passionate fan following. Although few other vampires can live up to his sterling example, several other sympathetic vampire protagonists do grace, with their sometimes uneasy consciences, the annals of modern vampire fiction.

One person's vampire hero, though, can be another person's worst nightmare, and sometimes it can be difficult to tell the good vampires from the bad, especially when they all leave large body counts behind. But one characteristic of vampires, we recall, is their ability to change shape. So perhaps we should not be too surprised when they transform from monsters to heroes . . . and back again.

CHELSEA QUINN YARBRO
(b. 1942)

*Born and raised in Berkeley, California, Chelsea Quinn Yarbro has pub-
lished more than fifty books, sixty short stories, and a handful of essays
and reviews in almost three decades as a professional writer. Her work
covers many genres: horror, science fiction, fantasy, thriller, mystery, historical, romantic suspense, young adult, and westerns.*

*Yarbro is perhaps best known for her immensely popular vampire nov-
els featuring the Count Saint-Germain, the first of which,* Hôtel Transylvania *(1977), is excerpted here. The others include* The Palace *(1978),* Blood
Games *(1979),* Path of the Eclipse *(1981),* Tempting Fate *(1982),* Out of
the House of Life *(1990),* Darker Jewels *(1993),* Better in the Dark *(1993),*
Mansions of Darkness *(1996), and* Writ in Blood *(1997). She is writing
a trilogy of novels about Count Dracula's wives, the first of which is* The
Angry Angel *(1998).*

*The trick that both Yarbro and Anne Rice have accomplished—in-
venting heroic, admirable vampires—seems beyond comprehension. In the
presence of such protagonists, readers must reconcile their elegance with
the fact that they sustain themselves by taking the blood of other humans.
Still, Yarbro's Saint-Germain is charming and attractive, and the author
reassures us that he never takes more blood than he needs—and then
only from willing victims. Among his other skills, he has learned how to
temporarily outwit the requirement that vampires sleep in their native soil:
he has had that soil built into the soles of his shoes!*

Excerpt from
HÔTEL TRANSYLVANIA

Excerpt from one of a series of letters written by le Baron Clotaire de Saint Sebastien to the absent members of his Circle; undated:

. . . The chapel may be reached by a secret tunnel that leads from the Seine to the abandoned vaults of the monastery that stood near the river over five hundred years ago. You will find the entrance to the tunnel on the river side of Quai Malaquais between la rue des Saints Péres and la rue de Seine. The tunnel is reinforced with heavy stones, and you should bring a club with you, for there are many rats.

. . . On the other side of the burial vaults is the chapel. It is rumored that practices of our sort were in effect there as long ago as the reign of the Spider King, which is auspicious. Certainly it has seen more recent use, for La Voison mentioned it and several others like it in and around Paris, to many of that Circle, to which my grandfather belonged.

The chapel itself is almost directly under Hôtel Transylvania. I find myself amused by this contrast. Above us, our splendid equals will be playing at dice, and risking several generations' fortune on the turn of a card, thinking that they have found the answer to power and fame, while we, far under their feet, will perform the rituals that will bring us power as they do not know exists, and the control of France more potent than the throne.

Let me warn you: apparently there is some means of access to the chapel from Hôtel Transylvania, although I have not discovered it, and it is doubtful that the owners of the Hôtel or the staff are aware of it. But you will admit that it would be most unfortunate if any of our number should use it, and even more important if any unlucky member of the Hôtel's staff should happen to discover our presence. For that, and other reasons, I will insist that each of you take turns standing guard. You will not be deprived of the delights of our sacrifice, or the use of our offering, who I find will be excellent. Even the slight taste I have had of her tells me that it will be a splendid thing to destroy her. But we must be secret. Reflection on the scandal that accompanied the last discovery of a Circle should make the need for these precautions obvious to you. One Affair of the Poisons is enough for France. I will not tolerate any of you being so clumsy as was Montespan.

As I write this last message the hour of one has struck. I charge you

to be at the chapel by the third hour of the morning, as we have planned. It may be a good thing that we have moved to the chapel ahead of the planned time for it reduces our chance of discovery and allows more leisure to make the offerings acceptable.

If you fail me in this, I will know you for my enemy, and will deal with you accordingly at my first opportunity. If you will not bow before Satan, you may still be of use to him, and to me. Think of the dismal fate of others who have stood against me, and let your decision reflect the benefit of your contemplations.

Until the third hour of the morning, then, and the first ritual, when we will offer on the altar the body of one who has betrayed me, be certain that you are in my thoughts—for advantage and luxury beyond your fondest hopes, or destruction, as you choose. It is my honor to be

Your most devoted
Baron Clotaire de Saint Sebastien

Water darkened the stones of the tunnel, and on the uneven flags that served as flooring, there was a thin film of slime, making it difficult to walk. A pervasive fetid odor filled the close air, making even the torches seem dimmed by the stench.

"Do not drop him!" Saint Sebastien ordered to the men who followed him through the tunnel.

Achille Cressie, who bore the shoulders of Robert de Montalia, complained, "Why did you have to drug him? We should have bound him."

"So that you could be entertained by his dear words, Achille?" Saint Sebastien's tone was poisonously sweet.

This did not have the expected effect on Achille, who chuckled unpleasantly. "You should have heard him in the tack room. How he despised himself when his flesh warmed to me."

De les Radeux, who held de Montalia's legs, gave a deprecating sigh. "It is all very well for you to boast of your prowess, Achille, but you will not let anyone watch, or share." He slid on the watery ooze, cursing.

"Pay attention!" Saint Sebastien barked out the order.

"He is heavy," de les Radeux insisted, sulking.

"All the more reason for you to keep your mind on what you are doing and away from your vain rivalry with Achille. If you cannot do as you are told, you are of no use to me."

De les Radeux muttered an imprecation under his breath, but steadied his grip on the drugged Robert de Montalia, going the rest of the way into the vault in silence.

The air was somewhat better there, not so close, and since the ancient stones were farther away from the river, the vault did not have that clammy cold that had made the tunnel so unbearable. Yet, it was a gloomy place. In the niches around the walls were the partially mummified remains of monks who had died three hundred years before. A closer look showed that most of the bodies had been profaned and that the crucifixes that had lain in their skeletal fingers had been replaced by phalluses, and that where consecrated oil had marked their foreheads as those belonging to God, there were now dried reddish stains in the symbol of Satan.

Saint Sebastien held his torch higher, and went quickly through the vault, arriving at last at a thick door set in the wall. The door was somewhat out of place in the Romanesque setting, for its design was recent, the strong iron hinges and other fittings still showing traces of oil to prevent rust, and the carving on the door indicated to what perverse use the chapel beyond had been put.

The door yawned open on nearly silent fittings, revealing the first area of the chapel beyond. Saint Sebastien sighed as he held the door for Cressie and de les Radeux. It would be an easy matter now. They had escaped detection, and there was no evidence that the chapel had been found and cleansed of the demonic presence.

Saint Sebastien walked farther into the chapel, his torch bringing light to the crude murals that adorned the walls, showing all the excesses of Satanic worship. Saint Sebastien smiled at one particularly horrendous representation, then went to the altar, saying to the panting men behind him, "Here, I think. Strip him and tie him down. I do not want to have to subdue him again."

De les Radeux said at his surliest, "I am honored to do this." He glared at the altar, at Saint Sebastien, at the man he carried. This was not at all what he had anticipated. He had been told that the ceremonies of the Circle were grand occasions. His uncle Beauvrai had dwelt lovingly on the complex gratifications that were offered for every desire as well as the opportunity to advance in power through these practices. But here he was in a cold stone room, under the ground, carrying le Marquis de Montalia and bowing and scraping to Saint Sebastien as if Saint Sebastien were king or archangel and he was the lowest peasant in France. To make matters worse, the damp had quite ruined his satin coat and fine white-silk hose. He wished now that he had had the foresight to keep his riding boots on.

With a last grunt, de les Radeux and Achille Cressie hoisted Robert de Montalia onto the altar, and set about pulling his clothes off, a task that proved to be surprisingly difficult.

It took Saint Sebastien about ten minutes to recite the required incantations as he lit the fifteen torches that lined the walls. The brightness grew, but the flickering of the torches made that brightness unsteady, a leaping, irregular illumination that gave weird life to the grotesque paintings on the walls.

A noise beyond the door brought Saint Sebastien's attention to the task at hand. He called out the password and waited for a response. The proper words came back, and he went to open the door.

Jueneport stood there, Madelaine in his arms. "Where do you want her?"

Saint Sebastien studied the limp figure. "I think we must put her where she can watch what we do to her father. Perhaps there." He motioned to the inverted crucifix that hung over the altar.

"It doesn't look safe to me," Jueneport said slowly. "She's strong enough to pull it out of the wall."

"I see your point." Saint Sebastien considered for a moment longer. "We could tie her there. She would then see what is done to her father, and we would see what is her reaction. An excellent combination." He had pointed to the screen that had once guarded part of the sanctuary, when the chapel had been used by the monks and not the Circles who had come to own it.

"It is strong," Jueneport agreed. "Very well. I imagine there are ropes available?"

"Behind the altar. Take what you need."

Jueneport nodded, then went to where de les Radeux and Achille Cressie worked to secure Robert de Montalia to the altar. Achille worked more slowly, pausing every now and then to run his hands over the nude body, an unpleasant light in his face as he said, "We could bind his organ as well. That way, his pain would be doubled, as would our sport."

De les Radeux shot him a look of tolerant disgust. "Is your lust all that goads you to this, Achille? Have you no other desires?"

The laughter that greeted these questions made Saint Sebastien turn, angered. "None of that, Achille, or I will forbid you to take part in the celebration."

Achille pouted, then shrugged and negligently returned to his task.

Now there was another knock at the door, and the passwords were once again exchanged. De la Sept-Nuit came in, his eyes searching for and finding the pathetic figure of Madelaine. He gestured to the bag he held. "These are the robes, mon Baron. They are all prepared, and need only your curse before we don them."

Saint Sebastien traced the pentagram in the air and said a few syllables of backward Latin. "You may dress whenever you like. Make sure your own garments are out of the way."

"I will." De la Sept-Nuit went away to a side alcove and returned several minutes later in the pleated silk robe of the Circle. It resembled a soutane, but the pleated silk clung to the body in a way no priestly garb did, and the neck opening ran the length of the robe to the hem, so that the material opened to reveal the body as de la Sept-Nuit walked across the chapel.

"I have put your robe aside," de la Sept-Nuit said. "Yours is the red with the embroidery, is that not so?"

"Yes. If you will take this torch and put it in place by the altar. I will invest myself. Are the bracelets there as well?"

"Two of silver, one of black glass. They're with the robe. You will find them. They are still wrapped as you want them to be."

"I am pleased to hear it. That is to your advantage."

De la Sept-Nuit shook his head. "You know what reward I would most enjoy." He waved a languid hand toward Madelaine, whom Jueneport had finished binding to the heavy screen. She was naked, and bruises were beginning to show on her flesh.

"Perhaps. With Tite dead, perhaps." He strolled away to put on his robes.

When he returned, the rest of the Circle had arrived and were concluding the preparations for the first ceremony. Châteaurose was now a little the worse for drink, but he knew the motions well enough that he would complete them without hazard.

"Have the sacrifices wakened yet?" Saint Sebastien asked as he came down the aisle toward the altar. He was gorgeous now in the heavy red silk which hung open showing his lean, hard body that had been only lightly touched by age. Gone was the polish that marked his public dealings, and in its place was a terrible mastery, made even stronger by the signs of office he wore around his neck, the sign of the pentagram and the obscene crucifix.

"Not yet, though the woman is stirring."

"They must be awake in twenty minutes. See to it that they are." He turned away and ignored the efforts of his Circle to force Madelaine and her father to be roused.

Beauvrai strode over to Saint Sebastien. "Well, Clotaire, how is your revenge?" Out of his ridiculous court finery, he was no longer the foppish fool he often appeared to be. In the black-silk robe none of his absurdity remained, and only the malice in him shone at full force, no longer hampered by his outward trappings.

"I have not tasted it yet. But soon. Soon."

"What for Robert? Have you thought of it?"

"Of course." He fingered the two medallions that hung halfway down his chest. "It will please you, mon Baron."

"I hope so." He turned aside, saying under his breath, "That nephew of mine is rather an ass, Clotaire."

"He seemed so to me as well," Saint Sebastien agreed at his most silky. "One would think he was too foolish to live."

"My point precisely." He bowed to Saint Sebastien and walked off to take his place in the first rank of worshipers.

At last Achille Cressie thought to bring two pails of water, and these he threw over Madelaine and Robert de Montalia. He was satisfied as he heard the woman stutter and her father gag. "I think we are ready," he said, very satisfied.

"That is good. We are very near the hour." Saint Sebastien came forward and plucked painfully at Madelaine's breasts and her cheeks. This brought a quick cry in response, and Saint Sebastien was reassured. "Yes, my dear," he said softly, caressingly, "it is I. You have not fled me."

Madelaine half-opened her violet eyes, and felt herself turn an icy cold that had little to do with the water that had drenched her. "Saint-Germain," she whispered in her desperation.

Saint Sebastien achieved a magnificent sneer. "So you long for that hoaxing fop, do you?" He reached out and slapped her face. "It is not that impostor who has you now." He turned away from the fury in her face and walked to the altar.

"He is awake," Achille told Saint Sebastien. "You have only to touch him to see the disgust in his face." He demonstrated this in superb imitation of Saint Sebastien's grand and evil manner.

"You have done well, Achille. I may let you enjoy yourself again before we dispatch Robert." He put one insolent hand on Robert's cold flesh. "How sad, my friend, that I cannot offer you a blanket. But you have my promise that I will see that you are warmed in other ways. You know that I always keep my promises."

Robert, whose jaw had tightened steadily through this new indignity, spat once, most accurately, at Saint Sebastien, then forced himself once again to stoic silence.

"You will make it worse for yourself, Robert." Saint Sebastien stood back, then lifted his arms and called out to the members of the Circle, who waited, robed and silent, before him. "We are met in the name of Satan, that we may grow in his power and his great strength, which is the strength of the great lie. We meet that we may join him in power, be with him in potency and in savagery, and to that end we bring him sacrifices."

"We bring him sacrifices," the Circle chanted.

"Lives, paid in blood, in degradation."

"In blood and degradation."

Madelaine, her arms aching from the bonds that held her to the screen, her body already hurt from the cruelty of the men gathered in the debauched chapel, felt herself sway in her bonds, almost overcome with fear and wretchedness. And she knew that for her the heinous men had not even begun to do what they were capable of doing. She remembered that there would be forty days for her destruction. She told herself in the back of her thoughts that they could not succeed, that she would be missed, and her father, that someone would find her, save her. Again she felt her soul reach out for Saint-Germain, filled with her yearning for him as much as with her panic-stricken desire for escape. But she did not know if she could dare to hope, not with the chanting growing louder.

"This forsworn one, your betrayer, Satan!"

"Your betrayer!"

"Brought back again to make expiation for his duplicity." Saint Sebastien held aloft a curiously curved dagger, letting the blade flash in the quivering torchlight.

"Your betrayer!"

Saint Sebastien put the point of the dagger against Robert de Montalia's chest, and with concentrated precision he cut the pentagram into his skin. "He is marked as yours, Satan!"

"Marked!" This triumphant shout covered the groans that Robert could not hold back.

"For your strength is not to be spurned, and your power is not mocked!"

"Power and strength are yours alone!"

Madelaine shook her head, as if the very motion would shut out the sounds that assaulted her. She could not look at her father as he steeled himself against further outrage, and she would not look at Saint Sebastien. The chanting got louder.

"Let him taste of your wrath!"

"Let him taste of your wrath!" came the shout from the Circle as Saint Sebastien brought the blade swiftly down and held up Robert's ear as a gory trophy. A great cry from the Circle combined with Robert de Montalia's scream, and the noise continued rising like a wave as Saint Sebastien put the ear to his mouth and licked it. The Circle surged forward, hysteria pulling them toward the ghastly spectacle. Saint Sebastien motioned for silence, the dagger held high as he waited.

His dramatic effect was quite destroyed when a voice spoke from the rear of the chapel, a voice that was beautifully modulated, and tinged with a slight Piedmontese accent. "I am glad I am in time, gentlemen," said le Comte de Saint-Germain.

Relief, more weakening than her terror had been, filled Madelaine, turning her very bones to water. The tears she had held back welled in her eyes, and a pang sharp as Saint Sebastien's knife lodged itself in her breast.

The members of the Circle turned, each member's face showing that dazed stupidity that often comes with being wakened from a sound sleep. Their movements were jerky, and the momentum of their ferocity faltered.

Saint-Germain came down the aisle toward the terrible altar. All of the elegant frippery of manner had vanished with his splendid clothes. Now his movements suited the tight riding coat of black leather worn over tight woolen breeches that were also black. His high boots were wide-cuffed, and the simple shirt under the coat was adorned with Russian embroidery showing a pattern of steppe wildflowers known as tulips. He carried no sword or other weapon, and was alone.

Saint Sebastien watched him, wrath showing in his narrowed eyes and malicious smile. He nodded, motioning his Circle to keep back. *"Ragoczy,"* he said. "I did not believe. I did not recognize . . ."

Saint-Germain inclined his head. "I have told you before that appearances are deceiving."

"But that was thirty years ago." He moved closer, the dagger held tightly in his hand.

"Was it? I will take your word for it." If he knew that he was in danger, nothing but the hot stare of his eyes suggested it.

"Your father, then?" Saint Sebastien closed in on Saint-Germain, almost near enough to strike.

"I was not aware that I had changed so much in that time." He had taken in the chapel and its uses when he entered it, and now he was prepared to deal with Saint Sebastien on his own ground. He touched the small locketlike receptacle that hung on a chain around his neck.

Saint Sebastien had already raised his dagger, and was about to make a sudden rush, when Saint-Germain's arm shot out, seized Saint Sebastien's shoulder, not to hold him back, but to pull him forward, sending him hurtling past Saint-Germain to crash into the stack of ruined pews at the back of the chapel.

Saint-Germain glanced toward Saint Sebastien, then directed his penetrating eyes to the members of the Circle who stood around the altar. "How absurd you are," he said lightly. "You should see yourselves standing there in your fine robes, with your manhood, if you can call it that, peeking out at the world like so many birds." He waited for the hostile words to stop. "You are foolish. Do you think that you will enhance your place in the world, obtain power and position, by following Saint Sebastien's orders? It is *his* position and power that your profane offices enhance. It is *his* desires that are met. And you, thinking that you get these things for yourselves, give yourself to him without question. If I were the one you worship, I would think poorly of your practices."

Beauvrai was the first to object. "You think we're stupid, you, who came here with nothing to protect you. . . ."

Saint-Germain held up the locket on the chain. "I beg your pardon, Baron. I have this. You are not so far removed from the faith you were born to that you cannot recognize a pyx."

The Circle, which had been growing restless, now became hushed again.

"You are asking yourselves if this is genuine." He held the pyx higher. "You may try to touch it if you like. I understand the burns are instantaneous." He waited, while the silk-robed men held back. "I see."

A sudden noise behind him made him turn, and in that moment he cursed himself for not being sure that Saint Sebastien was unconscious, for now the leader of the Circle was rushing toward Madelaine, and although he no longer carried a dagger, there was a wickedly broken piece of planking in his hands, and this he held ready to strike.

At that moment, the hush, the almost somnambulistic trance that had held the Circle members to their clumsiness and to Saint-Germain's control, ruptured with the explosiveness of a Dutch dyke bursting to let in the sea. With an awful shout, the men in the silken robes flung themselves at Saint-Germain.

Excerpt from a note written by l'Abbé Ponteneuf to his cousin, le Comtesse d'Argenlac, dated November 5, 1743:

. . . From my heart of hearts I pray God that He will comfort you and open your eyes to the glory that awaits all good Christians beyond the grave and the shadow of death. It is my duty to write this letter to you, my poor cousin, but even now my pen falters and I cannot find it in me to tell you what has befallen. I beseech you to marshal your heart to greet this terrible news with true fortitude, for all of us who know and love you cannot but wish that you would never have to endure the ordeal that is now before you.

It was rather less than an hour ago when a coach called for me, to take me to a church on the outskirts of the city. You may imagine my surprise at this unlikely request, for it is not usual to have such a request forthcoming at so late an hour. But I have not been a priest for twenty years without learning to accept what God sends me without complaint. So it was that I went in the coach to the church to which I have already alluded. We arrived in good time, and I was immediately ushered into the sanctuary, where an awesome sight met my eyes. There, laid out before me, were the bodies of three men. One was a mountebank, from the look of him, and I did not know anything of him. Another was one of Saint Sebastien's servants, whom I recognized by the livery. Saint Sebastien is such an unrepentant sinner of all the Deadly Sins that I did not know the man himself, but his master is not likely to have set his feet on a path toward Our Lord and His Sweet Mother.

It is the third man I must speak of, and it stops my heart to say this. The third man was le Comte d'Argenlac, your own beloved husband, whom you have loved so tenderly, and who has always been your staunch protector. It is further my most unpleasant duty to inform you that he did not die by accident or an act of God. He was, my unfortunate cousin, cold-bloodedly slain by a person or persons unknown.

The curé at this church has given me the use of his study that I might send you news immediately. His understanding is not great, but he is a good man, and I have told him that le Comte is known to me, and that it is only appropriate that you, as my cousin, should hear of this tragedy from one who has the knowledge of your particular circumstances.

Do not let yourself be overwhelmed. Pray to Mary for the saving of your husband's soul. You will find that such religious exercise does much to alleviate your grief, which must surely consume you otherwise. I have often remarked that when God made Woman as helpmeet to Man, He made her prey to whims and weaknesses that her mate does not know. The excellent solace of Scripture will help you to control those emotions which must fill your breast as you read this. . . .

I will take it upon myself to see that le Comte's body is removed to his parish church immediately, and that such notice as must be given of his death be delivered to the proper authorities. If you are not too incapacitated by this terrible event, perhaps, you will allow me to visit you and read with you the Great Words that will assuage your sorrow.

In the name of God, Who even now welcomes your beloved husband to the Glories of Paradise, I am always

Your obedient cousin,
L'Abbé Ponteneuf, S.J.

ANNE RICE
(b. 1941)

Born Howard Allen O'Brien, Anne Rice was raised in New Orleans and later attended San Francisco State University. A prolific writer, she works in more than one genre and under more than one name; she writes as Anne Rampling for her mainstream fiction, and as A. N. Rocquelaire for her works of sadomasochistic pornography. However, she is best known for the Vampire Chronicles, written under her own name. The first volume in this series, Interview with the Vampire (1976), was heralded as bringing a new direction in vampire fiction, and established her as the foremost, and the most ambitious, writer on vampire themes in the world. In this series, which also includes The Vampire Lestat (1985), The Queen of the Damned (1988), The Tale of the Body Thief (1992), and Memnoch the Devil (1995), she has created an epic genealogy of the vampire gods and shown them living among us as a superbly beautiful, mostly immortal, endlessly youthful and good-looking race. Their lovemaking has proved titillating to readers, perhaps speaking to the psychological hungers of people sidelined from contemporary culture.

Another fascinating element in Rice's work, and one exploited by Bram Stoker in Dracula, is the way in which the deadly amorous adventures of her characters are occasionally framed by religious discourse, imparting a glow of high seriousness to her novels.

As with Stoker's Dracula, the vampire of this short story—who is the master referred to in the title—remains a mysterious figure, visible only to Julie, the story's protagonist. The alluring power of a house also plays a role, as Julie becomes entranced with the Rampling estate, defying her father's dying wish that the place be torn down.

THE MASTER OF
RAMPLING GATE

Rampling Gate: It was so real to us in those old pictures, rising like a fairytale castle out of its own dark wood. A wilderness of gables and chimneys between those two immense towers, grey stone walls mantled in ivy, mullioned windows reflecting the drifting clouds.

But why had Father never gone there? Why had he never taken us? And why on his deathbed, in those grim months after Mother's passing, did he tell my brother, Richard, that Rampling Gate must be torn down stone by stone? Rampling Gate that had always belonged to Ramplings, Rampling Gate which had stood for over four hundred years.

We were in awe of the task that lay before us, and painfully confused. Richard had just finished four years at Oxford. Two whirlwind social seasons in London had proven me something of a shy success. I still preferred scribbling poems and stories in the quiet of my room to dancing the night away, but I'd kept that a good secret, and though we were not spoilt children, we had enjoyed the best of everything our parents could give. But now the carefree years were ended. We had to be careful and wise.

And our hearts ached as, sitting together in Father's booklined study, we looked at the old pictures of Rampling Gate before the small coal fire. "Destroy it, Richard, as soon as I am gone," Father had said.

"I just don't understand it, Julie," Richard confessed, as he filled the little crystal glass in my hand with sherry. "It's the genuine article, that old place, a real fourteenth-century manor house in excellent repair. A Mrs. Blessington, born and reared in the village of Rampling, has apparently managed it all these years. She was there when Uncle Baxter died, and he was last Rampling to live under that roof."

"Do you remember," I asked, "the year that Father took all these pictures down and put them away?"

"I shall never forget that!" Richard said. "How could I? It was so peculiar, and so unlike Father, too." He sat back, drawing slowly on his pipe. "There had been that bizarre incident in Victoria Station, when he had seen that young man."

"Yes, exactly," I said, snuggling back into the velvet chair and looking into the tiny dancing flames in the grate. "You remember how upset Father was?"

Yet it was simple incident. In fact nothing really happened at all. We couldn't have been more than six and eight at the time and we had gone to the station with Father to say farewell to friends. Through the window of a train Father saw a young man who startled and upset him. I could remember the face clearly to this day. Remarkably handsome, with a narrow nose and well drawn eyebrows, and a mop of lustrous brown hair. The large black eyes had regarded Father with the saddest expression as Father had drawn us back and hurried us away.

"And the argument that night, between Father and Mother," Richard said thoughtfully. "I remember that we listened on the landing and we were so afraid."

"And Father said *he* wasn't content to be master of Rampling Gate anymore; *he* had come to London and revealed himself. An unspeakable horror, that is what he called it, that *he* should be so bold."

"Yes, exactly, and when Mother tried to quiet him, when she suggested that he was imagining things, he went into a perfect rage."

"But who could it have been, the master of Rampling Gate, if Father wasn't the master? Uncle Baxter was long dead by then."

"I just don't know what to make of it," Richard murmured. "And there's nothing in Father's papers to explain any of it at all." He examined the most recent of the pictures, a lovely tinted engraving that showed the house perfectly reflected in the azure water of its lake. "But I tell you, the worst part of it, Julie," he said shaking his head, "is that we've never even seen the house ourselves."

I glanced at him and our eyes met in a moment of confusion that quickly passed to something else. I leant forward:

"He did not say we couldn't go there, did he, Richard?" I demanded. "That we couldn't visit the house before it was destroyed."

"No, of course he didn't!" Richard said. The smile broke over his face easily. "After all, don't we owe it to the others, Julie? Uncle Baxter who spent the last of his fortune restoring the house, even this old Mrs. Blessington that has kept it all these years?"

"And what about the village itself?" I added quickly. "What will it mean to these people to see Rampling Gate destroyed? Of course we must go and see the place ourselves."

"Then it's settled. I'll write to Mrs. Blessington immediately. I'll tell her we're coming and that we can not say how long we will stay."

"Oh, Richard, that would be too marvelous!" I couldn't keep from hugging him, though it flustered him and he pulled on his pipe just exactly the way Father would have done. "Make it at least a fortnight," I said. "I want so to know the place, especially if . . ."

But it was too sad to think of Father's admonition. And much more fun to think of the journey itself. I'd pack my manuscripts, for who knew, maybe in that melancholy and exquisite setting I'd find exactly the inspiration I required. It was almost a wicked exhilaration I felt, breaking the gloom that had hung over us since the day that Father was laid to rest.

"It is the right thing to do, isn't it, Richard?" I asked uncertainly, a little disconcerted by how much I wanted to go. There was some illicit pleasure in it, going to Rampling Gate at last.

" 'Unspeakable horror,' " I repeated Father's words with a little grimace. What did it all mean? I thought again of the strange, almost exquisite young man I'd glimpsed in that railway carriage, gazing at us all with that wistful expression on his lean face. He had worn a black greatcoat with a red woollen cravat, and I could remember how pale he had been against that dash of red. Like bone china his complexion had been. Strange to remember it so vividly, even to the tilt of his head, and that long luxuriant brown hair. But he had been a blaze against that window. And I realized now that, in those few remarkable moments, he had created for me an ideal of masculine beauty which I had never questioned since. But Father had been so angry in those moments . . . I felt an unmistakable pang of guilt.

"Of course it's the right thing, Julie," Richard answered. He at the desk, already writing the letters, and I was at a loss to understand the full measure of my thoughts.

It was late afternoon when the wretched old trap carried us up the gentle slope from the little railway station, and we had at last our first real look at that magnificent house. I think I was holding my breath. The sky had paled to a deep rose hue beyond a bank of softly gilded clouds, and the last rays of the sun struck the uppermost panes of the leaded windows and filled them with solid gold.

"Oh, but it's too majestic," I whispered, "too like a great cathedral, and to think that it belongs to us." Richard gave me the smallest kiss on the cheek. I felt mad suddenly and eager somehow to be laid waste by it, through fear or enchantment I could not say, perhaps a sublime mingling of both.

I wanted with all my heart to jump down and draw near on foot, letting those towers grow larger and larger above me, but our old horse had picked up speed. And the little line of stiff starched servants had broken to come forward, the old withered housekeeper with her arms out, the men to take down the boxes and the trunks.

Richard and I were spirited into the great hall by the tiny, nimble figure of Mrs. Blessington, our footfalls echoing loudly on the marble tile, our eyes dazzled by the dusty shafts of light that fell on the long oak table and its heavily carved chairs, the sombre, heavy tapestries that stirred ever so slightly against the soaring walls.

"It is an enchanted place," I cried, unable to contain myself. Oh, Richard, we are home!" Mrs. Blessington laughed gaily, her dry hand closing tightly on mine.

Her small blue eyes regarded me with the most curiously vacant expression despite her smile. "Ramplings at Rampling Gate again, I can not tell you what a joyful day this is for me. And yes, my dear," she said as if reading my mind that very second, "I am and have been for many years, quite blind. But if you spy a thing out of place in this house, you're to tell me at once, for it would be the exception, I assure you, and not the rule." And such warmth emanated from her wrinkled little face that I adored her at once.

We found our bedchambers, the very finest in the house, well aired with snow white linen and fires blazing cozily to dry out the damp that never left the thick walls. The small diamond pane windows opened on a glorious view of the water and the oaks that enclosed it and the few scattered lights that marked the village beyond.

That night, we laughed like children as we supped at the great oak table, our candles giving only a feeble light. And afterwards, it was a fierce battle of pocket billiards in the game room which had been Uncle Baxter's last renovation, and a little too much brandy, I fear.

It was just before I went to bed that I asked Mrs. Blessington if there had been anyone in this house since Uncle Baxter died. That had been the year 1838, almost fifty years ago, and she was already housekeeper then.

"No, my dear," she said quickly, fluffing the feather pillows. "Your father came that year as you know, but he stayed for no more than a month or two and then went on home."

"There was never a young man after that . . ." I pushed, but in truth I had little appetite for anything to disturb the happiness I felt. How I loved the Spartan cleanliness of this bedchamber, the stone walls bare of paper or ornament, the high luster of the walnut-paneled bed.

"A young man?" She gave an easy, almost hearty laugh as with unerring certainty of her surroundings, she lifted the poker and stirred the fire. "What a strange thing for you to ask."

I sat silent for a moment looking in the mirror, as I took the last of the pins from my hair. It fell down heavy and warm around my shoulders. It felt good, like a cloak under which I could hide. But she turned as if sensing some uneasiness in me, and drew near.

"Why do you say a young man, Miss?" she asked. Slowly, tentatively, her fingers examined the long tresses that lay over my shoulders. She took the brush from my hands.

I felt perfectly foolish telling her the story, but I managed a simplified version, somehow, our meeting unexpectedly a devilishly handsome young man whom my Father in anger had later called the master of Rampling Gate.

"Handsome, was he?" she asked as she brushed out the tangles in my hair gently. It seemed she hung upon every word as I described him again.

"There were no intruders in this house, then, Mrs. Blessington?" I asked. "No mysteries to be solved . . ."

She gave the sweetest laugh.

"Oh, no, darling, this house is the safest place in the world," she said quickly. "It is a happy house. No intruder would dare to trouble Rampling Gate!"

Nothing, in fact, troubled the serenity of the days that followed. The smoke and noise of London, and our Father's dying words, became a dream. What was real were our long walks together through the overgrown gardens, our trips in the little skiff to and fro across the lake. We had tea under the hot glass of the empty conservatory. And early evening found us on our way upstairs with the best of the books from Uncle Baxter's library to read by candlelight in the privacy of our rooms.

And all our discreet inquiries in the village met with more or less the same reply: the villagers loved the house and carried no old or disquieting tales. Repeatedly, in fact, we were told that Rampling was the most contented hamlet in all England, that no one dared—Mrs. Blessington's very words—to make trouble here.

"It's our guardian angel, that old house," said the old woman at the bookshop where Richard stopped for the London papers. "Was there ever the town of Rampling without the house called Rampling Gate?"

How were we going to tell them of Father's edict? How were we going to remind ourselves? But we spoke not one word about the proposed disaster, and Richard wrote to his firm to say that we should not be back in London till Fall.

He was finding a wealth of classical material in the old volumes that had belonged to Uncle Baxter, and I had set up my writing in the little study that opened off the library which I had all to myself.

Never had I known such peace and quiet. It seemed the atmosphere of Rampling Gate permeated my simplest written descriptions and wove its way richly into the plots and characters I created. The Monday after our arrival I had finished my first short story and went off to the village on foot to boldly post it to editors of *Blackwood's Magazine*.

It was glorious morning, and I took my time as I came back on foot.

What had disturbed our father so about this lovely corner of England, I wondered? What had so darkened his last hours that he laid upon this spot his curse?

My heart opened to this unearthly stillness, to an undeniable grandeur that caused me utterly to forget myself. There were times here when I felt I was a disembodied intellect drifting through a fathomless silence, up and down garden paths and stone corridors that had witnessed too much to take cognizance of one small and fragile young woman who in random moments actually talked aloud to the suits of armour around her, to the broken statues in the garden, the fountain cherubs who had had not water to pour from their conches for years and years.

But was there in this loveliness some malignant force that was eluding us still, some untold story to explain all? Unspeakable horror . . . In my mind's eye I saw that young man, and the strangest sensation crept over me, that some enrichment of the picture had taken place in my memory or imagination in the recent past. Perhaps in dream I had re-invented him, given a ruddy glow to his lips and his cheeks. Perhaps in my re-creation for Mrs. Blessington, I had allowed him to raise his hand to that red cravat and had seen the fingers long and delicate and suggestive of a musician's hand.

It was all very much on my mind when I entered the house again, soundlessly, and saw Richard in his favorite leather wing chair by the fire.

The air was warm coming through the open garden doors, and yet the blaze was cheerful, made the vast room with its towering shelves of leatherbound volumes appear inviting and almost small.

"Sit down," Richard said gravely, scarcely giving me a glance. "I want to read you something right now." He held a long narrow ledger in his hands. "This was Uncle Baxter's," he said, "and at first I thought it was only an account book he kept during the renovations, but I've found some actual diary entries made in the last weeks of his life. They're hasty, almost indecipherable, but I've managed to make them out."

"Well, do read them to me," I said, but I felt a little tug of fear. I didn't want to know anything terrible about this place. If we could have remained here forever . . . but that was out of the question, to be sure.

"Now listen to this," Richard said, turning the page carefully. " 'Fifth of May, 1838: He is here, I am sure of it. He is come back again.' And several days later: 'He thinks this is his house, he does, and he would drink my wine and smoke my cigars if only he could. He reads my books and my papers and I will not stand for it. I have given orders that everything is to be locked.' And finally, the last entry written the morning before he died: 'Weary, weary, unto death and he is no small cause of my weariness. Last night I beheld him with my own eyes. He stood in this very room. He moves and speaks exactly as a mortal man, and dares tell me his secrets, and he a demon wretch with the face of a seraph and I a mere mortal, how am I to bear with him!' "

"Good Lord," I whispered slowly. I rose from the chair where I had settled, and standing behind him, read the page for myself. It was the scrawl, the writing, the very last notation in the book. I knew that Uncle Baxter's heart had given out. He had not died by violence, but peacefully enough in this very room with his prayer book in his hand.

"Could it be the very same person Father spoke of that night?" Richard asked.

In spite of the sun pouring through the open doors, I experienced a violent chill. For the first time I felt wary of this house, wary of our boldness in coming here, heedful of our Father's words.

"But that was years before, Richard . . ." I said. "And what could this mean, this talk of a supernatural being! Surely the man was mad! It was no spirit I saw in that railway carriage!"

I sank down into the chair opposite and tried to quiet the beating of my heart.

"Julie," Richard said gently, shutting the ledger. "Mrs. Blessington has lived here contentedly for years. There are six servants asleep every night in the north wing. Surely there is nothing to all of this."

"It isn't very much fun, though, is it?" I said timidly, "not at all like swapping ghost stories the way we used to do, and peopling the dark with imaginary beings, and laughing at friends at school who were afraid."

"All my life," he said, his eyes fixing me steadily, "I've heard tales of spooks and spirits, some imagined, some supposedly true, and almost invariably there is some mention of the house in question feeling haunted, of having an atmosphere to it that fills one with foreboding, some sense of menace or alarm . . ."

"Yes, I know, and there is no such poisonous atmosphere here at all."

"On the contrary, I've never been more at ease in my life." He shoved his hand into his pocket to extract the inevitable match to light his pipe which had gone out. "As a matter of fact, Julie, I don't know how in the world I'm going to comply with Father's last wish to tear down this place."

I nodded sympathetically. The very same thing had been on my mind since we'd arrived. Even now, I felt so comfortable, natural, quite safe.

I was wishing suddenly, irrationally, that he had not found the entries in Uncle Baxter's book.

"I should talk to Mrs. Blessington again!" I said almost crossly, "I mean quite seriously . . ."

"But I have, Julie," he said. "I asked her about it all this morning when I first made the discovery, and she only laughed. She swears she's never seen anything unusual here, and that there's no one left alive in the village who can tell tales of this place. She said again how glad she was that we'd come home to Rampling Gate. I don't think she has an inkling we mean to destroy the house. Oh, it would destroy her heart if she did."

"Never seen anything unusual?" I asked. "That is what she said? But what strange words for her to use, Richard, when she can not see at all."

But he had not heard me. He had laid the ledger aside and risen slowly, almost sluggishly, and he was wandering out of the double doors into the little garden and was looking over the high hedge at the oaks that bent their heavy elbowed limbs almost to the surface of the lake. There wasn't a sound at this early hour of the day, save the soft rustle of the leaves in the morning air, the cry now and then of a distant bird.

"Maybe it's gone, Julie," Richard said, over his shoulder, his voice carrying clearly in the quiet, "if it was ever here. Maybe there is nothing any longer to frighten anyone at all. You don't suppose you could endure the winter in this house, do you? I suppose you'd want to be in London again by then." He seemed quite small against the towering trees, the sky broken into small gleaming fragments by the canopy of foliage that gently filtered the light.

Rampling Gate had him. And I understood perfectly, because it also had me. I could very well endure the winter here, no matter how bleak or cold. I never wanted to go home.

And the immediacy of the mystery only dimmed my sense of everything and every place else.

After a long moment, I rose and went out into the garden, and placed my hand gently on Richard's arm.

"I know this much, Julie," he said just as if we had been talking to each other all the while. "I swore to Father that I would do as he asked, and it is tearing me apart. Either way, it will be on my conscience for ever, obliterating this house or going against my own father and the charge he laid down to me with his dying breath."

"We must seek help, Richard. The advice of our lawyers, the advice of Father's clergymen. You must write to them and explain the whole thing. Father was feverish when he gave the order. If we could lay it out before them, they would help us decide."

It was three o'clock when I opened my eyes. But I had been awake for a long time. I had heard the dim chimes of the clock below hour by hour. And I felt not fear lying here alone in the dark but something else. Some vague and relentless agitation, some sense of emptiness and need that caused me finally to rise from my bed. What was required to dissolve this tension, I wondered. I stared at the simplest things in the shadows. The little arras that hung over the fireplace with its slim princes and princesses lost in fading fiber and thread. The portrait of an Elizabethan ancestor gazing with one almond-shaped eye from his small frame.

What was this house, really? Merely a place or a state of mind? What was it doing to my soul? Why didn't the entries in Uncle Baxter's book send us flying back to London? Why had we stayed so late in the great hall together after supper, speaking not a single word?

I felt overwhelmed suddenly, and yet shut out of some great and dazzling secret, and wasn't that the very word that Uncle Baxter had used?

Conscious only of an unbearable restlessness, I pulled on my woollen wrapper, buttoning the lace collar and tying the sash. And putting on my slippers, I went out into the hall.

The moon fell full on the oak stairway, and on the deeply recessed door to Richard's room. On tiptoe I approached and, peering in, saw the bed was empty, the covers completely undisturbed

So he was off on his own tonight the same as I. Oh, if only he had come to me, asked me to go with him.

I turned and made my way soundlessly down the long stairs.

The great hall gaped like a cavern before me, the moonlight here and there touching upon a pair of crossed swords, or a mounted shield. But

far beyond the great hall, in the alcove just outside the library, I saw
unmistakably a flickering light. And a breeze moved briskly through the
room, carrying with it the sound and the scent of a wood fire.

I shuddered with relief. Richard was there. We could talk. Or perhaps
we could go exploring together, guarding our fragile candle flames behind
cupped fingers as we went from room to room? A sense of well-being
pervaded me and quieted me, and yet the dark distance between us seemed
endless, and I was desperate to cross it, hurrying suddenly past the long
supper table with its massive candlesticks, and finally into the alcove before the library doors.

Yes, Richard was there. He sat with his eyes closed, dozing against the
inside of the leather wing chair, the breeze from the garden blowing the
fragile flames of the candles on the stone mantel and on the table at
his side.

I was about to go to him, about to shut the doors, and kiss him gently
and ask did he not want to go up to bed, when quite abruptly I saw in
the corner of my eye that there was some one else in the room.

In the far left corner at the desk stood another figure, looking down at
the clutter of Richard's papers, his pale hands resting on the wood.

I knew that it could not be so. I knew that I must be dreaming, that
nothing in this room, least of all this figure, could be real. For it was
the same young man I had seen fifteen years ago in the railway carriage
and not a single aspect of that taut young face had been changed. There
was the very same hair, thick and lustrous and only carelessly combed
as it hung to the thick collar of his black coat, and the skin so pale it
was almost luminous in the shadows, and those dark eyes looking up
suddenly and fixing me with the most curious expression as I almost
screamed.

We stared at one another across the dark vista of that room, I stranded
in the doorway, he visibly and undeniably shaken that I had caught him
unawares. My heart stopped.

And in a split second he moved towards me, closed the gap between us,
towering over me, those slender white fingers gently closing on my arms.

"Julie!" he whispered, in a voice so low it seemed my own thoughts
speaking to me. But this was no dream. He was real. He was holding to
me and the scream had broken loose from me, deafening, uncontrollable
and echoing from the four walls.

I saw Richard rising from the chair. I was alone. Clutching to the door
frame, I staggered forward, and then again in a moment of perfect clarity
I saw the young intruder, saw him standing in the garden, looking back
over his shoulder, and then he was gone.

I could not stop screaming. I could not stop even as Richard held me
and pleaded with me, and sat me down in the chair.

And I was still crying when Mrs. Blessington finally came.

She got a glass of cordial for me at once, as Richard begged me once more to tell what I had seen.

"But you know who it was!" I said to Richard almost hysterically. "It was he, the young man from the train. Only he wore a frockcoat years out of fashion and his silk tie was open at his throat. Richard, he was reading your papers, turning them over, reading them in the pitch dark."

"All right," Richard said, gesturing with his hand up for calm. "He was standing at the desk. And there was no light there so you could not see him well."

"Richard, it was he! Don't you understand? He touched me, he held my arms." I looked imploringly to Mrs. Blessington who was shaking her head, her little eyes like blue beads in the light. "He called me Julie," I whispered. "He knows my name!"

I rose, snatching up the candle, and all but pushing Richard out of the way went to the desk. "Oh, dear God," I said, "Don't you see what's happened? It's your letters to Dr. Partridge, and Mrs. Sellers, about tearing down the house!"

Mrs. Blessington gave a little cry and put her hand to her cheek. She looked like a withered child in her nightcap as she collapsed into the straight-backed chair by the door.

"Surely you don't believe it was the same man, Julie, after all these years . . ."

"But he had not changed, Richard, not in the smallest detail. There is no mistake, Richard, it was he, I tell you, the very same."

"Oh, dear, dear . . ." Mrs. Blessington whispered, "What will he do if you try to tear it down? What will he do now?"

"What will who do?" Richard asked carefully, narrowing his eyes. He took the candle from me and approached her. I was staring at her, only half realizing what I had heard.

"So you know who he is!" I whispered.

"Julie, stop it!" Richard said.

But her face had tightened, gone blank and her eyes had become distant and small.

"You knew he was here!" I insisted. "You must tell us at once!"

With an effort she climbed to her feet. "There is nothing in this house to hurt *you*," she said, "nor any of us." She turned, spurning Richard as he tried to help her, and wandered into the dark hallway alone. "You've no need of me here any longer," she said softly, "and if you should tear down this house built by your forefathers, then you should do it without need of me."

"Oh, but we don't mean to do it, Mrs. Blessington!" I insisted. But she was making her way through the gallery back towards the north wing. "Go after her, Richard. You heard what she said. She knows who he is."

"I've had quite enough of this tonight," Richard said almost angrily. "Both of us should go up to bed. By the light of day we will dissect this entire matter and search this house. Now come."

"But he should be told, shouldn't he?" I demanded.

"Told what? Of whom do you speak!"

"Told that we will not tear down this house!" I said clearly, loudly, listening to the echo of my own voice.

The next day was indeed the most trying since we had come. It took the better part of the morning to convince Mrs. Blessington that we had no intention of tearing down Rampling Gate. Richard posted his letters and resolved that we should do nothing until help came.

And together we commenced a search of the house. But darkness found us only half finished, having covered the south tower and the south wing, and the main portion of house itself. There remained still the north tower, in a dreadful state of disrepair, and some rooms beneath the ground which in former times might have served as dungeons and were now sealed off. And there were closets and private stairways everywhere that we had scarce looked into, and at times we lost all track of where precisely we had been.

But it was also quite clear by supper time that Richard was in a state of strain and exasperation, and that he did not believe that I had seen anyone in the study at all.

He was further convinced that Uncle Baxter had been mad before he died, or else his ravings were a code for some mundane happening that had him extraordinarily overwrought.

But I knew what I had seen. And as the day progressed, I became ever more quiet and withdrawn. A silence had fallen between me and Mrs. Blessington. And I understood only too well the anger I'd heard in my father's voice on that long ago night when we had come home from Victoria Station and my mother had accused him of imagining things.

Yet what obsessed me more than anything else was the gentle countenance of the mysterious man I had glimpsed, the dark almost innocent eyes that had fixed on me for one moment before I had screamed.

"Strange that Mrs. Blessington is not afraid of him," I said in a low distracted voice, not longer caring if Richard heard me. "And that no one here seems in fear of him at all . . ." The strangest fancies were coming to me. The careless words of the villagers were running through my head. "You would be wise to do one very important thing before you retire," I said. "Leave out in writing a note to the effect that you do not intend to tear down the house."

"Julie, you have created an impossible dilemma," Richard demanded. "You insist we reassure this apparition that the house will not be destroyed, when in fact you verify the existence of the very creature that drove our father to say what he did."

"Oh, I wish I had never come here!" I burst out suddenly.

"Then we should go, both of us, and decide this matter at home."

"No, that's just it. I could never go without knowing . . . 'his secrets' . . . 'the demon wretch.' I could never go on living without knowing now!"

Anger must be an excellent antidote to fear, for surely something worked to alleviate my natural alarm. I did not undress that night, nor even take off my shoes, but rather sat in that dark hollow bedroom gazing at the small square of diamond-paned window until I heard all of the house fall quiet. Richard's door at last closed. There came those distant echoing booms that meant other bolts had been put in place.

And when the grandfather clock in the great hall chimed the hour of eleven, Rampling Gate was as usual fast asleep.

I listened for my brother's step in the hall. And when I did not hear him stir from his room, I wondered at it, that curiosity would not impel him to come to me, to say that we must go together to discover the truth.

It was just as well. I did not want him to be with me. And I felt a dark exultation as I imagined myself going out of the room and down the stairs as I had the night before. I should wait one more hour, however, to be certain. I should let the night reach its pitch. Twelve, the witching hour. My heart was beating too fast at the thought of it, and dreamily I recollected the face I had seen, the voice that had said my name.

Ah, why did it seem in retrospect so intimate, that we had known each other, spoken together, that it was someone I recognized in the pit of my soul?

"What is your name?" I believe I whispered aloud. And then a spasm of fear startled me. Would I have the courage to go in search of him, to open the door to him? Was I losing my mind? Closing my eyes, I rested my head against the high back of the damask chair.

What was more empty than this rural night? What was more sweet?

I opened my eyes. I had been half dreaming or talking to myself, trying to explain to Father why it was necessary that we comprehend the reason ourselves. And I realized, quite fully realized—I think before I was even awake—that *he* was standing by the bed.

The door was open. And he was standing there, dressed exactly as he had been the night before, and his dark eyes were riveted on me with that same obvious curiosity, his mouth just a little slack like that of a school boy, and he was holding to the bedpost almost idly with his right hand. Why, he was lost in contemplating me. He did not seem to know that I was looking at him.

But when I sat forward, he raised his finger as if to quiet me, and gave a little nod of his head.

"Ah, it is you!" I whispered.

"Yes," he said in the softest, most unobtrusive voice.

But we had been talking to each other, hadn't we, I had been asking him questions, no, telling him things. And I felt suddenly I was losing my equilibrium or slipping back into a dream.

No. Rather I had all but caught the fragment of some dream from the past. That rush of atmosphere that can engulf one at any moment of the day following when something evokes the universe that absorbed one utterly in sleep. I mean I heard our voices for an instant, almost in argument, and I saw Father in his top hat and black overcoat rushing alone through the streets of the West End, peering into one door after another, and then, rising from the marble-top table in the dim smoky music hall you . . . your face.

"Yes . . ."

Go back, Julie! It was Father's voice.

". . . to penetrate the soul of it," I insisted, picking up the lost thread. But did my lips move? "To understand what it is that frightened him, enraged him. He said, 'Tear it down!' "

". . . you must never, never, can't do that." His face was stricken, like that of a schoolboy about to cry.

"No, absolutely, we don't want to, either of us, you know it . . . and you are not a spirit!" I looked at his mud-spattered boots, the faintest smear of dust on that perfect white cheek.

"A spirit?" he asked almost mournfully, almost bitterly. "Would that I were."

Mesmerized I watched him come toward me and the room darkened, and I felt his cool silken hands on my face. I had risen. I was standing before him, and I looked up into his eyes.

I heard my own heartbeat. I heard it as I had the night before, right at the moment I had screamed. Dear God, I was talking to him! He was in my room and I was talking to him! And I was in his arms.

"Real, absolutely real!" I whispered, and a low zinging sensation coursed through me so that I had to steady myself against the bed.

He was peering at me as if trying to comprehend something terribly important to him, and he didn't respond. His lips did have a ruddy look to them, a soft look for all his handsomeness, as if he had never been kissed. And a slight dizziness had come over me, a slight confusion in which I was not at all sure that he was even there.

"Oh, but I am," he said softly. I felt his breath against my cheek, and it was almost sweet. "I am here, and you are with me, Julie . . ."

"Yes . . ."

My eyes were closing. Uncle Baxter sat hunched over his desk and I could hear the furious scratch of his pen. "Demon wretch!" he said to the night air coming in the open doors.

"No!" I said. Father turned in the door of the music hall and cried my name.

"Love me, Julie," came that voice in my ear. I felt his lips against my neck. "Only a little kiss, Julie, no harm . . ." And the core of my being, that secret place where all desires and all commandments are nurtured, opened to him without a struggle or a sound. I would have fallen if he had not held me. My arms closed about him, my hands slipping in the soft silken mass of his hair.

I was floating, and there was as there had always been at Rampling Gate an endless peace. It was Rampling Gate I felt around me, it was that timeless and impenetrable soul that had opened itself at last. . . . A power within me of enormous ken . . . To see as a god sees, and take the depth of things as nimbly as the outward eyes can size and shape pervade . . . Yes, I whispered aloud, those words from Keats, those words . . . To cease upon the midnight without pain . . .

No. In a violent instant we had parted, he drawing back as surely as I.

I went reeling across the bedroom floor and caught hold of the frame of the window, and rested my forehead against the stone wall.

For a long moment I stood with my eyes closed. There was a tingling pain in my throat that was almost pleasurable where his lips had touched me, a delicious throbbing that would not stop.

Then I turned, and I saw all the room clearly, the bed, the fireplace, the chair. And he stood still exactly as I'd left him and there was the most appalling distress in his face.

"What have they done to me?" he whispered. "Have they played the cruelest trick of all?"

"Something of menace, unspeakable menace," I whispered.

"Something ancient, Julie, something that defies understanding, something that can and will go on."

"But why, what are you?" I touched that pulsing pain with the tips of my fingers and, looking down at them, gasped. "And you suffer so, and you are so seemingly innocent, and it is as if you can love!"

His face was rent as if by a violent conflict within. And he turned to go. With my whole will, I stood fast not to follow him, not to beg him to turn back. But he did turn, bewildered, struggling and then bent upon his purpose as he reached for my hand. "Come with me," he said.

He drew me to him ever so gently, and slipping his arm around me guided me to the door.

Through the long upstairs corridor we passed hurriedly, and through a small wooden doorway to a screw stairs that I had never seen before.

I soon realized we were ascending the north tower of the house, the ruined portion of the structure that Richard and I had not investigated before.

Through one tiny window after another I saw the gently rolling landscape moving out from the forest that surrounded us, and the small cluster of dim lights that marked the village of Rampling and the pale streak of white that was the London road.

Up and up we climbed until we had reached the topmost chamber, and this he opened with an iron key. He held back the door for me to enter and I found myself in a spacious room whose high narrow windows contained no glass. A flood of moonlight revealed the most curious mixture of furnishings and objects, the clutter that suggests an attic and a sort of den. There was a writing table, a great shelf of books, soft leather chairs and scores of old yellowed and curling maps and framed pictures affixed to the walls. Candles were everywhere stuck in the bare stone niches or to the tables and the shelves. Here and there a barrel served as a table, right alongside the finest old Elizabethan chair. Wax had dripped over everything, it seemed, and in the very midst of the clutter lay rumpled copies of the most recent papers, the *Mercure de Paris*, the London *Times*.

There was no place for sleeping in this room.

And when I thought of that, where he must lie when he went to rest, a shudder passed over me and I felt, quite vividly, his lips touching my throat again, and I felt the sudden urge to cry.

But he was holding me in his arms, he was kissing my cheeks and my lips again ever so softly, and then he guided me to a chair. He lighted the candles about us one by one.

I shuddered, my eyes watering slightly in the light. I saw more unusual objects: telescopes and magnifying glasses and a violin in its open case, and a handful of gleaming and exquisitely shaped sea shells. There were jewels lying about, and a black silk top hat and a walking stick, and a bouquet of withered flowers, dry as straw, and daguerreotypes and tintypes in their little velvet cases, and opened books.

But I was too distracted now by the sight of him in the light, the gloss of his large black eyes, and the gleam of his hair. Not even in the railway station had I seen him so clearly as I did now amid the radiance of the candles. He broke my heart.

And yet he looked at me as though I were the feast for his eyes, and he said my name again and I felt the blood rush to my face. But there seemed a great break suddenly in the passage of time. I had been thinking, yes, what are you, how long have you existed . . . And I felt dizzy again.

I realized that I had risen and I was standing beside him at the window and he was turning me to look down and the countryside below had unaccountably changed. The lights of Rampling had been subtracted from the darkness that lay like a vapor over the land. A great wood, far older and denser than the forest of Rampling Gate, shrouded the hills, and I was afraid suddenly, as if I were slipping into a maelstrom from which I could never, of my own will, return.

There was that sense of us talking together, talking and talking in low agitated voices and I was saying that I should not give in.

"Bear witness, that is all I ask of you . . ."

And there was in me some dim certainty that by knowledge alone I should be fatally changed. It was the reading of a forbidden book, the chanting of a forbidden charm.

"No, only what was," he whispered.

And then even the shape of the land itself eluded me. And the very room had lost its substance, as if a soundless wind of terrific force had entered this place and was blowing it apart.

We were riding in a carriage through the night. We had long long ago left the tower, and it was late afternoon and the sky was the color of blood. And we rode into a forest whose trees were so high and so thick that scarcely any sun at all broke to the soft leafstrewn ground.

We had no time to linger in this magical place. We had come to the open country, to the small patches of tilled earth that surrounded the ancient village of Knorwood with its gabled roofs and its tiny crooked streets. We saw the walls of the monastery of Knorwood and the little church with the bell chiming Vespers under the lowering sky. A great bustling life resided in Knorwood, a thousand hearts beat in Knorwood, a thousand voices gave forth their common prayer.

But far beyond the village on the rise above the forest stood the rounded tower of a truly ancient castle, and to that ruined castle, no more than a shell of itself anymore, as darkness fell in earnest, we rode. Through its empty chambers we roamed, impetuous children, the horse and the road quite forgotten, and to the Lord of the Castle, a gaunt and white-skinned creature standing before the roaring fire of the roofless hall, we came. He turned and fixed us with his narrow and glittering eyes. A dead thing he was, I understood, but he carried within himself a priceless magic. And my young companion, my innocent young man passed by me into the Lord's arms. I saw the kiss. I saw the young man grow pale and struggle to turn away. It was as I had done this very night, beyond this dream, in my own bedchamber; and from the Lord he retreated, clutching to the sharp pain in his throat.

I understood. I knew. But the castle was dissolving as surely as anything in this dream might dissolve, and we were in some damp and close place.

The stench was unbearable to me, it was that most terrible of all stenches, the stench of death. And I heard my steps on the cobblestones and I reached to steady myself against the wall. The tiny square was deserted; the doors and windows gaped open to the vagrant wind. Up one side and down the other of the crooked street I saw the marks on the houses. And I knew what the marks meant. The Black Death had come to the village of Knorwood. The Black Death had laid it waste. And in a moment of suffocating horror I realized that no one, not a single person, was left alive.

But this was not quite right. There was some one walking in fits and starts up the narrow alleyway. Staggering he was, almost falling, as he pushed in one door after another, and at last came to a hot, stinking place where a child screamed on the floor. Mother and Father lay dead in the bed. And the great fat cat of the household, unharmed, played with the screaming infant, whose eyes bulged from its tiny sunken face.

"Stop it," I heard myself gasp. I knew that I was holding my head with both hands. "Stop it, stop it please!" I was screaming and my screams would surely pierce the vision and this small crude little room should collapse around me, and I should rouse the household of Rampling Gate to me, but I did not. The young man turned and stared at me, and in the close stinking room, I could not see his face.

But I knew it was he, my companion, and I could smell his fever and his sickness, and the stink of the dying infant, and see the sleek, gleaming body of the cat as it pawed at the child's outstretched hand.

"Stop it, you've lost control of it!" I screamed surely with all my strength, but the infant screamed louder. "Make it stop!"

"I can not . . ." he whispered. "It goes on forever! It will never stop!"

And with a great piercing shriek I kicked at the cat and sent it flying out of the filthy room, overturning the milk pail as it went, jetting like a witch's familiar over the stones.

Blanched and feverish, the sweat soaking his crude jerkin, my companion took me by the hand. He forced me back out of the house and away from the crying child and into the street.

Death in the parlor, death in the bedroom, death in the cloister, death before the high altar, death in the open fields. It seemed the Judgment of God that a thousand souls had died in the village of Knorwood—I was sobbing, begging to be released—it seemed the very end of Creation itself.

And at last night came down over the dead village and he was alive still, stumbling up the slopes, through the forest, toward that rounded tower where the Lord stood with his hand on the stone frame of the broken window waiting for him to come.

"Don't go!" I begged him. I ran alongside him crying, but he didn't hear. Try as I might, I could not affect these things.

The Lord stood over him smiling almost sadly as he watched him fall, watched the chest heave with its last breaths. Finally the lips moved, calling out for salvation when it was damnation the Lord offered, when it was damnation that the Lord would give.

"Yes, damned then, but living, breathing!" the young man cried, rising in a last spasmodic movement. And the Lord, who had remained still until that instant, bent to drink.

The kiss again, the lethal kiss, the blood drawn out of the dying body, and then the Lord lifting the heavy head of the young man to take the blood back again from the body of the Lord himself.

I was screaming again, *Do not, do not drink.* He turned and looked at me. His face was now so perfectly the visage of death that I couldn't believe there was animation left in him, yet he asked: What would you do? Would you go back to Knorwood, would you open those doors one after another, would you ring the bell in the empty church, and if you did would the dead rise?

He didn't wait for my answer. And I had none now to give. He had turned again to the Lord who waited for him, locked his innocent mouth to that vein that pulsed with every semblance of life beneath the Lord's cold and translucent flesh. And the blood jetted into the young body, vanquishing in one great burst the fever and the sickness that had wracked it, driving it out with the mortal life.

He stood now in the hall of the Lord alone. Immortality was his and the blood thirst he would need to sustain it, and that thirst I could feel with my whole soul. He stared at the broken walls around him, at the fire licking the blackened stones of the giant fireplace, at the night sky over the broken roof, throwing out its endless net of stars.

And each and every thing was transfigured in his vision, and in my vision—the vision he gave now to me—to the exquisite essence of itself. A wordless and eternal voice spoke from the starry veil of heaven, it sang in the wind that rushed through the broken timbers; it sighed in the flames that ate the sooted stones of the hearth.

It was the fathomless rhythm of the universe that played beneath every surface, as the last living creature—that tiny child—fell silent in the village below.

A soft wind sifted and scattered the soil from the new-turned furrows in the empty fields. The rain fell from the black and endless sky.

Years and years passed. And all that had been Knorwood melted into the very earth. The forest sent out its silent sentinels, and mighty trunks rose where there had been huts and houses, where there had been monastery walls.

Finally nothing of Knorwood remained: not the little cemetery, not the little church, not even the name of Knorwood lived still in the world. And it seemed the horror beyond all horrors that no one anymore should know of a thousand souls who had lived and died in that small and insignificant village, that not anywhere in the great archives in which all history is recorded should a mention of that town remain.

Yet one being remained who knew, one being who had witnessed, and stood now looking down upon the very spot where his mortal life had ended, he who had scrambled up on his hands and knees from the pit of Hell that had been that disaster; it was the young man who stood beside me, the master of Rampling Gate.

And all through the walls of his old house were the stones of the ruined castle, and all through the ceilings and floors the branches of those ancient trees.

What was solid and majestic here, and safe within the minds of those who slept tonight in the village of Rampling, was only the most fragile citadel against horror, the house to which he clung now.

A great sorrow swept over me. Somewhere in the drift of images I had relinquished myself, lost all sense of the point in space from which I saw. And in a great rush of lights and noise I was enlivened now and made whole as I had been when we rode together through the forest, only it was into the world of now, this hour, that we passed. We were flying it seemed through the rural darkness along the railway toward London where the nighttime city burst like an enormous bubble in a shower of laughter, and motion, and glaring light. He was walking with me under the gas lamps, his face all but shimmering with that same dark innocence, that same irresistible warmth. And it seemed we were holding tight to one another in the very midst of a crowd. And the crowd was a living thing, a writhing thing, and everywhere there came a dark rich aroma from it, the aroma of fresh blood. Women in white fur and gentlemen in opera capes swept into the brightly lighted doors of the theater; the blare of the music hall inundated us, then faded away. Only a thin soprano voice was left, singing a high, plaintive song. I was in his arms, and his lips were covering mine, and there came that dull zinging sensation again, that great uncontrollable opening within myself. Thirst, and the promise of satiation measured only by the intensity of that thirst. Up stairs we fled together, into high-ceilinged bedrooms papered in red damask where the loveliest women reclined on brass bedsteads, and the aroma was so strong now I could not bear it, and before me they offered themselves, they opened their arms. "Drink," he whispered, yes, drink. And I felt the warmth filling me, charging me, blurring my vision, until we broke again, free and light and invisible it seemed as we moved over the roof-tops and down again through rain drenched streets. But the rain did not touch us; the falling snow did not chill us; we had within ourselves a great and indissoluble heat. And together in the carriage, we talked to each other in low, exuberant rushes of language; we were lovers; we were constant; we were immortal. We were as enduring as Rampling Gate.

I tried to speak; I tried to end the spell. I felt his arms around me and I knew we were in the tower room together, and some terrible miscalculation had been made.

"Do not leave me," he whispered. "Don't you understand what I am offering you; I have told you everything; and all the rest is but the weariness, the fever and the fret, those old words from the poem. Kiss me, Julie, open to me. Against your will I will not take you . . ." Again I heard my own scream. My hands were on his cool white skin, his lips were gentle yet hungry, his eyes yielding and ever young. Father turned in the rain-drenched London street and cried out: "Julie!" I saw Richard lost in the crowd as if searching for some one, his hat shadowing his dark eyes, his face haggard, old. Old!

I moved away. I was free. And I was crying softly and we were in this strange and cluttered tower room. He stood against the backdrop of the window, against the distant drift of pale clouds. The candle-light glimmered in his eyes. Immense and sad and wise they seemed, and oh, yes, innocent as I have said again and again. "I revealed myself to them," he said. "Yes, I told my secret. In rage or bitterness, I know not which, I made them my dark co-conspirators and always I won. They could not move against me, and neither will you. But they would triumph still. For they torment me now with their fairest flower. Don't turn away from me, Julie. You are mine, Julie, as Rampling Gate is mine. Let me gather the flower to my heart."

Nights of argument. But finally Richard had come round. He would sign over to me his share of Rampling Gate, and I should absolutely refuse to allow the place torn down. There would be nothing he could do then to obey Father's command. I had given him the legal impediment he needed, and of course I should leave the house to him and his children. It should always be in Rampling hands.

A clever solution, it seemed to me, as Father had not told *me* to destroy the place, and I had no scruples in the matter now at all.

And what remained was for him to take me to the little train station and see me off for London, and not worry about me going home to Mayfair on my own.

"You stay here as long as you wish, and do not worry," I said. I felt more tenderly towards him than I could ever express. "You knew as soon as you set foot in the place that Father was all wrong. Uncle Baxter put it in his mind, undoubtedly, and Mrs. Blessington has always been right. There is nothing to harm there, Richard. Stay, and work or study as you please."

The great black engine was roaring past us, the carriages slowing to a stop. "Must go now, darling, kiss me," I said.

"But what came over you, Julie, what convinced you so quickly . . ."

"We've been through all, Richard," I said. "What matters is that we are all happy, my dear." And we held each other close.

I waved until I couldn't see him anymore. The flickering lamps of the town were lost in the deep lavender light of the early evening, and the dark hulk of Rampling Gate appeared for one uncertain moment like the ghost of itself on the nearby rise.

I sat back and closed my eyes. Then I opened them slowly, savoring this moment for which I had waited too long.

He was smiling, seated there as he had been all along, in the far corner of the leather seat opposite, and now he rose with a swift, almost delicate movement and sat beside me and enfolded me in his arms.

"It's five hours to London," he whispered in my ear.

"I can wait," I said, feeling the thirst like a fever as I held tight to him, feeling his lips against my eyelids and my hair. "I want to hunt the London streets tonight," I confessed, a little shyly, but I saw only approbation in his eyes.

"Beautiful Julie, my Julie . . ." he whispered.

"You'll love the house in Mayfair," I said.

"Yes . . ." he said.

"And when Richard finally tires of Rampling Gate, we shall go home."

EDWARD BRYANT
(b. 1945)

Born and raised in Wyoming, Edward Bryant received his college education at the University of Wyoming. That state is the setting for several of his short stories, collected as Wyoming Sun *(1980).*

Bryant has written primarily short stories, beginning with "They Come Only in Dreams" (1970). His first collection of short stories, Among the Dead and Other Events Leading up to the Apocalypse, *was published in 1973, and his second,* Cinnabar, *in 1976—the latter being a collection of related short works about a future California city. His work is complex and sometimes dark, as illustrated by the story "Shark" (1973), in which an unhappy young woman wants to have her brain transplanted into a shark. His novels include* The Man of the Future *(1990),* The Cutter *(1988),* Fetish *(1991), and* The Thermals of August *(1992). He is a contributor to the* Wild Cards *series of superhero shared-universe novels; edited the anthology* 2076: The American Tricentennial *(1977); and is one of the regular book reviewers for* Locus *magazine. Bryant sometimes writes under the pseudonym Lawrence Talbot.*

"Good Kids" is a cocky tale of streetwise children old beyond their years. The children's snappy dialogue is suave and fluent and sounds authentic. The story's climax is at once surprising, bloody, and satisfying. A pleasant surprise tucked into the text that follows is just how much, and how deftly, Bryant has borrowed from the story of the king vampire, Stoker's Dracula.

GOOD KIDS

"*That* blood?" said Donnie, appalled. "That's grossss."

Angelique was peeking over her shoulder at the lurid paperback vampire novel. "Don't draw out your consonants. You sound like a geek."

"I'm not a geek," said Donnie. "I'm only eleven years old, you jerk. I get to draw out my esses if I want to."

"We're all too goddamned bright," said Camelia gloomily. "The last place I went to school, everybody just played with dolls or talked all day about crack."

"Public schools," Angelique snorted.

Donnie flipped the page and squinted. "Yep, he's lapping up her menstrual blood, all right. This vampire's a real gink."

"Wonderful. So her arching, lily-white swan throat wasn't enough," said Cammie. "Oh boy. I can hardly wait till *I* start having my period."

The lights flashed and the four of us involuntarily glanced up. Ms. Yukoshi, one of the Center's three night supervisors, stood framed in the doorway. "Okay, girls, lights out in three. Put away the book. Hit those bunks. Good night, now." She started to exit, but then apparently changed her mind. "I suppose I ought to mention that this is my last night taking care of you."

Were we supposed to clap? I wondered. Maybe give her a four-part harmony chorus of "Thank you, Ms. Yukoshi"? What was appropriate behavior?

"No thanks are necessary," said Ms. Yukoshi. "I just know I need a long, long vacation. Lots of R and R." We could all see her sharp, white teeth gleaming in the light from the overhead. "You'll have a new person to bedevil tomorrow night. His name is Mr. Vladisov."

"So why don't we ever get a good WASP?" Cammie whispered.

The other two giggled. I guess I did too. It's easy to forget that Camelia is black.

Ms. Yukoshi looked at us sharply. Donnie giggled again and dog-eared a page before setting the vampire book down. "Good night, girls." Ms. Yukoshi retreated into the hall. We listened to the click and echo of her stylish heels moving on to the next room, the next island of kids. Boys in that one.

"I wonder what Mr. Vladisov will be like," Donnie said.

Angelique smiled. "At least he's a guy."

"Good night, girls." Donnie mimicked Ms. Yukoshi.

I snapped off the lamp. And that was it for another fun evening at the renovated brownstone that was the Work-at-Night Child Care Center and

Parenting Service. Wick Pus, we called it, all of us who had night-shift parents with no other place to put their kids.

"Good night," I said to everybody in general. I lay back in the bunk and pulled the covers up to my chin. The wool blanket scratched my neck.

"I'm hungry," said Angelique plaintively. "Cookies and milk aren't enough."

"Perhaps you want some blooood?" said Donnie, snickering.

"Good night," I said again. But I was hungry too.

The next day was Wednesday. Hump day. Didn't matter. No big plans for the week—or for the weekend. It wasn't one of the court-set times for my dad to visit, so I figured probably I'd be spending the time reading. That was okay too. I like to read. Maybe I'd finish the last thousand pages of Stephen King's new novel and get on to some of the stuff I needed to read for school.

We were studying urban legends and old wives' tales—a side issue was the class figuring out a nonsexist term for the latter.

We'd gone through a lot of the stuff that most of us had heard—and even believed at one time—like the hook killer and the Kentucky Fried Rat and the expensive car that was on sale unbelievably cheap because nobody could get the smell out of the upholstery after the former owner killed himself and the body wasn't discovered for three hot days. Then there was the rattlesnake in the K-Mart jeans and the killer spiders in the bouffant. Most of that didn't interest me. What I liked were the older myths, things like keeping cats out of the nursery and forbidding adults to sleep in the presence of children.

Now I've always liked cats, so I know where my sympathy lies with that one. Kitties love to snuggle up to warm little faces on chilly nights. No surprise, right? But the bit about sucking the breath from babies' lungs is a load of crap. Well, most of the time. As for the idea that adults syphon energy from children, that's probably just a cleaner way of talking about the incest taboo.

It's a way of speaking metaphorically. That's what the teacher said.

I can see why adults would want to steal kids' energy. Then they could rule the world, live forever, win all the Olympics. See what I mean? So maybe some adults do. You ever feel just how much energy is generated by a roomful of hyper kids? *I* know. But then, I'm a kid. I expect I'll lose it all when I grow up. I'm not looking forward to that. It'll be like death. Or maybe undeath.

It all sounds sort of dull gray and drab, just like living in the book *1984*.

The thing about energy is that what goes out has to come in first. Another lesson. First Law of Thermodynamics. Or maybe the Second. I didn't pay much attention that day. I guess I was too busy daydreaming about horses, or maybe sneaking a few pages of the paperback hidden in my vinyl binder.

Don't even ask what I'm going to do when I grow up. I've got lots of time to figure it out.

Mr. Vladisov had done his homework. He addressed us all by name. Evidently he'd sucked Ms. Yukoshi dry of all the necessary information.

"And you would be Shauna-Laurel Andersen," he said to me, smiling faintly.

I felt like I ought to curtsy at least. Mr. Vladisov was tall and courtly, just like characters in any number of books I'd read. His hair was jet-black and fixed in one of those widow's peaks. Just like a novel. His eyes were sharp and black too, though the whites were all bloodshot. They didn't look comfortable. He spoke with some kind of Slavic accent. Good English, but the kind of accent I've heard actors working in restaurants goofing around with.

Shauna-Laurel, I thought. "My friends call me SL," I said.

"Then I hope we shall be friends," said Mr. Vladisov.

"Do we have to call you 'sir'?" said Angelique. I knew she was just being funny. I wondered if Mr. Vladisov knew that.

"No." His gaze flickered from one of us to the next. "I know we shall *all* be very close. Ms. Yukoshi told me you were all . . ." he seemed to be searching for the correct phrase. ". . . good kids."

"Sure," said Donnie, giggling just a little.

"I believe," said Mr. Vladisov, "that it is customary to devour milk and cookies before your bedtime."

"Oh, that's not for a while yet," said Angelique.

"Hours," chimed in Donnie.

Our new guardian consulted his watch. "Perhaps twenty-three minutes?"

We slowly nodded.

"SL," he said to me, "will you help me distribute the snacks?"

I followed Mr. Vladisov out the door.

"Be careful," said Angelique so softly that only I could hear. I wondered if I really knew what she meant.

Mr. Vladisov preceded me down the corridor leading to the playroom and then to the adjacent kitchenette. Other inmates looked at us through the doorways as we passed. I didn't know most of their names. There were about three dozen of them. Our crowd—the four of us—was pretty tight.

He slowed so I could catch up to his side. "Your friends seem very nice," he said. "Well behaved."

"Uh, yes," I answered. "They're great. Smart too."

"And healthy."

"As horses."

"My carriage," mused Mr. Vladisov, "used to be pulled by a fine black team."

"Beg pardon?"

"Nothing," he said sharply. His tone moderated. "I sometimes slip into the past, SL. It's nothing."

"Me," I said. "I love horses. My dad says he'll get me a colt for my graduation from middle school. We'll have to stable it out in Long Island."

Mr. Vladisov didn't comment. We had reached the closetlike kitchen-ette. He didn't bother to turn on the light. When he opened the refrigerator and took out a carton of milk, I could see well enough to open the cabinet where I knew the cookies were stored.

"Chocolate chip?" I said. "Double Stuf Oreos?"

Mr. Vladisov said, "I never eat . . . cookies. Choose what you like."

I took both packages. Mr. Vladisov hovered over the milk, assembling quartets of napkins and glasses. "Don't bother with a straw for Donnie," I said. "She's not supposed to drink through a straw. Doctor's orders."

Mr. Vladisov nodded. "Do these things help you sleep more soundly?"

I shrugged. "I 'spose so. The nurse told me once that a high-carb snack before bed would drug us out. It's okay. Cookies taste better than Ritalin anyway."

"Ritalin?"

"An upper that works like a downer for the hypers."

"I beg your pardon?"

I decided to drop it. "The cookies help us all sleep."

"Good," said Mr. Vladisov. "I want everyone to have a good night's rest. I take my responsibility here quite seriously. It would be unfortunate were anyone to be so disturbed she woke up in the early morning with nightmares."

"We all sleep very soundly," I said.

Mr. Vladisov smiled down at me. In the dim light from the hall, it seemed to me that his eyes gleamed a dusky red.

I passed around the Double Stuf Oreos and the chocolate-chip cookies. Mr. Vladisov poured and distributed the glasses of milk as solemnly as if he were setting out communion wine.

Cammie held up her milk in a toast. "We enjoyed Ms. Yukoshi, but we know we'll like you much better."

Mr. Vladisov smiled without parting his teeth and raised an empty hand as though holding a wine glass. "A toast to you as well. To life everlasting, and to the dreams which make it bearable."

Angelique and I exchanged glances. I looked at Donnie. Her face was saying nothing at all. We all raised our glasses and then drank. The milk was cold and good, but it wasn't the taste I wished. I wanted chocolate.

Mr. Vladisov wished us a more conventional good night, then smoothly excused himself from the room to see to his other charges. We listened hard but couldn't hear his heels click on the hallway tile.

"Slick," said Angelique, nibbling delicately around the edge of her chocolate-chip cookie.

"Who's he remind me of?" mused Cammie. "That old guy—I saw him in a play once. Frank Langella."

"I don't know about this," said Donnie.

"What don't you know?" I said.

"I don't know whether maybe one of us ought to stay up all night on watch." Her words came out slowly. Then more eagerly, "Maybe we could take turns."

"We all need our rest," I said. "It's a school night."

"I sure need all the energy *I* can get," said Cammie. "I've got a geography test tomorrow. We're supposed to know all the capitals of those weird little states west of New Jersey."

I said, "I don't think we have anything to worry about for a while. Mr. Vladisov's new. It'll take him a little while to settle in and get used to us."

Cammie cocked her head. "So you think we got ourselves a live one?"

"So to speak." I nodded. "Metaphorically speaking . . ."

So I was wrong. Not about what Mr. Vladisov was. Rather that he would wait to get accustomed to how things ran at Wick Pus. He must have been very hungry.

In the morning, it took Donnie forever to get up. She groaned when Cammie shook her, but didn't seem to want to move. "I feel shitty," she said, when her eyes finally opened and started to focus. "I think I've got the flu."

"Only if bats got viruses in their spit," said Cammie grimly. She gestured at Donnie's neck, gingerly zeroing in with her index finger.

Angelique and I leaned forward, inspecting the throat.

Donnie's brown eyes widened in alarm. "What's wrong?" she said weakly.

"What's wrong ain't pimples," said Cammie. "And there's two of them."

"Damn," said Angelique.

"Shit," said Donnie.

I disagreed with nobody.

The four of us agreed to try not to get too upset about all of this until we'd had time to confer tonight after our parents dropped us off at the Center. Donnie was the hardest to convince. But then, it was her throat that showed the pair of matched red marks.

Mrs. Maloney was the morning shift lady who saw us off to our various buses and subways to school. Mr. Vladisov had gone off duty sometime before dawn. Naturally. He would return after dark. Double naturally.

"I'm gonna tell my mom I don't want to come back to the Center tonight," Donnie had said.

"Don't be such a little kid," said Cammie. "We'll take care of things."

"It'll be all right," Angelique chimed in.

Donnie looked at me as though begging silently for permission to chicken out. "SL?"

"It'll be okay," I said as reassuringly as I could. I wasn't so sure it would be that okay. Why was everyone staring at me as though I were the leader?

"I trust you," Donnie said softly.

I knew I was blushing. "It'll be all right." I wished I knew whether I was telling the truth.

At school, I couldn't concentrate. I didn't even sneak reads from my Stephen King paperback. I guess I sort of just sat there like a wooden dummy while lessons were talked about and assignments handed out.

I started waking up in the afternoon during my folklore class.

"The thing you should all remember," said Mrs. Dancey, my teacher, "is that myths never really change. Sometimes they're garbled and they certainly appear in different guises to different generations who recount them. But the basic lessons don't alter. We're talking about truths."

The truth was, I thought, I didn't know what we were all going to do about Mr. Vladisov. That was the long and short of it, and no urban myth Mrs. Dancey tempted me with was going to take my mind off that.

Time. Things like Mr. Vladisov, they figured they had all the time in the world, so they usually seemed to take things easy. Given time, we'd figure something out. Cammie, Donnie, Angelique, and me. We could handle anything. Always had.

"Shauna-Laurel?" It was Mrs. Dancey. Talking to me.

I didn't know what she had asked. "Ma'am?" I said. "Sorry."

But it was too late. I'd lost my chance. Too much daydreaming. I hoped it wouldn't be too late tonight.

Donnie's twin red marks had started to fade when the four of us huddled in our room at the Center to talk.

"So maybe they *are* zits," said Cammie hopefully.

Donnie irritably scratched at them. "They itch."

I sat on the edge of the bunk and swung my legs back and forth. "Don't scratch. They'll get infected."

"You sound like my mother."

"Good evening, my good kids." Mr. Vladisov filled the doorway. He was all dark clothing and angular shadows. "I hope you are all feeling well tonight?"

"Aren't you a little early?" said Angelique.

Mr. Vladisov made a show of consulting his watch. It was the old-fashioned kind, round and gold, on a chain. It had hands. I glanced out the window toward the street. The light had gone while we were talking. I wondered where Mr. Vladisov spent his days.

"Early? No. Perhaps just a bit," he corrected himself. "I find my position here at the Center so pleasant, I don't wish to be late." He smiled at us. We stared back at him. "What? You're not all glad to see me?"

"I have the flu," said Donnie dully.

"The rest of us will probably get it too," Angelique said.

Cammie and I nodded agreement.

"Oh, I'm sorry," said Mr. Vladisov. "I see why this should trouble you. Perhaps I can obtain for you an elixir?"

"Huh?" That was Cammie.

"For your blood," he said. "Something to strengthen your resistance. Tomato juice, perhaps? or V-8? Some other healthful beverage?"

"No," said Donnie. "No thank you. I don't think so. No." She hiccupped.

"Oh, you poor child." Mr. Vladisov started forward. Donnie drew back. "Is there something I can do?" he said, checking himself in midstride. "Perhaps I should call for a doctor?" His voice sounded *so* solicitous. "Your parent?"

"No!" Donnie came close to shouting.

"She'll be okay," said Cammie.

Mr. Vladisov looked indecisive. "I don't know . . ."

"We do," I said. "Everything will be fine. Donnie just needs a good night's sleep."

"I'm sure she will get that," said Mr. Vladisov. "The night is quiet." Then he excused himself to fetch our milk and cookies. This time he didn't ask for volunteer help.

Cammie was stroking Donnie's hair. "We'll see nothin' happens. You'll be just fine."

"That's right," said Angelique. "We'll all stay up."

"No need," I said. "We can take turns. No use everybody killing themselves."

"Bad phrasing," said Cammie. "Taking turns sounds good to me."

I volunteered, "I'll take the first watch."

"Yeah." Cammie grinned. "That way the rest of us got to stay up in the scariest part of the night."

"Okay, so you go first and wake me up later."

"Naw, Just kidding."

I liked being friends with Cammie and the others. But then we were so much alike. More than you might think.

The daughter of a widowed Harlem mortician.

The daughter of the divorced assistant French consul.

The daughter of an ambitious off-Broadway director.

The daughter of a divorced famous novelist.

All of us denied latchkeys and dumped at Wick Pus. Handier than boarding school if a parent wanted us. But still out of their hair.

One of us used to love drugs. One of us was thinking about loving God. Another was afraid of being the baby of the group. And another just wanted peace and a horse. I smiled.

Donnie actually did look reassured.

After a while, Mr. Vladisov came back with our nightly snacks. He seemed less exuberant. Maybe he was catching on to the fact that we were on to him. Maybe not. It's hard to tell with adults.

At any rate, he bid us all a good evening and that was the last we saw of him until he came around to deliver a soft, "Lights out, girls. Sleep well. Sleep well, indeed."

We listened for his footsteps, didn't hear any, heard him repeating his message to the boys down the hall. Finally we started to relax just a little.

Through the darkness, Cammie whispered, "Three hours, SL. That's it. Don't knock yourself out, okay? Wake me up in three hours."

"Okay."

I heard Donnie's younger, softer whisper. "Thanks, guys. I'm glad you're all here. I'm even going to try to sleep."

"Want a ghost story first?" That was Angelique.

"No!" Donnie giggled.

We were all silent.

I listened for steady, regular breathing. I waited for anything strange. I eventually heard the sounds of the others sleeping.

I guess I really hadn't expected them to drift off like that.

And then I went to sleep.

I hadn't expected that either.

I woke up sweaty, dreaming someone was slapping me with big slabs of lunch meat. Someone *was* slapping me. Cammie.

"Wake up, you gink! She's gone!"

"Who's gone?" The lamp was on and I tried to focus on Cammie's angry face.

"Donnie! The honky bloodsucker stole her."

I struggled free of the tangled sheet. I didn't remember lying down in my bed. The last thing I recalled was sitting bolt upright, listening for anything that sounded like Mr. Vladisov skulking around. "I think he—he put me to sleep." I felt terrible.

"He put us all to sleep," said Angelique. "No time to worry about that. We've got to find Donnie before he drains her down to those cute little slippers." Donnie had been wearing a pair of plush Felix the Cat foot warmers.

"Where we gonna look?" Cammie looked about ready to pull Mr. Vladisov apart with her bare fingers with their crimson painted nails.

"Follow running blood downhill," I said.

"Jeez," Cammie said disgustedly.

"I mean it. Try the basement. I bet he's got his coffin down there."

"Traditionalist, huh?"

"Maybe. I hope so." I pulled on one Adidas, wound the laces around my ankle, reached for the other. "What time is it, anyway?"

"Not quite midnight. Sucker didn't even wait for the witching hour."

I stood up. "Come on."

"What about the others?" Angelique paused by the door to the hall.

I quickly thought about that. We'd always been pretty self-sufficient. But this wasn't your ordinary situation. "Wake 'em up," I said. "We can use the help." Cammie started for the door. "But be quiet. Don't wake up the supervisors."

On the way to the door, I grabbed two Oreos I'd saved from my bedtime snack. I figured I'd need the energy.

I realized there were thirty or thirty-five kids trailing just behind as my roommates and I found one of Donnie's Felix slippers on the landing in the fire stairs. It was just before the final flight down to the dark rooms where the furnace and all the pipes were. The white eyes stared up at me. The whiskers didn't twitch.

"Okay," I said unnecessarily, "come on. Hurry!"

Both of them were in a storage room, just up the corridor from the place where the furnace roared like some giant dinosaur. Mr. Vladisov sat on a case of toilet paper. It was like he was waiting for us. He expected us. He sat there with Donnie cradled in his arms and was already looking up at the doorway when we burst through.

"SL . . ." Donnie's voice was weak. She tried to reach out toward me, but Mr. Vladisov held her tightly. "I don't want to be here."

"Me neither," muttered Cammie from beside me.

"Ah, my good kids," said Mr. Vladisov. "My lambs, my fat little calves. I am sorry that you found me."

It didn't sound like he was sorry. I had the feeling he'd expected it, maybe even wanted it to happen. I began to wonder if this one was totally crazy. A psychotic. "Let Donnie go," I said, trying for a firmness I don't think was really showing in my voice.

"No." That was simple enough.

"Let her go," I repeated.

"I'm not . . . done," he said, baring his fangs in a jolly grin.

I said, "Please?"

"You really don't understand." Mr. Vladisov sighed theatrically. "There are two dozen or more of you and only one of me; but I am a man of some power. When I finish snacking on this one, I will kill most of the rest of you. Perhaps all. I'll kill you and I will drink you."

"Horseshit," said Cammie.

"You will be first," said Mr. Vladisov, "after your friend." He stared directly at me, his eyes shining like rubies.

"Get fucked." I surprised myself by saying that. I don't usually talk that way.

Mr. Vladisov looked shocked. "Shauna-Laurel, my dear, you are not a child of *my* generation."

I definitely wasn't. "Let. Her. Loose," I said distinctly.

"Don't be tiresome, my child. Now be patient. I'll be with you in just a moment." He lowered his mouth toward Donnie's throat.

"You're dead," I told him.

He paused, smiling horribly. "No news to me."

"I mean *really* dead. For keeps."

"I doubt that. Others have tried. Rather more mature specimens than all of you." He returned his attention to Donnie's neck.

Though I didn't turn away from Mr. Vladisov, I sensed the presence of the other kids behind me. We had all crowded into the storage room, and now the thirty-odd of us spread in a sort of semicircle. If Mr. Vladisov wondered why none of us was trying to run away, he didn't show it. I guess maybe like most adults, he figured he controlled us all.

I took Cammie's hand with my right, Angelique's with my left. All our fingers felt very warm. I could sense us starting to relax into that fuzzy-feeling receptive state that we usually only feel when we're asleep. I knew we were teaming up with the other kids in the room.

It's funny sometimes about old folktales (we'd finally come up in class with a nonsexist term). Like the one forbidding adults to sleep in the same room with a child. They had it right. They just had it backwards. It's *us* who suck up the energy like batteries charging . . .

Mr. Vladisov must have felt it start. He hesitated, teeth just a little ways from Donnie's skin. He looked at us from the corners of his eyes without raising his head. "I feel . . ." he started to say, and then trailed off. "You're taking something. You're feeding—"

"Let her go." I shouldn't even have said that. It was too late for making bargains.

"My . . . blood?" Mr. Vladisov whispered.

"Don't be gross," said Cammie.

I thought I could see Donnie smile wanly.

"I'm sorry," said Angelique. "I thought you were going to work out okay. We wouldn't have taken much. Just enough. You wouldn't have suspected a thing. Finally you would have moved on and someone else would have taken your place."

Mr. Vladisov didn't look well. "Perhaps—" he started to say. He looked like he was struggling against quicksand. Weakly.

"No," I said. "Not on your life."

And then we fed.

LAURA ANNE GILMAN
(b. 1967)

Born and raised in New Jersey, Laura Anne Gilman received her bachelor's degree from Skidmore College in Saratoga Springs, and then went into publishing. She has worked in the science fiction and mystery genres for the past decade as an editor for variety of talented writers, ranging from award-winning mystery author Dana L. Stabenow to cyberpunk writer Wilhelmina Baird.

Gilman's short fiction has varied widely within the fantasy/science fiction genres, from a quiet but charming character study in The Day the Magic Stopped (1995) to an intense story about love and magic in Lammas Night (1995) to a hilarious look at artificial intelligence in Don't Forget Your Spacesuit, Dear (1996) to a straightforward adventure tale involving a telepath in Highwaymen: Robbers and Rogues (1997). Gilman also co-edited a critically acclaimed alternate were-creature anthology entitled OtherWere: Stories of Transformation with Keith R. A. DeCandido (1996).

"Exposure," written for an anthology called Blood Muse (1995), is a very modern vampire tale. In it, the vampire, a professional photographer whose daily work involves him in decisions about light and dark, faces a challenge unique to his situation. Despite the story's whimsical tone, the serious nature of Westin's artistic problem is never lost sight of in the story. Anyone who has ever taken photography seriously will feel for him.

EXPOSURE

The timer clicked, a cicada in the dark. Lifting the tongs off their rest, he swirled the paper gently; watching, deeming Good to go by the rules, better to work by instinct. Finally deeming it complete, he lifted the sheet out of its bath, placing it in another shallow tub and turning the water on, cold, over it.

The music played, one cd after another, continuous shuffle so that he never knew what would come up next: Melissa Etheridge, Vivaldi, the exotic noises of a rain forest. It suited his mood, prepped him for the evening's work. For now the lilting strains of *The Four Seasons* kept him company. Tugging at his ear where it itched, he studied the image floating face-up at him. Satisfied, he lifted it between two fingertips, shaking some of the wetness off. Turning off the water, he transferred the print to his right hand and reached out to flick the toggle switch on the wall next to the room's exit. Stepping into the revolving door, he pushed the heavy plastic with one shoulder and emerged from the darkroom.

Blinking in the sudden fluorescent lighting, he cast a glance over his shoulder to make sure that the warning light had gone off, then carried the print over to the line strung across the far end of the studio. Clipping it to the line, he stepped back to examine the other prints already there. Several, most notably the three shots of the hookers talking over coffee, leaning intently across the table to get in each other's faces, pleased him. Others were less successful, but overall he was satisfied. Checking his watch once again, he took off the stained apron he wore, hung it on a hook beside the door, shut off the stereo, and went to take a shower. Time to go to work.

"Hey, Westin!"

He slung the bag more comfortably over his shoulder, and stopped to wait for the overweight Latino cop who chugged up alongside him. "Going out again tonight, huh?"

"As I've done every night this week," Westin replied. "And the week before that."

"But not the week before that," the cop said.

"But the entire month before that I didn't miss a single night. So why are you asking now?"

The cop ignored the slight edge to Westin's voice. "There's some weirdo out there, past few nights. Scared the hell out of a couple slits Tuesday, cut into their business too. Guy's wearing Pampers and some kinda bonnet, according to reports. If you happen to run into him . . ."

"I should take his picture for your album?"

"The brass'd be thankful. And ya gotta know the *Post*'d pay for that picture. Anyway, keep your eyes out."

"I always do," Westin said, holding up his camera. He watched with detached affection as the cop loped back to his post, holding up a wall in the upper hall of the Port Authority. Swaddling and a bonnet. That was a new one. He could certainly understand johns keeping away, but why were the hookers afraid of him? Westin thought briefly about following up on it, then put those thoughts away. If he came into the viewfinder, then would be the time to wonder. For now, there was the rent to pay. He stepped into the men's room to moisten his contact lenses, darkened to protect his hypersensitive eyes. Another thing to bless technology for. Even he couldn't take photographs through sunglasses.

Leaving the bustling noise of the terminal, he exited into the sharp cold night of Eighth Avenue and paused. Where to go? Where were the pictures, the images waiting for him to capture? He turned in a slow half-circle, ignoring the line of dinner-hour cabs waiting in front of him, letting his instinct pick a direction. There. The hot white lights were calling him.

Walking briskly, he cut crosstown, one hand on his camera, the other hanging loosely by his side. The sidewalk hustlers and gutter sharks watched him pass, recognizing a stronger predator. But the hookers, ah, the hookers were another story. They swarmed to him, offered him deals, enticements. He did love women so, their softness hiding such strong, willful blood. But he was not feeding tonight. At least, not of that. Tonight was for a different passion. Bypassing Times Square itself, he wandered the side streets, catching the occasional sideways stare from well-dressed theatergoers on their way from dinner to their entertainment. Only the expensive Konica hanging by his side kept them from assuming he was a panhandler. The long trench had seen better decades, and not even the Salvation Army had been able to find anything nice to say about his boots except for the fact that they had once been sturdy. And the less said about his once-white turtleneck, the better. But he preferred these clothes, using them the same way wildlife photographers hid within camouflaged blinds. He was stalking wildlife as well, a form that was more easily spooked than any herd of gazelles or a solitary fox.

For the next seven hours he took shot after shot of the ebb and flow of humanity around him, occasionally moving to a new spot when people became too aware of him or, more accurately, of the camera. His choices satisfied him. The elderly woman in rags stepping over a crack in the sidewalk with graceful poise. The businesswoman striding along, topcoat open to the bracing wind. Two too-young figures doing a deal with brazen indifference to the mounted policeman just yards away, and the cop's equal indifference to their infractions. The hooker holding a Styrofoam cup in her hands, allowing the steam to rise to her face, taking delicate sips. He loved them all, carefully, surreptitiously, with each click of the shutter, every zoom of the lens to catch their expressions, the curve of their hands, the play of neon across their skin. He could feel the beat of their blood, pulling him all unwilling, and he blessed the cold which kept their scents from him. He couldn't afford the distractions.

Stopping in a Dunkin' Donuts to pick up a cup of coffee, he dug in his trench pocket for a crumpled dollar bill to pay for it. "Why can't you carry a wallet?" he could hear Sasha complain. "That way when someone finally puts you out of your misery I'll know to collect the body." Lovely, long-suffering Sasha. But she forgot her complaints when he had a show ready for her pale white walls, secure in her status as Michael Westin's only gallery. For three long, hungry years she had supported him, and for the last eleven he had returned the favor. He understood obligation, and needing, and the paying of debts.

Finally he came to the last roll of film he had prepared for the night. He took it out of the pouch hanging from his belt and looked at it, black plastic against the black of his thin leather gloves. High-speed black and white, perfect for catching moments silhouetted against the darkness, sudden bursts of light and action. His trademark. One roll left. He still had time to shoot this roll before heading home, still subjects to capture.

Or he could try again, a little voice whispered inside his head. There was time.

Shaking his head to silence the unwanted voice, he removed the used film from the camera, marked it with the date, location, and an identifying number, then replaced it in the pouch. Still the unused film sat in his palm. He could reload the camera, finish the evening out. Or he could save it for the next trip, cutting the session short and going home. At the thought his lips curled in a faint smile. Home to where Danielle slept in their bed, her hair fanned out against the flannel sheets. She would be surprised to see him, surprised and pleased, if he knew his Dani.

Or you could try again.

"Damnit, enough!" He would be a fool to listen to that voice, a fool to even consider it. Hadn't the three attempts been enough to teach him that? If the third time wasn't a charm, then certainly the fourth was for fools. And his kind didn't survive by being fools.

But still the thought lingered, caressing his ego, his artist's conceit. He could picture the shot, frame it perfectly in his mind. The conditions were ideal tonight, the location tailor-made. It would be the perfect finish to this show, the final page of the book he knew Sasha would want to do.

Stuffing the thought back into the darkness of his mind, he deftly inserted the black cartridge, advancing the shutter until the camera was primed. He cast one practiced eye skyward. Four A.M., give or take fifteen minutes. He had another hour, at most, before he would have to head home, wrap his head under a pillow, and get the few hours of sleep he still required before locking himself in the darkroom to develop this night's work. Then dinner with Dani, and perhaps he would take tomorrow night off. Fridays were too busy to get really good photos. Better to

spend it at home, in front of a roaring fire, and his smooth-necked, sweet-
smelling wife and a bottle of her favorite wine.

You work too hard, she had fussed at him just last month, rubbing a
minty-smelling oil into his aching muscles after a particularly grueling
night hunched over the lightboard, choosing negatives. *Always pushing,
always proving. You don't have anything to prove.* But he did. Had to
take better photos, find the most haunting expressions, the perfect lighting.
All to prove to himself that he was the photographer his press made him
out to be, and not just some freak from a family of freaks, that his work
was the result of talent and dedication, not some genetic mutation, a
parasite on human existence.

Shh, my love, he could hear Dani whisper. *I'm here, and I love you.*
She would whisper that, baring her neck so that he might graze along
that smooth dark column, feel the pulsing of her blood . . .

He swore, cutting off those thoughts before his body reacted to the
thought of her strength, her warmth. Jamming his hands into the pockets
of his trench, he watched the street theater, looking for something that
would finish the evening on a positive note, leave him anxious to see the
proof page. But the street was empty for the moment, leaving him with
the little voice, which had crept back the moment his attention was distracted. *The perfect photograph,* it coaxed him. *Something so heart-
breakingly perfect that only you could create. Otherwise this exhibit is
going to end on a downer, and there's enough of that in this world,
isn't there?*

Cursing under his breath, he scared off a ragged teen who had sidled
up next to him. Westin watched the kid's disappearing backside with wry
amusement. It had been a long time since anyone had tried to mug him,
and he would have given the boy the twenty or so bucks he had in his
pocket, just to reward such *chutzpa.*

Checking the street one last time, he sighed and gave up. Time to call
it a good haul, and head on home. *To bed, perchance to screw, and then
to sleep.* Hanging the camera strap around his shoulder, he adjusted the
nylon webbing until the shoulder patch fit snugly against his coat. *There's
still film left,* the little voice said, sliding and seducing like a televangelist.
Can't go home with film left.

"I'll take shots of some of New York's Finest," he told himself. Fragile
humans, holding back the night. It would be a good image, and it would
please Miguel to be included. And Tonio, his partner. Kid was so green
his uniform squeaked when he walked. Veteran and rook, side by side,
against the squalor of the bus terminal. Maybe he'd catch them in an
argument. He could see that, frame it in his head. The possibilities grew,
flicking across the screen in his head fast enough to wipe all thoughts of
That Shot out of his head. By the time he reached the corner of Seventh
Avenue, he had it all planned out. Stopping to look up at the still-dark
sky, he thought he could see just the faintest hint of light creeping skyward

from the east. False dawn. At home, he would be watching the deer come down from the wooded area to eat his bushes. He had done an essay on them for National Wildlife which paid well enough to replace the rosebushes the hoofed terrorists had devoured the spring before.

Waiting at the light on the corner of Forty-first and Eighth, something made him tilt his head to the right. There. By the chain-link fence protecting an empty lot. A shadow that wasn't a shadow. His soothing thoughts broke like mirror shards, and he turned his head to stare straight across the street. Live and let live. The fact that he chose not to hunt—did not, in fact, have to—did not mean others might not. Only once had he made it his concern, when a kinswoman had gotten messy, leaving corpses over the city—*his city*. His mouth tightened as he remembered the confrontation that had followed. He hadn't wanted to destroy her—but he wasn't ready to end his existence yet either. And letting her continue was out of the question. Only fools saw humans as fodder. They were kin, higher in some ways, lesser in others, but in the balance of time, equal. He believed that, as his father had believed that, raising his children to live alongside the daylight-driven world as best they could, encouraging them to build support groups, humans—companions—that would offer so that they need not take. It was possible, his father had lectured them, to exist without violence. And so they had. And the daylight world had given him good friends, a loving wife—and the means to express the visions which only his eyes could see.

With that thought in mind, he turned slowly, looking up at the sky behind him. False dawn. It was almost upon him.

The perfect photograph. It would only take one shot. One exposure, and then it's done.

A scrap of memory came over him. "If 't were done, 't were best done quickly . . ." *Damn. Damn damn damn damn.*

It seemed almost as though another person took control; moved his body across the street, dodged the overanxious cabs turning corners to pick up the last fare of the night. Someone else walked across the bare floor of the terminal that even at this hour still hosted a number of grubby souls wandering, some slumped over knapsacks, asleep, some reading newspapers or staring down into their coffee as though it held some terrible answer. His hand powered by someone else reached for the camera, holding it like a talisman, a fetish. Standing on the escalator, he watched out of habit, his mind already on what he was going to do. He could feel it pulling him, a siren's song, and he cursed himself. But he couldn't stop, no more than the first three times he had tried. Tried, and failed.

Crossing over to the next level of escalators, he paused at the first step, willing his body to stop, turn around, get on the bus that would take him home. Only a fool would continue, only a madman. Looking down, he saw first one boot, then the other, move on to the metal steps, his left hand grasping the railing. With his right hand he fingered the camera's casing, stroking his thumb over the shutter button.

At the end of this escalator he stopped, hitting his free hand against the sign that thanked him in Spanish and English for not giving money to panhandlers. The pain made him wince. At least in that they were equal, humans and he. Pain was a bitch. He hit his hand again, then gave up. The siren call, as strong as blood, had him again, and he had no choice but to give in. If it was to be done, it had to be done fast. Get in, get out, go home. Punching the up button, he waited for the elevator that would take him to the rooftop parking lot.

He adjusted the camera in his hand, barely aware of the sweat that ran down the back of his neck and down the front of his shirt. Shifting closer to the roof edge, he leaned against the ornate masonry, bracing himself. A glint of light caught his attention and he squinted, the hair along his arm rising in protest. "One minute more," he told himself. "Just one damn more minute, you bitch, and I'll have you. Come on, come on, do it for me!" He swallowed with difficulty, wishing for the water bottle at arms' reach, as impossible as if it were on another planet.

Another flicker of light caught the first building, fracturing against the wall of windows. "Come on," he said under his breath, unaware of anything except the oncoming moment. He could feel it, a sexual thrill waiting to shoot through his body, better than anything, even the flush of the first draw of blood. This was why he was alive. This was it, this was the perfect moment . . . He drew the camera to his face, focusing on primal instinct. The light rose a fraction higher, and he was dropping the camera, running for the maintenance door, aware only of the screaming animal need to hide, survive, get away from that damn mocking bitch. The camera lay where it fell: abandoned, broken.

"Goddamn," Westin swore, shaking himself free of the memory. "Go home, Westin. It's a fucking picture. Not worth dying for." The woman exiting the elevator glanced at him, pulling her coat closer around her body as she swept past him, eyes forward in a ten-point exhibition of New York street sense. The first rule: never let them see you seeing them. He moved past her on instinct, not realizing until the doors had closed that he passed the Rubicon. "Well goddamn," he said again, but he was grinning. A predator's flash of too-white teeth, a grin of hungry anticipation. His fangs tingled, the veins underneath them widening in response to the rush of adrenaline coursing through his body.

The parking lot was mostly deserted—the late-night partiers having headed home, and the Jersey commuters not yet in. There were a handful of cars parked in the back for monthly storage, and one beat-up blue Dart pulled in as he stood there. He waited in the shadows until the driver, a heavy-set man wearing workboots and carrying a leather briefcase, passed by him into the elevator.

Going to the edge of the lot, he sat on the cold metal railing, hooking

one foot under the longest rung to keep himself from slipping five stories to the pavement waiting below. The air was noticeably colder here, the wind coming at him without buffer. Dawn was coming, damn her. He could feel it in every sinew of his body, every instinct-driven muscle screaming for him to find a dark cave in which to wait the daylight hours out.

Forcing himself to breathe evenly, he took control of those instincts, forcing them back under the layers of civilization and experience. There would be plenty of time to find a bolthole somewhere in the massive bulk of the Port Authority. He had done it before, here and elsewhere. It was all timing. Timing, he reminded himself, and not panicking.

Squinting against the wind, he swung his body into better position, facing eastward, toward the East River. Toward the rising sun.

Idiot, a new, more rational voice said in tones of foreboding. *Do the words crispy critter mean anything to you?* He shrugged off the voice, lifting the camera to his eye. There was only the moment, and the shot. His entire universe narrowed down to that one instant, his entire existence nothing more than the diameter of the lens. His fingers moved with a sure steadiness, adjusting the focus minutely, his body tense.

A particularly aggressive gust of wind shook the rooftop, making him lose the frame. Swearing, he fought to regain it, all the while conscious of seconds ticking by, each moment more deadly than the last. A taloned claw clenched in his gut, and sweat ran along his hairline and down under his collar. "Damn, damn, damn," he chanted under his breath, a mantra. The muscles in his back tightened, his legs spasming. But his arms, his hands, remained still, the muscles cording from the strain.

The first ray of light touched the rooftops, glinting deadly against empty windows. He swore again, his finger hovering over the shutter button. "Come on, baby," he coaxed it, a tentative lover. "Come here. That's it, you're so perfect."

Another ray joined the first, the faintest hint of yellow in the pure light. The hairs along his arms stirred underneath the turtleneck, his heart agitating with the screaming in his head to *get out get away you dumb fuck get OUT.* His hands remained steady, his eyes frozen, unblinking: waiting, just waiting. He could smell it now, that perfect moment, with more certainty than he'd ever known. Everything slowed, his breathing louder than the wind still pushing the building beneath him, his body quivering under the need for release.

A third ray sprang across the sky, then a fourth and fifth too fast to discern. Suddenly the rooftops were lit by a glorious burst of prism-scattered light, heart-stopping, agonizing, indelible. A ray flashed toward him, reflected by a wall of glass, and glanced off the brick barely a foot to the left. His forefinger oh so slowly pressed toward the shutter button while every muscle twisted in imagined agony. "Come on come on come on . . ." he whispered, holding himself back for the perfect second.

The smooth metal was underneath his fingertip when the first light caught him, slashing against his cheek, his chest, reaching through the skin into his vital organs.

He screamed, falling backwards in a desperate attempt to keep the deadly light from him, slamming to the cold cement floor even as his finger pushed, even as his ears heard the click of the shutter closing underneath the sound of his own primal voice.

His skin was burning, the blood seeping from the pores of his face and arms. The pain was everywhere, searing him, branding him. Tears tinctured with red washed a track down his narrow nose.

Crawling to his feet, Westin barely retained the presence of mind to shove the camera back into its padded carry-bag before dragging himself to the elevator and slamming his fist against the Down button. Blood dripped down his arm and onto the fabric.

The elevator opened in front of him. Westin pushed himself into the empty space, shaking. He leaned against the back wall and drew a deep breath, knowledge of his own stupidity battling with the sheer exhilaration of a different sort of hunt.

All too soon, the rush was over, and he was himself again, drenched in sweat and drying blood. In his memory, the sun rose like some killer angel, and he knew his actions for what they were—vanity.

But he would do it again.

ACKNOWLEDGMENTS

Allen, Woody: "Count Dracula." Copyright © 1971 by Woody Allen. Reprinted by permission of Random House, Inc.

Beaumont, Charles: "Blood Brother." Copyright © 1961 by HMH Pub. Co., renewed 1989 by Christopher Beaumont.

Brown, Frederic: "Blood." Copyright © 1955 by Frederic Brown.

Bryant, Edward: "Good Kids." Copyright © 1989 by Edward Bryant. First appeared in *Blood is Not Enough*, edited by Ellen Datlow.

Carter, Leslie Roy: "Vanishing Breed." Copyright © 1970 by Leslie Roy Carter. First published in *Curse of the Undead*, edited by Margaret L. Carter.

Casper, Susan: "A Child of Darkness." Copyright © 1989 by Susan Casper.

Charnas, Suzy McKee: "Unicorn Tapestry." Copyright © 1988 by Suzy McKee Charnas.

Cheever, John: "Torch Song." From *The Stories of John Cheever* by John Cheever. Copyright © 1947 by John Cheever. Reprinted by permission of Alfred A. Knopf Inc.

Derleth, August: "The Drifting Snow." Copyright © 1997 by Arkham House Publishers.

Ewers, Hanns Heinz: "The Spider." Copyright © 1921 by Hanns Heinz Ewers.

Gilman, Laura Anne: "Exposure." Copyright © 1995 by Laura Anne Gilman.

King, Stephen: *Salem's Lot*. Reprinted with permission. Copyright © 1976 Stephen King. All rights reserved. Originally published in *Playboy* magazine.

Lee, Tanith: "Bite-Me-Not or Fleur de Feu." Copyright © 1984 by Tanith Lee.

Leiber, Fritz: "The Girl With the Hungry Eyes." Copyright © 1989 by Fritz Leiber.

Matheson, Richard: *I Am Legend*. Copyright © 1954, renewed 1982 by Richard Matheson. Reprinted by permission of Don Congdon Associates, Inc.

Moore, C. L.: "Shambleau." Copyright © 1933 by Popular Fiction Publishing Co., renewed 1961 by C. L. Moore. Reprinted by permission of Don Congdon Associates, Inc.

Oates, Joyce Carol: *Bellefleur*. Copyright © 1980 by Ontario Review Press. Reprinted by permission of John Hawkins & Associates, Inc.

Rice, Anne: "The Master of Rampling Gate." Copyright © 1983 by Anne O'Brien Rice. Originally published in *Redbook*. Reprinted by permission of author.

Strieber, Whitley: "The Hunger." Copyright © 1981 by Andrew Strieber.

Yarbro, Chelsea Quinn: *Hôtel Transylvania*. Copyright © 1978, 1988 by Chelsea Quinn Yarbro.

Zelazny, Roger: "The Stainless Steel Leech." Copyright © 1963 by Roger Zelazny.